KILLMAN
CREEK

OTHER TITLES BY RACHEL CAINE

Stillhouse Lake Series

Stillhouse Lake

The Great Library

Paper and Fire

Ink and Bone

Ash and Quill

Weather Warden

Ill Wind

Heat Stroke

Chill Factor

Windfall

Firestorm

Thin Air

Gale Force

Cape Storm

Total Eclipse

Outcast Season

Undone

Unknown

Unseen

Unbroken

Revivalist

Working Stiff
Two Weeks' Notice
Terminated

Red Letter Days

Devil's Bargain
Devil's Due

Morganville Vampires

Glass Houses
The Dead Girls' Dance
Midnight Alley
Feast of Fools
Lord of Misrule
Carpe Corpus
Fade Out
Kiss of Death
Ghost Town
Bite Club
Last Breath
Black Dawn
Bitter Blood
Fall of Night
Daylighters

Stand-Alone Titles

Prince of Shadows

KILLMAN CREEK

A Stillhouse Lake Thriller

RACHEL CAINE

THOMAS & MERCER

Text copyright © 2017 by Rachel Caine, LLC
All rights reserved.

Published by Thomas & Mercer, Seattle

www.apub.com

Amazon, the Amazon logo, and Thomas & Mercer are trademarks of Amazon.com, Inc., or its affiliates.

ISBN-13: 9781542046411
ISBN-10: 1542046416

Cover design by Shasti O'Leary Soudant

Printed in the United States of America

KILLMAN CREEK

1

GWEN

On the twelfth night since my ex-husband escaped prison, I am in bed. Not sleeping. Watching the play of light and shadow on the curtains. I'm lying on a narrow foldout cot and feeling every twinge of spring poking through the thin mattress. My kids, Lanny and Connor, occupy the two full-size beds in this midpriced motel room. Midpriced is the best I can afford right now.

The phone is a new one. Another disposable, with a brand-new number. Only five people have the number, and two of them are asleep in the room with me.

I can't trust anyone outside that vanishingly small circle. All I can think of is the shadow of a man walking through the night—walking, not running, because I don't believe Melvin Royal is on the run, though half the police in the country are hunting him—and the fact that he is coming for me. For us.

My ex-husband is a monster, and I thought he was safely contained and caged, awaiting execution . . . but even from behind bars he ran a campaign of terror against me and our kids. Oh, he had help, some of it from inside the prison, some outside; how wide and deep it went is still in question, but he also had a plan. He maneuvered me, through targeted fear and threats, into the place he'd wanted me: a trap we'd survived, but only just.

Melvin Royal stalks me in the brief darkness when I close my eyes. *Blink*, and he's on the street. *Blink*, and he's walking up the stairs of the motel to the second floor's open walkway. *Blink*, and he's outside the door. Listening.

The buzz of a text arriving on my phone makes me flinch so hard it hurts. I grab for the device as the room's heater rattles on; it's loud, but it's efficient, and warmth glides through the room in a slow, welcome wave. I'm grateful. The blankets on this cot aren't up to much.

I blink my tired eyes and bring the phone's screen into focus. The message says **Number Blocked**. I turn it off, and put it under my pillow, and try to convince myself that it's safe to sleep.

But I know it isn't. I know who's texting me. And the double locks on the motel room door don't seem nearly enough.

I am twelve days out from rescuing my children from a murderer. I am exhausted, sore, and plagued with headaches. I am heartsick and tired and anxious and most of all—*most of all*—I am angry. I need to be angry. Being angry will keep us all alive.

How dare you, I think at the phone beneath my pillow. *How fucking dare you.*

When I've stoked my anger to a boiling, almost painful, temperature, I reach beneath my pillow and pull out the phone again. My anger is a shield. My anger is a weapon. I click the message firmly, expecting what it will hold.

But I am wrong. The text message is not from my ex-husband. It reads, **YOU'RE NOT SAFE ANYWHERE NOW**, and it is followed with a symbol I recognize: Å.

Absalom.

Shock diffuses my anger, sends it flowing in hot, electric waves through my chest and arms, as if the phone itself lashed out. My husband had help—help manipulating us, help abducting my children—and Absalom was that help . . . a master hacker who manipulated me into the trap Melvin had planned for him. I'd dared hope that maybe with the end of that plot, Absalom wouldn't have more to threaten us with.

I should have known better.

For a moment I feel a wave of sheer, visceral terror, like all the childhood fears of ghosts have been proven real, and then I take in a deep, slow breath and try to think through the impossibility of dealing with this . . . again. I am guilty of nothing more than defending myself from a man who wanted to kill me, who gained my trust over the course of years, and gradually led me to the place meant for my execution.

But that doesn't make the message on the screen go away.

Absalom has someone else coming for us. The thought runs through me like a lightning bolt, dries my mouth, makes all my nerves fire at once, because *it feels right*. Something has been bothering me all these long days while we've been in hiding and moving for our safety . . . the feeling that we're being watched, still. I'd put it down to paranoia.

What if it isn't?

I try to get up quietly, but the cot creaks, and I hear Lanny, my daughter, whisper, "Mom?"

"It's okay," I whisper back. I stand and slip my feet into shoes. I'm fully dressed in comfortable pants and a loose sweater and heavy socks, and I put on my shoulder holster and parka before I unlock all the security measures and step out into the chill.

It's overcast and cold here in Knoxville. I'm not used to the city lights, but just now they comfort me a little. I don't feel quite as isolated. There are people here. Screams will be heard.

I call one of the few numbers in my phone. It rings just once before it's picked up, and I hear the ever-tired voice of Detective Prester of the Norton Police Department—the town nearest where we lived, no, *live*, because we will go back to Stillhouse Lake, I swear we will—say, "Ms. Proctor. It's late." He doesn't sound happy to hear from me.

"Are you one hundred percent sure that Lancel Graham is dead?"

It's an odd question, and I hear the creak of what is probably an office chair as Prester sits back. I check my watch. It's after one in the morning. I wonder why he's still at work. Norton is a sleepy little town, though it's got its fair share of crime to deal with. He's one of two detectives on staff.

And Lancel Graham used to wear a Norton PD uniform.

Prester's reply is slow and cautious. "You got some pressing reason why you think he isn't?"

"Is. He. Dead?"

"Dead as they come. I watched them pull organs out of his corpse on an autopsy table. Why are you asking at—" He hesitates, then groans, as if he's just checked the time, too. "No fit time in the morning?"

"Because it kind of freaks me out to get yet another threatening text."

"From Lancel Graham."

"From Absalom."

"Ahh." He draws that out, and he does it in such a way that I am immediately put on my guard. Detective Prester and I are not friends. We are, to some extent, allies. But he doesn't fully trust me, and I can't really blame him. "'Bout that. Kezia Claremont's been doing some digging. She says it's possible Absalom's not a *he*. More of a *them*, maybe." I respect Kezia. She'd been Officer Graham's patrol partner, at least some of the time, but unlike Lancel Graham, she's fiercely honest. It had been a pretty devastating shock to her, finding out her partner was a killer.

Not as much as it had been for me.

My voice is tight and angry, for all that. "Why the *hell* didn't you warn me? You know I'm out here with my kids!"

"Didn't want to panic you," he says. "No proof yet. Just suspicion."

4

"In the time you've known me, Detective, do you find I am prone to blind panic?"

He lets that go without a comment, because he knows I am right. "I still say it'd be better for you to come back home to Norton, let us protect you here."

"My husband turned one of your cops into a murderer." I have to swallow a ball of sick fury. "You left Graham alone with my kids, remember that? God only knows what he could have done to them. Why the hell would I trust their safety with you?"

I still don't know everything about what Lancel Graham did when he abducted my children. Neither Connor nor Lanny will tell me anything about it, and I know better than to push them. They've been traumatized, and though the doctors had said they were in good health, and nothing more had been physically done to them, I still wonder what kind of psychological damage they've endured. And how it will bend them in the future.

Because bending them, shaping them, breaking them is what Melvin Royal wants. It's the kind of thing he takes a deep, unsettling delight in doing.

"Any word about Melvin?" *Mel,* a little voice in me, timid and ghostly, still whispers. He never liked being called Melvin, only Mel, which was why I now make it a point to only use his full name. A petty kind of power is still power.

"Manhunt is pretty heavy all over, and of those who broke out, about seventy-five percent are already back behind bars."

"Not him."

"No," Prester agrees. "Not him. Not yet. You planning on running until he gets caught?"

"That was the plan," I say. "But that plan just changed. If Absalom has more people to send after us, then they're going to find me for him. It's what he wants. It's why he's out. Running just prolongs this nightmare, and it means I don't have any control of my life. I'm not giving that up to him. Ever again."

There's that squeak of his office chair again. This time I'm almost certain he's leaning forward. "Then what the hell are you doing, Gwen?"

He still calls me that, by my new identity, and I appreciate it. The woman who'd been known as Gina Royal, wife of an especially horrible serial killer, is gone, another corpse Melvin left behind him. She's better off dead. I am Gwen now. Gwen isn't taking any more shit.

"I don't think you'll like it, so I'm going to spare you the details. Thanks, Detective. For everything." I almost mean it. Before he can ask any more questions, I shut off the phone and stick it in my coat pocket and stand there in the moist, chilly wind a moment. Knoxville hasn't quite shut down for the night yet, and I catch hints of music from passing cars on the street, see human shadows moving behind curtains in other motel rooms. A TV flickers across the courtyard, visible through cracked curtains. A plane passes overhead, slicing the sky.

I hear the door to the room open, and Lanny steps out. She's put on some shoes and her jacket, but beneath that she's still in her pajamas. That relaxes a little anxious fist inside me. If she'd changed into her jeans and loose flannel shirt as well as running shoes, it would have been a sign she was afraid.

"The brat's still asleep," she says as she leans on the rail next to me. "Tell me."

"It was nothing, baby."

"Bull crap, Mom. You don't get out of bed and make outside calls for nothing."

I sigh. It's cold enough that the wind drags the breath out in a faint, white plume. "I was talking to Detective Prester."

I see her hands tense on the rail, and I wish I could take this away from her, this fear, this constant and crushing sense of oppression. But I can't. Lanny knows as much as anyone how dangerous our situation is now. She knows most of the truth about her father. And I have to rely on her, at the tender age of almost-fifteen, to bear up under that weight.

"Oh," my daughter says. "Was it about him?"

Him means her father, of course. I give her a slight, hopefully reassuring smile. "No news yet," I say. "He's probably a long way from here. He's a hunted man. Most of the prisoners who escaped with him have already been caught. He'll be back behind bars soon."

"You don't believe that."

I don't. I don't want to lie to my daughter, so I just change the subject. "You need to go back to sleep, sweetheart. We're moving early in the morning."

"It is the morning. Where are we going?"

"Somewhere else."

"Is this how it's going to be?" Her voice is quietly fierce this time. "God, Mom, all you do is *run*. We can't just let him do this to us! Not again. I don't want to run. I want to *fight*."

She did. Of course she did. She was a brave kid who'd been forced to face ugly truths about her dad when she was just ten, and it wasn't surprising that she's still angry at her core.

She's also right.

I turn toward her, and she twists to look me in the face. I hold her gaze as I say, "We are going to fight. But tomorrow you're going to go somewhere safe, so I can be free to do what has to be done—and before you argue with me, I need you to stay with your brother and make sure he's protected. That's your job, Lanny. That's *your* fight. All right?"

"*All right?* You're dumping us off on somebody else now? No, it's not okay! Please tell me it's not Grandma."

"I thought you loved your grandmother."

"I do. As Grandma. Not to stay with. You want us to be safe? She can't protect us. She can't protect anybody."

"I'm going to make certain she doesn't have to. Meanwhile, your father will be watching *me*, because finding me is his top priority." I

7

pray that to be true. It's a huge gamble, but there is a very limited circle of people I can trust to look after my kids. My first instinct is to take them to my mother, but I also have to admit it: my daughter is right. My mom is not a fighter. Not like us. And this is an entirely different level of danger.

I don't tell her yet, because I need to think it over, but Javier Esparza and Kezia Claremont have offered to guard my kids if I need them. They're a formidable couple. Javier is a retired marine and runs a gun range; Kezia's a police officer, tough and smart and capable.

The drawback is, they live outside of Norton, and relatively close to Stillhouse Lake. That beautiful, remote place started out for me as a refuge, a sanctuary, but it turned into a trap, and now I don't know that I can ever feel safe there again. We certainly can't go back to our lakeside house; we'd be easy targets.

Javier's place, though, isn't at the lake. It's a remote, fortified cabin, and I intuitively believe that Melvin, and Absalom, would look everywhere but the place we'd just fled.

"Are you leaving us with Sam?" Lanny asks.

"No, because Sam's coming with me," I tell her. I haven't asked him yet, but I know he will; he wants to find Melvin Royal as desperately as I do, for just as personal a reason. "Sam and I are going to find your father and stop him before he hurts anyone else. Before he can even think of hurting you and your brother." I give her time to think about it, and then I say, "I need you to help me, Lanny. This is the best option we have, other than running and hiding again. I don't want to do that any more than you do. Please believe that."

She looks away and, with studied indifference, shrugs. "Sure. Whatever. You still make *us* do it." All the running we've done before has been necessary. It had been the right thing to do at the time. But I understand how terribly hard it has been on my kids to live in constant vigilance.

"I'm so sorry, honey."

"I know," she finally says, and having made that pronouncement, she gives me a quick, unexpected hug and goes back into the motel room.

I stay out there for a while in the cold, thinking, and then I dial Sam Cade's phone number and say, "I'm outside."

It only takes him about a minute to step out on the narrow second-floor walkway beside me; his room is right next to ours. Like me, he is fully dressed. Ready for a fight. He leans on the railing right where Lanny stood and says, "I don't suppose this is a booty call."

"Funny," I say, casting him a sideways look. We aren't lovers. Not that we aren't, in some ways, intimate; I think that eventually we might circle around to it, but neither of us seems to be in a hurry to get there. We have baggage, God knows. Ex-wife of a serial killer, constantly under threat from Melvin's groupies, his allies, the baying hounds of Internet vigilantes.

And Sam? Sam is the brother of one of my ex-husband's victims. Melvin's last victim. I can still see that poor young woman's body strung up by a wire noose. Tortured and murdered for pure, sadistic pleasure.

We're complicated. When I first met Sam, I'd believed he was a friendly stranger, no connection to my old life. Finding out that he had deliberately tracked me, stalked me, in hopes of finding evidence I'd been complicit in my husband's crimes . . . that had nearly broken everything.

He knows now that I'm not guilty, and never was, but there are still deep cracks between us, and I don't know how to fill them, or if I should. Sam likes me. I like Sam. In another life, without the rancid shadow of Melvin Royal between us, I think we could have been happy together.

For now, my vision is limited to surviving and ensuring the survival of my children. Sam is a means to an end.

Which, thankfully, he completely understands. I'm sure he sees me exactly the same way.

"What's up?" he asks me, and I dig the phone out, pull up the text, and pass it over. "Shit. But Graham's dead, right?" I hear the same free-fall disorientation in his voice, but he recovers faster. "They're sending someone else?"

"Maybe more than one," I tell him. "Prester says Absalom might be some kind of hacker collective. Who knows how many people they have in their network? We need to be even more careful now. I'm dumping this phone and buying a new one. We use cash, we stay off cameras as much as we can."

"Gwen, I can't keep doing this. Hiding isn't—"

"We're not hiding," I tell him. "We're hunting."

He straightens and turns to face me. Sam's not a big man, nor overly tall; he's got a lithe strength, and I know he can handle himself in a fight. Most of all—and this is everything to me now—I know that I can trust him. He isn't Melvin's creature, and he never will be. I can't say that of many people anymore.

"Finally," he says. "So, the kids?"

"I'll call Javier. He offered to take them before, and we can trust him."

Sam's already nodding. "It's a risk leaving them behind," he says, "but not as much as trying to protect them while we're going after Melvin. Sounds right." He pauses. "Are you sure about this?" He asks it almost gently. "We could leave it to the cops. The FBI. We probably should."

"They don't know Melvin. And they don't understand Absalom. If it's a collective, they could hide Melvin indefinitely while they track us down for him. We can't afford to wait it out, Sam. Hiding doesn't work." I take in a sharp breath of the cold air and let it out as a warmed stream of fog. "Besides. I want him. Don't you?"

"You know I do." He looks me over impersonally. Assessing a fellow soldier. "You're sure you don't need more rest?"

I laugh a little bitterly. "I'll rest when I'm dead. If we want to get to Melvin before the cops do, we're going to have to be tougher than him, and faster, and better. And we're going to need help. Information. You said before you had a friend who might be able to assist?"

He nods. There's a hard set to his jaw and a glitter in his eyes. Sam's not usually easy to read, but in this moment I see all his rage and heartbreak. Melvin is free out there, free to stalk and kill more women like Sam's sister. Melvin will kill again. If I know anything about my ex-husband, I know he will want to go out in a blaze of selfish, murderous, Grand Guignol fury.

The FBI is after him. The police of every state adjoining Kansas are as well. But it's unlikely that they'll turn him up quickly in the Midwest, because the first thing Melvin has done, I am certain, is to make his way southeast, toward us.

Absalom tracked us this far, and that means that Melvin won't be across the country, or across a distant border to a nonextradition country. He might not be here yet, but he's coming for us. I can smell it in the wind.

"We'll go at seven in the morning," I tell him. "I want the kids to rest a little more. All right?" I look at my phone. "I'll call Kezia and Javier to set everything up."

In a quick move, Sam takes my phone and slips it into his pocket. "If Absalom has this number, you can't use it to set up the kids' shelter," he says, and I immediately feel stupid I didn't think of it. I must be more exhausted than I think. "I'll wipe calls and contacts and leave it for someone else to steal. Better it stays on and leads Absalom on a false trail for a while." He nods across the street, at a lit-up convenience store. "I'll go get one new phone tonight. We use it to call Javier and dump it immediately. We don't buy any more phones close to this location; that's the first place Absalom will search for purchases."

He's right on every point. I need to think like a hunter now, but I can't forget that I'm also prey. Melvin made me vulnerable before by luring me, manipulating me, to end up where he wanted me to be. Now we need to do the same to him.

For years, I clung to a terrible fiction of a marriage—a life in which Melvin Royal controlled every aspect of my reality, and I failed to realize or fear it. Gina Royal, the old me, the vulnerable me . . . she and the kids were Melvin's camouflage for his secret, terrible life. On my side of the wall, I had only known that it all seemed so *normal*. But it never was, and now that I've left Gina Royal behind, I clearly see that.

I'm not Gina anymore. Gina was tentative and worried and weak. Gina would be afraid that Melvin would come hunting for her.

Gwen Proctor is ready for him.

I know in my heart that it all comes down to us. Mr. and Mrs. Royal. In the end, it always has.

2

LANNY

My little brother, Connor, is too quiet. He's barely said a word all day, and he keeps his head down. He's gone behind those walls he builds up, and I want to kick them all down and drag him out and get him to scream, hit the wall, do *something*.

But I can't even exchange two words with him without Mom's radar picking up trouble . . . at least, not until after the door closes behind her, and she's outside on the motel balcony. I know my mother. Mostly I love her. But sometimes she doesn't help. She doesn't know how to let her shields down anymore.

Connor's awake. He's good at pretending to be asleep, but I know his tells; for two years when Mom was away—in jail and at trial, accused of being my dad's accomplice—we'd shared a room because Grandma didn't have much space, even though I was ten and he was seven and we were too old to be sharing a room. We'd had to be each other's allies, watch each other's backs. I'd gotten used to knowing when he was really out, and when he was just pretending. He never did cry much, not as much as I did. These days, he doesn't cry at all.

I wish he would.

"Hey," I say. I make it quiet, but not too quiet. "I know you're faking it, loser." He doesn't answer. Doesn't move. His breathing continues smooth and even. "Yo, Squirtle. Don't play."

Connor finally sighs. "What?" He sounds totally awake. He doesn't even sound annoyed. "Go back to sleep. You're grumpy when you don't get your not-beauty rest."

"Shut up."

"Hey, you wanted to talk. Not my fault you don't like what I say." He sounds normal.

He's not normal.

I flop back on the bed. The bed smells like the dollar store, like old sweat and nasty feet. This whole room smells like the dollar store. I hate it. I want to go home . . . and home is the house Mom and Connor and I worked to make so nice. The one with my own bedroom, and a wall I painted with purple stenciled flowers. The one with Connor's bugout zombie defense room.

Our house sits right on Stillhouse Lake, and it represents something I thought we'd never have again: security. My memories after the day we had to leave our first home—the one in Wichita—were a blur of plain rooms and gray cities, for years. We never stayed anywhere long enough to feel like we were *home*.

Stillhouse Lake was different. It felt permanent, like life was really starting again for all of us. I had friends. Good friends.

I had Dahlia Brown, who started out being the kind of girl I hated and ended up being my best friend in the world. It hurt to leave her back there, like some discarded, broken toy. She didn't deserve that. I don't deserve it, either. I had a sort-of boyfriend, but it's a little bit of a shock to realize I don't really miss him at all. I haven't thought about him.

Only Dahlia.

We'd left our house just as it was, and I wonder if it's been completely trashed by now. Probably. News of just who we are, who our dad is, had broken in the middle of all the craziness with Officer Graham, and I remember what happened to our old places when people found out. Spray paint on the walls. Dead animals on the doorstep. Broken windows and vandalized cars.

People can be really shitty.

I can't help but imagine what our house by Stillhouse Lake might look like now, if people took out their anger on it instead of us. It makes my chest get tight and my stomach boil. I roll over on my side and angrily punch the cheap pillow into better shape. "Who do you think that text was from?"

"Dad," he says. I don't miss the slight inflection, the tiny hitch, but I don't know what it means. Anger? Fear? Longing? Probably all those things. I know something my mom probably doesn't: that Connor doesn't really, *really* get why Dad is a monster. I mean, he does, but he was seven when our lives spun out; he remembers a father who was sometimes awesome to him, and he misses that. I was older. And I'm a girl. I see things differently. "Guess now she's going to go after him." Now I hear a different intonation. One that I recognize.

So I dig. "Makes you mad, doesn't it?"

"Like it doesn't you? She's going to dump us like strays," he says. This time, the cold, flat tone isn't subtle at all. "Probably with Grandma."

"You like staying with Grandma," I say. I'm trying to be upbeat about it. "She makes us cookies and those popcorn balls you like. It's not exactly torture." I'm horrified the second the word drops off my lips, but it's too late. I'm angry with myself, a searing red flash that sizzles in my nerves like they've turned into firecracker fuses. In the next second I'm back in a cabin high up in the hills, being dragged down into a basement. Locked in a tiny little cell not much bigger than a coffin, along with my brother.

I know my mom wonders what happened to us in that basement. Connor and I haven't talked about it, and I don't know when, or if, we will. She'll try to make us, sooner or later.

I just want to be able to close my eyes and not see that winch and the wire noose that dangled from it, and those knives and hammers and saws glinting on the pegboard mounted on the walls. That room outside the cell looked just like my dad's garage workshop—the pictures I've seen of it, anyway. I know what happened there. I know what could have happened to us, in Lancel Graham's replica dungeon.

Most of all, I wish I could forget the stupid *rug*. Somehow, Graham found an exact replica of my dad's rug. Well, it was really *my* rug, because it was one of my first memories: a soft spiral-braided rug in pastel greens and blues. I loved that rug. I would lie facedown on it and scoot around on the floor, and Mom and Dad would laugh, and Mom would pick me up and slide the rug back in place by the door, and it was *love*, that stupid rug.

One day when I was about five, the rug disappeared from the spot in the hall, and Dad put a new one there. It was fine, I guess. It had a nonskid back, so nobody would go sliding around on it. He told us he'd thrown the other one away.

But on the day that our lives ended, the day Dad became a monster, that rug, *my* rug, was on the garage floor, right under the winch and the noose and the swinging body of a dead woman. He'd taken a piece of my life and made it part of something awful.

Seeing one *just like it* in Lancel Graham's horror basement broke something in me. When I close my eyes at night, that's what I see. My rug, made into a nightmare.

I wonder what Connor sees. Maybe that's why he doesn't sleep. When you sleep, you give up the choice to control memory.

Connor hasn't responded to my torture gaffe, so I stumble on. "You seriously want to go with Mom if she's hunting Dad?"

"She acts like we can't take care of ourselves," he says. "We can."

I agree that *I* can, but I'm also old enough to face the ugly truth about our dad and what he can do. I don't want to have to fight him. The whole idea hurts, and it terrifies me. But I also don't want to be left on my own with Connor, responsible for keeping both of us safe. I almost want Grandma, even if her cookies are kind of terrible and her popcorn balls too sticky. Even if she treats us like we're toddlers.

I shift the blame. "Mom's never going to let us fight him. You know that."

"So off to Grandma's house we go. Like Dad can't guess *that*."

I shrug, but in the dark I know he can't see me. "Grandma's moved and changed her name, too. It'll be just for a while, anyway. Like a vacation."

It's eerie how Connor doesn't move, doesn't shift. I never hear so much as a rustle of those stiff motel sheets from him. Just a voice in the dark. "Yeah," he says. "Like a vacation. And what if Mom never comes back for us? What if *he* comes back for us? Do you think about that?"

I open my mouth to confidently tell him *that's never going to happen*, but I can't. I can't get it out of my mouth, because I'm old enough to know that Mom isn't immortal, or all-powerful, and that good doesn't always win. And I know—Connor knows—that our dad is *incredibly* dangerous.

So I finally say, "If he does find us, we get away from him. Or we stop him, any way we can."

"Promise?" His voice suddenly sounds his age. Only eleven. Too young to deal with this. I forget how young he is, sometimes. I'm nearly fifteen. It's a big gap, and we've always babied my little brother.

"Yeah, doofus, I promise. We're going to be okay."

He lets out a long, slow breath that's almost a sigh. "All right," he says. "You and me, then. Together."

"Always," I tell him.

He doesn't say anything else. I can hear Mom talking in a low voice to someone outside; I think it's Sam Cade. I listen to the soft blur of their voices, and after a while I hear that Connor's breathing has deepened and slowed, and I think he's finally, really asleep.

That means I can sleep, too.

◆ ◆ ◆

Mom surprises us at oh-my-God in the morning with doughnuts and cartons of milk; she and Sam are already up and dressed, and they have coffee. I ask for some. I get shut down. Connor doesn't bother. He drinks his milk and mine, when I pass it to him while Mom isn't looking.

She surprises us when she tells us she's *not* sending us off to Grandma, all the way up the coast. Instead, she's sending us back to Norton. Not home, but close. And I can't help but feel a little relieved, and at the same time a little anxious, too. Being *almost* home seems dangerous in a whole lot of ways . . . not so much because Dad would find us, but because I immediately realize it means I can't really go home, to our old house. To my room. Being so close and *not home*? That's kind of worse. Worse still: Dahlia. I can't talk to her. Can't text her. Can't even let her know I'm there. That's the definition of *suck*.

But I don't tell Mom that.

Connor perks up a little when he realizes that instead of weeks with Grandma, he gets to hang out with Javier Esparza, who is a quietly awesome badass. His presence always feels strong and reassuring, and I don't doubt he can defend us. Connor needs a guy to bond with. He and Sam Cade got close, but I know Sam's got his own battles. He's going with my mom, no question about that.

So we'll be staying at Mr. Esparza's cabin, which he sometimes shares with Norton police officer Kezia Claremont. Also a quiet badass. They're totally sleeping together, which I guess we're not supposed to know. I approve of Kezia, though. It also means we have twice the firepower protecting us. I know Mom's doing it for that reason, but I'm still glad, for Connor's sake. I hope having Mr. Esparza around might break him out of his rigid silence.

Packing isn't much of a problem. We've been running for so long, Connor and I are both pros at throwing our stuff in bags and being ready to go in moments. Actually, Connor doesn't even have to do that. He packed early, while I was still asleep. We keep score on things like that, and he silently points to his bag to let me know he wins. Again. He's got his nose in a book already, which is his way of blocking out any attempts to converse. Plus, he loves books.

I wish we had that in common. I make the promise to myself, again, to borrow some from him.

We're in the car and navigating traffic on a foggy highway half an hour from the moment Mom sets the doughnuts down.

I doze, mostly, with my headphones blocking out the nonconversation. Mom and Sam are being very quiet. Connor's turning pages. I amuse myself by making a new playlist: SONGS TO KICK ASS AND TAKE NAMES. It's a boring drive, and the pounding rhythm of the music makes me want to go for a run. Maybe Mr. Esparza will let me do that when we get to his cabin, though I kind of doubt it; we're under house arrest, again, hiding from all the boogeymen in the shadows—not just of the real world of Dad and his friends, but all the amped-up Internet trolls. One pic, and somebody will paste me all over Reddit and 4chan again, and things will get very, very bad, very fast.

So probably no run.

We drive for a couple of hours, then stop at a big-box store, where Sam buys four new disposable phones; I'm temporarily thrilled to discover he had to buy *real smartphones*, even though they're still kind of clunky. No flip phones available. These are plain black, nothing special. We unshell them in the car and trade numbers. We're all used to this by now. Mom liked to buy me and Connor different colors of phones, just so we wouldn't get them mixed up, but Sam didn't think of that;

19

all four phones are the same. Mom confiscates mine and Connor's and does her Mom thing, which locks off all the Internet functions before she gives them back and disables as much as she can. Normal course of business. She's never wanted us to see the flood of ugliness out there about Dad, and about us.

I slide the phone into my pocket, plug my headphones into my iPod, and crank up the music. I am jamming to Florence + The Machine when I realize that Sam hasn't started the car. He's got a slip of paper out, and he's entering a phone number into his own device, then making a call.

I move my headphones out of my ear and pause the music in mid-wail to listen.

"Yes, hi, is Agent Lustig available?" Sam listens for a few seconds. "Okay. Can I leave a message for him? Ask him to call Sam Cade. He'll know the name. Here's my number . . ." He reads it off to her from the package. "Ask him to call me soon as he's able. He'll know what it's regarding. Thanks."

He hangs up and starts the car, and as we pull out onto the road and drive on, I realize he's not planning to share with the class. So I take one for the team. "Who's Agent Lustig?"

"Friend of mine," Sam tells me. He's honest with us, or at least, as honest as he thinks he can be. That's something I really like about him.

"Why are you talking to the FBI? He is FBI, right?"

"Because they're tracking your dad," he says. "And also, we need to understand something about Absalom. I'm hoping that the FBI might have more information."

I know about Absalom, and I frown. "Why?"

"Because Absalom might have someone else besides Graham to send after us," he says, after a glance at Mom to confirm it's okay to tell me about that. "And they might have traced us this far. Which is why we're using new phones now."

Mom finally chimes in. "Absalom could be a group, not just a person. If so, they could be helping your dad stay hidden, while also working to find us for him."

"If there's danger, why are you taking us back to Norton? Why can't we just stay with you?" Connor asks. He lowers his book but keeps the place with a finger between the pages.

"Seriously?" Mom is trying to sound amused, but she just sounds grim. "You know the last thing I'm going to do is take you anywhere near trouble. My job is to keep you away from it. Besides, this has been hard enough on you already. You both need to be somewhere safe, and you need rest."

And you don't? I think it, but I don't say it, which is weird for me. Instead, I say, "You don't have to go, you know. The cops are chasing him. So is the FBI. Why can't you just stay with us?"

Mom takes her time with the answer. I wonder if she even understands it herself.

"Sweetheart, I know your father," Mom says. "If I'm out in the open, it means he might do something stupid and expose himself to come after me. And that means he gets caught faster, and fewer people get hurt. But I can't take that risk if you're with me. Understand?"

Sam again says nothing. I'm watching his hands on the steering wheel. He's pretty good at covering up what he thinks and feels, but not *that* good, because I see the slight whitening of his knuckles.

"Yeah," I say softly. "I get it. You're bait." I fiddle with my iPod but don't put the headphones back in. "Are you going to kill him?" I don't know what I want to hear.

"No, sweetie," Mom says. But I don't hear any conviction behind it. I know that Sam wants to put a bullet in Dad's head. Maybe more than one. And I get it. I get that Dad is a monster who needs to be slayed.

But Dad is also a memory to me. A strong, warm figure tucking me into bed and placing a kiss on my forehead. A laughing man whirling me around in the sun. A father kissing my boo-boo finger and making

21

it better. A giant shadow scooping me up off that soft braided rug and folding me in warm, protective arms.

I look away, out the window, and I don't argue with any of it. Thinking about my father, both as the monster and the man, makes me feel short of breath and sick, and I don't know how I'm supposed to feel. No, that's a lie: I know I'm supposed to hate him. Mom does. Sam does. Everybody does, and they're right.

But he's my dad.

Connor and I don't talk about this—not ever—but I know he feels this, too . . . the way it pulls and rips inside to try to match up these two very different things. I think about that colorful old rug again, a piece of home inside a monster's den. I can't decide if that was him trying to still be *Dad*, or if the monster was all there ever was, and *Dad* was a mask he wore to mock us.

Maybe it's both. Or neither. It's exhausting, and I put the music back on and try to drown it all out.

I sleep for a while. When I wake up, we're close. Sam turns the car off the main freeway and onto smaller state highways, and we glide through a dozen small towns before the turnoff comes for Norton, and Stillhouse Lake. I watch that buckshot-riddled old sign glide by with a pain deep in my stomach. I want to jump out of the car and run down that road, run straight for home and throw myself into my bed and pull the covers over my head.

We avoid heading into Norton proper and instead take a side road off into the deeper woods. It's mostly mud and ruts, and bumpy; even Connor finds it too hard to read with all the jolts, and he slides a bookmark in place with a stubborn sigh of frustration. We go maybe half a mile and then loop around a broad turn to come up to a small, old, neatly maintained cabin surrounded by high iron fencing.

Javier Esparza is sitting on the porch. He's at least a dozen years older than I am, if not more; he's dressed in a khaki-green T-shirt and dark jeans, and he looks more like a soldier than people in uniform. As he stands up, I see that he's got a shotgun in easy reach. He's also wearing a semiautomatic handgun in a holster on his belt—more obvious than the way my mom wears hers, in a shoulder rig currently concealed under her leather jacket. He's also got a big killer of a dog—a rottweiler—lying panting at his feet.

As Mr. Esparza stands up, so does the dog, all muscle and attention focused right on us.

Mom gets out of the car first, and I see Mr. Esparza relax slightly. He looks down at the dog and says something in Spanish, and the dog sinks back down. Peaceful, but still watching. "Hey, Gwen," he says to my mother, coming forward to open the gate. "Any trouble?"

"Nothing," she says.

"Nobody following?"

"Nope," says Sam as he exits the driver's side of the car. "Not behind or ahead. And no drones."

I shoot a raised-eyebrow look at my brother across the trunk of the car as we're getting out and mouth, *Drones?* I say, "Are we living in a stupid spy movie now?"

"Nope," Connor says without even a trace of a smile. "It's a horror movie."

I swallow my smart-ass comeback and go to the trunk to grab my bag. Connor takes his. The open trunk lid is momentarily hiding us from the adults, so I say quickly, "Are you okay? For real?"

My brother freezes for a second, like a visual stutter, then looks over at me. His eyes are clear. He doesn't look upset. He doesn't look anything, really. "No," he says. "And you're not, either, so stop trying to be in charge."

"I *am* in charge," I tell him loftily, but he's hit me for sure with that one. I ignore him, because that's the best thing I can do right now, and walk over to stand next to Mom. I'm watching the dog, who's watching me. They can smell fear. I've had a bone-hurting dread of big, loud, angry dogs since one lunged at me when I was four.

I decide to stare him down.

Connor, stepping up, pokes me in the back. Hard. I wince and glare over my shoulder, and he says, "Dogs don't like that. Stop glaring at him."

"What are you now, the Dog Whisperer?"

"Settle, you two," our mom says, and I throw an elbow back—silently—to make sure Connor knows to leave me alone. He dodges with the born ease of an annoying little brother. "Javier, thanks for doing this. I can't begin to tell you what it means to me. I only have three people in the world I'd trust with my kids right now, and you and Kez are on that list."

I still can't get over that she calls him Javier, just like that. Standing this close to him (even though that isn't particularly close), I can't imagine that. But I silently say it to myself to try it out. *Javier.* Sam's old enough to be my dad, and he's, well, Sam. Mr. Esparza is . . . different. He's cool. He's the kind of guy I know I ought to have a crush on, and maybe I did for half a second early on . . . but I don't anymore. That's easier since we're going to be living with him.

I don't like being off balance, so I do what comes naturally to me. I glower at Javier Esparza, as if I can't believe I'm being afflicted with him, let my hair hide half my face, and groan like my bag carries a million pounds of bricks. "Do we get bedrooms? Or do we have to sleep in the barn with the chickens or whatever?" When I'm feeling uncomfortable, I attack. It makes people step off and gives me time to find my way. I don't wait this time. I just charge straight for the porch, and I'm two steps into that when I remember the dog.

The dog who comes up from the wood floor like he's spring-loaded and fixes those big, scary eyes on me. I feel rather than hear his very low growl. I stop myself, suddenly very aware that I'm exposed. *Stupid, stupid, stupid.*

Mr. Esparza hasn't moved, but now he slowly extends a hand to the dog, and the rumbling stops. The rottweiler licks his chops and sits, polite and panting again. I don't buy it, not for a second. "Maybe let me introduce you to Boot. Hey, Boot. Play nice."

Boot barks. It's a full-chested thing that hits me in ways that make me want to run, but I don't. Barely. Boot stands up, flows down the stairs, all sleek fur and muscle, and circles around me. I stay still, not sure what I'm supposed to be doing. Finally, Boot comes to a stop in front of me and sits.

"Uh . . ." I say. Which is genius. But I can't think of anything else. My mouth is dry. I'm afraid to even look at the dog. "Hi?"

I slowly, slowly lower my bag to the ground. Boot doesn't move. He stares at me as I hold out my hand to him, then turns and looks at Mr. Esparza as if he's saying, *Is she serious with this crap?* before sniffing my fingers and giving them a dismissive little lick. He snorts, as if he doesn't like my bodywash or something, and then turns and flops himself down in the shade to put his chin on his paws. He seems thoroughly disappointed. I guess he was looking forward to a good, solid fight to start his day.

Boot and I have a lot in common.

I keep my head down and don't look at Mr. Esparza at all as I say, "Can I go inside now?"

"Sure," he says. He sounds calm, and ever so slightly amused. I keep my eyes on Boot as I pick up my bag and walk slowly across the open space to the steps.

"Good dog," I tell Boot. He looks away, but he gives me a little twitch of a tail wag. Then I'm up the steps. There's an old weathered chair, and a shotgun still braced in the corner by the door. I have an almost crazy urge to touch it, but Mom would go apeshit if I do, so I just open the cabin door and step inside.

"Great," I say sourly, looking at my options. It isn't big. I guess it's fine; there's a fire burning in the hearth to take the chill off, and the sofa looks big and comfy. So do the chairs. A little dining table next to an equally little kitchen, everything neat and clean.

There are three doors off the main room: bathroom (one, oh God), and two small bedrooms. I throw my bag on the first bed I see and collapse facedown on it. Take in a deep breath.

It smells like pine and crisp linen, and I hug the pillow for dear life. That, at least, is right. Very right.

"Hey," says Connor from the doorway. "Where am I supposed to sleep?"

"Don't care," I mumble into the pillow. "I claim this land for Atlanta."

"Don't be a b—"

"If you say the word I'm thinking, I'm going to kick your ass, Connor."

"Meanie," he says instead, which is kiddie enough to make me laugh, especially the dignified way he says it. "I need to sleep *somewhere*."

"You get the other room," says Mr. Esparza from behind him, and a quick glance shows me he's smiling. "The bigger room, since Lanny already picked this one."

"Hey!" I get up fast, but I'm too late; Connor is already scrambling for the other room. I glare through a veil of black hair at Mr. Esparza. "Not fair!" He shrugs. "Wait . . . where are *you* sleeping?"

"Couch," he says. "It's okay. I'm used to worse, and it folds out into a decent bed."

He thinks like Mom, who always takes the room closest to the door . . . putting herself between us and whatever might be coming.

"Hope you don't snore," I shoot back.

"Oh, I do," he says. "Like a wood chipper. Hope you have earbuds."

I *think* he's kidding. Maybe. I don't want to ask in case he isn't. I just flop back on the bed like I've been shot and stare at the ceiling. Pretty bland. The room is . . . blah, but clean, and it smells nice. I have a couple of personal things in the bag. Connor has a buttload of books. Maybe I can steal some.

Mr. Esparza turns away, and I see Mom stepping inside the main room with Sam Cade. "Javi, you're sure this is okay?" She suddenly sounds uncertain. Which is not like Mom. "I know this is a ridiculous favor to ask. I'm putting you in danger, and putting you out at the same time . . ."

"It's fine," Mr. Esparza says. "Be nice to have some guests for a while. Look, this cabin might look like a shack, but it's reinforced. I've got alarms and lights. I've got Boot and guns and training. They're going to be okay. I'm going to see to that." He pauses, and I see the look he gives Sam. I'm not sure what it means. "Going after your ex is a dumbass idea, Gwen."

"Yeah, it is," she says. "But I spent years hiding, and look what happened. He manipulated me. He put me right where he wanted me. But he's on the run now, and hunted, and I am *not* letting him come after my kids again."

This is the first time I've heard Mom say it so directly. I mean, I know that's on her mind; she needs to be between us and him. I get it. I'm just worried about what is going to happen.

Mom comes into my room and sits down on the bed next to me. I don't want to have The Goodbye Talk, so I start unpacking.

"You always unpack first thing, everywhere we go," Mom says, and I hesitate as I'm folding up a shirt. "Did you know that?"

"Whatever," I say. I open the dresser drawer. It's empty, lined with cedar that wafts up in a warm cloud. I'm going to smell like a tree. Awesome. I stash my pile of underwear and socks, then put shirts in the second drawer.

"Connor never does," Mom says. "He leaves everything in the bag."

"Yeah, well, he's always ready to run. I like to feel like I'm not." Even though I am. Even though I know exactly where everything I have is, and I can have my bag packed in less than a minute in an emergency.

I take the rest of the shirts out of the bag and refold the wrinkles out, then put them away.

"I thought you'd gotten rid of all of those," she says, and I realize she's talking about the faded Strawberry Shortcake T-shirt that I'm putting away. It looks weird, I admit, in my gloomy drawer full of blacks and reds and navy blues. I'm not a Strawberry Shortcake kid anymore. I'm wearing loose cargo pants with zippers and flapping rings, a big bowling shirt, black, with a giant embroidered sugar skull on the back. My hair is dyed the color of midnight, and worn long and straight. I didn't put on any eyeliner today. I miss it.

"Yeah, well, I like the way the shirt feels," I tell her, then shut the drawer on the girl I used to be. "There. Home sweet home. You're dumping us here for how long?"

There are spikes in it, but she doesn't flinch. "I don't know. I know it's going to be hard, but I need you not to contact your friends in Norton. All right?"

Yeah, right, like any of my friends would want to talk to me now. I'm not just the Town Weirdo. I'm evil by association. Besides, they're all in school. "What are we supposed to do about classes?"

"I'm sorry," Mom says. "I know how much this hurts. But it's temporary. Javier and Kezia will make sure you get lessons while I'm gone. I'm hoping it'll be a week, maybe two at the most. But I need you to—"

"Be responsible, take care of Connor, yeah, yeah, I know." I roll my eyes, because we're clearly at that part of the conversation. "Hey, maybe we can hunt our own food. That'll be fun. Squirrel soup. Yummy."

I dig into the bag. On top is a picture of the three of us, laughing, standing in front of the cabin on Stillhouse Lake. Sam took it. It was a good day. I set it on top of the dresser and stand there, fidgeting with it, trying this angle and that. My mom hasn't taken my bait. I'm not surprised. I finally say, "You told us you weren't going to shoot Dad."

"I'm not setting out to do that," she says, which is pretty honest, all things considered.

"I wish you would," I say. "I wish he was dead already. They should have killed him back in Kansas. That's why they call it death row, right?"

28

I try hard to keep my voice even and my shoulders from hunching in. "He's going to murder somebody else, isn't he? And maybe us, if he can."

"That's not going to happen." Mom says it gently. I can tell she wants to give me a hug, but she's become an expert at Lanny Language, and she stays at arm's length. I don't want a hug. I want a fight. She's not going to give it to me, which sucks. "He's going to be caught, and he's going back to jail. And when it's time, then the state will carry out his sentence. That's the right way to do it. Otherwise it's just revenge."

"What's wrong with revenge? Didn't you see the pictures of the bodies? If that was me hanging in that noose, Mom, wouldn't you want revenge?"

She freezes. Just . . . shuts down. I think because she doesn't want me to know how much revenge she'd want to get. Then she blinks, and she says, "Did Connor see those pictures?"

"What? No! Of course not, I'm not stupid. I wouldn't show those to him, and not the point, Mom. The point is, Dad doesn't deserve to live, does he?"

"I'm emotional about him. So are you. That's why it shouldn't be us who decides what happens to him." She's talking the talk, but I can tell she's not feeling it. She wants him super dead, so much that it makes her shake. But she's making an effort not to raise me that way. I guess that's good.

I dump the bag upside down, and stuff rains out on the bed. Makeup, mostly. A scrapbook that comes with an ostentatious, probably easy-to-open lock on it that Connor said he could jimmy with a paper clip. A diary, also locked. I like to write longhand, on paper. I like to think it survives, when stuff on the Internet is just pixels that can disappear in a second. Gone like it never existed.

"Lanny. My job is to get between your dad and you. So that's why I'm going. You understand that?"

I fiddle with a tube of lipstick—Crimson Shadow—and set it on the dresser. "And I'm the one who stands between him and Connor," I tell her. "I get it. I just hate it, that's all. I hate that no matter what we do, how hard we try, it's always all about *him*."

Mom puts her arms around me this time and hugs. Hard. "No. It's about making him meaningless, finally. We are not his. We are *ours*."

I hug her back, but fast, and then I'm out. I flop down on the bed and put my headphones around my neck. "And when do I get my laptop back, Warden?"

"When this is done."

"I know what not to do. You could put parental controls on it, even."

She smiles. "And you're a smart kid who can crack those two seconds after I'm out the door, so no. I'm sorry, but not until this is over."

I give her The Look. It bounces off without effect.

"I'll call tonight," she tells me, and I shrug, like it's no big deal if she doesn't. Except it is. We both know it.

When I get my makeup set up to my satisfaction, I find that Mom has gone out to the living area and is at the kitchen table. She's sitting across from Connor. Javier has put a glass of water in front of my brother, but he's ignoring it. All his attention is on the page he's reading. Mom takes his glass of water and sips, but he ignores that, too. "Must be a good story," she says. I settle into one of the armchairs near the windows. I was right. Comfy. I sling a leg over one arm and watch the show, which consists of my mom trying to gently get behind Connor's walls, and Connor pretending she isn't even there.

He finally gives in enough to say, "It is." He carefully inserts a battered bookmark between the pages of his book, closes it, and puts it down on the table. "Mom. Are you going to come back?" I can see his eyes. I'm worried about how they look. I don't really know what my brother is thinking about anymore. Since Lancel Graham took us, he hasn't felt safe; I know that. He'd put such faith in Mom to keep us completely secure, to keep the world away, and for him, that failure had been epic. Hadn't been her fault, and she'd come for us like I knew she would.

But I don't know how to fix my brother.

Mom says all the right things, of course, and she hugs him. He breaks away quickly, which he always does . . . Connor isn't much of a hugger, especially when other people are around. But it's more than that.

Mom kisses me on the forehead, and I give her a hug, a real one, but I don't say anything. Sam, who's been quietly leaning against the door, comes over to me and says, "Hey. Take care of your brother, okay?" Sam is a good man. I was wary for a long, long, *long* time, but I've seen him do quietly amazing things for us, including fighting to save us when our lives were on the line. I believe him when he says he cares.

I also believe it's hard for him, because our asshole dad killed his innocent sister, and when he looks at us he can't help but see some part of Melvin Royal in me and Connor. I study myself for hours in the mirror sometimes, picking out bits that resemble Dad. My hair's more like Mom's. But I think the shape of my nose is more like Dad's. And my chin. I've looked up how old I have to be to get plastic surgery, just to remove any trace.

Connor sometimes looks exactly like pictures of our father when Dad was a kid. I know it bothers my brother a lot. I know he spends a lot of time obsessing about whether he will turn out . . . bad.

Mom needs to get him help. Soon. And if she won't, I will.

"I'll take care of him," I tell Sam, then give it a shrug for good measure as if it's no big deal. But Sam gets it.

"And yourself, tough chick."

"Who you calling *chick*?" I demand, giving him a grin. We don't hug again. We bump fists, and he goes to do the same with Connor.

Then he and Mom are gone, out the door, and we go out on the porch with Javier Esparza and Boot the dog to wave goodbye. Well, Boot doesn't wave. He still looks unhappy he didn't get to chew my face off. I give him a guarded pat on the head. He snorts again, but then he turns to Connor, and without the slightest evidence of fear, my brother sits down next to the dog and scratches him between the ears. Boot closes his eyes and leans against him.

Boys, I think, and roll my eyes.

I watch Mom and Sam get in the car. I watch them drive away. My eyes are clear and dry, and I'm proud of that.

Mr. Esparza says he's going to make chili dogs for lunch. He puts Connor to work chopping up onions.

I go to my room, shut the door, and weep into my pillow, because I am as afraid as I've ever been in my life that I will never see my mother again.

And that Dad's going to find us.

3

SAM

Gwen is still too quiet, an hour out onto the road. I can feel the pain vibrating the air around her.

"You okay?" It's an inadequate question, but I have to try. There's something haunting in the blank way she's staring out the window at the flickering trees, like she's trying to hypnotize herself into something like peace.

"I just abandoned my kids," she says. Her voice sounds strange. I shoot her a quick look, but the road is narrow and curved, and I can't spare much focus from keeping the SUV on the road. "Left them with . . . strangers."

"They aren't strangers," I say. "Come on. You know they're good people. They'll do everything they can to keep the kids safe."

"I should have stayed with them." I can tell that she's aching to ask me to turn the car around. "I just want to take my kids in my arms and never let them out of my sight again. I'm terrified . . ." Her voice fades out for a few seconds, thin as fog, then comes back stronger. "What if I never come back to them? What if they're taken while I'm gone?"

She sounds so shaken that I pull the SUV off on the shoulder, in the blue shadow of trees. "Do you want to go back?" I cut the engine and turn to look at her. Not judging, but worrying. If this is going to work, I need to be sure that she's up to it. I won't blame her if she isn't, but deep in my heart I know I have to go, with or without her. Melvin Royal is out there, and he's going to come for Gwen, and those kids. This used to be about revenge for me, about getting justice for my sister, Callie, but now it's something more.

"Of course I want to go back," Gwen says, then takes in a deep breath. "But I can't, can I? If I don't fight for my kids and protect them now, how can I ever look them in the eyes again? He's going to come for them. And I need to be in his way when he does."

Gwen's all raw pain, wired in place with steely control. Looking at her, you'd never doubt that she means what she says. And I don't, not about Melvin Royal. She will face him head-on. And she won't run.

"We're going to kill him," I say. It isn't dramatic, and it isn't a question. "We understand each other, right? We're not in this to find him and call the cops and put him back in jail. The man will keep hurting you any way he can for as long as he lives. And no way am I letting him go on doing that."

I don't mean to betray that much, but there it is. If I feel love for this woman, it's a harsh kind of love, dangerous to both of us until the ghost of Melvin Royal is finally put to rest.

"Yes," Gwen agrees. "We're going to kill him. It's the only way to be sure the kids are safe."

I nod slowly, then give her a smile. The one that answers me is grief and guilt and apology all together. "I have to confess, I never thought I'd be talking about becoming a straight-up murderer. Funny the things you learn about yourself, when you're pushed."

Gwen puts a hand on my arm, and I feel it through the cloth, hot as a brand. I let go of the steering wheel and slide my hand into hers. Our fingers twine. We don't say anything for a long, long moment, and the peace of the wild country road, the trees, the distant call of birds, is so far from the darkness inside that it feels like another world away.

A ringing cell phone shatters the silence, and we both go for our pockets. "Mine," I say, and because I recognize the number that shows up on the screen, I answer. "Hey, Mike. What's up?"

"The hell you think is up, Sammy, I called you to shoot the shit? Business, son. I got a couple of leads on possible Absalom members. You want to take one?"

"Sure," I say. "I take it this isn't official."

"Officially, I haven't got enough to ask any of these sons of bitches what time of day it is, so you take it however you want. You want the tip or not?"

I have no pen or paper, so I make an air scribble with one hand, and Gwen takes the hint; she comes up with a pen and the rental agreement for the SUV. I listen to the two options that Mike Lustig reads out and make an instant choice. I jot it down. "Got it. We'll take the closest one to us, in Markerville."

"You go careful, yeah?"

"Yeah," I tell him. "You, too."

Mike hangs up without a goodbye, which is just his style. I hand the written note to Gwen.

"Arden Miller, Markerville, Tennessee," she reads off. "Man or woman?"

"Don't know."

"And where's Markerville, besides in Tennessee?"

Having a name, a direction, makes this feel real now. Momentum. I give her a sudden, broad grin and put the SUV in gear. "Don't know that, either. First stop: buy a map." That would sound weird to most people these days, but neither of us can afford to risk using the Internet. Not with Absalom watching everything.

The longer we can stay off the grid and off anyone's radar, the better.

◆ ◆ ◆

The map we buy doesn't have Markerville on it, and I end up asking an old man sitting in a rocking chair outside the store, which is as rural as it gets. He squints his eyes at me—faded gold coins that used to be a dark brown, I think—and shakes his head. "Nobody got no business in Markerville," he tells me. "Place been gone for years. Even the post office closed up shop back in the sixties. Nothing there but falling-down shacks."

It doesn't sound promising, but I get directions anyway. It's a fair drive, at least a few hours, and it's already getting dark by the time we hit the outskirts of Nashville.

"You want to keep driving, sleep in the car, or get a room?" I try to make sure there's nothing in the question to suggest that it's a come-on, because God knows, this isn't the time even if there's some possibility of it. "Two rooms, I mean."

Gwen's the practical one. "One room, two beds will do," she says. "Someplace cheap. No point in getting to Markerville tired and having to wait for sunup, right?"

"Right," I say. "Cheap. Got it."

A half hour later, I spot a place called the French Inn, a drive-in motel that saw its best days back in the fifties, at the latest. It's a plain U-shaped brick affair, slightly raised up a hillside, and it has all the curb appeal of a mortuary. There are two cars parked in the small lot, and a total of about twenty rooms, all first floor.

I give her raised eyebrows. "Norman Bates called, he wants his shower curtain back."

Gwen laughs, and it sounds real. Warm. "Looks delightful."

"Bedbug Central it is," I say, then turn the wheel. We bump into the parking lot, which is just as rough as the paint job on the room doors, and park in one of the many free spaces. "Wait here. If there's a camera, I don't want you on it." Gwen's more recognizable than I am, and with any luck, Absalom hasn't got their asses in gear scouring for pictures of my face yet. I add a Florida Marlins cap I found in the last convenience store, pull it low, and head inside. Before I close the door, I give her a straight look. "Doors locked."

"Always."

She's also armed, and a great shot, and I'm not particularly worried about leaving her out here alone. Gwen Proctor won't go anywhere. Not quietly. And if some random predator decides to take her down, he's got a surprise in store.

The motel office is as unenthusiastic as you'd expect, and I wonder about the slack-faced man behind the counter; he has the dead-fish eyes of someone who's seen it all and covered most of it up. I take the greasy plastic-tabbed key and hand over cash, and I'm back out the door in two minutes.

We leave the car where it's parked, since it's near a floodlight, and take everything of any value out. We have the third room, and when I unlock the door and swing it open, there's a familiar smell of bleach and despair that radiates out. Soul-crushing. At least when I flick on the light there aren't any visible cockroaches scuttling for cover, and everything seems clean enough, though I wouldn't care to run a black light over the surfaces.

Less than reassuring are the furnishings, which look like the world's worst garage sale, and the water stains on the sagging ceiling. There are, as requested, two beds, and I motion Gwen to take the one nearest the bathroom for no better reason than it's farther from the door. I watch as she lifts the drab bedspread, which drapes all the way to the carpet, and bends over to look underneath. She grabs a flashlight from her pack and checks it again.

"What exactly are you looking for?" I ask her.

"Creepy dudes," she says. "Dead bodies. Stashes of methamphetamines. Who knows?"

Checking suddenly sounds like a damn good idea, so I borrow the flashlight. While I'm down there peering at a mummified condom and at least three beer bottles, and regretting life choices, I use the cover to ask, "Night or morning shift in the bathroom? Because I'm guessing this place only has enough hot water for one coffeemaker and a two-minute shower every few hours."

"I'll take night," Gwen says. "You need in there first?"

I straighten up and shake my head, and Gwen avoids looking at me directly. She grabs her bag and takes it with her into the bathroom, and I hear the door shut and lock.

I can either sit here and listen to her undressing, or I can do something useful.

I choose to go get us some food.

When I come back, Gwen's done with her shower, the room's desperate smell has been replaced with a warm, fruity scent, and she's fully dressed again except for shoes. I approve. Sleeping vulnerable here isn't a plan I'd recommend. I hand over a bag with a burger and fries, along with a canned soda, and we sit on opposite beds silently refueling for a while.

"I should have asked," she says. "Was that your FBI friend on the phone? Mike?"

I nod without replying. The hamburgers are a crime against beef patties, but I choke down the last bites anyway. I need the fuel.

"And why exactly is an FBI agent helping us out . . . ?"

"Because sometimes I do him favors. And he owes me at least three right at this moment. Besides, he's low on bodies to follow up leads, and he thinks I'm probably more reliable than the state troopers."

"Only probably?"

I shrug. "Mike's not a guy who trusts anyone completely. He wasn't really detailed about his tip, so what you saw is what he gave me. Arden Miller, Markerville. He didn't have an address, and said we wouldn't need one. If it really is a ghost town, that's probably true."

"And how does Arden relate to Melvin?"

"Lustig heads up a task force that investigates dangerous Internet groups. Absalom's on his radar, and apparently, Arden has something to do with them."

"So are we dealing with a hermit? A survivalist? What?"

"Not a clue," I say. "But we will be really damn careful."

"Yeah, about that. Before we head straight for the town, let's take time to do some research on Arden Miller and see if we can put together a decent game plan for this place. We can hit the local library in the morning. I'll take the Internet searches, you take the book searches . . . ?"

"It's a plan," I say. We've finished the burgers by then, both of us wolfing them down at a speed that meant we were actively trying to avoid tasting them. I take the wrappers to the trash, and while I'm up, I take a good look at the door. There's a flimsy chain lock that's clearly been ripped out several times, and neither the door nor the frame looks sturdy enough to resist a stiff breeze, much less a solid kick.

"How's the bathroom?" I ask her. "Security-wise?"

"There's a window, but it's small and barred, and no fire release."

"Let's not start any fires." I drag over a chair upholstered in baby-shit brown and wedge it under the door handle. It might not help much, but it's better than nothing.

"What time in the morning do you want to get up?" Gwen asks me. Her voice sounds a little tight. Nerves. It's a normal enough question, but it feels like something you ask a spouse, or a lover, and we both feel the implication hanging in the air. I walk to my bed, take the clip-on holster from the back of my jeans, and put it on the bedside table. Gwen's shoulder holster is already hooked over the bedpost, like a particularly edgy piece of bondage gear.

Yeah, maybe don't go that way, I tell myself. I lean over and start unlacing my boots.

"Seven's early enough," I tell her. "Or whatever time the werewolves attack."

"I think we're more in zombie territory," she says. She's sitting cross-legged on top of the covers, but she gets up, folds back the sheets, checks for bugs, and then crawls in. "Okay, well, good night." Sounds awkward. Feels the same.

My second boot hits the floor. I move them under the nightstand, in easy grabbing distance if I need them, and lean back against the pillows. The mattress is lumpy and tired. It matches my mood. "Good night, Gwen." It sounds ridiculous.

We're both silent for a long few seconds. The laughter starts deep in my guts, as ridiculous and infectious as shaken champagne, and when I can't help it anymore, I let it out.

Gwen laughs, too. It feels good, cleansing, and in the aftermath, even the drab room seems brighter. "Sorry," I finally manage. "It just seems so *polite*. Fuck, we're adults, aren't we? Why is this so . . ."

"Good question," she says, rolling over on her side to look at me. It silences the last of my laughter. "Why is it?"

"You know why," I tell her.

"Just once, I'd like to hear you say it."

"Because there are dead people standing between us," I say, and instantly, all that brightness is gone, and the truth is so frightening that it *feels* like a ghost, sending my skin into shivers and goose bumps. "My sister, for a start."

She doesn't flinch from it. "And all those women I should have been able to help. Even Melvin's half brother—he committed suicide, did you know that? Between the small-town shunning and the Internet basement heroes, he couldn't take it anymore." She swallows, and I wish I hadn't started this now. "The last post he put up on his social media said that it was my fault, that if I'd been a good enough wife, Melvin wouldn't have—"

"That's bullshit," I interrupt. I sound angry, and I don't mean to. "It was never your fault. Blaming you was just petty." I let a second go by. Then another, because I'm standing on the precipice of admitting something I never intended to. I take the plunge. "I tracked Melvin's brother. Just like I tracked you. I knew where he lived. I knew where all of you lived."

Gwen freezes, and I can see that she hesitates. She doesn't really want to ask, but as always, she doesn't turn away, either. "Did you send him hate mail, Sam?"

I'm staring at the irregular, rusty water stain on the ceiling. It looks like Australia. My hesitation lasts too long before I work up the courage to say, "Yeah, I did. I sent some to you, too. Seemed easy, at the time. Felt like justice. But all it was doing was destroying you in slow motion, one envelope at a time. And I'm sorry for that, God, Gwen, I'm *sorry*."

My voice sounds painfully raw on that last, and I know she can hear that. And know that it's as genuine as the laughter that started this.

Out of the corner of my eye, I see Gwen stand up. She sits on the edge of my bed and takes my hand. In a Hollywood movie, the music would come up, we'd kiss, and all of a sudden passion would explode and there'd be some soft-porn montage, all gold-lit skin and awkward angles.

But this is real, and it hurts, and instead of that, I just tell her, half in a whisper, about the hate I used to feel. It's like lancing an infected wound. I tell her about how I obsessed about exacting bloody justice. It isn't romantic. It's appalling. But as with the laughter, when it's done, there's a strangely clean feeling in the air.

She squeezes my hand at the end and says, "You were hating him all that time. Not me. At least now we've both set our targets right."

There's a rare grace in what she's just done. It's forgiveness, and pity, and understanding, and without even thinking about it, I move her hand to my mouth and gently kiss her fingers. I could sketch every inch of her from memory. The shape of her hand is burned on mine in tactile perfection.

I let her go. I don't say anything. I can't.

Gwen waits for a few seconds, and when I don't move, she goes back to her bed. I hear the covers rustle. Dark takes over when she switches off the light.

I sleep badly, and my dreams are haunted by a figure jumping from the roof of a six-story building in downtown Topeka. I'd read the newspaper articles about the suicide. Melvin's brother had gone to work, dressed in a brand-new suit. He'd walked up to the roof and removed his tie and shoes. He'd left them in a neat arrangement with his watch, wallet, and a letter apologizing to his boss for the mess before stepping off the roof on a cloudless June day, two years ago.

But when I see the face of the man in my dreams as he falls, it's not Melvin's brother.

It's me.

4

GWEN

After a full day at the public library ransacking their shelves and the Internet—and paying robber-baron rates for printouts—we have a folder that's remarkable for its thinness, but it's all the info we've found on both Markerville and Arden Miller. There are fourteen Arden Millers that we've located, but only two in Tennessee, and one of them is in a nursing home—not likely to be the one we're looking for. The Arden Miller that's left is a tall redhead, thirty-three years old, who for someone that age has a strange absence of social media. We've found a few photos tagged with her in them, but not many, and in none of them is she plainly visible. In the best one, she's wearing a floppy sun hat and giant sunglasses and is partly turned from the camera, holding the hat against a breeze.

I have no idea why we're looking for her, or why in God's name she'd be living out in the middle of nowhere in a town deserted for forty years.

Or, for that matter, why Mike Lustig wants us to look for her, except that there is some connection to my ex-husband's case.

We spend the night again at Motel Hell, and I thank God that we've eased the tension between us; it feels cleaner now. Simpler. And when I sleep, for the first time in a long time, I feel safe. That's quite an achievement, since the French Inn feels like it's been the silent witness to hundreds of crimes over the years.

The next day, the drive out to Markerville takes us into remote areas of wilderness, where it would be easy to believe you're the only one left on earth, except for the ever-present contrails of planes passing far overhead as they glide the atmosphere. The route takes a series of progressively narrower and more forbidding turnoffs, heading up into hills that are rough and unforgiving for hikers and SUVs alike.

I've been doing rough calculations on mileage, and I warn Sam when we're close; we pull over and park the truck off a little dirt track, behind trees. It's well concealed from the road, and we take a hiker's route up toward where Markerville once stood. According to the records, it had never actually thrived; when the railroad had stopped coming, the few businesses that had opened there failed, and most residents moved on or died clinging to their broken-down houses. The last casualties were the post office/general store and the antiques store, which had apparently been left abandoned with the doors open and a TAKE WHAT YOU WANT sign on the window. We'd found a clipping mourning the town in the self-satisfied way that city dwellers have about the woes of rural folk, and then . . . nothing.

We don't expect to find much, and when we ease through the trees into midafternoon sun to look down at the little valley where the town had been, it looks like a movie set. The four-building main street still stands, probably because it's built of brick, but most of the other wooden buildings are some flavor of leaning, weathered, collapsing, or wreckage. Disaster in slow motion. We hunker down and observe for a while, but nothing moves except birds and, twice, a lean and slinking cat. A door hanging on one hinge creaks shrilly in the wind.

"If she's here," I say, "she's got to be in the brick structures. Right?"

"Right," Sam agrees, then stands up. "Let's make an agreement right now: we don't shoot unless we get shot at. Okay?"

"Can we make exceptions for knives? Clubs?"

"Sure. But nonfatal wounds. We need to question Arden, not haul her dead."

It puts us at a serious disadvantage, but he knows that.

As we go down the hill, I catch sight of glass glinting behind some leaning boards, and I pull Sam to a stop to point. It's a car. It's not some relic left behind from the glory days, either; this looks to be a fuel-efficient midsize no more than five years old. I'm lucky to spot it. Someone's gone to some effort to keep it concealed. From the glimpses I can make out, it doesn't seem neglected. More like it was parked there recently.

I alert Sam, and we ease around to take a look. The hood is cool when I cautiously lay a hand on it. I'm careful of tripping any alarm sensors . . . and then I think about that. I exchange a look with Sam, and we are once again perfectly in sync.

"Do it," he says.

I yank hard on the door handle—locked—and the quiet is ripped apart by a wailing, honking banshee that rattles painfully in my ears. Sam and I fall back to the shadows and wait; it isn't a long delay before a slender red-haired woman runs from the open doorway of one of the brick buildings, tosses aside boards, and glares at the car. The alternating hazard and headlights turn her face white, then gold, and she fumbles keys from her coat pocket and turns off the alarm.

In the silence, I say, "Arden Miller?"

She nearly falls down, she backpedals so fast, but Sam's moved to block her retreat, and she bounces off him and into the car, practically climbing up the hood. I see the fear chasing over her face. "Leave me alone!" she shouts, then pushes off to rush at me, hoping to break past.

I calmly pull my gun and level it at her, and she stops in a spray of twigs and leaves and pebbles. Her hands shoot up like they're on strings.

"Don't kill me," she says, bursting into wrenching, terrified tears. "Oh *God*, don't kill me, please, I can pay you, I can give you money, I'll do anything—"

"Relax," I tell her. There's a command in my tone, which I realize is counterproductive. I ease it down. "Miss Miller, nobody's going to hurt you. Deep breaths. Relax. My name's Gwen. That's Sam. Okay? Relax."

The third repetition seems to get through, finally, and she gulps a breath and nods. She doesn't match her photo much. The hair is still red, but it's in a short, sassy bob, and she has on thick glasses that magnify her blue eyes. She's a conventionally pretty woman, but there's something about her . . .

It takes me a moment to spot it. Arden Miller didn't start life as biologically female, but her transition is very nearly perfect. She moves correctly, carrying her weight in the right places. If she's had plastic surgery done, it's flawless. She looks more feminine than I do, and acts it, too.

"Did they send you?" she asks, transferring her tear-filmed stare from me, to Sam, and back to me. "I don't have them! I swear I don't, please don't hurt me, I'll tell you!"

"Don't have what?" Sam asks, and she flinches. I give him a little hand motion to back off, and he does. I holster my weapon.

"Tell you what, Arden, let's just sit down. Is there somewhere you'll feel more comfortable?"

She sniffles, dabs at her eyes with the care of someone who knows not to smear her mascara, and says, "Inside. I mean, it's not much. I come here to work."

"Okay," I say. "Let's go inside."

◆ ◆ ◆

Arden's *work*, it turns out, is stunning. I don't know a lot about art, but even I can tell that what she's creating here with paint and canvas is phenomenal—she's documenting destruction, breakdown, beauty.

She's taken Markerville and made it astonishing instead of morbid. There are six canvases propped against walls to dry. She's working in the old post office/general store, which still has—against the odds—glass in the front window, and it gets eastern light. She has lanterns burning now, and she's found an old sofa that's reasonably clean. I think she sometimes stays here all night; there's a rolled-up sleeping bag and a tidy collection of camping gear. Arden's made use of the old rolltop desk—surely a collector's item—that hulks against the far northern wall, and it holds a laptop. No Wi-Fi out here, so she probably uses a disposable cell phone for a connection, and an anonymizer to go online. It's what I'd do.

Arden's already feeling better, in here; the sight of her paintings, her space, gives her steadiness and strength. She leads us to the couch, and she and I sit, while Sam studies the paintings. Arden keeps glancing toward him, but she focuses on me.

"What do you want?" she asks me anxiously. "Did they send you?"

"Nobody sent us," I tell her, which isn't quite true, but close enough. "We just thought you might be able to help us, Arden."

Her back straightens a little, and I don't miss the wary flash in her eyes. "With what?"

"Absalom." I drop the word deliberately, and I see the pure, stark panic flare through her. She holds herself very still, as if she might break. I take a chance, a blind one. "They've been after me, too. And him. We need to find out how to stop them."

The breath goes out of her in a rush, and she folds her arms over her chest. Defensive, but not against me. "I stay off the grid, mostly," she says. "So they can't find me. You should, too."

"I try," I tell her, and then I play another hunch. "When did you leave the group?"

This time, she barely even hesitates. I sense that she's been desperate to tell this story, and for simple human contact. Friendship, even if it's temporary. "About a year ago," she says. "I was never in the inner circle, you know. It was just a game at first. Trolling pedos. Taunting people who deserved it. Or we thought deserved it, anyway. And we got paid for doing it, too."

This time, I am the one who sits back, because this is something I've *never* considered. "Paid? By whom?"

Arden laughs. It sounds like a rustle of leaves in a dry, dead forest. "Like I'd know. Good money, though. And I was fine with it until . . . until I found out *why* we were doing it. It wasn't like they advertised it to the rank and file like me, but one of the higher-ups slipped and mentioned it."

I swallow. I feel desperately in need of water for some reason, as if I've been crawling through a desert. I'm in strange territory now. "I don't understand."

"Look, we certainly did it for the lulz, no question; we were good at it, too, which was why they recruited us for the special projects. I thought it was some kind of crusade, you know? Pure. But they sent us after people when they stopped paying blackmail money. They sent us to punish them into cracking open the bank again," she says. "We were just virtual leg breakers. When people dig in their heels, the hounds like me come off the chain. I know I'm a bitch, but come on." Arden laughs again. It doesn't sound any happier. "The idea somebody was making hard cash off ruining people—that's just wrong."

"It's better to ruin them for free?" I ask. I feel a little dazed.

This time, I get an apologetic shrug. "If you're doing wrong and you're on the Internet, you have to expect some of that, don't you?"

I like Arden, but this baffles me. It's a blind spot, an assumption that cruelty is fine in the right context. *Doing wrong.* Everyone's done wrong to someone. Even now, she can't see the toxic effects of having that easy access to a victim.

I have to start rearranging the whole image I have of Absalom. I've been thinking of them as manipulative fanatics, in it for the sheer bloody chaos of destruction, and some of them certainly fit that description. What Arden is describing, though . . . this is bigger. More cynical. Had Melvin paid them to go after me? How? He hadn't had access to cash in prison. Maybe he'd traded favors.

Dealing with dedicated, incredibly psychopathic trolls was one thing. Dealing with them when it was their *job* to come after me might be even worse.

"Arden." I lean forward, putting out all the good intentions and sincerity I can. "Why did Absalom turn against you?"

Her face contorts into a grimace, and she sweeps a hand up and down her body. "They found out," she says. "A lot of them hate women. *All* of them hate trans women. They started posting about me. I fought back. When they kept at it, I downloaded a bunch of their payment records from the server and told them I'd put it out public if they came after me. I thought it would stop them." She looks away. "I had a friend staying over that day. I went out to get us Chinese food. When I came home, my apartment was on fire. The whole building went up. Seven people died."

"And . . . you don't think that was an accident," I say. "I'm so sorry."

She nods and fights back another wave of tears. "They thought they got me, for a while. But I've been moving around, finding places to stay low. One good thing, I took up painting, and the gallery I showed them to says I'm pretty good at it. I need to sell these and get out of the country. Maybe it'll be easier somewhere else. Sweden, maybe."

"These files you took," I say. "Arden . . . do you still have them?"

I'm praying she says yes, but she gives me a sad look and shakes her head. "They were stored on a thumb drive," she says. "It went up with everything else. I don't have anything to hold over them now. I'm scared to death, Gwen. Aren't you?"

"I am," I tell her. "Are you sure you don't know anything that can help me find them . . . ?"

She thinks about it. Picks at a stray red hair on her jeans and lets it drift down in a ray of sunshine. Watches it fall.

"I know one thing," she says. "The asshole who was the angriest about me, I know where he lives. That was the last thing I found before I was afraid to push it anymore."

I glance at Sam. He turns to look at us and nods. "Then . . . would you tell us? Let us go after him for you?"

Arden folds her hands together in her lap and sits up straight. She meets my gaze, and there's defiance in there. Anger. Fear. But mostly, there's resolve.

"I wasn't a good person," she says. "I hated myself, and I thought the world was shit and everybody deserved what they got. I wanted to see everybody hurt the way I did. But I'm not like that anymore. And I'm sorry for all the people I went after online. I never meant—" She stops and shakes her head. "I know that doesn't mean much. But if you can get this guy, maybe that's a step in the right direction. You got a pen?"

I've left pen and paper in the car, but Arden just shrugs, goes to the rolltop desk, and pulls out supplies. She writes, walks back, and hands it to me. I blink, because I'm expecting an address.

"GPS coordinates," she tells me. "It maps to a cabin in Bumfuck, Georgia. But you be careful, Gwen. You be *really* careful. I was a terrible person, but this guy's *evil*. I get the creeps just thinking about him."

"Thank you," I say, then put the paper away. I get up and hesitate. "Will you be okay?"

Arden looks up at me. Her eyes are clear, her perfect jaw set. I recognize the look. I've seen it in the mirror. It comes when you own your fear and use it as fuel. "Not yet," she says. "But someday. Yeah. I will be."

I offer her my hand, and we shake. Sam comes closer, and I see Arden's body tense a little. She's gun-shy with men, and I wonder how much abuse she's already taken. But he just extends his hand, too, and she finally completes the gesture.

"You're really good," he tells her. "Keep doing this. And keep safe."

She gives him a faint, cautious smile. "I will. You, too. Both of you."

I call the kids from a pay phone that is sticky with sweat and other things and smells like spilled beer. Connor is as tight-lipped as ever, and Lanny adopts a cool, distant attitude that tells me how angry she is about me being gone. I hate it. I hate that I've had to leave them. *It won't be long. This might be the break we need.*

Maybe I'll let Sam go on without me, I think as I hang up. But though it makes me ache with guilt, I also know I probably won't. I *need* to stop Melvin.

Just a few more days.

It takes us another full day to get near the GPS coordinates Arden's provided, and I hope they're not random numbers she scribbled down to get rid of us . . . but she's right, they do lead us to the ass end of nowhere in Georgia, which is as remote as it gets. After some discussion, Sam calls in to his friend Agent Lustig, and we tell him what we know from Arden; Lustig says he'll check it out when he has the manpower.

We decide that might be never, and that we don't care to wait.

We sleep in the SUV for a few hours down on a logging road, and when Sam finally wakes me up, it's night. Chilly, too, and damp. There's a light freeze in delicate crystal lace over our windshield.

"We should get moving," Sam says. "See if this guy's home."

"Tell Lustig we're going in," I say.

"Mike will tell us not to."

"Well, then he can get his ass out here and stop us."

Sam smiles, dials the phone, and gets voice mail. He gives Lustig a brisk account of where we are and what we plan to do, and then he turns the phone off and puts it in his pocket. I silence mine, too.

"Ready?" he asks me. I nod.

And we go.

It's a hard hike up a steep, difficult slope, and if we hadn't known where we were heading, we'd have missed it entirely.

I kneel behind a screen of Georgia underbrush, in the shadow of a looming pine tree. It's a small cabin, two rooms at most, and it's well kept up. Gingham curtains in the windows. A neat stack of firewood waiting to make the place warm and cozy. Nobody's burning a fire tonight. No smoke coming from the chimney.

A light flickers on in the main room. *Someone's home.* Sam's made me agree to observe and report, and only go in if we're sure no one's inside; after Arden's warning, neither of us wants to be in a violent confrontation with a sociopath. So we're going to have to wait for him to leave . . . or come back later. As cold as I am, I'm in favor of the latter option, because it's murderously dark already, and there's a wind with a viciously icy edge to it that brings tears to my eyes. Every breath burns like a paper cut. And I'm sore and stiff, and I want to go home and hug my kids forever.

But I focus during the long hours that follow as lights flicker on and off inside the cabin, as the TV comes on and switches off. *Leave,* I beg the man inside, but that doesn't happen. In my mind, I run through what we'd like to get out of this. A handwritten list of the real names of other Absalom hackers would be nice. Never happen, of course. But I'd settle for online handles, which we *might* be able to get the FBI to track. Sam's friend in the Bureau could get us useful information. But at the very least, we've identified a suspect for Mike Lustig to grill. That has to count for something.

In the cabin, a radio is playing. Something low and quiet. Jazz, I think. Maybe it's stereotypical, but I expected thrash metal for a hacker.

Coltrane seems out of character, somehow. I only really notice because the music shuts off, and about a minute after, the light goes out in the front window. From where I kneel, I can't see the side, but I can see the light that's being cast out over the ground in a golden spray. I see when it, too, cuts out.

Our mark is going to bed. *Finally.* I check my phone for the time. It's nearly two in the morning.

Sam is noiselessly rising to his feet, and I try to do the same. I'm athletic and strong, but creeping around in the dark forest isn't among my particular skill sets. I just try not to do anything obviously stupid. He makes a throat-cutting gesture; he wants to punt this and try again tomorrow. We have to find a time when our man isn't at home, to avoid any confrontations. I understand why, but it's so frustrating to be so *close* and not get answers. Any answers.

You don't want to hurt anyone, Gwen, I tell myself. That's my better angels talking. My demons are telling me that I absolutely do, that I want to put a gun to this man's head and demand to know *what right* he thinks he has to make my life, and the lives of my innocent children, a living hell. What kind of sick bastard takes the side of a cold-blooded psychopath who tortures and kills innocent young women? And gets *paid* for it?

I don't want to leave. I want to go in there and ask. But I know that Sam is right, and I'm fiercely and terribly emotional about all this. I want my ex-husband dead, because every moment he's out in the world is another moment he's hurting people. And coming for my kids, and for me.

I force myself to agree with a nod to Sam that, yes, we will break off our approach and come back tomorrow.

A blur of movement catches my eye, and I snap my head to the right, in time to see a small rabbit break cover and race across the open space in front of the cabin. Behind it comes a black cat intent on its prey. Neither of them makes a sound. Life and death, happening right in front of us.

The fleeing rabbit is about a quarter of the way across the clearing when suddenly a light flares on, blindingly bright, aimed to illuminate the entire semicircle at the front of the house. *Motion light.* I drop back into my crouch, and I can see Sam doing the same. I'm mentally kicking myself for missing the fixture, but it was hard to see until it ignited like a ball of white fire; it's set far back under the peak of the eaves, and when I raise a hand to try to block the glare, I think I can see that it's contained behind some kind of wire mesh.

Won't be easy to reach, disable, or fool.

The rabbit loses the race halfway across the yard. The cat pounces, and the rabbit makes a sound that's eerily like a scream as it's seized by the back of the neck. The little shriek cuts off when the cat viciously shakes it, biting down. Good, efficient murderers, cats.

Having killed it, the cat drops the limp bag of fur on the ground, bats it with a paw for a while, then strolls off. Leaves it where it lies.

I think of my ex.

The motion light clicks off again in another thirty seconds after the cat is gone, and I look over at Sam. He seems grim, studying the scene, and finally shakes his head. He's thinking this cabin is a very bad place. It has an aura of—I don't know how else to say it—*darkness*. I can imagine bad things being done here. I can almost feel the ghosts crowding around me. What has this faceless man done? Arden sure seemed terrified of him.

I wonder for the first time if our man is alone in this cabin. Does he share my ex-husband's tastes? Does he have a captive in there? If we walk away, who else might we leave to suffer?

There is no good answer here. We're in the wrong, legally; the info we have on this man is thin, and there's no proof he's done anything wrong. We're trespassing. Maybe stalking, since we've been watching this place for hours. We still haven't caught so much as a glimpse of the person who owns the place.

Something's been nagging at me all this time, and now, suddenly, it goes from a whisper to a shout. *He should have looked out.*

The security light had flashed on. If he was that paranoid about people approaching, *he should have looked out.*

I tell myself that maybe he's distracted, in another room, maybe on the toilet, but that still doesn't make sense. The cabin isn't that big. He still would have pulled the curtain, or opened the door and reactivated the security light to check the surroundings.

All those lights, coming on and going off since sunset. And it has a *pattern.* I see it now as I replay it in my memory.

It's all on timers. Jesus. There's nobody in there.

I could be wrong, of course, but I don't care. Watching that rabbit die, seeing that spray of blood fly in the air as the cat shook it, makes me remember the pictures that *this* man sent to me, him or one of his slimy little friends. Pictures that dishonor the victims of my husband's crimes, digitally map the faces of my children onto murder and rape victims, show them posed in degrading and horrible ways. This man is a coward. He hides out here in the wild and torments my family, and I am *right here*, and I'm not going to walk away without letting him know he's not safe. Not from me. Not anymore.

Regardless of the motion light, I stand up, and I run for the front door.

The light blazes on again before I'm more than two steps out of cover, but I don't hesitate. I hear Sam moving behind me; he hasn't shouted my name, and I'm a little surprised he's followed. I know he'll be angry. We cross the open space and flatten out against the wall on either side of the front door. After what seems an eternity, the light clicks off again, and I have to blink away the bright afterimages.

"The hell are we doing?" Sam whispers.

"Going in!"

"Gwen, no!"

"Yes!"

There isn't time for a long debate, and he knows it. He sends me a look full of fury and frustration, but he pivots, balances, and slams his boot into the door just at the lock. The door shudders, but it doesn't open. He tries again. And again.

Nothing. The door's meant to withstand worse than us.

But the windows aren't.

I go around to the side. The window there is locked, but we're in this now, and I'm not about to hesitate. The glass proves to be breakable, even though it's thick and double-paned, and once I've shattered enough of it, I reach inside, flip the catch, and slide it open to climb inside.

I pull the gun that I've kept holstered until that moment. Sam's already got his own weapon ready as he slithers through behind me and rolls back up to his feet.

There's no sound. No light. I glimpse a lampshade and frantically feel around for the switch; it blazes on when I find it, and we're confronted with a couple of plush chairs, a hooked rug, a small table on which the lamp sits, some bookcases with a jumble of contents, a kitchen with a tiny stove and refrigerator that look like they date back to the 1950s.

There's no one here.

Sam's still moving. There's a door to our right, and he opens it and covers the room with his gun while I flip on an overhead light.

There's a twin bed. Neatly made with a forest-green blanket for a cover. Behind a small divider, there's a shower and toilet.

And there's no one here at all.

Sam ducks into the small bathroom, then out again. "The shower's still got some moisture in it. It's humid, so that might be left over from earlier today." He gives me that *look*. "You got lucky, Gwen. He could have been in here."

"Come on, he had everything on timers, which meant he wasn't," I snapped. "Handling this with kid gloves isn't going to get us anywhere, Sam. And it won't protect my kids."

Sam shakes his head, but he can't fault my feelings . . . he loves my kids, too, I know that. Our friendship is, by any standards, peculiar; it shouldn't exist, and sometimes I feel like it's skating on thin ice over a terribly dark fall. But he wants what I want. That will never change.

Standing in this stranger's cabin, I can feel that sense of darkness again. This man leads a hidden life. I don't know what variety of depravity he practices, but I know it will be something awful.

It's hard to look at this normal place, the calm neatness of it, when he's dedicated his life to destroying other people's. I'm angry. Probably too angry. I want to smash everything. And what's stopping me? Truth is, we're already committing a crime just by being inside. Breaking and entering. Vandalism seems like a reasonable add-on.

"Look around," I tell Sam. "There has to be something we can take with us. Something to tell us what he's into, and maybe, if we're lucky, he'll have correspondence with Melvin."

Sam nods, but he pointedly checks his watch; if there was some kind of alarm system, we're already in trouble. I doubt there is, though. Someone who makes a practice of living so far away from civilization doesn't depend on 911. *Our security provided by Smith and Wesson.* If he was here, or anywhere near, he'd have opened fire on us already. We're safe. For now.

"Papers," I tell him. "Electronic records. Anything that looks like it could be of use, okay? Ten minutes."

"Five," he says, and then he leaves me to it.

There's a small desk shoved into the corner of this small room. Like everything else, it's painfully neat and clean, made of burnished maple in plain country style. I open drawers, then pull them out and dump them to look behind and underneath. We can't conceal our intrusion here. Might as well do a thorough job of it.

I find nothing I can immediately identify as important. Receipts, mostly. Printed papers that seem not very illuminating. I grab everything and shove it into my backpack.

I'm wearing gloves, so I've left no prints behind; I put everything back in the drawers and slot them back in place. I check the closet. There's a gigantic gun safe, but as I'm staring at it, I see a shoe box up on top. I open it. More receipts. I cram those into my backpack. One drifts down behind the safe, and as I'm groping blindly back there for it, my fingers brush the sharp edges of something that doesn't quite belong.

I push it, and it moves.

Magnetic. I detach it from the safe and pull it out. It's a shallow box with a sliding top, like the old hide-a-key my grandmother used to put in the wheel well of her car.

This one holds a USB.

I never would have found it if I hadn't dropped a page behind the safe. It was in a space that would have been missed in a search, and the gun safe is too huge and heavy to move without major effort.

I retrieve the fallen page, and I put that and the USB in the backpack.

"Got anything?" Sam calls.

"Receipts, some printouts, and a thumb drive," I say. "No computer, just a power cord. He must have taken that with him. You?"

He appears in the doorway. I can't read his expression, but something about it makes me step back from the closet and come toward him. "You'd better see this," he says. I know I'm not going to like it, but I follow him out into the main room. Everything in its place. Everything clean and orderly. I wonder if this man has a military background, because every surface gleams. If there are fingerprints here, I can't spot any.

Sam opens up a closet. It looks like a normal pantry, just deep enough to reach into. Eight shelves, top to bottom, packed with canned goods and sundries. Whoever this Absalom asshole is, he likes canned tuna and quick-prep casserole kits.

Sam puts a finger to his lips and pushes on the shelves. They swing back without so much as a squeak, and behind that is a set of stairs. Motion lights click on, revealing a wall with cheap faux-wood paneling, and below, at the bottom of the steps, like a living thing, crouches a steel door with a key lock. I feel the darkness of it breathe up through the chilly air, and for a moment I don't move. I can't. I feel like it's watching me, assessing me for weaknesses.

I'm paralyzed by flashbacks to my ex-husband's torture chamber, so carefully hidden inside my own house. To the basement of Lancel Graham's tumbledown cabin up in the hills above Stillhouse Lake, where he lovingly re-created that horror.

This feels like something just as bad.

We go down slowly, careful of our steps; Sam's probably concerned about noise, but I'm not. I'm worried about hidden traps and tripwires. This place feels like death. Like threats and consequences.

"Stop," I whisper, when Sam takes the last step down. He's about four feet from the door. He listens, and pauses, and looks at me. I keep staring at the steel face of the thing, and I slowly shake my head. "This is wrong. Don't."

"Gwen—"

"Please, Sam." I feel sick, and I am shaking now. The urgency hurts. "We've got to go. Now. Right *now*." I am not psychic, have no trace of any kind of power or gift, but I have instincts. Instincts I ignored for years with Melvin Royal. I should have known what he was doing, what kind of horror show was going on under my roof. I never did, at least not in any conscious way.

Never again. I don't know what will happen if Sam touches that door, but I can feel it's wrong. This is a job for the FBI now, not a couple of renegade amateur thieves. This place feels claustrophobic, and I feel like I'm being watched.

Sam accepts my decision, and that's a gift I can't measure; most men, I believe, would have ignored me and gone straight on ahead. As a consequence, we are almost to the top of the stairs when, with a whispering sigh, the door at the bottom of the stairs cracks open. There's a faint, almost inaudible click.

Sam pauses. I don't know what's coming out of that door, and I don't want to know. I grab Sam, lunge forward—past the shelves, out of the closet—and drag him along with me.

Sam has just cleared the doorway when *something* picks us up and throws us, violently, across the room. I lift and cross my arms in front of my face, draw my legs up in an instinctive attempt to protect my brain and belly, and I hardly feel it when I hit the wall. I definitely don't feel hitting the floor, because suddenly I'm just *there*, lying on wood and looking up as a blast of orange light floods the room. I don't understand what it is. I feel a wave of heat, and then the roof is, strangely, moving away from me, like a giant has picked it up. The lights we've turned on blow out like candles, and I'm looking at stars and trees and then everything, everything, is on fire.

5

GWEN

I come conscious again, coughing, with someone pouring water on my face. The water's cold, and I'm shivering, and I roll over and cough helplessly for a few moments. Awareness starts somewhere in me, reporting pain in my back, in my leg, in my arm. My brain's good at analyzing these things, and it tells me it's nothing too serious. I hope it's not lying to me. My head hurts as well, and that seems of more concern. My mouth tastes like an ashtray, and I grab blindly for the water bottle that's been splashing my face and rinse out my mouth. I spit it out on the ground, then chug thirstily. That's probably a mistake. The thick weight of water hits my stomach hard.

I roll up to my knees, sway a little, find my balance, make it to my feet. I'm in the clearing, near the tree line. Sam is kneeling next to me, and he looks worse than I feel—bloody from a cut on his head, shaking, favoring one side as he tries to get up. I help him. He winces and presses a hand to his ribs.

"How did we—" I turn back toward the cabin.

It's an inferno. I lose my words when I see it, and the reality that we were *in there* comes down on me. I stare, mesmerized. *How did we get out?*

"I pulled you out. What the hell, Sam?" says a new voice. It belongs to a man standing a distance away, who's watching the blaze. He's more than six feet, wearing a black tufted parka, which I envy right now, and as he shifts, a gold badge on a chain around his neck catches the light. *Cop,* I think, and I freeze. But the badge is different. I can't immediately identify it. My eyes won't focus finely enough. He's African American, and his voice has a slow southern accent that makes him sound amiable, though I can see him studying me, calculating, weighing my worth. He's also wearing a bulletproof vest under the parka, I realize, as the wind blows a hot gust from the burning cabin and flaps it back.

FBI. It's right there on his vest.

"Mike Lustig," he says. "And you're both a pair of goddamn idiots. What happened?" He directs that last part past me, and Sam winces as he shifts position.

"Is that a general question, or do you want something specific?"

"You said you were going to *look around*. What the fuck did you do?"

My brain clears a little. Mike Lustig. Sam's FBI friend. He has an escalating curse level. I wish he'd lower his volume, because my ears are ringing constantly, and my head pounds like a bass drum.

"There was some kind of booby trap," I tell him. "Down in the basement. We didn't open the door, but someone else did. We were lucky to get out of that hallway before it blew."

"Not luck," Sam says. "You smelled a trap, and I didn't."

Mike looks from one of us to the other. "And you don't know what was in the hidden room?"

"No."

"Damn," he says. "He could have had anything down there. A captive, even."

I go cold. "Are you saying that . . . that there was someone down there? Someone we could have rescued?"

Mike just looks at us. Sam shifts finally and says, "Jesus, Mike. What did you know about this guy?"

Lustig ignores the question. "I need to get you to town for a checkup. That cut needs stitches. Favoring your side, too. Broken ribs? How about you, Ms. Proctor?"

"Stop changing the subject!" Sam shouts.

Mike looks past us at the burning cabin. The damage, I realize, is already beyond repair; the place is falling in on itself. He sighs. "This is going to attract attention. Engine company's probably on the way already; they take fire seriously up in these hills. Come on. I'll brief you in the car." He turns and walks away, into the trees, and for a long second, I just stand there, trying to understand what has happened, what the hell is going on. Nothing's making sense. Maybe that's shock; maybe that's the fact my brain has been severely rattled inside its bone cage.

It takes Sam's hand on my shoulder silently urging me along to make me follow, and I keep looking back at the raging inferno, the sparks spitting high at heaven.

What was in that room? Who the hell are these people? They're not just hackers. It's not just a blackmail ring, either.

I'm not sure if I'm brave enough to want to know the answer.

◆ ◆ ◆

We sit in the back of the FBI agent's SUV, which is both a comfort and a worry; I'm fairly certain these doors won't pop open at the pull of a latch. He provides us with strong, dark coffee from a thermos before he steps out to make some calls. I drink it thirstily, more for the warmth than the taste. Sam doesn't say much. Neither do I. We watch the fire, still visible through the trees, and the garland of blinking red-and-blue lights snaking up-mountain toward us.

I finally say, "So that's your friend. Agent Lustig."

"Yeah, we served together," Sam says. "He joined the FBI; I re-upped." He's staring out at the fire, but his gaze cuts suddenly toward Lustig, who is on the phone outside the vehicle. Lustig is pacing back and forth, possibly just to keep warm, but I can't help but think he's also betraying some anxiety. "He knows something he didn't tell us."

"I gathered that," I say, and I wince when I shift to relieve an ache. It wakes something sharper. Still not broken, I think, but I've definitely stressed everything. "Has it occurred to you that maybe he's using you as much as you think you're using him?"

I think he isn't going to respond, but he does. He says, without looking away from Lustig, "He's a good guy."

"He's going to get us killed," I say.

"No," Sam says, and he looks directly at me now. "*You* nearly got us killed. We were supposed to stay outside, not go charging in. *You* wanted to do that."

He's right. I'm angry because he's right, and I know that's a terrible reaction to have, so I bite my lip and manage to stop myself from escalating the argument. I'm tired, I hurt, and I have the awful feeling that we started something here that's out of our control. And what did we get for it? Not much. A backpack stuffed with receipts that probably won't lead anywhere.

My voice comes out a little shaky when I say, "What do you think was in the room—"

"Don't go there," Sam says, putting an arm around me. It's unexpected, and welcome. We both reek of foul-smelling smoke, but I don't mind. "We can't know what he was hiding down there, and he damn sure wasn't about to let us find out."

"What if it was someone—"

"No," he says. "You'll rip your guts out if you do that. Don't."

I sense he doesn't want to imagine it. I do, because I must: a young woman, maybe the age of Melvin's chosen victims. Locked up, tied up maybe. Left to burn if anyone comes close to finding her.

"Maybe it was him," I say. "Maybe he was down there, and he opened the door."

"That's a happier thought," Sam agrees, but he shakes his head. "I was looking at the door when it opened. The knob didn't turn. There was nobody on the other side. It was like a . . . remote-control release."

"You mean we tripped some kind of sensor?"

"Maybe. But . . . maybe someone was watching us. Waiting for us to take the bait. And when we didn't . . ."

That was right; I felt it click together inside. I'd had an overwhelming sense of being watched on those stairs. And I'd been right. *Someone* had been behind a camera. Probably had watched us going through the whole house. It was only after we'd found the hidden basement room that he'd taken action, though. "He was watching," I agree. "And he was off-site. He had a remote control to open that door and set off the explosion. He must have been close by."

"Not necessarily. He could have all of it routed through an app." He gives me a fleeting trace of a smile. "The way you set up the cameras on your house."

He's right. I'd used Internet-capable cameras to monitor my house at Stillhouse Lake, and I could access and watch remotely from anywhere. The tools were common, and commercially available. "And the door?"

"Some Wi-Fi security apps let you lock and unlock doors," he says. "He was probably watching us from the moment we broke in. Once we'd found the secret stairs, he waited for us to go down and open the door. That was probably booby-trapped; maybe he has some kind of disarming signal for the bomb he sends before he goes in himself. When we didn't take the bait—"

"He triggered it for us," I finish. "So he could be anywhere. We've got nothing."

"Not necessarily," he says, nodding to the packs we've got dumped in the floorboards between our feet. They're stuffed with papers. It's something. I hope. "Gwen, remember—"

Whatever he's about to tell me, he's interrupted by Lustig, who yanks the door open and says, "Okay, here's what's about to happen. All hell is going to break loose and rain down shit on us. County sheriffs, fire, ambulance. I'm going to claim federal jurisdiction. You two get taken to the hospital, but you *do not move* until I get there. And you *do not* answer questions until I get there. Understood?"

"Mike," Sam says. "What the hell did we get into?"

The look Mike Lustig gives him is a two-parter: one says, *Not here*, and then flicks to me to indicate I'm not someone he wants to be letting in on the story. And why would he? Mike knows who I am. Who my ex-husband is. He probably doesn't trust me any farther than he can throw a Sherman tank. That's fair. I don't trust him *at all*, and the fact that he's got a badge and a gun and these doors don't open from the inside makes me itch all over. He's Sam's friend, sure. But he isn't mine. My trust isn't contagious.

Lustig shuts the door again, cutting off a cold blast of wind that carries an edge of ice with it, and leans against the SUV as the first responder—a black-and-white county-sheriff SUV—rounds the curve and pulls to a stop beside us. No sirens, but the pulsing flare of the lights turns everything raw and cold in bursts, renders everything alien, even Sam's face. I try the door. It doesn't open. My heart thumps faster, and I look around for something, anything, I can use. Reflex. *I can slither over the seat to the front and get out that way,* I reassure myself. There might even be an extra gun in the glove compartment. If not, I can be out and running in seconds, and in these woods, in the dark, they'd have a hell of a time tracking me down.

It's an academic exercise, this escape plan. I do it for every situation when I feel the least bit out of control. It helps. I've practiced the art of evade, attack, escape for years now in my head, and I've trained for it. My life—and the lives of my kids—depends on it.

"So what's our story?" I ask Sam. "Because the truth isn't going to fly. Not for this."

"Stick as close to it as we can," he says. "We came looking for answers. Found the door wide open. Went in to see if someone was hurt, discovered the secret room, got the hell out just in time."

It doesn't paint us as innocent, but it doesn't indicate we brought dynamite and blew the place to smithereens, either, which I'm completely behind. I nod. *Door is wide open.* I visualize it in my mind, imagining our cautious approach, calling out, looking for someone who's hurt. I imagine it until it seems so real it could be true, and then I keep on imagining it until it *is* true, and the other thing is a distant possibility. It's the only way to consistently, convincingly lie: you have to believe it.

So I make myself believe it. Of course, if the door doesn't burn completely, and they can determine it was locked, then we're screwed. But given the inferno, I think we're safe on that score.

More vehicles crowd around us, penning us in: two fire trucks, a single ambulance, another official-looking SUV, maybe from the forest service. The firefighters are carrying loads of hose into the woods up toward the blaze, and I hear the buzz overhead of a light aircraft; they're spotting for spread of the fire.

It takes the better part of an hour before the glow of the fire is completely out, and then the night is lit only by the still-burning strobes of the emergency vehicles and flaring headlights. All the different sources paint everything a semiconsistent purple, with pops of blues and reds out of sequence. I keep my eyes closed after a while, and so I'm surprised when the door beside me is yanked open. I straighten up fast and realize I'm looking at a young, slender African American man in an ill-fitting paramedic's uniform. "Ma'am," he says, and his Georgia accent is already in full force. "I need to check you over. Can you walk for me over to the ambulance?"

"Sure," I tell him, getting out of the SUV with a little burst of relief. No escape required, after all. At least, not yet. Another paramedic is guiding Sam, and we end up perched together on the step of the ambulance as we're checked out. Sam is diagnosed with a mild concussion and cracked ribs; he's tagged for transport to the hospital. My headache earns me the same privilege, but no way do I want to leave our bags behind in Mike Lustig's SUV, or rob us of getaway transportation. I decline. While they put Sam in the ambulance, I move our stuff back to our own rented vehicle, which is thankfully pulled far enough off to the side that I can back it around the blockage.

I'm halfway out when Mike Lustig steps into my path, and I have to brake hard to avoid giving him a bumper kiss; once I'm stopped, he steps around to my driver's side door and taps on the window. I roll it down. "I'm heading for the hospital," I tell him. "And I'll wait there."

"Fine," he tells me. "You two need to be right about this. You ready?" His gaze tells me I'd better be. I nod. "Don't leave the hospital. I'll be there soon as I can."

I nod, and then I back up and turn to follow the ambulance down the winding mountain road, away from the ashes of what we'd hoped to discover.

◆ ◆ ◆

The first thing I do, once the doctors have checked me, is sit down and call Javier, even though it's now nearly five in the morning. I don't tell him about the fire, or the near miss. I just tell him we're okay. He can tell we're at a hospital, though thankfully he doesn't ask many questions, and I don't have to lie.

"How are they?" I ask him. I've woken Javier up, and I feel bad about it, but hearing his voice is an immense relief. "Are they adjusting?"

"I don't know yet," he says, which is honest. He's keeping his voice down, and I hear the rustle of clothes and footsteps. I imagine him putting on a coat and stepping out onto his porch, because I hear the slight hiss of wind over the phone speaker, and the creak of wood as he sits down on the chair he keeps there. "Jesus, it's freezing tonight. The kids are fine, but I can't say they're happy. It's setting in on them that you're in danger. Lanny's dying to get out of the house. Connor just . . . reads. Is that normal?"

"More or less," I say. "Tell them I love them, will you?"

"Sure." He hesitates for a few seconds, and then he yawns. It's contagious, and I do, too, and realize how exhausted I am, again. "You're not okay, Gwen. I can tell."

"I'm okay enough."

"You coming back soon?"

"I don't know," I tell him softly. "I'm trying."

When I hang up, I find my chest is tight, my throat sore with unshed tears.

Eight long ER hours later, Sam's injuries have been confirmed as cracked ribs and a minor concussion. I've been warned my head will hurt like a son of a bitch for about a day (and it already does, despite a generous application of over-the-counter painkillers). By the time Sam's ribs have been wrapped and we've been relieved of payments we can't afford, we find three beefy white men in uniform waiting for us in the hallway. They're virtually identical, all with the blocky build of guys whose glory days came as high school linebackers; they've all got buzz cuts and tans that end at their collars and cuffs. Mike Lustig, in his FBI body armor and badge and blackness, stands apart, leaning against the wall with his arms folded. In the better light here, he has a long, friendly sort of face, one that seems prone to breaking into ironic smiles more than angry frowns.

Can't say the same for the Georgia bulldogs. They all look impassive at best, outright antagonistic at worst.

"Mr. Cade? Mrs. Royal?"

"It's Ms.," I automatically correct, and then I take in that he's called me by my old name. "Not Royal. My name is Gwen Proctor."

"My info says Gina Royal," the spokesman says, with a grim little twist of his lips that I don't mistake for a smile. "You come with me, *Miz*."

I glance at Mike Lustig. He shrugs. "I got no dog in this fight," he says. "Go on."

Sam and I exchange a quick look, and I nod to let him know it's fine. I don't *know* if it's fine, but there's no point, and no benefit, to staging a war here in the hallway. I walk with the officer around the corner to a quiet waiting room, and he gestures me to a corner seat. It's the farthest one from the exit, but I automatically calculate the ways out, just for practice. Agent Lustig hasn't followed us.

Interestingly, the officer excuses himself almost immediately and shuts the door. I check my watch and start counting. I expect he'll let me cool my heels for at least an hour. It's standard technique. The more off balance and tired a subject is, the better the chances of a slipup.

Georgia's playbook clearly says two hours are the optimum, because it's nearly three when the officer returns. He squeezes himself into the chair next to me, too close for comfort. I imagine he means to intimidate. It just annoys me. If he really knows who I am, then surely he understands I have a whole different scale of intimidation. He smells like sweat and smoke, which means he was up at the cabin, or what's left of it. There's a small stained area on his left sleeve that looks like old blood, and now that I've seen it, I can't quite look away. Did he get it helping someone? Or punching someone? Though sometimes, you have to punch one person to help another.

"So," I say to him, "Officer—"

"Turner, ma'am."

"Officer Turner, was calling me by a dead name a power play, or just a mistake?"

He leans back with a creak of plastic, and he considers me with the expressionless eyes of someone who's been in law enforcement for years. He's considering which approach to take: bully, or country-boy charm. Neither will work, but it's a little interesting to watch his internal debate.

He decides to go with country-boy charm, and when he speaks again, his voice is warmer, with a touch more drawl, and he's even managed a bashful smile. "I admit, ma'am, I thought that might throw you off balance. I apologize if I upset you. Mind if we start over?"

"Sure," I tell him, with a smile every bit as false. "What can I do for you, Officer Turner?"

"I just need you to start from the beginning and tell me how you came to be up there around that cabin, ma'am. How you got the idea to go up there, what happened, that sort of thing."

I sigh. "I don't suppose I could coax a cup of coffee out of you for it, could I?"

He falls for it, though only to the extent of going to the hallway, motioning to someone, and presumably ordering up my caffeine. He's all smiles when he comes back. I summon up one in answer, though I'm not feeling it. "Now," he says, settling in again, "you were saying?"

I toy with just answering *I wasn't*, and asking for a lawyer; I'm still not sure I don't really need one. The evidence can read a lot of ways, and neither Sam nor I planned on having to answer these questions. So I say, "Mind if I ask one question first?"

He considers, then nods. "Go ahead."

"Did you find any bodies in there?"

More considering, and then a slow shake of his head. "Can't rightly say. So what exactly brought you up to that cabin, Ms. Proctor?"

He's allowed to lie to me, of course. It's a time-honored tradition in interrogations, although I haven't yet been advised of my rights. Which is telling.

I stick to my story, the first part of which is true: that we were hoping to discover some information about someone who was helping my ex-husband evade capture. That gets an eyebrow raise, but no comment. It's exactly what Sam's going to say. We've already determined that truth is our best defense, up to a point . . . any other explanation is going to invite suspicion, with my obviously sinister ex in the background. I tell him about the open door and how we cautiously ventured inside. Just as I rehearsed it.

"And what did you find?"

"Nothing," I lie, easy as breathing. I'm not giving up what we brought out of there. "We didn't have time."

"You just . . . went on in?"

"The door was open," I say blandly. "We thought he might have been hurt or in trouble."

"Never crossed your mind a guy like that might shoot you dead for walking in on him?"

I shrug. Don't answer. Stupidity isn't a crime. He has nothing to coax out of that, except the fact that both Sam and I were armed, of course. But legally. Trespassing is a thin charge, at best. He won't bother, unless he thinks he can pin something bigger on top of it.

Officer Turner alters his body language into let's-be-frank. For him, it involves leaning forward, resting his elbows on his thighs, and tenting his big hands together. "Ms. Proctor," he says, "right now, local officers in Tennessee are going through your house up there at Stillhouse Lake, looking for anything that links you to your ex-husband. Your phone records are being analyzed. We know you went to see him before he broke out. You got something you want to get off your chest now, before those results come to light? Might do you some good."

Amateur. I went through years of this, from interrogators far better— and worse—than he is. I gaze at him thoughtfully for a moment, and then

I say, "I hate Melvin Royal. He's *hunting me*, Officer Turner. Do you know how that feels? Do you really think I want to help him? Because if you stand me in front of him and give me a gun, I will not hesitate to put a goddamn bullet in that man's head."

I mean every word of it, with an intensity that takes even my own breath away.

Turner slowly leans back, hands smoothing flat against his thighs. He's got those lightless, merciless eyes that all cops seem to share, the ones that are constantly taking in everything and giving back nothing. For all his awkwardly folksy manner, he's a shark.

There's a knock at the door, and Turner gets up to retrieve two flimsy cups. He hands one to me, and I gratefully wrap cold hands around it. The coffee is a crime in itself, but at least it's warm, and it cuts the astringent hospital smell. This place stinks of fear and despair and boredom, of unwashed people whose body odor has soaked into the couches. There's a tiny, sad little play area in the corner for kids. It's currently deserted, but I think of Lanny and Connor, only ten and seven when a car smashed into Melvin's garage and revealed his horrors to the world. In my gut, they'll always be that age. That vulnerable, shattered age.

"You want to tell me what was in that basement?" I ask Turner, cutting my eyes suddenly to him. It startles him a little. "Because our guy didn't want anybody to see it. Whatever it was."

"It's pretty well destroyed," he tells me. "Ain't nobody going to get down there to take a good look for a while. Going to be hours before it's safe. We might still find bodies."

I hope not, too. Desperately. I nod, then drink the rest of my coffee in a thirsty rush. "Right. Well, I'm going to go now. Thanks for the coffee." He stands up with me, blocking my way. I stare at him and slowly allow the corners of my lips to curl, just a little. "Unless you'd like to arrest me . . . ?"

He's got nothing concrete, and he knows that. He's bluffing when he says, "Sit down, Ms. Proctor. We've got more to talk about."

I don't answer. I just walk toward him. At the last moment, he moves. Illegal detention wouldn't do him any favors, and he's smart enough to know I can't be buffaloed into thinking he's got cause. Yes, there's a burned-out cabin. Yes, I was inside. But there's ample evidence that the place had been booby-trapped, and I was lucky to escape alive, and they've got lots of tantalizing evidence to analyze that doesn't have anything to do with me and my maybe-but-not-provable illegal entry.

I don't break stride passing him. From behind me, he says, "We'll be talking, *Mrs. Royal.*" That's just spite, and I don't dignify it by looking back at him. I keep going, and as soon as I pass the door frame, I feel a weight lifted. I take in a sharp breath, filtered by the fresh scent of the coffee I've just finished, and I dump the cup and go in search of where they've put Sam.

He's still closeted with another officer, and when I look around for Mike Lustig, he's nowhere to be found. I don't much like that. I don't like that he's abandoned us here to fend for ourselves. I find a seat and wait, watching the door and watching the clock hands crawl. Sam's conversation goes on at least twice as long as mine does, and it's nearly six when he finally appears. He doesn't look bothered, and he's finishing coffee. He downs the rest in a gulp and tosses the empty cup, then stops beside me. "You okay?" I ask him.

"Nothing I can't deal with," he says. There's a storm circling behind his eyes. I wonder what the cop said to him. Must not have been pleasant.

"Where's your friend Mike? Fat lot of good he did us."

"Yeah," Sam says. "He had to leave and go back to the scene."

"So what did he tell you, if he told you anything?"

"To go home," Sam says. "And forget this ever happened." Go back to Stillhouse Lake, I'm sure he means. Hunker down, guns at the ready, for my husband to come for us. But when I try to imagine that, I can't see us managing to defend ourselves. I see Melvin appearing, like some evil spirit, behind us. I see him killing Javier and Kezia. I see Sam dead on the floor.

I see me and my kids, alone against the darkness that is their father. And I am not confident that I can save them.

"We can't just give up," I say. "Let's take a look at what we got first. Will Lustig tell us what they find in the basement up there?"

"Maybe," Sam says, which doesn't fill me with enthusiasm. "I might have burned a bridge on that one. We'll see. No, don't apologize." I've already opened my mouth to do just that, and I shut it, fast. "I'd burn every bridge I ever built to get to Melvin. Understand that."

I wonder if he includes the bridge that we've so carefully built between the two of us. I think I understand Sam, most of the time. But when it comes to this . . . maybe I'm fooling myself. Maybe, despite everything he's done for me and my kids, despite the fact that I've allowed myself to be open and vulnerable around him, and he's shown every sign of appreciating that . . . maybe, ultimately, if it comes to a choice between me and getting to Melvin, he'll step over me to get a grip around my husband's throat.

Fair enough. I might just do the same thing. Probably best we don't discuss it.

There's a gauntlet of uniforms around, but we aren't blocked on our way out. Our car is still there in the lot, and still locked. Sam lets out a held breath as we turn onto the main road, and he accelerates—within the speed limit—heading south. "Right," he says. "Let's get the hell out of here. Where we headed?"

"Next town over," I tell him. "Let's stay local, but not right under their noses. Find us a motel." I start to say *something midpriced*, but then I stop myself. That's my natural inclination, but if Melvin's been alerted to this event, he and Absalom will be looking for us. It's a small pool of choices in this area. They'll try everything cheap and anonymous first. "Find us a bed-and-breakfast. Something off the beaten path."

He nods and tosses me a pamphlet. "Grabbed it from the gift shop in the hospital," he says. "Should be some ads in there."

6

CONNOR

Officer Graham told me, *Never tell about this*, and I haven't. Not because
I don't know Officer Graham was a bad guy—I know that. He scared
the hell out of us. He hurt us when he dragged us out of our house, too.

But I'll never tell because of what he gave me. I know Mom would
take it away, and I'm not ready for that to happen.

I leave the phone Lancel Graham gave me turned off. I tried to
use it back in the basement in that cabin where he was holding us, but
there wasn't a signal. I turned it off and removed the battery when Mom
found us because I didn't want it ringing, and I didn't want anybody
tracking us with it.

I don't really know why I haven't just thrown it out, or buried it, or
told someone I have it . . . except that it's *mine*.

Officer Graham said, *This is from your dad, and it's just for you,
Brady. Nobody else.*

My dad sent me something, and even though I know I should get
rid of it, I can't. It's the only thing I have from him. I sometimes imagine him standing in a store, looking at all the phones and choices, and

finding one he thought I'd like. Maybe that's not what happened, but that's how I imagine it. That he cared. That he put some thought into it.

It's lucky that it looks almost like the cheap phone I already carry. They're both disposables, but I've learned to tell them apart by touch—the one Mom gave me feels a little rough under my fingers, and Dad's feels as smooth as glass. They use the same charger. I keep both of them charged up by putting one under the bed charging when I'm carrying the other one.

But I don't turn Dad's on. I just keep it off, with the battery in my pocket, ready to go.

I've just taken Dad's phone out of my pocket—not to use it, just look at it—when Lanny leans in the door of my room and says, "Hey, did you go in my room?"

I'm already feeling guilty, and the second I hear her voice it feels like there's a spotlight on me, bright white and very hot. I drop Dad's phone and watch as it spins across the floor and up against her foot. My mouth goes dry. I'm scared to death that she's going to immediately frown and say, *This isn't your phone—where did you get it*, and it'll all be over, and everybody will be mad that I didn't turn it over first thing, and they'll all give me those *looks* again. The ones that wonder if I'm really like him.

But all Lanny does is snort, say "Way to go, Butterfingers," and kick it back to me. I pick it up and jam it into my pocket. My hands are shaking. I shove Mom's phone, still on the charger, into the shadows under the bed with my foot. She hasn't seen it, I can tell. "Did you go in my room or what?"

"No," I tell her. "Why?"

"My door was open."

"Well, I didn't do it."

Lanny crosses her arms and looks at me with that frown that means she's not buying it. "Then why do you look guilty?"

"I don't!" I tell her, and I know that makes me *sound* guilty. I'm not a very good liar.

"Did you take something? Because you know I'm going to look!"

I don't think. I just get up, shove her back, and close the door. It locks, which is good, because she immediately starts jiggling the knob.

"I'm not talking to you!" I yell at her, and I lie down on my bed.

I take my dad's phone out of my pocket and turn it over and over again in my fingers. The screen's dark.

I stare for a long time before I reach in my pocket and get the battery out. I open the back and slide it in, then put my finger on the "Power" button. Lanny's gone away, probably to complain to whoever cares that I'm being a brat. Normally that would be Mom. Normally.

I press gently on the button, but not enough to actually make it start up. What happens if I turn it on? Will Dad know? Will he call me? Why did he want me to have this at all?

But I know why. Because he can track the phone if it's on. He could find us, and Mom, and I can't do that.

But it takes time, part of me says, the part that memorizes all the risks and tells me what's safe, and what isn't. *He won't be able to track you if you just turn it on, check it, and take the battery out again. It's not magic.*

That might be right. It's probably right. I could turn it on and see if he called me, or texted. That would be okay, wouldn't it? I wouldn't have to *read* anything. Or listen to a voice mail. I'd just check.

I brush my finger over the button, again. Hold it a little longer this time. Not long enough, I think, because when I let go, the screen is still dark.

And then it buzzes in my hand, like something about to sting me, and the screen lights up and spells out HELLO in bouncing letters, then SEARCHING FOR SIGNAL.

I can't breathe. My heart hurts, and I lean forward like someone's already punched me in the stomach, but I can't look away from the screen as it fades, and comes back, and it's a clunky little collection of icons almost too small to see, but I can tell that there aren't any phone calls. No voice mails.

No texts.

I select the **CONTACTS** icon. There's one number programmed in. *Dad's number.*

I should stop right now. I should stop and give this phone to someone else. An adult, not Lanny, because Lanny would just bash it with a rock. If Mr. Esparza and Ms. Claremont have Dad's phone number, maybe they can find him before he hurts someone. Before he finds Mom, or Mom finds him.

You're killing him if you do that. I don't like the voice in my head. It's quiet, but it's firm. And it sounds like me, but grown up. *If they don't shoot him the second they see him, they'll take him back to prison. Back to death row. That means killing him. You'd be the one doing it.*

I don't like it, but the voice is right, too. I don't want to have to think about how *I* was the reason my dad got killed, put down like a sick dog. Because this time, I would be the reason if I turned over this phone.

He trusted me not to do that. He *trusted* me.

I've had the phone on too long. I quickly press and hold the "Power" button until the screen says, in cheesy waving letters, **Goodbye,** and little pixeled fireworks go up, and the whole screen goes black. I pull out the battery. My hands are shaking.

I didn't send him a message. I didn't call him. I didn't do anything wrong, but I feel sick and light-headed and I'm shaking all over like I've caught the flu.

I almost fall off the bed when Lanny knocks on the door. It sounds super loud, but it isn't, I realize in the next second. She's being nice. She says, "Hey, Connor? I'm going to make Rice Krispies treats. The kind with peanut butter and chocolate, your favorite. You want to come help me?" There's a beat of silence. "I'm sorry, Squirtle."

I desperately want my sister right now. I want to not feel so alone and out of control. So I shove Dad's now-inactive phone back in my pocket, open the door, and give her what I'm sure is a totally dumb smile. It feels fake on my face. "Okay," I say, then shut my door behind me. "As long as I get the first three squares."

"First *two*."

"I thought you were sorry."

"Two says I'm sorry. Three says I'm stupid."

It feels all right. Everything *should* feel all right here; Mr. Esparza is outside on the porch, reading a book, and Ms. Claremont is getting ready to go to work for a few hours. The house is warm and friendly and full of smiles.

I feel like I'm the one who's wrong, like the phone in my pocket is a bomb just waiting to go off and destroy everything.

I look at Ms. Claremont as she picks up her bag. She gives me a quick, wide smile that fades when she looks at me closely. Lanny's moving to get stuff out of the kitchen cabinets, so her back is turned, and I'm not trying to look happy anymore.

"Connor?" Ms. Claremont keeps her voice low. "You okay?"

I could do it. I could take the phone out of my pocket and hand it to her and confess everything, right now. This is my chance.

But I think about the documentary I saw on YouTube about a man strapped down on a table in prison, and poison put in his arm so he died, and I think about my dad.

And I say, "I'm fine, Ms. Claremont."

"Kez," she tells me, again. She's said that the last four times. Maybe she really means it.

"Kez," I say, then force another smile out. "I'm okay. Thanks."

"Okay, but if you're not, you know I'm a call away, right?"

My fingertips tap the phone in my pocket. "I know."

7

GWEN

Sam's tourist pamphlet is worth its weight in gold. There's a perfect candidate for our stop for the night, and when I check the folded paper map, I find that it's about twenty miles away—far enough to be off the radar, and couples oriented enough to be the last place Melvin—or Absalom, for that matter—would look. *Desperately charming,* I think.

When we arrive there, we find that's exactly the right description. It's lovely and neat and perfectly trimmed, with a small parking lot. It's too dark to see beyond the lights mounted outside, but I imagine the mist rises heavy in the mornings to give the whole place a magical look. It looks like a typical B and B sort of establishment, an expensive hobby for retired financial analysts who sink a fortune into renovating an old but magnificent house in the middle of nowhere. They've certainly spared no expense, I find as we walk inside: it's clean, gracious, full of well-kept antiques. It smells of fresh oranges.

The lady standing behind the antique counter is not what I expect. Midthirties, I think. She's of Indian extraction, wearing a truly lovely sari of royal blue trimmed in ornate gold, her hair drawn back in a neat bun, and she smiles with real welcome. "Hello," she says. "Welcome to Morningside House. Are you looking for a room?" Her voice carries a slight, crisp midwestern accent, without any trace of a southern drawl. There's a very slight shadow beneath the smile, a little wariness in her eyes. I wonder how hard life has been for her here in deep redneck country. Very, I imagine.

"Yes, thanks," Sam says, stepping up as she opens a register book. He scribbles down names, but in unreadable scrawl. "One room's fine. Two beds."

She gives us a quick once-over, reconsidering whatever her earlier presumption had been. "Ah. Well. Unfortunately, all my one-room arrangements have a single bed. But I do have a two-bedroom suite." She lifts her hand to indicate the nearly empty parking lot and gives a sad little shrug. "I can offer you a substantial discount."

She names the shockingly cheap price, and we pay it in cash, which she doesn't seem to find too strange. She doesn't ask for identification. She's probably sick to death, I think, of people demanding to see her own. On impulse, I hold out my hand to her. She looks at it in surprise, then takes it and shakes. "Thanks for making us welcome," I tell her. "This is a beautiful place."

She brightens and beams as she looks around at the carefully tended room. "Yes, we like it," she says. "My husband and I bought it five years ago. We spent two years renovating. I'm glad you like it."

"Very much," I say. "I'm Cassandra, by the way." I choose a name at random, and it doesn't escape me that it's out of a Greek tragedy.

"Aisha," she tells me. "My husband, Kiaan, is in the back—" She has to break off, because a door behind the counter slams open, and a small figure rushes out and skids to a halt when he spots us. A heartbreakingly cute little boy, with wide dark eyes and a shy smile that he immediately hides in the folds of his mother's sari.

She sighs and picks him up with that automatic grace of mothers everywhere, then balances him against her hip. "And this is Arjun," she says. "Say hello, Arjun."

He utterly refuses this, with the stubbornness of a typical kid his age, but he stares at me and Sam with undisguised fascination. I wave to him, and he gives a little hand wave back before hiding his face again. But he's still smiling. I remember that age so well, and it almost hurts. I feel the weight of Connor in my arms suddenly. The familiar pressure on the point of my hip. The soft caramel smell of his hair and skin.

The same door that Arjun burst through opens again, and it's an older girl of about fourteen, willowy and wearing jeans and a pale-pink shirt. Her hair is worn long and straight in a shimmering curtain, held back with jeweled pins. She gives us a curious glance, then takes possession of Arjun. "Sorry, Mom," she says. "He got away from me." She looks resigned more than irritated.

"It's all right," Aisha says. "Please tell your father we have guests. And put on the scones."

Sam looks at me and mouths *scones*, with raised eyebrows, and it's all I can do not to laugh. We've been bedding down in crap motels and in the SUV, and this lush, fragrant place seems like heaven right now.

As the daughter disappears through the door again, Aisha leads us up two flights of polished steps to the second door, which she opens before handing me and Sam identical keys, dangling from silver tags that read MORNINGSIDE HOUSE. "I'll send the scones up soon," she tells us. "Have a good night."

With that, she's gone, closing the door with a soft click. I automatically shut the bolt—it's a sturdy one, vintage—and then turn to look at what we've bought for ourselves.

It's great. The sitting room has two comfortable sofas, old enough to fit the theme but with none of the stiffness I usually associate with antiques. There are lovely little tables and a modern flat-screen TV, two desks (a rolltop and a smaller flat one) with antique roller chairs at each. There's a padded bench beside a large picture window that I'm sure will provide a spectacular view of the mountains come morning, but for now, I'm all too aware of the darkness outside, and the fact that we're nearly visible from space in the illumination of the room. I pull the curtains, then turn to Sam with a smile. "So?" I spread my hands to indicate the room.

He's studying the workmanship on a Tiffany-style lamp, all drooping, graceful purples and greens that mimic wisteria. "We lucked out," he says, then straightens. Winces. Dumps his backpack in a wing chair near the fireplace. "This is amazing. And there are scones."

"Bet breakfast is fabulous, too."

"Probably."

We look at each other for a few seconds, and then I put my backpack on the desk. I dig out the papers, find the USB, and take out my laptop. There's an Internet sign on the wall that gives me a password, but I don't bother. I don't want to be connected yet. I plug in the power cord, then turn the USB drive over and over in my fingers. My laptop's on, ready to go, and somehow, I still hesitate.

I feel Sam's warmth behind me, and he says, "We have to know." He doesn't sound any more eager about it than I feel.

I slide the USB stick into my computer, and a window pops up. Files, available for review. Some of them are documents. Some, ominously, are video files. A few are just audio.

Best to get the worst over with first, I think, and I click on the first video file.

At first, it's hard to make out what it is I'm watching, but when I realize, I involuntarily flinch backward, and then I spin the chair sideways and stare at the crisp, soothing fabric of the window curtains instead of the screen. I hear Sam murmur, "Ah, goddamn," and hear him turn away, too. I have the volume low on the laptop. It doesn't completely mute the harrowing, awful screams. I am shaking, I realize; my pulse is suddenly a jackhammer in my head, and my hands are quivering until I clench them hard enough to hurt. The room feels colder, and suddenly I smell cold dirt and mold and that awful stench of blood and metal that rolled out of my shattered garage that day, years ago, when Melvin Royal's hidden life finally saw the sun.

Sam reaches past me and presses keys to stop the screaming, and I'm so glad I could sob, but I don't. I just breathe. I keep doing that until I feel safe enough to turn and look at the computer again.

Sam's walked away a few steps now, head down, hands fisted at his sides. Like me, he's living in the past, but our pasts are different. I don't know where his has taken him, but I know from the tense set of his shoulders, the harsh, rapid breathing, that it's somewhere I wouldn't want to be.

"They're going to find bodies," he says, and I agree with him. I'm horribly glad that we didn't open that door and see what lay beyond. I'm grateful that horror wasn't the last sight I had on earth. Sam's voice is rough and low, and I close the laptop and get up. I go to him, but I don't touch him. I just stand there, facing him, until he looks up. There's a distance in his eyes that's both painful and self-protective. "I can't—" He stops. Just . . . stops. I know he's thinking about his sister, Callie's, torturous, horrific death. About the photos my ex-husband took, all those pictures that were blown up and shown to the court. He liked photographing what he called *the process*. In the first photo, she's scared, alive, untouched. What's left by the last is . . . unimaginable. And though Sam wasn't in the courtroom for it, he's seen the records. The video taken at the crime scene.

Even for a combat veteran, which he is, it's too much.

"Hey," I say softly, and this time, I do touch him. Just a light brush of fingers on his sleeve, not bare skin. There need to be barriers between us right now. "Sam. Stay with me."

I see him snap back, as if his soul has catapulted into his body, and he blinks and focuses back on me. For an instant I see a wash of emotion so powerful I can't guess what it is. Love? Hate? Revulsion? And then it's gone.

Sam Cade nods, reaches out, and takes my hand in his. It's unexpected, and I tense just a bit, but he's careful, and the warmth of his skin eases some silent, animal howl inside. "We don't need to watch the rest right now," he tells me. "Not now. Okay?"

"Okay," I say. I'm grateful he isn't going to make me do that, or do it to himself. There's bravery, and then there's punishment. Not masochism, because neither one of us gets any kind of release from facing this demon. It's just more scars. More damage. "How about the paper files?"

"Yeah, that's an idea," he says. We let go of each other and divide up the crumpled papers that we rescued from the inferno. They still smell of smoke, and—I just now realize—so do we. My hair feels crisp at the ends. We were so, so lucky.

My phone buzzes in my pocket. I frown and check it. It's not a number I recognize. I ignore it.

Another second later, Sam's cell buzzes. He locks gazes with me, then puts the phone to his ear. "Hello?"

I freeze as I watch him, looking for clues in his expression, his body language. I see a slight frown, and—paradoxically—a relaxing in his shoulders. Then he says, "Hey, Mike? How'd you get Gwen's number? I didn't call you from it." He puts the call on speakerphone and lays the device on the polished wooden table between us.

"How you think?" Mike Lustig asks, and his deep voice makes the small speaker rattle. "You were both unconscious at the scene. I copied her number down while you both were out. Not surprised Ms. Proctor skipped my call, by the way. I hear she's a tough nut."

"And she's on speaker," Sam says.

"Figured that. How do, Ms. Proctor?"

"Cut the country charm, Agent Lustig," I say. "I'm not in the mood. So what did you find at the cabin?" I brace myself. Hard. The memory of that awful video grazes me, and I flinch away from it. As I'm asking the question, Sam gets up and goes into the right-hand bedroom, which seems odd until I realize he's looking for a window with an angle on the road we came up. He returns, shaking his head. No sign of police coming our way.

I'm waiting for the obvious, for Lustig to tell us that they've found a torture room, bodies, horrors . . . but he says, "Nothing much. Some file cabinets, tough to salvage anything out of them but ashes. Some camera equipment and such. Some old-school videotape, but it's melted to shit; the lab's working on it, remains to be seen if they get anything. We won't know for months, most likely, if they come up with a result. I'm trying to light a fire under them—so to speak—but every case they work on is a priority, so it's not likely we're getting the express lane."

I'm so surprised I don't know what to think. *But we saw* . . . I reach forward and stab the "Mute" button on Sam's phone. Then I say, "They didn't find shackles, chains, winches? Then that video wasn't filmed there. Not in that basement!"

Sam's standing near me now, rocking back and forth on the balls of his feet, as if he can't quite bear to be still. "Son of a bitch," he says. "Then why burn the place?"

"File cabinets," I remind him. "Maybe there were documents in there that linked him to the videos. Or had info about Absalom. We still don't know how big this group is, do we?" I wonder if Arden knows. It might be important to talk to her again—but I think and hope that she's already gone. I imagine her landing in Stockholm and walking away free. I hope that's where she is.

I hope Absalom hasn't found her.

Before Sam can comment, Mike Lustig says, "Y'all still there? Take me off 'Mute,' because if you're having a chat without me, that's just rude."

I'm starting to like Mike Lustig. Cautiously, which is the only way I like anyone now. I hit the button to add him back to the conversation.

"Sorry," I say. I almost mean it. "So we're back to square one, then? No more leads from the cabin?"

"Look . . ." He stops, then sighs, and I can almost see him shaking his head. "I took a chance you two would keep your heads and not go charging in to make a mess of things, *which you did*. Why in the hell would I give you any more leads even if I have one? I like my job. Damn hard to keep it if there's an obvious line to draw from you reckless fools to me."

He is not, I notice, saying that he intends to cut us out. He's saying, *Don't drag me down with you*. That's a different thing entirely. Mike Lustig is a hell of a good friend, I think, and I wonder if Sam will mind when I ask him how the two of them got to be so close. Mostly, he doesn't care if I dig into his past . . . but then, mostly, I don't ask.

"So," Sam says, "why the hell *would* you give us any more leads? Great question, man. Do you want to know the answer?"

"I might."

"Because we're about to move your investigation along. We have a USB that came out of that cabin. And receipts. You've got ashes."

I whip my head around to stare at him, but it's too late to stop him. He's not just let the cat out of the bag; he's set the bag on fire, and the cat's over the state line. I mouth, *What the hell?* at him, but he doesn't take his gaze from the phone.

"Hmmm." Lustig draws that out, a rumble that rattles the phone on the table. "Don't suppose you plugged it in somewhere to take a look at what might be on that stick."

"Might have."

"Don't suppose you found anything interesting on it, then."

"Might have done that, too. Look, Mike, I'll hand it to you, no strings, but you have *got* to share the rest of what you know. We can stop this bastard if we work together. If you keep us out—"

"If I'd kept you out, *as I should*, then I'd have had that damn thumb drive, and the chain of evidence would be intact!"

"Most likely," I say, leaning forward, "you or your guys would have opened that door downstairs and blown themselves up, all the evidence would be ashes, and not a damn thing useful would have come out of it. We didn't make that mistake because we understand who we're dealing with."

His voice hardens just a touch, skimming off the charm. "And you think I don't?"

"Have you met Melvin Royal?" I ask. I feel a cold ball forming in my stomach, heavy as lead, just from having his name on my tongue. "Interviewed him? Interrogated him? Even been in the same room with him?"

"No."

"I lived with the man for *years*. I slept next to him. I saw him when he was angry and happy and stressed. I know how he thinks."

"Respectfully, ma'am, if you knew how he thought, you'd have known what was swinging in your own goddamn garage."

It's sharp, but I've felt that piercing observation before. I don't let it stop me. "There's a difference. I have the knowledge of him *now*, and what I knew *then*. And each informs the other. I'm an asset, Agent Lustig. You're going to need me." I take in a slow breath. "Because Melvin Royal isn't like the other killers you hunt. If he was, you'd have already found him, wouldn't you? You caught all the others he escaped with."

He's silent on that. I catch Sam's eye. We have a lot to talk about, but he just nods in agreement with me for now.

"Hey, Mike?" Sam says, crouching down to a height nearer my chair. Like me, he still reeks of smoke and sweat. It's more suffocating in this clean, pleasant room. "Don't shut us out. You'd rather have us where you can see us. We make great bait. Right?"

"You're killin' me," Lustig says, and then I hear him moving. I hear the crackle of wind in the speaker, and the sound of passing traffic. "Tell me where you are. I'll come pick up the USB, and we'll talk."

I hit the button to mute the call instantly and say, "No way in hell—"

"I wouldn't," Sam assures me, and unmutes. "Tomorrow, Mike. We'll meet wherever you want. Call in the morning."

He hangs up before Lustig can answer. We both look at the phone, waiting for it to ring again, but it doesn't. After a full minute, Sam stands up. He looks as tired as I feel. "He could have traced it," I tell him.

"Yeah, I know," he says. "But unless something shifts in a major way, he won't. I'm taking a shower. If SWAT's here when I come out, at least I'll be clean for jail."

I have to laugh. He's right. We have to trust Lustig this far, if no farther. And now that Sam's said it, the idea of a hot shower sounds meltingly good. For a dizzying moment our gazes meet and hold, and I wonder what it would be like to stand in the shower with him, fully naked with another person for the first time since . . . since Melvin. It's an involuntary thing, the picture that comes into my head, and it makes my breath catch, my pulse trip.

Then Sam looks away and says, "I'll go first."

"Such a gentleman."

"Damn right." He walks away to the bedroom on the left, the one nearest the stairs, and closes the door behind him—no, he almost does, and then it opens again, and he leans out. "Don't watch that fucking video without me, Gwen."

He knows me too well. He knows that I'd force myself to do it, now that we know it was filmed somewhere other than that basement. I'd make myself watch it for clues, anything that might tell me where it was done, and by whom. Maybe familiarity would provide some kind of buffer from the human suffering captured on it.

I nod, but I don't promise, and he disappears. I hear the shower start. I don't open the video, but I do grab a pair of blue nitrile gloves from a pack I carry in my bag, then take a handful of papers and move them back to the coffee table. Preserving fingerprints is probably useless; whatever evidentiary value these had ended when we stole them from the cabin. But being careful wouldn't hurt anything, either.

The papers look like the normal life of just about every person on earth—receipts for supplies, an online order for electronic games and gadgets, bills for electricity and propane. They're all billed to a bland corporate name that the FBI can track, if that leads anywhere at all. I assume, due to the lack of a bill, that the water and septic were his own. Some clothing orders, all male, in sizes I note down on a sheet of rose-pink paper from the desk, though I am certain that finding the owner of that cabin is going to be difficult, if not impossible. A job for the FBI, for sure, now that he's alert and on the run. This man, I think, is quite the record keeper; he not only buys in bulk, but he tracks every single purchase. There doesn't seem to be any differentiation between the trivial—like bulk orders of toilet paper and paper towels—and what might be important, like the purchase of sets of steel chain in varying lengths. I start separating the pages out into what is likely nothing, and what might be something. The distant, steady drum of the water in Sam's shower calms me, and by the time it shuts off, I almost feel centered again.

When he opens the door and comes out, he's wearing what must be a hotel-provided bathrobe and slippers, and his sandy-blond hair has been toweled dry but is still slick at the ends. He looks warm and at ease. "Sorry," he says, indicating the clothes with a sweep of his hand. "Mine need a wash. They reek."

"Mine do, too," I say. "Don't suppose they have a laundry service . . . ?" We have extra clothes in our backpacks, but I don't know when we'll next have a shot at cleaning things. So he goes to call the front desk while I head to the shower.

It's magnificent, and I linger in the water, letting the pounding spray on the top of my head drive out the images I glimpsed on that video. I want to call the kids again. I want to make sure they're okay, even though I've already done that, even though I know that they'd look at it as half-crazy behavior. I get out of the shower and dry off, find the robe—lush and fluffy—and slide my feet into the clean, new slippers.

This feels like a kind of luxury I've never really known before. I can see how someone could get used to it.

I hear my phone buzz, and I grab it. I check the number, which at a glance seems familiar—Mike Lustig's, from before?—and I click on and say, "Hello?"

I get dead air, and a rattle of static after, and my defenses come up fast. "Mike?"

"Mike?" says a voice on the other end, and I freeze. I forget to move, though I have a sudden urge to throw the phone away like I've grabbed a spider. "Who's Mike? Are you cheating on me *again*, Gina? That's disappointing."

I close my eyes, and then I open them again, because I don't want to be trapped in the dark with him: Melvin Royal, serial killer, ex-husband, father of my children. I've sunk down on the edge of the bed without knowing it; my legs have lost their strength. I stare blindly at the cheerful pale-yellow wall, the framed print of a peaceful Monet garden, but all I can see is shattered bricks, a gaping dark maw where a wall had been. The cracked egg of the two-car garage that Melvin used as a workshop.

The odor of death and rot, metal and terror.

The swaying body hanging from the wire noose of a winch.

I have the sudden, horrible sensation that Sam's dead sister is right behind me, looming close. Melvin's conjured that ghost, but I'm the one who's haunted.

The icy stillness in my chest releases, and I'm suddenly flooded with heat, blood, rage. My hand shakes, and I take a firmer grip on the phone now. "Where are you, Melvin? Come on, tell me. You're not afraid of me, are you?"

I know instinctively how much he'll loathe that idea, and sure enough, it sparks an immediate reply. Not as controlled as the first. "You?" The barked word, and laugh, has so much contempt in it that it's like a knife across my skin. But my skin's thicker now, and the edge doesn't draw blood. "No, Gina. I'm not afraid of you. How's the weather in Georgia, by the way?" *Gina*, not Gwen. He'll always call me that.

"Cozy," I say calmly. "How's hiding like a cornered rat?"

"Oh, I'm not hiding, sweetheart." His tone drops into a range that feels wrong. A little frightening. "I'm looking up at that warm square of light where you are. If you turn out all the lights, you'll see me. Pull back the curtains, Gina. Take a good look."

My free hand fists itself in the bedclothes, a violence the lovely room doesn't deserve, and I take in a deep, slow breath tinted with the faint scent of lavender. "The hell I will," I say. "Because you're a god-damn liar. You're not here. You have no idea where I am."

"Prove it. Go and look."

"Fuck off with your mind games, Melvin. You're *not there*. If you were, you'd be knocking on the door."

I bolt to my feet, because *at that very moment*, there's a knock. Brisk. Three taps on the main entrance.

I hang up the call, drop the phone, and lunge to open my bedroom door. "Sam! Don't!" I grab my handgun from the shoulder holster slung over the chair, and he pauses, already in the act of unlocking. I rush to put my back to the wall. My heart's pounding, and although I do *not* believe Melvin is the boogeyman he wants me to think, the timing is too eerie. I calm myself, then nod to Sam. I'm ready, but I hold the gun at my side, pointed down.

He opens the door and steps quickly back, and I see our nice host-ess standing there in her blue sari, smiling. There's another advantage of having the gun down; I can quickly slip it into a pocket of the robe before she turns her gaze toward me. "Please excuse me, I came for your clothes . . . ?"

I'd forgotten all about the laundry, and I feel incredibly stupid. Hot and cold at once. I go and grab mine. Sam stuffs them in with his and hands her the crinkling plastic bag, and she gives us a nod and a smile and moves away. She turns back as he begins to close it. "Oh, wait, sir," she says, stepping back. Behind her is her daughter, with a silver tray. "Your scones."

"Sorry it took so long," the daughter says. "I hope you like them."

They look delicious, and I say so and thank her. I wince as Sam closes and locks the door again. "Sorry," I say. "I'm jumpy." My heart's racing. My hands are shaking. Melvin has put poison in my veins, like the call was a snakebite.

"Yeah, got that," he says as he grabs a treat from the tray I'm holding in both hands. He doesn't miss the tremors. "What is it?"

I don't want to tell him, not yet, so I slide the tray onto the other, empty table, shake my head, and go back to the bedroom. I put my gun back in its holster. I turn the light off in the bedroom, and after a second of hesitation, I walk to the window and slide the closed curtain aside, just enough to look.

There's a deck down on the first floor, with round wooden tables and chairs arranged in precise formation around them. The shade umbrellas are tightly folded. Beyond the deck, the lawn rolls down a hill and into underbrush, and beyond that, a forest and climbing hills. It's a pretty place.

There's no one down there. Not a soul stirring.

I turn back to the bed as the phone buzzes for attention. This time, I accept the call and say nothing. Just wait. The silence stretches, and finally, Melvin says, "Made you look." I can hear the smile in his voice. Smug. Relentless.

"I'm not afraid of you, you murderous shit," I tell him. "Fuck off."

He hangs up. I sense that Sam's hovering near my doorway, not quite asking, and without raising my head I say, "That was him. I'm sorry. I let him gaslight me. Won't happen again."

"Hey." I do look up, finally, and his face is tense, but there's compassion there, too. Concern. "None of this is your fault, Gwen. It never was. Remember that."

I nod, but my heart isn't in it. I was uniquely situated to stop a monster, for *years*. It's impossible not to feel that. To know in my bones that I bear part of that blame, if only in my own mind. "He said he was here," I say. "Outside. And then I heard the knock—"

"Bad timing," Sam says. "Story of our lives. How the hell did he get your number?"

I take a deep breath and shake my head. I don't know, but I can guess. Absalom. The Georgia cops demanded our cell numbers. That info got entered somewhere in a system, and Absalom would have been looking for those reports. *He knows we're in Georgia,* I think, and my pulse jumps again. *We shouldn't stay here. We should run.*

But that's the old Gina, whispering to me. I'm done running. I'm hunting.

I tell Sam that Melvin knows we're in the state, because I can't *not* tell him that, and I feel a little weight come off me when he shrugs. "Have to expect that. We did send up a nice big flare at that cabin. He doesn't know we're here. You're right. He was gaslighting you."

"So should we go?"

"Do you want to go?" I silently shake my head. "Then we should get a decent night's rest."

Sam comes into the room, but not far. Leans against the doorpost. We're so careful with distance, the two of us; we understand the minefield of memory and deceit and a bloody, sorrowful past.

And it doesn't mean that the desire to step into that minefield isn't real, too. I can feel the pull between us, slow and steady, a constant tension that we keep dialed down to a low hum, for the sake of safety. We might sleep in the same space, but we don't sleep *together*. I know we're both thinking about it on some level, especially in this calm, lovely place, stripped down to robes that untie so easily.

What dries my mouth and shakes my confidence is that I wonder if this powerful attraction I feel toward him right now is the rebound reaction of having heard Melvin's voice. I want comfort. I crave safety. And

I know that seeking that in the arms of another man—even Sam—is dangerous. My safety has to be found within myself.

Sam's probably not doing as much self-analysis, but then again, he isn't coming forward, either. He stays safely on his side of the line.

"Could still be something in those receipts," Sam says, and I think it's just to say *anything* to break the silence. "Some of the supplies he bought don't look right. We didn't see any heavy chain in the house, did we? Saws?"

Those aren't unusual purchases for a rural cabin, but still, he's right. We didn't, not inside the cabin, anyway. I'd think Mike Lustig would have mentioned if he'd found them down in the wreckage of the basement. "You're thinking he bought them for someone else . . . ?"

"I'm thinking that this could be the beginning of a long thread we can follow. Don't you?"

I nod. I suddenly flash on something, and I get up and walk back to the rolltop desk. Sam follows and stands near as I quickly thumb through receipts, looking for the most innocuous thing of all.

Paper towels. Toilet paper. The bulk purchases are on the same online order for other household things, like air freshener and bleach, in quantities normally reserved for large businesses. I don't even know why it's attracted my attention.

I stare at it for a second, not quite sure what it is that I'm seeing in it. Probably nothing. People buy things in bulk. Paper towels don't go bad. So why does it bother me?

"Shit," I say out loud when I finally see it. I hold the page out to Sam and watch him go through the same exact process. It takes about the same amount of time. We're well matched, Sam Cade and I.

"The address," he says. "This didn't get sent to the cabin."

"No," I agree. And even though I'm reluctant, I say, "You'd better call Mike."

96

Mike Lustig cheers up considerably when he hears our news. He wants a fax, but we compromise and send the address to him instead. Or rather, I do that. Sam is busy mapping the address from the invoice on the Internet; he's careful to launder our connections through anonymizers to disguise our IP address, and I don't even have to remind him to do it. Google Maps shows us the location. It's a nothing-much sort of industrial address in Atlanta. I've been half expecting a remailing place, but this looks like a warehouse, as anonymous as all the other ones squatting near it. No cars visible in the snapshot of time that the map vehicle passed by it. Concrete and metal, rusting and dented. Isolated, too, by tall barriers of weeds that have grown up, in, and through the sagging chain-link fence. NO TRESPASSING signs, buckshot-scarred into near illegibility.

This place doesn't need volume-store levels of toilet paper.

"Jesus," I say, staring over his shoulder at the still image. "What the hell is this?" But I'm afraid I already know. My voice goes soft. "Do you think that's where—"

"Where they filmed? I don't know," he says.

Mike calls back in five minutes. He doesn't sound happy. "I can go with you to check this place out, but there's not a hope in hell I can get a search warrant based on what you've got," he says. "Seeing as how you appropriated the evidence and any judge who isn't pass-out drunk can see I don't have a legal leg to stand on. Tell you what: tomorrow, you bring that goddamn drive and the paperwork, and you give it to me. We'll take a nice long walk around the perimeter of this place, and I'll put my people to work digging up ownership. Maybe we can come at this from a different direction that gets us into court."

He's frustrated. I don't blame him. The FBI is overstretched, handling crime and terrorism at the same time, and he doesn't need the complication we've given him. Then again, he's probably aware that we've given him a tremendous gift, too. At least, I hope so.

"Right," Sam says. "Where do you want us to meet you?"

Lustig rattles off an address, which happens to be in a suburb of Atlanta. A six-hour drive from where we are tonight. We agree on a 10:00 a.m. rendezvous. That means we need to be up and driving before dawn, but that doesn't bother either of us much. I feel lighter when Sam closes off the call. I feel dizzy with it. *Yes. Finally.*

Without thinking, I put my hand on Sam's shoulder. He reaches up and puts his fingers over mine. His touch feels so unexpected, so warm, that I realize how chilled I am. *Why not,* I think, and I am almost giddy with it. The kids are safe. We've got a short rest in a beautiful, calm, secure place.

He looks up at me, and I see the spark. I feel it.

He smiles a little sadly. "I know," he says. It's not exactly a question. Not exactly a statement. But it's a toe across the line, inviting me to match him.

And I want to, *so much*. I look at Sam, and I think that in another life I would have met this man, and liked him, and loved him, and we would have been something good. Something lasting.

But this is not that world.

I lean forward and kiss him gently on the lips, and it's sweet and soft and lovely, and it doesn't feel like mines, or traps. It feels right.

But it also feels wrong. It feels like the ghosts are screaming, and my ex is laughing, and *I can't do this*.

So I leave. Fast. I hear Sam say my name, but I don't look back. I go into the bedroom. I shut and lock the door. *Lock* it—against Sam, against myself, against the memory of Melvin crawling into the bed we shared at night. I get beneath those lavender-scented covers, still wrapped in my robe, and I ache; I ache for all the lost things, the lost moments, the cost of ever choosing Melvin Royal, even though I was young and naive and virginal when he romanced and married me. Because some mistakes you have to keep paying for, forever. Marrying a monster like Melvin . . . that's a mistake that never, ever goes away.

I can allow myself to be happy when this is done. When *he's* done. Maybe.

Or I will be dead. But at least I will have paid in full.

When I close my eyes, I see Melvin standing down that hill, just in the shadow of the trees with his eyes shining like silver coins. Smiling. And I whisper, "Just wait there, you son of a bitch. I'm coming for you."

I'm coming.

8

SAM

Why the *fuck* did I push her?

I say Gwen's name, but she doesn't respond. I want to say all the things bouncing around inside my aching head, like *I need you* and *I'm not going to hurt you*, but the fact is that although both those things are true right now, I can't guarantee they'll be true in the morning. The need part, probably. I've felt that since . . . since when? I'd memorized her face from the online photos first, and I damn sure hadn't needed her then. She'd been an empty set of pixels, something to pour my rage into. I'd looked at a thousand pictures of her and felt nothing but contempt and blind hatred. *This woman helped kill Callie.* I remember thinking that, over and over again. I remember wanting to hurt Gina Royal, pay her back for every wound my sister had to suffer.

I dedicated the better part of two full years to tracking her, paying for intel, following just behind her until finally she settled at Stillhouse Lake with the kids, and I could slip into the landscape. Blend in. Watch her as she went about her business. I became a member of the same gun range, both to keep up my practice and to see her up close, in situations where she wasn't as on guard.

I don't know when I started seeing past the still photo. Maybe it was the grateful, thoughtless smile she gave me when I held the door for her; I don't think she even clocked who I was, just that I was a friendly stranger. Maybe it was watching the way she shredded the target, and afterward, the look in her eyes—that shimmer of grief and rage. I knew that feeling.

Maybe it was seeing her with her kids, laughing, interested in what they had to say, sharply protective of them. I was careful. I watched from a distance, trying to catch her with her mask down, trying to see the monster underneath, the one who'd allowed my sister to die so horribly. Who was complicit in the inhuman crimes of the man she'd married, and stayed with. The man who'd abducted, tortured, and raped my sister while I was overseas, fighting for our country.

But I didn't see a woman who covered up for a monster. Instead of Gina Royal—whom I'd never once met—I saw Gwen Proctor, a woman with a faint resemblance to that other person. Someone who had a full, human personality. Who treated others kindly, if a little guardedly.

That was when I realized that those Internet trolls I hung out with online, the ones who were trying to track her movements, competing to be more aggressive, more vindictive . . . they were wrong. Wrong about who she was. What she deserved. Wrong about her kids. What else had they been wrong about? Her role in the killings?

I remember the day she opened her door to me. Her son had gone missing from school, and I'd found him nursing a bloody nose down at the lake. I'd seen the relief at finding him safe, and then that flash of pure, terrified rage that I might have done something to her child. Then the gratitude when she judged I was being honest, that I hadn't done anything but be a responsible adult.

I'd told myself I stayed around them to gather evidence of her guilt, but from that moment on it hadn't been true.

Need came later, but it came on slowly. Softly. Against my will.

I'm not prepared to say I love her. But I am willing to admit to myself that it's more than curiosity, more than liking, more than the kind of one-night-stand lust that you get over in the morning.

There are moments when it feels like I've always known her. And then, like tonight, there are moments when I feel like I don't know her at all. Like she's a mystery I'll never solve, wrapped in barbed wire and thorns and roses.

I think about what she said. *Melvin Royal called her.* How he'd gotten the number is a mystery, but then again, he's still working with Absalom. Maybe they'd located footage of me in the convenience store where I'd bought the disposable phones. Maybe then they'd tracked us from the rental car agency, where we'd used a fake ID. The Georgia police. Maybe, maybe, maybe. It's useless to speculate *how*, but the important question is . . . *why*? First, always, it's to torment her, and it's worked. He's unsettled her. Thrown her off balance.

Which means we are getting close to him now. Melvin deflects. Misdirects. Hits *there* and moves *here*. Classic tactics, but done with the slick, unnerving confidence of a true sociopath. I can't play chess with him; I don't even have whatever sick board he's using. But I can understand that this isn't really about Gwen. She's a piece he moves, or tries to, when it suits him. She's no longer a pawn, like she'd been when he married her, but a more powerful piece: a bishop, a rook, a queen.

Me? I am a knight. I move in unforeseen directions. Which is why, after I hear Gwen close and lock her door, I dig earbuds out of my backpack, plug them in, and start up the torture video.

This time I make myself watch it without blinking, without stopping. It's long. A full fifteen minutes of torture, degradation, and horror. A human figure suspended by the hands from a chain, anchored to the floor by another two more. Splayed out and defenseless to do anything but bleed and scream. The video's jerky and poorly lit, but now I am paying attention, walling myself off from the horror of it and focusing on details. *This is not a person,* I tell myself. *This is an echo. A collection of light and shadow.* I am reducing that suffering person to the same pixels to which I once reduced Gwen. Stripping away the humanity because that is the only way I can save myself and still watch this unrelenting horror. I'm watching it for details. For the room. Anything I can use to possibly identify a location, the victim, or the perpetrators.

My first assumption—and, I'm sure, Gwen's first assumption—is completely wrong. The person who's screaming, suffering, and dying in this video is *male.*

And this isn't torture done purely for the sake of sadism. It's an interrogation.

I can't really hear the questions; the sound is terrible, garbled and echoing, which—I quickly note down—means a large, metallic room of some kind, maybe that warehouse we've already identified. I can't make out the answers the man's giving, either, mixed in as they are with microphone-overwhelming shrieks, with gasps and coughs and bloody mumbling. I close my eyes and reverse the video, starting from the beginning. Listening for questions and answers.

I finally get a few.

How long have you been tracking us?

Months.

Did you really think we wouldn't catch you?

Please stop, for God's sake . . .

Who are you working for?

I open my eyes, because I finally understand his last response. Just one word. A name.

I write it down, sit back, and stare at it.

Then I pick up the phone and call Mike Lustig. It's late—nearly two in the morning—but I know he'll answer. He does, on the second ring, with no trace of grogginess. "You know what time it is, my man?" he asks, but it's done in place of a hello. I don't answer the rhetorical question.

"You recognize the name Rivard?"

There's a long, long pause before Mike says, "Could be thousands of them, but the only one that springs to mind is Ballantine Rivard, owns Rivard Luxe. Been a tabloid staple for—how long? Forty years? The Howard Hughes of retail. Lifetime member of the billionaire boys club, with Buffett, Gates, Trump . . . Been locked up in his tower for years now."

"Couldn't be anybody else?"

"Depends on the context, but it's a pretty rare name."

"The context is, the man who's being tortured in the video we got out of that cabin says he was hired by someone named Rivard. We already know Absalom specializes in blackmail. Somebody that rich could be a hell of a target."

"Could be," Mike agrees. "You'd better be goddamn sure before we go after that particular pale whale. You sure you want to keep involving *her*?"

"I'm sure." *Her* means Gwen. Mike isn't convinced of her innocence. Like most people, he can't fathom how she couldn't have known something, since Melvin was bringing victims home to the garage just on the other side of their kitchen wall.

That's where we differ. I got sucked under on the Internet. I got indoctrinated by the echo chamber of like thinkers who set out to believe Gina Royal was guilty, and I swallowed it completely. I was blinded by my own hatred to the extent of planning just exactly how to kill Gina Royal. Not a merciful end. One that would deliver back to her all the pain and suffering that Callie had endured.

I had a cold, hard lesson in how easy it could be to lose your way, get lost in the shadows of your own rage and other people's delusions. I understand how Gina Royal might have been blind to her husband's horrors. She had been innocent. Too innocent to understand the depth of evil on the other side of that wall.

But I know Mike won't understand that. Not yet.

"You still with me, son?" Mike says. He means *son* in the sense that other people say *brother*. We're similar ages, though he comes across as much older. "'Cause you're keeping me from my bed."

"Not your wife?"

He laughs. "Vivian's dead asleep. After all these years of me being a field agent, she can sleep through a bomb blast, bless her. Don't make for much spontaneous late-night fun, though." He sobers quickly. "Don't let that woman get too close to you, Sam. You've got a weakness."

"I know," I say. "See you in the morning."

"Hell, yes, you will. Now go to sleep."

He hangs up.

I shut down the computer, take out the USB, and after a moment's thought, put it in a zippered pocket of my backpack. I take the pack with me into my bedroom, then shut and lock the door.

I don't want Gwen getting up and doing the same thing I just did. I'd rather spare her that, even though she might hate me for it.

Only one of us needs to live with those images. I've got the thing that matters out of all that pain.

Ballantine Rivard. Rich, eccentric old man who retired years ago from the company he founded—Rivard Luxe—and hasn't been seen outside his tower fortress since. No obituaries that I could find before I called Mike Lustig. The man was still alive and kicking.

Tomorrow we are going to find him and ask him why he hired a man to infiltrate Absalom.

And what he knows about Melvin Royal.

◆ ◆ ◆

Gwen and I have coffee out of warm, heavy mugs downstairs in the B and B's dining room. It's far too early for breakfast to be ready, but we wolf down the rest of the now-cold, still-delicious blueberry scones from the night before. The proprietor's up, and presents us with our carefully folded clean laundry, which we add to our packs, and we're gone long before the first light of dawn even begins to blush the horizon. As Morningside House disappears behind us, I hope they do well. They deserve to. Maybe someday, we'll come back for a real weekend retreat, once all this horror show is done.

The drive to Atlanta goes smoothly, and we're already inside the city limits when Mike Lustig finally calls. He gives directions to a downtown coffee shop, which mostly involves various iterations of "Peachtree," and when we find it, it's almost exactly 10:00 a.m.

Mike's sitting calmly at a table in the busy place, with a huge to-go cup sitting in front of him as he checks his phone like the twenty-or-so other people in the place. He's not visibly FBI just now; he's wearing a nice sports jacket, black pants, and a dark-gold tie. The jacket almost disguises the gun he wears in a rig at his hip, but every cop, local or state or fed, has that same habit of scanning the room like a laser, looking for anomalies. The scan catches and holds on us, and he nods at me.

"Hey," he says. "Get your own damn drinks. I don't even have a budget for my own."

I take a risk. I leave Gwen at the table with him and get in line for the coffees; I make them simple and keep an eye on the table. To all appearances, Mike and Gwen are having a civil conversation.

Appearances are wrong.

I get there with the coffee and set Gwen's down in front of her, and I see the hard shimmer in her eyes. I'm familiar with that look, and the unyielding set of her chin. They're staring at each other without speaking, and I slip into the chair to make it a triangle and say, "So I see we're getting along."

"Oh yeah," Mike says to me in an offhand kind of way that I know from experience means nothing in particular. "Ms. Proctor here was just telling me in detail why I don't know how to handle her ex-husband. So you go on, ma'am, and tell me all about how to do my damn job."

106

I can't tell if Mike's actually mad, or just pretending to be. Mike has made an art form out of separating how he looks from what's inside; back in the war zone, he was able to smile like a son of a bitch and drink all night with the guys, and then tell me as we were staggering home that he'd spent the whole night wanting to scream and rip his eyeballs out. I was never able to hide it that well.

"Let's not," I say, then take a too-fast, too-big swig of boiling-hot coffee. My tongue stings and goes mercifully numb. "You got info for us about this warehouse address?"

"Yeah," he says. "You want to tell me how the hell Ballantine Rivard figures into it?"

"Wait," Gwen says. "You mean *the* Ballantine Rivard?"

Mike gives me a questioning look. "You got that video for me?"

"Yep. But I wouldn't watch it here," I tell him. Mike is wondering what I've told her. I confessed going through the recording on the drive over, and we've gotten that inevitable argument out of the way. She's made it clear she's not happy with my choice to take that on for her, but she understands why I did it. "She knows I watched it."

"Uh-huh." Mike taps on his phone for a few seconds, then turns it outward to show a photo of an old white man, hair wispy around his skull, black-rimmed glasses framing watery brown eyes. He has a face like a basset hound, but somehow it manages to convey cleverness, too. Maybe it's the focus in the eyes on whomever, out of frame, he's addressing. He's wearing a dark-blue silk suit and tie. Hand-tailored, probably. He looks perfectly stylish despite being in a motorized wheelchair. "Ever seen him in person?" he asks her, and she immediately shakes her head.

"I only know the name. I don't exactly shop at Rivard Luxe."

"Yeah, you wouldn't, unless you were a one percenter who thought Neiman Marcus was too down-market," Mike says. "It's a department store for people with so much cash they use it for carpet. Upside to only selling to the stupidly rich: they never stop buying, no matter how much everybody else starves. Rivard turned a few million into about ten billion in ten years. He's worth upward of forty billion now."

"And the man who died in that video probably worked for him," I say. "Or at least, he said he did. Rivard makes sense both as a blackmail target and as somebody with the resources to try to fight back on his own terms."

"And . . . we think those people in the video torturing him are from Absalom. Right?"

"No idea," Mike says, "since I haven't seen the damn thing yet." He holds out his hand. I unzip my backpack and hand it over. Gwen's eyes narrow, and I see her biting back an impulse to say something cutting to me. I'm sure it'll come later. We'll have a good argument about how I don't have any right to protect her, and she'll be correct. But Gwen doesn't need my permission, and I don't need hers, and sooner or later she'll protect me, too. She already has, more than once.

The USB drive disappears like a magician's assistant with a quick, fluid motion of Mike's hand. *Now you see it, now you don't.* I'm glad I made a copy and put it up in cloud storage. Just in case. "And the documents?" he asks. Gwen's turn; she hands them over in a manila folder. He seems satisfied with that, though he gives the rest of the papers a good going-over, too, once he puts on a pair of evidence gloves. The paper with the warehouse address is on top, and he nods. "Okay, then. Let's drink up and do this thing."

My coffee is still too hot to give it another attempt, and Gwen doesn't seem to want hers at all. Pity, but I dump both cups on the way out the door. Mike follows us, and I frown back at him. "You're not taking your own car?"

"Nope," he says. "My official car has monitoring." And, I realize, he doesn't want it showing up on any routine GPS checks the FBI might do. He crams himself into our backseat, which isn't easy to do with those long legs, but then again, he must manage it in airplanes, and the FBI damn sure doesn't pay for business class. While I'm getting the car started, he takes out his phone and powers it off. "You should shut both of yours off, too," he tells us. "Trust me."

I hand mine to Gwen, and she takes care of both. Lustig gives me quiet, terse directions as we glide through Atlanta; we leave the gridlock of downtown and head out into a less affluent part of town. It turns industrial, and then it turns into rusted, mostly abandoned structures that look ready to fall down in another stiff wind. The few people I see are homeless, or hopeless. A group of sullen young men in what passes for Atlanta winter wear sit on a corner and watches us drive by with impassive interest. The gang signs are everywhere.

I drive past the address, turn the next corner, and park. "We'd better take everything with us," I say. "Not the place you leave stuff in view."

"Good plan," Mike says. "Common wisdom is, you don't park in this neighborhood unless you leave somebody behind to watch the ride."

"You volunteering?" Gwen asks drily, then gets out. I know she's armed underneath that leather jacket. My gun is in a pancake holster on my left side; I like cross-body draw because it gives me time to assess before the weapon's in my hand. Too many shots get fired before the brain catches up. "So. How do we want to do this?"

I lock the rental and mentally kiss the deposit goodbye. "Split up?"

"No," both Mike and Gwen say. They exchange a look, as if surprised they agree on anything. "Outer perimeter only," Mike says. "Start at the back, work our way 'round. We see *anything* sketchy, we're out, and we sit on the place until I can get some guys here."

"What are you going to tell them?" Gwen asks as we start walking. To our right is an old, boarded-up convenience store. There are eyes looking out between the boards, so it's probably being used as a squat. "Since all your evidence is inadmissible."

"I'll say we heard sounds of a person in distress," Mike says. "Which, when we find this video, won't be too hard to believe. I'll drop it inside, some point."

"You seriously think that's going to play."

He shrugs. "Gets us a step farther. Right now, progress is all I got."

We turn right at the alley, which makes my skin tingle and hair prickle painfully on the back of my neck. With two-story crumbling warehouses on either side, it looks like a place shadows gather. I'd rather not get knifed out here. Mike isn't wearing a protective vest, either. This feels like an ambush waiting to happen.

The first warehouse we pass on the right-hand side is concrete blocks, so it's surviving better, though the corrugated roof has rusted heavily. The chain-link fence is cut in two places. But the next warehouse, the one we came for, looks worse. Yet this chain link is new and shiny, and there's a loop of barbed wire across the top to keep out anyone thinking of hopping it. The **No Trespassing** signs are new and bright red, lacking the gunshot spatter that I'd seen on the ones in front in Google Street View. I wonder if someone has been out to renew all of it. Probably.

"Over here," Gwen says, pulling on the chain link right at the farthest pole. It rattles, and when I come over, I see that it's been cut and fastened with a couple of paper clips. I work them free, and Gwen shoves the opening back. It's big enough to crawl through.

I look at Mike. He holds up both hands. "Not my circus," he says. "You take care."

He's using us. Still. But I get why. I watched the video. I have a dim sense of what lies behind Mike's calm face and unflickering smile.

I want to rip my fucking eyeballs out, he'd said, leaning heavily on me as we staggered back to our quarters that night. *I want to scream until I throw up.*

All night, he'd been smiling that same smile.

9

GWEN

Inside the perimeter fence, it feels like we're alone on the face of the earth, and I instinctively check around me for escape options. It's not good. One exit, behind us. I prefer multiple ways out. If I have to, I can scale that fence, sacrifice the jacket to provide some protection from the cutting wire edges. *What if he's in there . . .*

He isn't, I tell myself firmly. Though, honestly, what better place for Melvin Royal to be holed up? A deserted warehouse, with his followers to bring him food and comforts and victims. It's so eerily possible that I slow, nearly stop, and earn a look from Sam. He doesn't see it. He's intent on finding clues.

I'm terrified we're about to find something much, much more dangerous.

It feels like the zombie apocalypse has arrived inside this yard. The Atlanta sky has grown cloudy above us, and the coverage is low enough that I can't see jets cutting through to remind me that the world still turns. I hear nothing but the wind hissing through the fence and the rattle of graying plastic trash as it listlessly drifts and flutters. The area where we stand was a parking lot once, but it's long surrendered to the assault of weeds, grass, and weather. It's a minefield of up-jutting, broken asphalt, mixed in with dead or dying stalks. *Easy to lose footing in here. Impossible to run safely.* Even from here, I can see the shiny padlock on the back door. The clasp that holds it looks newly installed.

"Gwen?" asks Sam, who's retreated to stand next to me. "You okay?"

I don't want to do this, I want to tell him. I want to remind him that I was right about the basement. But I know the difference between a genuine instinctive warning and the chaotic product of fear. So what if Melvin's squatting here? There are two of us, both good shots, both with reason to see him dead. It means my nightmare could be over in a few minutes instead of days, or weeks, or never.

"Okay," I tell him, and I make myself give him a nod. I'm still simmering about him watching that horror show of a video alone, because it feels like protection, like a man making decisions for me. We'll have that conversation later. For now, it's business. "Let's do this. Careful of the footing."

We move around the side. Wherever the corrugated siding might have peeled away, it has been nailed back; the nail heads are still bright, no sign of corrosion. Windows way up high, broken, but also unreachable; no handy stacks of crates or discarded ladders we could use to boost up to them, and even if I get on Sam's shoulders, I'll be several feet short of the goal. This is starting to look like a waste of time, I think, and then I see a side door. Like the back, someone's put a new lock in place; unlike the back, they didn't bother to swap out the original steel clasp. The nails look old. Rusted.

I point it out to Sam, and he nods. He reaches into his backpack and pulls out the kind of multitool pocketknife they don't allow at airports anymore; he chooses the thickest blade and uses it to pry the nails, and it doesn't take much for the entire clasp, lock still stoutly fixed, to swing away. It's almost silent.

Sam stops me and hands me a pair of blue nitrile gloves; he puts on a pair himself. Smart. The last thing we want to do is leave fingerprints here. The fewer traces, the better.

I open the door and step inside, carefully and as silently as I can manage, and despite all my focus and control, I can feel sweat beading on my forehead, under my arms, on my back. I'm trembling with the thunder of adrenaline dumping into my body, and I'm flat-out terrified that I'm about to see Melvin's pallid face looming out of the shadows, eyes as empty as a doll's as he reaches for me. The fear is so real that I have to take a second to imagine locking it behind a door, where it can pound and rage without damage.

He's not here.

But if he is here, I'll kill him.

It's a mantra I think to myself, and it helps.

The floor is gritty, cracked concrete, but at least I don't need a flashlight to see my footing; the milky light that filters in shimmers on floating dust, but it provides enough light to see that this part of the warehouse is open space, littered here and there with rusted parts, a discarded engine, and a pile of old debris.

"Watch your feet," Sam whispers to me, a thread even I can barely catch. "This place is a tetanus factory."

He's right. We've both got on thick-soled boots, but I keep watch for nails, broken glass, anything like that. Broken glass is often used as a cheap alarm system by squatters in these places, and nails are hammered through boards and placed points-up as home defense. Last thing I want to do is step on one of those improvised booby traps.

We stop and listen. Except for the whistle of the breeze blowing and creaking through the roof and windows, there isn't much to hear. No movement at all. But there's a *smell*. Rust. Blood. Decay. It's so familiar, so loathsome, that I feel dizzy.

Melvin's signature perfume.

There's an open doorway ahead, and I make my way carefully toward it. I stay out of the line of sight of anyone on the other side, and I halt when I see what looks like a pile of clothes along one side of the wall beyond. I draw my gun, and Sam does the same. He moves to flank me on the other side of the door and raises three fingers. He counts down, and we both pivot in, smooth and quiet.

I almost run into the dangling chains. I flinch back at the last second, and I can't help the silent explosion of breath that comes out of me, but at least it isn't a cry. I look down. More chains, anchored in fresh, shiny steel loops driven into the concrete. The chains above are hooked to a pulley system, and I follow the line of the rope back to a tie-off on the wall beyond me.

The floor is thick with old blood, long ago clotted and dried to a rough, flaky crust of black. Still some flies, but nowhere near as many as would have stormed this place when the gore was fresh. I'm trying not to feel anything, but the door I've shut on my fear is breaking under the strain. I'm sweating, shaking, and I feel like I can't breathe. I'm a second away from hyperventilating, and I know I need to calm down.

Focus, I tell myself. *Lock it up. Don't think about it.* I know why I'm freaking out. It's too similar to what I saw in my husband's garage, even down to the smell. I'm having flashbacks, and I just want to leave here.

But I can't.

"Gwen," Sam says. He isn't bothering to be quiet this time. When I turn, he's crouching over the pile of clothes, and I move to join him.

The smell of decomposition hits me within one step, far worse now, and I know what I'm going to see before I make it out in the dim light.

The body's been here a long time, long enough to have been reduced to ragged, chewed meat by scavengers. About half skeleton-ized. What skin remains on him—I assume it's the same man we saw on that video—is thin and dry as wax paper, and the maggots are long gone. They've left their pupa casings in a scatter like dropped rice.

"How long—" My voice isn't steady. I stop talking. Sam looks up at me.

"The weather's cold now, but it was probably still warm when he was killed. So maybe a couple of months." Sam is silent a moment, head bowed, and then he gets up. "Look around. If there's anything else here—"

I try to ignore the corpse, but it's difficult. I feel it constantly, as if its dead, empty eye sockets are tracking me. The rest of this part of the warehouse consists of a pile of old desks that yield nothing but rat droppings and a curling, ancient stack of forgotten invoices twenty years old, and probably of no interest.

But there's an office at the far end, and as Sam checks his side of the room, I head for it. There's a metal door with a wide glass panel, reinforced with wire mesh; it's been pocked and cracked, but it's still holding firm. I try the door handle.

Locked. But the lock looks old, original to the door, and a few solid kicks bust it wide open. One of the hinges pops free at the bottom, and the door lists drunkenly and scrapes the floor for balance.

Someone was using this place. It's still dilapidated and dusty, and spiders have claimed the filing cabinets along the back wall as their hunting ground, but on the other end of the room, an old-fashioned desk with the clunky, functional lines of World War II surplus is relatively clean. There are scuffs in the dirt on the floor, but no meaningful footprints.

There's some paper stacked on one corner—plain copy paper, no watermarks, no writing. I try a trick I learned from old Nancy Drew novels; I gather up a handful of the fine, powdery dust and sift it onto the top sheet, then gently slide it around to see if it will reveal any hidden depressions.

Nothing.

I start pulling open drawers. I startle some spiders, and am startled in turn, but eight-legged predators are the last thing I'm afraid of right now.

In the next-to-last drawer, I find a man's wallet. It's well worn, shaped to someone's rear, and I put it on the desk surface and open it up carefully. No spiders erupt from it, but I see a bristle of cash in the back divider. Plenty of cash, at least two or three hundred. I don't count it. I look at the license that's slotted into the plastic case in front on the left side. It's a Louisiana driver's license for a man named Rodney Sauer. I take a cell phone picture of the address on the license; it's in New Orleans. Behind the license are the usual mundane plastic squares of modern life: debit cards, credit cards, a couple of loyalty cards for supermarkets and big-box stores.

On the right, I find a picture of a plump, contented blonde woman cuddling two adorable kids. On the back, it says, in childishly awkward cursive, *Love to Daddy from Mommy, Kat, and Benny*.

I have to catch my breath against the pain in my chest. Does this pretty, happy woman know he's dead? Did he just vanish into thin air one bright summer day? Do the kids still ask when he's coming home?

I slip the picture back in and keep looking. I find a small stash of business cards marked with Rodney Sauer's name and what looks like an official law-enforcement star embossed in thick black ink.

He's not a cop. He's a private investigator. I pull one of the cards free and put it in my pocket.

There's nothing else of any use in the wallet. If Rodney had a notepad, voice recorder—anything like that—it's not here.

They left everything that wasn't useful to them, including Rodney.

"Gwen?" Sam asks quietly from the door. I nod and drop the wallet back in the drawer, shut it, and leave.

We go past the body, through the other room, out the side door and into the cloudy afternoon, which is the brightest, friendliest thing I've ever seen. I feel sickly dizzy, and I gulp in air to steady myself. My adrenaline level is toxic, and now that I'm out of there, I'm shaking all over.

Lustig's waiting for us at the fence. I still have my weapon out, I realize, and I put it back in the holster. Lustig holds the links back for us as we climb out, then carefully fastens them back with the paper clips.

116

We tell him. The only thing we've left is boot prints, and our path is clearly new, not contemporary to the horror show that played out in that place. We make our way back to the car—which is, thankfully, still intact, though the locks have been jimmied, and the radio's been jacked right out of the console—and at a pay phone halfway across the city, I make a phone call to report a body.

"Thanks," Lustig says, as I hang up. "Now, call me." He reads his number off to me, and I put in another handful of quarters for that call, too. I leave him the same message, and tell him there's some link to an ongoing FBI case. I hang up and look at him questioningly, and he gives me a thumbs-up. Since his phone is still off, he can't be tied to this location. He's now covered on receiving an anonymous tip.

Back in the car, on the way to the coffee shop, I begin to feel a little better. My skin feels warmer, my nerves less jangled. I know I'll dream about the dreadful stillness of that place, the way that it masqueraded as peace. By tonight there'll be police tape up, and crime scene investigators, and Mike Lustig will be whipping up a reason for local FBI involvement. Maybe they can track the ownership of the building, but I doubt it will lead anywhere significant. Absalom doesn't own that place. They probably don't even have any ties to it, beyond using it when the owners aren't looking. Corporations aren't great at checking over dilapidated buildings. If someone did inspect, they'd see the fresh signs, the new fencing, the new padlocks, and assume someone else in the company had taken care of it already. Bureaucracy at work.

Absalom lives in the cracks. Like cockroaches, and Melvin.

"So what now?" I ask, turning to look at Sam. He glances at Mike.

"We drop him off," Sam says. "And then we pay a visit to Ballantine Rivard."

"What makes you think he'll see you two?" Lustig asks.

"We're going to tell him what happened to his guy."

10

CONNOR

The Rice Krispies treats truce between me and my sister lasts until afternoon, and then I screw it up. By then, Lanny's already moody and grumpy and snapping at me every time I breathe. Glaring at me like I'm personally to blame for the fact she's stuck here in this cabin without much to do. I'd try to get her to read, but the last time I did, she threw the book at me and called me a nerd, which is a name I usually don't mind, but not the way she said it.

She begs, seriously *begs*, for Internet permission, which Mr. Esparza finally, reluctantly grants, but only for thirty minutes, and he warns her he's set up the parental controls just the way Mom requested. Not surprised; Mom's serious about that stuff, and she has good reason.

I drift over and watch what she's doing, because Lanny's in a weird mood, and I don't know why.

She just pulls up pictures, that's all. School pictures of her friends, out of her secret cloud account Mom doesn't know about. After about two minutes of staring, I realize every picture has the same person in it.

I lean over her chair and say, "Are you crushing on your best friend?"

Lanny goes nuclear. Her face turns streaky scarlet, she shoves me back against the counter, she yells, "Leave me alone," then flees into her bedroom and slams the door hard enough that the pictures flap on the walls.

I look at the picture of Dahlia Brown. She's pretty. I always thought she was. "Totally crushing on you," I tell the picture. No wonder Lanny was so crazy. She probably didn't want anybody to know, and here I was, knowing.

The front door opens, and Mr. Esparza looks in, sees me, and says, "What was that?"

I shrug. "Nothing." He knows it isn't nothing, but I clear the browser and shut the laptop and pick up my book instead of telling him anything else, and he finally shuts the door. He's cleaning a gun out on the porch, all the parts laid out on a clean towel, and I can smell the oil he uses from in here.

Lanny's got a secret. I feel a surge of glee about that, but I won't tell. We don't do that. We don't spill on each other, not unless it's life or death. This isn't, but she probably feels like it is. I feel kind of bad about embarrassing her. And she made me Rice Krispies treats.

I go back and open the laptop, find the pictures again, and print one out. I write on the back of it: *It's okay if you like her, you know.* I slide it under my sister's door, close down the computer again (because if I didn't, I might sit down and look up stuff I know I shouldn't, like news about the search for Dad), and step outside onto the porch. Mr. Esparza's bent over working on the barrel of a shotgun, but when he sees me, he straightens up and groans a little. "Getting colder out here," he says. "She all right?"

I nod. I don't tell him she's got a secret girlfriend. "She's in her room," I tell him.

He gives me a long look, and I make sure I'm staring somewhere else. "And you? You all right, Connor?"

I shrug. I don't know how to answer that. What does *all right* look like?

"You know you can talk to me if you need to."

I settle onto the steps, and Boot the dog comes and flops next to me. I stroke his head, and he licks his chops and rests his head on my leg. It's heavy. I've never seen him really mad, but I can imagine it's pretty scary.

"You know about my dad," I say. I'm staring at the trees beyond the fence. They're rustling and swaying in the wind, and overhead the clouds look like moving metal.

"Yeah, a little bit." Mr. Esparza's being careful about that. He probably knows a lot more than a little. "Doesn't feel good, does it?"

"What?" I know what he means. But I don't want to let him think that.

"Thinking your dad's done something terrible."

I shake my head. I don't know if I'm just generally saying *It doesn't feel good*, or rejecting something else. I don't know how I feel anymore. "Mom doesn't talk about it."

"Do you want to talk about it?"

"No."

Mr. Esparza nods and goes back to working on his gun. It's familiar. I remember Mom doing that same thing, carefully breaking the guns apart, cleaning and oiling and putting them back together. He's neater about it than Mom. Everything's lined up straight on the cloth. "You mind if I talk about it?"

I shrug again. Can't stop adults from doing what they want. And I'm curious, anyway.

"I know about what he did. They had it in the papers, online, on the news. Not that I was following the story, but I couldn't avoid it. Everybody said it had to be some kind of monster to do things like that. You hear people say that?"

I nod this time. I heard it. Lots.

"He's not a monster," Mr. Esparza says. "He has a monster inside him."

"What's the difference?"

"It's still okay to think of him as a person, if you want to. But just don't forget: he's still got the monster."

"Like he's possessed," I say. "Like in the horror movies." Not that Mom lets us watch horror movies. But I sometimes watch them with my friends, when she doesn't know.

"Not exactly. Possessed people can't help what they do. Your dad made choices." Mr. Esparza hesitates, and I can tell he has to choose his words carefully. "You know I used to be a marine, right? A soldier?"

"Yeah."

"I've seen people make those choices. Maybe they love their families. Love their pets. But that doesn't stop them from being monsters when they get the chance. People are complicated. It'd be easy to call your dad a monster, because then it's easy to talk about killing him, because we kill monsters, right? But he wasn't always a monster to you. I get that. And it shouldn't be easy to kill. Ever."

I finally look at him. "You killed people, though."

Mr. Esparza's hands are steady when he picks up another part and cleans it, but he's looking at me. I can only stand a second of that, and I watch his hands instead. "Yeah," he says. "*Es verdad.* You know what that means?"

"It's true."

"Right. I killed people. And I'll kill again if I have to, to protect others. But having that ability, that's a responsibility, and I can't take it lightly."

"But it's not that way for my dad."

"No," he agreed. "It's not. For him, it's fun. He likes it. And that's why your mom is so careful with you. Understand?"

"He wouldn't kill me, though."

Mr. Esparza doesn't say anything to that. He lets me think about it. Everything he's said makes sense. I know he's right. But at the same time, it's not what I *feel*. I feel like Dad . . . cares.

"How long do you think we're going to have to stay here?" I ask. That makes his smooth, practiced motions hesitate for a second. He's done cleaning now. He's starting to put the gun back together.

"I don't know." At least he's honest about it. "But however long it is, you're going to be safe here. I promise."

"Who's the better shot, you or Ms. Claremont?"

"I am. It's my job. Hers is solving crimes. But she's pretty good."

"Will you teach us to shoot? Me and Lanny?"

"If your mom agrees," he says. "And if you want to learn."

I nod, and I think for a couple of seconds. Then I stand up, dislodging Boot's head from my leg. "Can I just walk around in the yard? I don't want to be inside all the time."

"Sure, just don't go outside the fence without me, okay?"

I nod. "Me and Lanny need to have something to do that isn't just . . ."

"Sitting around inside? Yeah, I know that," Mr. Esparza says. When he sighs, it comes out in a thick, misty plume. "I'm working on it. Maybe we'll do some camping, fishing, that stuff. What do you think?"

I think it sounds cold and lonely, but he's trying, and I nod. "Maybe we can go to another town and see movies sometime? Like, Knoxville?"

"Maybe," he says. "Hey, if you're staying out here, put your coat on. Gloves, too. I don't want you catching cold."

"That's not how you catch cold," I tell him, very seriously. "You have to get a virus."

He laughs. "I know. But it's still good advice."

I go back inside, put on my coat and gloves, and when I go out, Mr. Esparza is done reassembling the shotgun, and heads back inside to get warm. Boot doesn't seem bothered at all by the chill, but then, he's wearing fur. He happily jumps off the porch and runs around with me. We play fetch for a while, and then I sit down on the far side of a tree trunk. I pick the side of the house that has the fewest windows. Boot paces around, looking at me. I guess other people find him scary—I know Lanny does—but to me he's comfort. He doesn't look at me like I'm a bomb about to go off, or somebody about to break like a soap bubble. He thinks I'm normal.

It's good to have some privacy. No one looking at me, monitoring how I'm *feeling*. They all want to help, I know that. But I don't want it. Not right now.

I'm far enough from the cabin that nobody can hear me with the windows closed. With the tree at my back, they can't stare at me, either. Boot flops down beside me and puts his head on my leg again, and I pet him for a few minutes.

I finally slip my hand in my pocket and take out the phone and the battery. I turn it over and over in my fingers. I know it's bad. Real bad.

But I'm half-bad anyway, right? My dad's half of me. He has a monster inside.

Having a phone that connects me directly to Dad is a little like playing with matches. It's thrilling and scary at the same time, and yet once you start, you can't stop yourself.

Until you get burned.

I've thought about what would happen if I called him. I've imagined what he's going to say to me. How his voice will sound. How surprised and pleased he'll be to know I kept the phone. *Hello, son,* he'll say to me. *I knew you could do it.*

I still remember him saying that to me—*I knew you could do it*—when he taught me to swim at the local pool. I was scared to death, but he stayed with me. Held me up while I thrashed at the water until I could stay up by myself. He taught me how to float on my back.

He also took me swimming out at one of the lakes where they later said he put dead people. I know I should hate that, but I remember what a good day it was, how happy he was to take me out on the boat, how we'd do backflips off into the cold, murky water and race each other in laps around the boat. He let me win. He always let me win.

The reason I remember all that so clearly is that he was almost never paying attention, so when he was, when he was really *Dad*, those were the brightest, happiest days of my life.

It only occurs to me now that Mom and Lanny were never with us for swimming. It was always him and me. It never occurred to me to ask why.

Don't do it, I tell myself again. I've been thinking it constantly. *Give Mr. Esparza the phone. Or Ms. Coleman. It might help catch Dad and send him back to jail.*

But if I do that, it just means Dad's one step closer to death.

I look at Boot. "Hungry?" I'm sort of joking, and sort of not. "Help a fella out?" At least if the dog eats the phone, it won't be my fault. None of it would.

He licks his chops and drops his head to my thigh again. Not interested.

I slip the back open and put the battery in. I turn it on, watching the dancing **HELLO**, and wait until the screen comes up. *You don't have long,* I tell myself. *Figure out what you want to do, and do it.*

I don't want to call him. I'm not ready to call him. It's too much.

So instead, I start typing a text.

hi dad i miss u

I stare at it for a long time. I can feel Boot's drool soaking into my pants. It's getting even colder, and I can see my breath on every exhale. I start counting, one breath for every letter I just typed.

Then I start deleting.

hi dad i miss
hi dad i
hi dad

I stop. I should turn off the phone and strip the battery and throw it all away, somewhere into the woods where it'll get rained on and short out, and it'll be like I never had it at all.

I can't do this. I shouldn't do this. It's bad. It's *dangerous*.

But it's like the impulse to light those matches. This time, Lanny won't walk in and yell at me to stop before I burn the house down.

There's nobody but Boot, gazing up at me with sad eyes.

I press the "Send" button.

The second I do it, I know it's wrong, and I wish I could take it back. I feel sick, and I grip the phone so hard I think I might break it. *Turn it off. You have to turn it off.* Boot looks at me like he can tell I'm upset; he gets up and sits taller so he can lick my face. I can hardly feel it, but I put my arms around him and hug him, tight.

He whimpers a little and wiggles in my grasp. *I'm going to turn it off and throw it away,* I promise, even though I'm not sure who I'm really promising it to. Me? Lanny? Mom? I slide the cover off. I reach for the battery.

And then it's too late, because the phone shakes in my hand.

I let go of Boot, and I open the phone and stare at the words on the screen.

hi son

I should throw it away. I know I should. I'm not crazy.

But just looking at the phone, I can hear his voice. I can feel the way he hugged me on the good days, the days when everything was right. I don't think about the other days, most of them, when Dad drifted through the house like a ghost and looked at us like strangers.

Sometimes, he'd go days without talking to us. Sometimes, he wouldn't be there at all. Working, Mom always said, but I could feel how worried she was that he wouldn't come home.

This message feels like Good Dad. I'm back home, and I'm not scared anymore, and everything is finally . . . safe.

Just this once, I think. *I'll get rid of the phone tomorrow.*

That's how it starts.

11

GWEN

After leaving the warehouse, we head back to the coffee shop. Nursing more caffeine, and I ask for a phone book from the counter lady, who gives me a disbelieving look and finally unearths a water-stained copy that must be nearly ten years old from the back of a cabinet. I don't tell her why I'm such a Luddite, and she doesn't ask, thank God.

The directory gives me the phone number and street address for Rivard Luxe.

I work through six choose-a-number menu options before I reach the cool, disinterested voice of an operator, who calmly informs me that Mr. Rivard is not available for calls. I expect that. I say, "Please send a message to him and ask him if he's missing an investigator he hired a few months ago. If he is, I've found his man. He's dead."

There's a short silence while the operator parses that out, and she doesn't sound quite so serene when she replies. "I'm sorry, did you say *dead?*"

"Absolutely. Here's my phone number." I read it off to her. I'll have to buy a new disposable after this, but that's an acceptable trade-off, because I was planning to do that anyway. "Tell him he has one hour to call me back. After that, I won't answer."

"I see. And . . . your name?"

"Miss Smith," I say. "One hour. Understand?"

"Yes, Miss Smith. I'll see he gets the message right away."

She sounds off balance enough that I believe her. I hang up and raise my eyebrows at Sam, who nods. We're well aware that he could do a variety of things, including calling the Atlanta police, and we're fully prepared to ditch the phone into the trash the second we see a cruiser. We watch the comings and goings of patrons. Nobody pays attention to us. The hot topics are, as in most coffee shops, schoolwork, writing, politics, and religion. Sometimes all at once.

Ten minutes later, my phone rings. "Please connect me to Miss Smith."

"I'm Miss Smith," I tell him. "Who's this?"

"Ballantine Rivard." He has a southern accent, but it isn't Georgia. It's an unmistakable Louisiana drawl, rich as cream sauce.

"And how can I be sure it's you, sir?"

"You can't," he says, and he sounds amused about it. "But since you reached out to me, I suppose you'll have to take your chances."

He's right. I can't prove I'm talking to the right man, but what choice do I really have? "I want to talk to you about the man you hired. The one who's gone missing."

"The dead man, according to your discussion with Mrs. Yarrow."

"Yes," I tell him. "He's dead. I can tell you what I know, if you meet with us."

"If you knew anything at all about me, you'd know I don't meet with anyone." He still sounds polite, but there's a new firmness. I can sense I'm losing him. "Please call the police with your story, Miss Smith. I have no money for whatever scheme you're—"

"I'm not looking for money," I interrupt him. I decide to take a chance. "I'm looking for Absalom. And I think you are, too."

There's an electric silence that stretches on forever before he says, "You have my attention. Talk."

"Not on the phone," I say. "We'll come to you."

Sam is watching me intently, coffee forgotten now. He's as surprised as I am that the great Ballantine Rivard returned my call, and that he's still on the phone.

"You'll be thoroughly searched," Rivard says. "And you'd best not be wasting my time, or I promise you, I'll have you arrested without a second thought. Do you understand?"

"Yes."

"Then come to the Luxe building, downtown Atlanta. I assume you are in town?"

"Yes."

"And what are your real names? The ones on your identification you will be showing my people?"

I don't like doing it, but he's right; I'm going to have to show ID. "Gwen Proctor," I tell him. "And Sam Cade." I know that he'll have minions Googling us in seconds, providing him with a complete dossier of every news report ever written about Gwen Proctor, and Gina Royal. It'll be a thick enough file. Sam's will be far thinner.

If he recognizes the name, he doesn't show it. "You'll leave everything with security. Phones, tablets, computers, notes, paper, clothing. We'll give you something temporary to wear. If you don't agree with those conditions, don't show up, Ms. Proctor. If you do, I'll see you promptly at one thirty."

That doesn't leave us much time. We've left Lustig, or rather, he's gone off to do what he needs to do. He didn't ask what we intended to get up to the rest of the day. That might have been a mistake on his part.

I say goodbye and hang up, then put the phone on the table between us.

"You got us an invitation to the Ivory Tower," Sam says. "My God."

"To what?"

"That's what they call the Luxe building," he tells me. "Rivard's been living at the top of it for twenty years now. Hasn't left it in a while, especially after his son's death."

"How did his son die?"

"Suicide," Sam says. "Broke Rivard's heart, according to the tabloids."

"Oh, and you read the tabloids?"

"I'm as weak as the next guy when it comes to celebrity gossip."

"I'm not judging," I say, and for the first time, I feel a real smile forming. "So you're the Rivard expert of the two of us. What do you think will impress the man?"

Sam sips coffee. "Honesty," he says. "And I think you've already got that part down."

"Glad you think so. They're going to strip-search us," I say. He chokes on his coffee. "Just being honest."

◆　◆　◆

It's not *quite* a prison search—I've had plenty of experience—but Rivard's people are clearly serious about their work. Our phones are taken. Backpacks, including my laptop and our phones. We're asked to strip to our underwear, searched, and then allowed to put on some dark-blue velour tracksuits in just the right sizes with RIVARD LUXE embroidered in gold thread over a crest on the front. Not quite business casual, but I'm willing to bet that they're exorbitantly expensive. Matching slippers, and they're so comfortable it's like walking on clouds.

We go up in a private elevator that looks salvaged from the height of the Gilded Age, a work of art in itself. A security man rides up with us and hands us badges on black cords. "You'll need to wear these at all times," he says. "Stay inside the designated areas. If you go beyond those, the badges will sound an alarm."

"And how will we know where the designated areas are . . . ?"

"Assume you should ask before you go anywhere at all," he says. He looks like a former military man, one with a fairly high rank, too, and he's used to being in charge. I glance over and see that Sam is fidgeting with the zipper on the front of his tracksuit. This is not his kind of outfit. He sees me looking and shrugs.

"I feel like a Russian mobster," he says.

"Wrong shoes," Mr. Security says, and I have to laugh. Then I have to consider how many of that type he's ushered up here.

We arrive at a large, round entry hall. One end of it is crusted in a multicolored glass window, a mix of modern and deco, which shows a man reaching up toward the sun. It's a mesmerizing piece of art, and it's enormous. Worth, I presume, several million dollars. Or ten or twenty thousand of these tracksuits we're wearing. I'm not sure just how Rivard counts money.

Our security guard leads us forward through a grand double-doored entrance, into another room that I suspect only exists for circumstances like this: meetings with strangers. It's built to impress. There's no desk, but there's a vast view of the city, obscured today by low, wispy clouds. Three grand sofas arc set in a triangle, with a table in the middle. The security man takes up a post near the wall and crosses his hands in front, looking like he can stand there for the next ten thousand years, and Sam and I wait, not sure where, or if, we should sit.

Ballantine Rivard rolls in exactly on time. His wheelchair is a marvel of aesthetic design, and it moves almost silently, except for the slight hiss of tires on the thick carpeting. In person, he looks younger than his pictures, and he's changed out the black-rimmed glasses for a pair with a slightly blue tint to the lenses. Frameless. They make him look like he's about to go Formula One racing.

Ironically—or not—he's wearing the exact same tracksuit we are.

"Sit, sit," he says, giving us an impartial smile. "Gwen Proctor. Samuel Cade. Don't stand on ceremony." His honeyed tones don't fool me. This man didn't get to the top of this tower by being charming.

Sam and I sink down on the sofa, which feels brand-new. Not many people get to sit here, I think. We're rare exceptions, coming here at all.

"Can I offer you a drink?" He doesn't look behind him, but as if on cue, an impeccably dressed man in a tailored blue business suit walks in, carrying a silver tray loaded down with drink choices. Every one of them is alcoholic, and above my wildest dream budget.

"Scotch would be fine," Sam says, and I nod. Rivard wants to be hospitable, and we'll sip for courtesy.

The Scotch, of course, is heaven in a glass. I try to keep the sips shallow.

"Now," Rivard says, as he's given his own glass, which the man in the suit has mixed with expert ease from three different liquors. "You have news of this investigator."

"I'll tell you what we know, but it needs to be private."

Rivard's eyes lock on me through the blue-tinted glasses. "Mr. Chivari. Mr. Dougherty. Please leave us."

The man in the blue suit does it without hesitation or question, but the security man says, "Sir, wouldn't you rather I stay—"

"Out, Mr. Dougherty. You may wait just beyond the door. I will be fine." There's a set to Rivard's jaw now, and a faint flush working up through the pallid skin of his neck, though his voice remains calm and slow. Dougherty gives us both a last, unhappy look, and then closes up the door after himself. "All right. We're alone now. And I can answer you without filters. Now. Tell me how you happened to find this man."

"You mean, Mr. Sauer?"

His eyes flicker just a little, but what it means, I don't know. "Yes. Where did you find him?"

"In a deserted warehouse," I say. I'm willing to let Sam take the lead, but he's laying back, watching. Absorbing information. "Why did you hire him?"

"You said the name Absalom," Rivard counters. "Explain how you know that name, please."

I force a smile. "Sure. But first you tell me how *you* know it."

"I've had some . . . issues. I'd rather not go into the details."

"Did it have to do with your son?" Sam asks, and I ease back to let him take the conversation.

I think for a few seconds that we've lost the old man, that he's going to summon his men to see us out . . . but Rivard heaves a sigh and looks off into the distance, out at the serene Atlanta skyline. "Yes. It had to do with my son," he says. His voice has a ring of sadness, and also frustration. "Very much to do with him. I lost him to suicide a few months ago, you know. My fault. It's not easy, raising wealthy children with a good sense of right and wrong. I should have done better, but that's my sin, not his. He had drug problems through the years, as I suppose you're aware; the tabloids covered it with a great deal of glee. He was in and out of treatment facilities . . . not unlike you, Mr. Cade. You also have some hospitalization in your past, don't you?"

Sam closes up. I've seen it before, this change, but it's still alarming, as if he's turned to glass, and only his eyes are still alive. Then the shell breaks, and he says, "I was hospitalized after Afghanistan."

"No shame in it, son. A lot of good men come back damaged from war."

Sam's not having Rivard's honey-coated condescension. His eyes have gone flat and cold. "I was treated for severe depression, and since you're only discussing it to demonstrate you dug into both our histories, why don't you just skip to the main course and talk about Melvin Royal?"

I'm glad he's countermoved. Hearing him say my ex-husband's name is a shock, but a bracing one. We've just controlled the pacing. And I see Rivard doesn't care for that much, from the slight tightening of his thin lips.

"All right," he says. "Let's do discuss the invisible serial killer in the room. Melvin Royal is on the loose, everyone is running in terror, and yet you, *Gina*, you aren't hiding. If anyone has cause, one would suppose it's you . . . unless you have a good reason not to be afraid of him. Which makes me believe that is how you know about Absalom."

"Fuck you," I say, which makes him wince from the incivility of it all. "You think I'm working with my ex? Sincerely, *fuck you*." I stand up, set my glass with a thump, and head for the door. Rivard smoothly angles his chair forward to cut me off, and I'm not *quite* angry enough to punch a rich old man who's wheelchair-bound. "Move."

"I was only seeing your reaction," he tells me calmly. "I do apologize if you were offended."

I'm staring straight into his eyes. "*If I was offended?* Fuck you and your Ivory Tower power-play bullshit. That sick bastard *is hunting me*. He's hunting *my children*. Either help, or get out of my way. Is that direct enough for you?"

Behind me, Sam stands, too. I hear his glass hit the table. "We don't need you," he tells Rivard. "Go to hell."

It's not quite *Fuck you*, but I'll take it. He's probably thinking about Mike Lustig, and not completely destroying this back channel, but I don't have any kind of patience. I am incandescent with rage. *Melvin's Little Helper* had her day in court, and I'll be damned if I'll let anyone say this to my face again.

Rivard blinks first. "All right," he says, then moves his chair out of my way. "You're welcome to leave if you like, I won't stop you. But I do apologize, Ms. Proctor. That was rude. But I had to be certain you weren't . . . one of them."

"Absalom, you mean," I say, and he nods. "It *was* Absalom you were after? That's who Sauer was looking into?"

"Yes." He takes a long breath. "My son suffered from, as they term it these days, affluenza. I would simply call him spoiled. It led to drug and alcohol addiction, which resulted in a variety of problems. All tiresomely predictable. A cliché." He waves that away. "Absalom targeted him, and they were unspeakably cruel in how they tormented him online. No reason at all. Simply because he was an easy target. Amusement, I suppose."

"How did they attack him?" I ask, but I think I already know. He takes another drink, then puts his glass down on the table to join ours. It means he's surrendering his last defense, I think.

"It started as postings. What do they call them on the Internet? Memes. One day he woke up and discovered he was the butt of a thousand jokes, and I can only imagine it devastated him; he never told me about it. He tried to handle it himself, and that only put fuel on the fire. They came after him like a pack of wild dogs. Put his personal details online. Posted stolen therapy records. They went further every day. My son had a three-year-old daughter. They first claimed he molested her, then forged paperwork that purported to prove it. Pictures. They posted these—horrible videos of—" Rivard's voice fails him, and for the first time, I feel sorry for him. I know this story. I've lived it.

He clears his throat. "The worst was, people believed it. There were websites formed around hounding him. Police investigated the claims of molestation. There was no truth to it, the case was dismissed, but that didn't stop the crusade. There were avalanches of vile letters. Faxes. Phone calls. He couldn't—he couldn't get away from it. After a while, I suppose he didn't even see the point of trying." Rivard's watery eyes suddenly shift to lock on mine. "*You* understand. I know you do, given what was done to you."

I slowly nod. From the day that Melvin's horror chamber was broken open, my kids and I have been targets. You never understand how vulnerable you are in this age of social media until something breaks against you, and then . . . then it's too late. You can shut down Facebook, Twitter, Instagram; you can change your phone number and your e-mail. Move to new places. But for dedicated tormentors, that isn't a barrier. It's a challenge. They enjoy hitting. They don't particularly care if the blows ever land, and it becomes a contest of who can post the most shocking, degrading material. The torrent comes from nowhere, and everywhere, and the hatred . . . it's like poison, seeping from the screen into your brain.

It doesn't take much of Absalom's brand of abuse to erode your sense of balance, your confidence, your trust in those around you. When your enemies are faceless, they are everywhere. Paranoia becomes reality. At any given moment, even now, I can log on and find a firehose of hatred directed at me, and at my kids. I can watch it happen in real time. It's a self-perpetuating engine of outrage.

So I can sympathize with the hopelessness Ballantine Rivard's son felt. I had days where ending things felt like the only way out of the trap. I'd survived, just barely. He hadn't. It isn't fair, or right, but it's dreadfully human, the way we tear each other apart.

"I'm sorry for what he went through," I tell Rivard. I let a beat go by before I come back to the topic. "How did he kill himself?"

Rivard's eyes go distant and blind. "He jumped from this tower. He had an apartment here. The glass was thick; he had to make a dedicated effort to break it. I believe he used a marble bust. Then he jumped. Twenty-eight stories."

I give that a respectful moment of silence before I continue, "And, after he died . . . you hired this investigator to track down the people who went after him?"

"No. I hired Mr. Sauer to investigate who was driving him to the brink of madness well before that. But Mr. Sauer disappeared just prior to my son's death." His hands tap restlessly on the armrests of his chair. Grip them tightly, until I can almost hear his knuckles crack.

Now we are getting to it. "Did he give you regular reports? Information?"

"Some," he says. "Not as much as I'd hoped. He was due back to me with more details on the day he vanished. And now it's time for you to explain to me how exactly you located my missing man."

We do. We leave Lustig out of it, but we tell him about the video we recovered—though not where we found it. Mike Lustig has the thumb drive, but Sam has taken the precaution of uploading it to the cloud, and he offers to play it for Rivard. Rivard provides a laptop, and Sam gives him the link. I don't watch. I try not to listen, but I hear when Sauer gives up the name *Rivard*.

Rivard stops the video. We are all silent for a moment, and then Sam says, "Do you recognize anyone? Any voices?"

"No," Rivard says. He sounds subdued and thoughtful. "And you found his body there?"

"Yes."

"Did you find anything else? Any clues?"

"Just his wallet. The police will have it all now." I consider mentioning the FBI, but I decide not to.

"Would you be willing to give us what you have on Absalom?" Sam asks. My impulse would have been to demand it, but Sam's right. Rivard's sense of entitlement responds better to what he considers politeness. Whatever works. My ego isn't at stake. "Mr. Rivard, I know you can hire a hundred investigators to go at this, but we're here. We're invested. And we're going forward with or without you, so you might as well join with us, don't you think?"

"You're proposing an alliance." He glances at me, then back to Sam. "You realize that I'm a very public figure. I would have to ask you to withhold any mention of my involvement. I can, however, offer you resources to help you along. You'll keep me informed of what you discover?"

"Yes," Sam says. "At every step." He sounds completely trustworthy. But then, he lied to me successfully, too, for quite a while. He's good at deception when he needs to be.

Rivard seems to accept that at face value. "All right. He gave me a few names. Most of who Absalom seems to recruit are just kids, fifteen and sixteen years old. Sociopaths, yes, but too young to be held criminally responsible, and followers, definitely not leaders. Of the adults Mr. Sauer was able to track down, two were already dead when he located their identities." Rivard takes in a raw breath. "He'd called that information in the morning he vanished, but I was hoping for more. He said he'd be back in touch. He wasn't."

I try to keep my voice quieter. Softer. More feminine, which is what Rivard seems to favor. "Will you give us the last name that Mr. Sauer reported to you?" I ask it carefully. Quietly. I don't look at him directly, for fear of raising his hackles again.

Rivard considers. He does it a long time. There's a knock—a discreet one—at the door, and it opens a small amount for the man in the blue suit to lean in. "Sir," he says. "It's almost time for treatments."

"So it is," Rivard says. "A moment, Mr. Chivari."

Chivari waits inside by the door. Rivard works in silence for a moment on the laptop. As he punches keys, he says, almost absently, "The last name I was given by Mr. Sauer is Carl David Suffolk. He lives in Wichita, Kansas. Your old home, I believe, Ms. Proctor. I leave locating him up to you. Ah. Here. I believe that there is one last thing that you should see."

He faces the computer out toward us. I glance at his face, then down at the screen, and Sam leans forward. I'm expecting to see something about Carl David Suffolk, but he's sucker punching me, and I don't even see it coming.

I recognize the house in the video. It's . . . it's mine. It takes me just an instant before that creeping sense of familiarity clicks in, and I feel like I'm drifting out of my body. For a second I think, *Someone must have fixed our garage*, but that's stupid; the garage was never fixed after the wreck that broke open that brick wall and poured out my husband's secrets. The house was torn down instead. There's a park there now. I've been to it.

But this video is of *our old house*, before. Before the world knew who we were, what Melvin was.

I don't know what I'm looking at, and I quickly glance up at Rivard's face.

"Wait for it," he says.

The video's a little rough, but perfectly clear. It's night, and the security lights fixed around the roof of our house—Melvin's insistence—are all dark just now. They were motion sensitive, I remember. There's a streetlight right at the curb that casts an unrelenting glow over the side of the house, and the one next door, and I remember how much trouble I went to, to find blackout curtains that Melvin liked because he hated sleeping in a room that wasn't dark, and . . .

I see an SUV come into the video frame. Its lights turn off, and it glides quietly into the driveway of our house.

That's our old minivan. I have a visceral memory of being in that vehicle, of driving it on the day that everything went wrong. That feeling of the world turning over sweeps through me again. I don't know why Rivard is showing me this, but I'm afraid.

The minivan triggers the motion light at the back of the house. Whoever's filming moves jerkily and gets an angle on the driveway as the vehicle pulls beneath the carport at the end. It's dark under the canopy. Brake lights flash, then go dark, and when the door opens, the video zooms forward and jumps around before fixing on the person getting out of the driver's side.

It's Melvin. Younger than the last time I saw him. Eerily *present*. He glances around, and as he does, I think, *He looks so normal. Just a normal man in a checked shirt and dad jeans. Just a normal monster.*

Then I realize that someone is getting out of the other side of the truck, and that someone is me.

No. It's Gina Royal.

She looks different than I do. Her hair is longer, curled, and styled. She's wearing a dress (*he always liked me in dresses*) that looks pale blue in the dim light. Heels. I don't remember the dress, but I feel sick to my stomach, looking at Gina, at a person I used to be. Her head is down. Her shoulders are rounded. I never, ever thought I was an abused wife; I never even saw the way he controlled me, bullied me, manipulated my life. But it's clear to me now as I look at the woman I used to be. Like seeing a ghost.

Melvin opens the rear door of the van and says something. Gina moves to the back, and I'm struck by a weird sense—the strangest yet—of unreality.

What am I seeing? I don't remember this. Any of it.

Melvin reaches in and slides something out.

It's a woman. A limp, unconscious woman. Her long hair sways as he lifts her under the arms, and Gina Royal picks up her feet. The young woman is wearing a gray top and blue shorts and running shoes, and Gina's grip fastens around the girl's ankles. She almost drops the weight as she fumbles to get the minivan's door closed.

I am numb. Silent. Stunned by a sense of utter *wrongness*.

Because I didn't do this.

It never happened.

And yet, I recognize the house. The vehicle. Melvin. Myself. The motion lights that snap on as I help Melvin Royal *carry a victim into our house*.

The numbness shatters as the light falls full on the face of the woman not-me is helping to carry in, and I hear Sam's groan, a deep, low sound like someone has reached inside and torn it out of him. It's his sister. Callie.

This isn't right, I think. My head feels odd and weightless, and the world is wrong; everything is wrong. I am not this. I have never been *this*.

The video goes dark.

Rivard closes the laptop and hands it back to his assistant with a calm nod of thanks.

I want to scream. Choke the bastard. Vomit. But instead I just sit, numb and frozen, waiting for the world to make sense again. *Could I have?* No. No, I would remember. I would know. I don't remember this.

I am not Melvin's Little Helper.

I finally lick my dry lips and say, "That isn't me." My voice sounds faint and weak and not my own. "It's not me." I feel cold and alone. I feel like I'm falling to the center of the earth.

"That was my sister," Sam says. "That was Callie—" Unlike me, Sam doesn't sound cold. He sounds *hot*, boiling, barely in control. I feel the sofa shift as he launches to his feet and stalks away. I don't turn to look, because I can't. I can't see the horror and revulsion in him right now. Rivard's pale eyes follow his progress. "Is that real?"

"No," I say. "It can't be. I didn't do that. Sam, I—"

"Is that real?" It's a shout, raw and horrifying, and it isn't directed at me, but I still flinch. He's talking to Rivard. If I turn just a little, I'll be able to see Sam's face. But I can't look. I don't look.

"No, I don't believe that it is," Rivard says calmly. "I believe this is an escalation of their ability to fake evidence. Still, you should know that this piece of artful fakery is out there on the dark web. So far, not many people have seen it, and fewer still understand what it implies." He activates the controls on his sleek, expensive wheelchair, and behind him, the big double doors open. Chivari holds one side. The security man, Dougherty, holds the other. I sit and watch, not sure what I'm supposed to do now, as Rivard turns his chair in a neat half circle. He stops and slowly rotates it back to meet my eyes. "Mr. Sauer discovered that one of Absalom's primary sources of income is making and selling a variety of false evidence . . . such as the falsified video of molestation they used against my son. When you called today, I purchased this particular piece of special-effects artistry from them."

"You . . . you *bought it*." I don't know what's happening. I feel ill and cold. "Why would you do that?"

"Perhaps I should say I purchased a *copy*. Because I believe in having leverage against those I don't know, and I don't know you, Ms. Proctor. Or you, Mr. Cade. Absalom clearly created this video with a plan, I believe, to discredit you should you ever decide to come against them. I can stop them by offering to buy it outright, remove it from the market;

the price is tremendous, but if you cooperate with me, I will pay it and ensure your safety. In return, here is *my* price: go to Carl David Suffolk and tell him that I want to speak with him. Tell him that I am willing to offer him a great deal of money to that end. I will give you a sealed message to give him regarding his payment. I believe it will induce him to accompany you back."

"Why? What are you going to do with him?"

"If it leads you to the rest of Absalom, and your ex-husband, what do you care?" he asks me. "I understand you might need a moment. Mr. Dougherty will see you back downstairs when you're ready. Good day, Ms. Proctor. Mr. Cade."

I don't want him to go. I don't want those doors to close. I don't want to be left alone, in silence, with Sam.

The minefield we reached across before, the one we didn't cross, has grown to miles of deadly traps, and I'm afraid to even look at him now. I sit back on the couch and wait for him to say something. He doesn't. The silence is unbearable.

Finally, I say, "Sam, I—"

"We should go." The words are an iron bar, slamming into my stomach, and I can't breathe. "We should find Suffolk. If anyone ever sees that video, you're finished."

I want to tell him that I didn't do it, that I never saw any of Melvin's victims, that I would *never* have helped him, *never*. But it sounds weak, and worse, it sounds like lies. Even my own confidence has been shaken by what I saw on that screen. Reality has bent and warped and shifted around me. And I don't know what's true and what's a lie anymore.

Sam walks past me to the door. He doesn't look at me.

I follow.

12

SAM

I can't look at her. Gwen. Gina. *Her*. After all the horrors we've seen, I thought I knew her. I thought she was . . . someone I could trust.

And now, sitting in the same car with her is hard to take. I want to scream and pull the ejection lever and get the *hell out of this*, because everything is poisoned and toxic and wrong. The sight of Callie's face has destroyed my world. Last time I saw her it was on a Skype call. I was in Afghanistan, getting ready to fly a mission. She was excited about something mundane—a new job she'd just landed, I remember now. A job she didn't even live to start. I hadn't known my sister, not for many years; we'd been separated when our parents died, adopted out separately. I'd never even seen her until I was deployed. I'd never seen her in real life at all. Only on video screens.

This was another distant picture of her, light from a dead star, and suddenly I remembered how her lips curled when she smiled, and how her eyes shone when she laughed, and how she'd had a cat named Frodo, and I want to kill this woman who's sitting so silently next to me. The one I don't know at all.

We're back in our street clothes, the Rivard Luxe tracksuits left in changing rooms. We have our backpacks, our weapons, our phones. We should be back to normal. We are anything but that.

I hurt all over, and I feel exhausted and wounded. We've left our rental behind—Rivard's security chief guaranteed it would be returned for us, and the damage fees paid—and we're in a Rivard-branded town car, heading for the airport. Not to the huge sprawl of Hartsfield, but to a smaller, more exclusive one: DeKalb-Peachtree. It's the sort of place the Atlanta rich keep their jets and helicopters, and for a moment I miss flying again, the sheer mindless freedom of being up there in the blue. Being a passenger sealed inside a cabin isn't the same.

I could walk away, I think. It's very clear to me, clear enough to touch. *I could get out at the next stoplight, hail a cab, get a flight, go anywhere but here. I owe her nothing. Rivard can't touch me.* The sight of Callie's unconscious face, knowing what would happen to her in the hours or days after that . . . it's broken something inside me. I thought I was tougher than this. I was wrong.

The only thing that makes me hesitate at the next red light is that it wouldn't be just Gwen I walk out on. There are her kids, too—innocent kids who never did a damn thing wrong, who were born to a killer and don't deserve to be torn apart by the wolves that are bound to come for them. If this video gets out, Gwen won't be safe, not anywhere, not ever. And the kids will be just as endangered. I think about Connor, the quiet, introverted kid who came out of his shell in our hours together nailing shingles on the roof of their Stillhouse Lake house; I think about Lanny, a bright, stubborn girl who hides wounds under armor. Brave kids. Good ones.

You're not their savior, I tell myself. *You don't owe them a thing.* That's true. I just want to feel whole again. I thought revenge would do it, when I first started all this. Then I thought I was finding something like peace without that bloody price.

Now, I don't know. I don't know if I'll ever be whole again.

I haven't been paying attention to the journey, but I'm dragged out of the dark places in my mind when the car slows down for a barrier. We're at the airport, and then we're through and onto the airfield. I'm familiar with small places like this; when I was a teen, I hung out at one, helping out with repairs and maintenance just so I could be around the planes. Once I was old enough, I built engines. Learned to fly. This place feels, unexpectedly, like home.

It's a little bit of sanity, just when I need it.

I finally risk a glance at Gwen. Her face is as pale and smooth as marble, but I'm struck by the fact that there are tear tracks on her cheek. Damp spots on her shirt collar. She's been silently crying, and it's a rare sign of weakness from her. If she senses me looking at her, she doesn't respond. She stares straight ahead, looking—at least, from her expression—into nightmares.

In that moment, she looks more like Gina Royal than I've ever seen before. All of Gwen's certainty and fierce, hard-won confidence is gone.

The car stops at a private hangar, and I get out. Take a breath of air tinged with the sharp, nose-burning smell of jet fuel and oil. I have that wild urge again to just turn my back, walk away, let my long-nursed rage bleed off into the cool air and *start over*. That video called everything into question. Everything I thought I ever knew about Gwen, and myself.

But it strikes me, as I hear her door open and turn to look at her, that Gwen is having the same crisis, only hers must go even deeper. All the way to the bone. She looks like she's seen into hell, and hell's leered back.

"You should go somewhere else," she tells me. "You can't trust me, Sam. I don't blame you. I wouldn't know what to think, either."

I ask her, point-blank, "Have you been lying to me? Were you helping him?"

She's violently shaking her head before the first few words are in the air. "No. No! I don't know what that was, but . . . *no!*" Her voice sounds unsteady, but fierce. She takes a deep breath and angrily swipes tears from her cheeks. "I'm going to find Suffolk. Are you coming or not?"

I look over at the sleek private plane that's waiting for us, a uniformed pilot standing by.

And I say, "For now."

◆ ◆ ◆

I'm not surprised to find that the interior of the G-7 is top-of-the-line custom work—leather recliners, polished wood tables and trim, original artwork on the walls. Rivard didn't name his company *Rivard Luxe* for nothing; he clearly likes his comfort. The plane holds, at most, twelve passengers; there are six recliners, and two sofas set facing each other that could hold another six comfortably. The pilot vanishes after telling us the flight time; another uniformed officer from the hangar scans our IDs, in case of emergency, and wishes us a good journey. Then a flight attendant I'm almost positive is a famous runway model boards and shows us menus. We have a choice of steaks from Bone's, or a custom lunch from Cakes & Ale, with dessert from Alon's Bakery. I'm not from Atlanta, but I was stationed close enough to know big-name restaurants.

I order the steak. Gwen just shakes her head. I reach out to stop the flight attendant and say, "Bring her something; she needs to eat." It isn't that I care, I tell myself. It's that she does me no good if she collapses. We're both running on adrenaline and anger and shock right now— well, to be fair, for me it's mostly anger—and that's not a good way to go into a situation that will probably turn out to be dangerous. I don't believe for a second that Rivard sent us because we're convenient. He could—and maybe has—hired others to do this job.

He's sending us because we're expendable. The cost of the best airplane food in existence and the jet fuel to get us there is the equivalent of buying us coffee to him.

My cell phone rings, and I flinch hard enough to pull a muscle. I'm strung too tightly. I hate that Gwen saw it.

"Yes?" I answer.

"Thought you'd want to know, possible sightings of Melvin Royal reported in Texas." It's Mike Lustig's voice on the other end. "You still in Atlanta?"

"Just leaving," I tell him, which at least has the benefit of being true. "Is it credible, you think?"

"Shit, you know nothing's credible until we have surveillance photos, fingerprints, or DNA," he says. "Trouble is, we've got a body in Texas that's surfaced with a similar profile, and it fits in geographically to the reports. Could be him."

I look at Gwen. Can't help the instinct. She knows I'm talking to Mike but doesn't know what it's about. Yesterday, she'd probably have asked.

Today, with the shadow of what just happened lurching between us, she says nothing and averts her gaze.

"Hey, Sam, you still with me? You got any reason to think he's got some support in Texas? Specifically, East Texas, up near the Louisiana border?"

"I don't know."

"Well, can you ask her?"

"Not right now," I say. "Is this recent?"

"Recent enough. Girl was abducted about six days ago. Body dumped in a bayou, found because a gator severed her leg where it was chained to a block. Gave the hunters who spotted her a hell of a shock. Last time she was seen alive was at a shopping center. Her ex liked to pick women off from places like that, didn't he?"

Callie was abducted from a local shopping-mall parking lot. I say nothing. Mike knows Melvin Royal's MO as well as I do.

"This vic had stun-gun marks," Mike says. "Same as most of his victims did. So it tracks. But Texas is a long way off from where we had other reports. Feels like a decoy to me. Not that we aren't looking into it; we are." He's quiet for a moment, waiting for me to say something. I still don't. "You don't sound right. Everything okay?"

"Sure," I say. "Just thinking. You talk to Ballantine Rivard?"

"I called. He's not available, air quotes and all. Got a feeling I'm going to have to go get court paper to open up the pearly gates."

"Don't think you'll get too much even if you do get inside," I say.

"Probably not, but I deal with rich asshole sociopaths all the time. I checked him out: the usual lawsuits for underpayment, improper dismissal, contract violations, that sort of stuff. I don't imagine anybody who runs a company this big has cleaner hands. His son was a damn mess, though."

"Yeah, I know." I'm distracted by the reappearance of the flight attendant with a cart. It's chock-full of ridiculously indulgent, high-priced liquor. "Listen, I've got to go. You be safe, Mike."

"You, too," he says. "You're not doing something stupid, are you?"

"Probably," I say, then hang up.

I order another scotch.

Gwen sticks with water. No ice. I suspect the taste of scotch is now associated with the memory of that video, and now that I think of it, the shimmering taste in my own mouth turns a little sour. I down it in a gulp and hand the tumbler back.

The flight attendant smiles at me without any real warmth and reaches beneath the cart to take out a sealed manila envelope. She hands it to me. "From Mr. Rivard," she says. "With his compliments."

She wheels the cart away, and I look across at Gwen. She sips water and says, "I suppose he likes you better."

Inside the envelope is a file folder. It's full of photocopies, and I glance at each page before I pass it on to her. Carl David Suffolk's Kansas driver's license, reproduced in color, doesn't do him any favors; he's a puffy, pale man with a receding hairline who's chosen to cultivate a goatee to cover up what's probably a weak chin. Beneath the license are his personal details: single, no kids. His bank account balance, which is healthy but not impressive.

The next page is a copy of his employee ID, in which he looks even less prepossessing. He works at a place called Imaging Solutions—copy shop, print shop, something like that. The rest of the file is a list of phone numbers he regularly calls and texts, and most of them have names beside them, as well as addresses. A few don't, which means they're disposable phones. Rivard's also included a list of screen names that Suffolk uses, along with the specific sites that they're associated with. Most are innocuous.

A few raise the hair on the back of my neck. Suffolk visits chat sites that mainly host children and teens. At his age, and childless, it's a pure red flag.

At the very end of the file, there's a handwritten note. It says:

In this envelope I have a sealed message, which I trust you to hand to Mr. Suffolk. It contains the details on payment I will make to him upon his agreement to go with you. If he does not agree, I suppose you should use your discretion.

As agreed, I have made the offer to buy the video from the dark web and remove it entirely. However, there is a significant complication. It seems the video has already been delivered to another untraceable buyer, and that, I cannot control.

There may not be any way to stop the video from seeing the light of day.

I don't like it. Instinctively, something tells me that Rivard is playing us, but I have no idea how, or why. Rich men don't look at people like us as human beings; we're pieces they move, levers they pull to get what they want.

There's a sealed, expensive-looking envelope at the back of the file with Suffolk's name written on it. I strongly consider opening it, but I don't. Yet.

We need a backup plan. So I text Mike Lustig. Hate to ask you for another favor, but what are the chances you can give me some backup?

Mike's reply is, Pretty good, but your debt is earning compound interest, my man. I fucking hate Wichita.

How the hell . . . I stare at his words, then text back, simply, ???

Did you really think I didn't know where you were, Sam? Come on. I've had eyes on you the whole time. How's that Rivard jet? Smooth? Hope so. Had to buy a goddamn economy-class middle seat. Flight out in half an hour.

I don't know whether to be angry that he's spied on us, or relieved that he hasn't kicked us loose. Right now, probably the latter. Where do we meet you?

You don't, Lustig says. After that, I get no response at all.

In ten minutes we're in the air, traveling as smoothly as gliding on ice, and the sky outside the oval windows is a fresh-washed blue, all the clouds below us.

I don't tell Gwen what Rivard has said in the letter, and I don't tell her about Mike Lustig. I let her enjoy the temporary peace, the expensive steak dinner, the fancy dessert, because I know that when we land, the peace will be over.

And the war may never stop.

13

LANNY

When I asked for the Internet, I really just wanted to check social media, see how everybody was doing. I wasn't going to post or anything, just lurk. Because I was bored.

And then I saw Dahlia's picture, and all of a sudden, I felt something crushing me inside. I missed her so much it hurt. I wanted to call her. I wanted to hear her voice and tell her what's happened, and I wanted . . . wanted all kinds of things, wild things that raced through my head while staring at her picture that made me uncomfortably warm inside. I'd been feeling that way before everything blew up out at our old house, and I'd been trying to figure out what it meant, and what to do about it. Now I think I know. But I can't do anything.

I'm so *close*. But not close at all.

Connor making fun of me is the last straw, and when I blow up at him, I mean it *so hard*. I race off to my room and cry into a pillow for a good fifteen minutes. By that time, I still feel wretched and alone, but I also am too exhausted to care. I curl up hugging my damp pillow and stare off into the distance. Outside the window, it's a cold afternoon, and it's chilly in here, too. I turn on the space heater and put on fuzzy socks and climb under the covers on my bed. My lower abdomen is aching. I check my calendar, but it's still a week until my period. I have enough tampons for this time, but I'm going to have to ask Kezia to get me more. I can't ask Javier. God, no. Number fifteen million of things my brother doesn't have to put up with.

It's an hour later when I get up, shuffle across the floor, and pick up the piece of paper that's been shoved under the door. I know it's from Connor, and his sharp-pointed printing makes me smile a little.

Dahlia's picture makes me want to cry all over again, but I put it on my nightstand, propped up so I can look at it. Maybe I can find a frame for it.

The lure of Rice Krispies peanut butter chocolate treats finally gets me to unlock the door and slump into the kitchen. Javier eyes me from where he's working on the computer. I can tell he's thinking about what to say, but I don't want to talk to anybody. I get my snack fast and start back to my room. But not fast enough.

"Hey," he says, "your brother's asked for more stuff to do. How do you feel about learning to shoot at the gun range?"

I nearly forget about feeling bad. "Seriously?"

"Yeah."

"Mom hasn't taken us."

"I'll clear it with her first. But would you be interested if she agrees?"

"Hell *yes*, I would!" The idea makes me feel about ten thousand times more in control. "When?"

"When I get her okay. Slow your roll, gunslinger, you're not shooting anything for a long while even if she says yes. Tell you what: we'll go to the range after it closes, and you're going to pick out a gun. I'll give you a choice of three. Then you're going to learn how to take it apart, clean it, and put it back together."

"Wait, that's all? I already know how to do that!" I've watched my mom clean hers a hundred times. He doesn't reply. I nibble on the treats. "Oh, come on. Really?"

"That's all we're going to do at first. Choose, disassemble, clean, reassemble. Okay?"

"But I want to do target practice!"

"I know."

"Why can't I?"

"Because this is how I do it. If you don't like it, we don't have to go at all."

He's as bad as my mom. I seriously think about saying so, but I don't, because I don't see how it gets me anywhere except staying here for another round of Monopoly.

"Fine," I say, but I say it in a way that makes it clear it isn't. "Sure. Whatever."

"Great." Javier shuts the laptop. "This isn't a game, Lanny. You understand that, right? A gun is a responsibility. The second you touch one, you assume the power of life and death, and you can't take that lightly."

"I know that!" His look says he doesn't think I really do. I try to look calm and adult, because I know that's what he wants. "Okay. I'll pick a gun. I'll learn how to do what you want. *Then* can I get to shoot?"

"When your mom says you can," he tells me. "But not tonight. One step at a time."

He's carrying a gun on his hip right now. It looks like the one Mom carries, so it's probably a 9mm semiautomatic. Mom's extremely careful with her guns, but every once in a while, I've been able to pick one up, feel the weight of it. He's right. There's something that changes when you have a gun in your hand. It feels reassuring and exciting, sure. But there's something else, too. I've never quite been able to say what it is.

Maybe when he finally lets me fire one, I'll know what I'm trying to tell myself.

It's a start, I tell myself. *Stop pushing.*

I don't like to be patient. I think I got that from Mom.

I lower my voice and say, "Have you talked to Mom in the past couple of days?"

"Yeah, for a little bit. She had to go before I could pass the phone on to you. She's okay."

"Did Mom say anything about . . . him?" I almost said *Dad,* but I know I shouldn't call him that. Not out loud. We all know who I'm talking about.

Javier shakes his head. "Nothing yet," he says. "There's no reason to think he's anywhere around here, but let's keep on as we're doing. Stay inside as much as you can stand. Stay offline. The longer we can keep where you are a secret, the better and safer for all of us."

"You could at least let me talk to my friends," I tell him. I really mean Dahlia. "They won't sell us out." *She* won't sell me out.

"And your friends tell other friends, and pretty soon everybody in Norton knows you're back. You think your mom isn't the best piece of gossip ever to hit this place? Nobody's going to pass up the chance to talk about it."

He's right, of course. The *friends* thing is half-hearted. Javier takes his job seriously. So does Kez—who's off at her real job as a cop right now, investigating some break-in around the other side of the lake. I hope it isn't our house. I worry about that . . . about the kids from school who might break in, trash our house, take selfies in my bedroom humping my pillow. Go through my stuff, not that I have a lot of stuff after all the years on the run. It still hurts to imagine what little privacy I've ever had being violated.

But maybe it isn't our house. Maybe the Johansens' big-ass flat-screen TV finally got jacked. Or their Mercedes SUV.

Maybe someone's ransacked Lancel Graham's old house; after all, we might be killers by association, but Graham really *did* kill people. If Graham's house gets trashed, I not only can't be sorry about it, I approve. He was a sick, evil man, and if Mom and Kez and Sam hadn't gotten to us in time . . . God only knows what would have happened. No. I know. It's what happened to his other two victims, and to all the girls my dad killed.

I try not to think about it.

Connor comes in from outside. He's been out awhile, because he's wearing a coat and gloves, and he sheds the outerwear and slumps on the couch, where he immediately picks up a book. He glances at me but doesn't say anything. Maybe he thinks we still aren't talking.

Maybe we still aren't.

"What time are we going?" I ask Javier, because at least it's a distraction.

"I said we'd check with your mom first."

"You also said I wasn't going to get to shoot any guns. So there's nothing to ask yet."

He gives me a look. "I'm calling. If I don't get her, I'll leave a message."

"Going where?" Connor asks. I ignore him.

"To the range. It closes at eight," Javier says. "I'll go in for closing, get everything done for the day, make sure everybody's cleared the building. Then I'll come back for you, Lanny. Kez can stay here with you, Connor."

"Wait, you're going to the range? Why can't I at least go along?" my brother asks, just as I knew he would.

"Because you're a kid," I tell him. "So, no. You can't go."

But Javier is watching him, and he says, "Do you want to?"

Connor shrugs. He keeps reading.

"Is that a yes?"

"Sure," he says. But I see the flush darkening the skin at the edges of his jaw, around his ears. Not quite a blush, but close. It's not in my brother's nature to show it, but he's excited about getting out of here, too. Maybe even about the guns, though he's always told me he doesn't like them.

I check the clock and groan. We still have hours to kill. I look over the games and finally plug Assassin's Creed into the game console and hip-scoot my brother out of the way. He gets up and goes to his room and shuts the door. Fine. Good. Though I'd kind of expected him to offer to play. He likes this game. That's why I picked it.

"Jerk," I say under my breath, starting it in single-player mode. Then I pause it, get up, and open his bedroom door without knocking, because I know that will piss him off.

His back is to me, and for a second I think I've walked in on him doing something *way* personal, but then I realize he's on his phone. "Are you calling Mom?" I ask him.

"No." There's a look in his eyes that surprises me.

"Who were you calling?"

"Nobody," he says.

"Because if you're calling Mom—"

"I'm not calling anybody!"

"Then—"

He explodes. It shocks me, because I know Connor has a temper, but it usually takes a long, long fuse to make it go off, and this is out of nowhere, and he's shouting. "Just get out, okay? Stop pretending to be Mom, you're not good at it!"

I back up, and he lunges forward and slams the door in my face. I have to jump back a few inches, or I'd have gotten it right in the nose. "Jesus!" I yell back and hit the door with the side of my fist. "Throw a tantrum, why don't you, you brat!"

He doesn't respond. I don't expect him to. I glare at the door for a few seconds, then turn. Javier's looking at me. "What?" I snap.

"Do you think it's okay when he barges into your room when the door is shut?" he asks.

"Hell, no."

"Then don't do it to him. I know your mom taught you better."

If he was even a *little* bit less nice I'd tell him to shut up, but I don't. I flop back on the couch, pick up the game controls, and start up. I'm not as good at this as my brother is, but I don't suck. For a while, I get pulled into the game world, and I'm glad for that, glad to leave everything behind and feel the walls around me fade out.

But it all comes back when Javier suddenly is right there, turning off the TV. "Hey!" I protest, because I was right in midjump, and now I'm going to lose a life, but he puts a finger to his lips, and his dark eyes are very fierce, and I shut up. Fast.

I hear something. Tires on gravel. Javier goes to the window and eases back the curtain. I can't tell for a second if it's okay or not, and then he eases his gun out of its holster and says, "Get your brother and stay out of sight. No noise. Go now."

"What is it?" I keep it to a whisper. My pulse is pounding, and I feel hot all over. Then cold. "Is it *him*?"

"I don't think so," he says. "But I still need you out of sight. Go."

I look around. We haven't left anything that would give us away in plain sight. I rush to Connor's room knock softly before I open the door. "Connor, come on, we have to—"

I don't finish, because although the book is lying tented upside down on his bed to mark his spot, he isn't there. I bend and look under the bed. Nothing. I check the small closet.

Then I feel a breeze on the back of my neck, and I look over and see that the window by the bed is open. The curtains are slowly moving from the wind.

Holy crap, no, you didn't.

There's no time to tell Javier, because I hear Boot's deep-chested barking outside. I sweep the curtain back and look out, but I don't see my brother anywhere. There's a small wooden crate under the window, perfect for climbing down on quietly. *Where the hell are you?* The old barn is the only thing in view, and I hesitate for only a second before I throw a leg out the window, duck, and step down onto the crate. It creaks a little, but it holds. I ease the window shut. Boot's low-throated growls and barks cover whatever noise I make, and now I hear Javier whistling him back to the porch. I step off the crate and run as quietly as I can across the open ground toward the barn.

Connor isn't in here, either.

The barn is full of tools and the usual junk that accumulates in rural areas—old parts, mostly—and if there ever was a loft, it's long gone. There's no place to hide in here.

It's too late to try to get back into the house, so I go back into the shadows and try not to think about the spiders that live in here. Or snakes looking for places to curl up for warmth. I crouch down and listen. I don't have a gun, but I grab a hay fork and hold on to it with both hands. If I have to fight, I will. I listen for the crack of a gunshot, or sounds of a fight. I don't hear anything but male voices. They're calm, I guess. It goes on awhile, and finally I hear an engine start up and the crunch of tires as the car turns around and leaves. I wait until I can't hear it anymore, then stand up and brace myself with the pitchfork, because my knees are shaking.

I go outside and look around, but I don't see any sign of my brother at all. I climb back in his window and peek out the door. Javier's just closing the front and locking it. Boot's inside, off the chain, and he saunters over and looks up at me.

"Who was it?" I ask Javier. My mouth is dry, and it hurts to swallow.

"Detective Prester," he says. "He says he was checking in on my health, seeing how I'd cut back my hours at the range. He smells a rat, though—"

I interrupt him in a rush. "Connor's missing!"

"What do you mean, *missing*?"

"He's not in his room. And he's not anywhere outside. I looked."

"How about the closets? The barn?"

"He isn't in—"

"Lanny, just check the closets!"

I open my door and look in all the places my brother might be able to hide, but there's nothing. I back out and am in time to see Javier yank back a gel mat that covers part of the kitchen floor—we stand on it every day, to wash dishes—and beneath it, there's a ring inset in the wood. I blink, because I had no idea that thing was even there. He hasn't mentioned it. I suppose he was saving it for emergencies.

When he heaves it open, I see that there's a set of wooden steps leading down into darkness, and a light hanging down with a pull cord. Javier yanks the cord as he plunges down the steps. Boot scrambles at the edge and barks, but he doesn't follow. Javier's only gone for a moment, and then he switches the light off and slams the trap shut as he exits. Kicks the gel mat over top of the door. "He's not down there. Did he say anything to you? Anything about where he'd go?"

"No," I say. "I mean, he likes to go out in the yard sometimes, but . . ."

He's gone before I can say anything else, and Boot scrabbles claws on the wood floor and takes off after him. I feel sick now. Shaky. I look again in my brother's room. In my room. I check absolutely everywhere.

He isn't here.

And when Javier comes back, looking grim, I realize the worst has happened.

My brother really is missing.

Calm down, I tell myself sternly. *He's just off pouting. He's mad at me. He's gone off to punish me.*

Would he, though? He knows the rules, and he knows Dad is out there loose. He knows Mom is too far away for us to find, so why would he try to run away to her? He has to be just angry and stupid. Maybe he's gone into Norton. I don't know.

I absolutely can't tell Mom I've lost him. When I find him, I'm going to hug him, and then I'm going to punch him so hard he'll never forget it. Then I'll hug him again. I want to tell Javier, *Please don't tell Mom*, but I can't. He feels responsible, too.

I go out on the porch. Boot's chain lays there in a long, piled coil. I stand next to it and look around. Javier's come all the way around the house by now, with Boot pacing at his side. He looks out over the fence at the woods around us, and I know what he's thinking: *Which way?* I have no idea.

"Can Boot find him?" I ask.

"Maybe. He's tracked game before. Maybe he can track Connor."

I go back inside to Connor's closet, and I come back with a particularly smelly T-shirt from the laundry pile. I hand it to Javier, who shows it to Boot. He sniffs it enthusiastically, then looks as us as if he has no idea what we want. I crouch down and say, "Find him."

I don't speak dog, and Boot just licks his chops and cocks his head at me. I take the T-shirt and shove it in his face again. He waddles backward and gives me a warning growl. "Please," I tell him. "Please."

He sits down and sneezes. Javier curses quietly in Spanish—he probably thinks I don't know what he's saying—but he reaches down and pets the dog, and says, "Sorry, boy, not your fault."

Boot still looks confused, but suddenly, his ears perk up. It's like he makes up his mind. He backs up, barks once, and takes a single muscular leap that clears the fence with at least six inches to spare. Javier's mouth drops open.

"Did you know he could jump the fence like that?" I ask.

"No. Damn."

Javier opens the gate and goes out to the gravel drive, where Boot is industriously sniffing the gravel, nose shoving aside rocks and blowing bits of dust. He circles around the entire drive, then takes off at a dead run down the road. Javier runs after him, and I fall in, gain, and pull even. I silently have to thank my mom for dragging me on all those jogging sessions around Stillhouse Lake. The gravel's not that easy to run on, but we don't slow down until Boot does, about halfway from the cabin to the main road. The gravel peters off to mud here, mostly dried. Boot does a figure-eight pattern, snuffling, and then comes back to a spot and sits down. Looks at us with a little bit of pity. *Stupid humans.*

I'm the one who spots the footprints at the side of the mud right by the trees. I recognize the tread. They're Keds, and that's what Connor was wearing.

I sprint off into the forest and hardly hear Javier's yell for me to *Wait, Lanny,* because I'm scared. I'm so scared that he's gone, or worse, that something happened to my brother and he's wandered back in here and collapsed, or . . .

I see Connor's face first. He's looking back toward the cabin, and the afternoon light through the trees falls right on him, and he looks sad and pensive and maybe a little bit guilty. He's just standing there.

Then he turns and looks at me, and says, "Lanny—"

I'm not listening. I'm skidding to a halt in front of him, grabbing him by the shoulders, and shaking him like I want to shake the idiot out of him. It's only then that I realize that Connor is crying. *Crying.*

I stop shaking him, and I gather him in my arms. Even though I've always been bigger than he is, I think he's never felt so small and fragile before.

He just collapses, and I go with him, and we're both on our knees, holding each other. Rocking back and forth and not saying a word. I don't know if either of us really *can* talk. Something's very wrong here, and I don't know what it is. I'm afraid to know.

Connor holds out his phone to me. His hands are shaking. Mom always makes sure she disables the Internet features and enables parental controls before she gives them to us, but I'm not super surprised to find he's hacked his way around that—he must have, because there's a video playing on the screen. Right as I take the device from him, it ends. "What is this?" I hear Javier arrive behind me, and Boot's there, whining and wedging himself in under Connor's arm to lick my brother's face. I swallow and sit back. Connor's arms go around the dog instead, as if he needs something to hold on to. "Connor? Do you want me to watch it?"

He nods silently. I hit "Play."

And when I see what's on it, the world changes. Forever.

14

Gwen

When we land in Wichita, it's late afternoon, and the sun's already sinking low. It's cold, with the icy bite of snow in the air, though the sky's still clear. I remember this kind of weather, how it meant to lay in a good supply of wood for the fire, and salt for the steps, and make sure the winter tires were good to go. Stepping off that Rivard Luxe jet, I feel like I'm hallucinating, stepping into the wrong decade of my life. The smell of this place makes me dizzy.

My phone buzzes. I've had it off for the flight, and it's just connected to the new roaming network. I check it, and see a text that says 911.

It's from Lanny.

I also have a voice mail from Javier, but I don't bother to listen. I stop right on the tarmac, two steps off the plane, and dial my daughter's number. I feel sick, and I get a surge of false relief when I hear her say, "Hello?"

"Sweetie, what's wrong?" I ask. I hear nothing. "Are you there? Honey? Hello?"

"You bitch," she says, and then she hangs up on me. Just like that. I think we've been disconnected, and then I start thinking worse things. She didn't sound like herself. She sounded cold. Angry. *Different.* And she's never called me that. Never.

Sam slows down as he descends the steps, because he's seen the look on my face. We lack the closeness we had before we went up that elevator in the Ivory Tower, but he can't seem to help being concerned. "What is it?" he asks. "The kids?"

I dial again. Lanny picks up but doesn't say anything. I hear noise, as if the phone's being handed off, and then Javier's voice says, "Gwen?"

"Oh, thank God, is everything okay there? I got a text and Lanny—"

"Yeah, look. You need to get back here." Javier doesn't sound right, either. I have a sickening idea that he's got a gun to his head, that they've all been taken prisoner, that Melvin Royal is leaning over and listening to every word we're saying. Is that possible? *Yes.* Horribly possible.

"Javier, if you're under duress, just say my name one time."

"I'm not," he says. It sounds clipped and angry, but not anxious. "Your kids need some answers. I need some answers. All right? When can you be here?"

"I don't understand. What happened? God, tell me, is everyone all right?"

"Yes," he says. I don't know whether or not to believe him. "Get back here."

"I—" I have no idea what's going on. "I will. Tomorrow by noon. I'm nowhere close, it'll take me some time." I wonder if Rivard will mind if I hijack his plane on the way back.

"Okay," he says. He sounds different, most certainly, from the man I left in charge of my kids. As if something's happened to change his mind about everything.

"Tomorrow," I promise, and he hangs up without a goodbye. Sam's standing by me now, frowning. I look up at him as I put the phone away. "Something's wrong. I need to get back to Javier's tomorrow."

"Are the kids all right?"

"I . . . hope so. I don't think they were being forced to call, nothing like that." I think hard about calling Connor, seeing if he'd be more willing to talk to me, but I don't. Something, some gut-level instinct, tells me that isn't a good idea. *Just get this done, and you can get back to them. Stop overthinking.*

The crew of the plane has seen us off with professional smiles, but they don't waste any time. As we're speaking, the stairway is pulled up behind us, the hatch shut, and now the plane is revving up to taxi off toward a hangar. Sam and I head for the small terminal. We go straight through, and I feel a strong sense, again, of déjà vu. I remember being here, picking up my mother on a flight in to visit her grandkids when they were little. That was before everything changed and life became a surreal, never-ending nightmare.

The carpet in the terminal is still exactly the same.

There's a taxi rank—more or less, if one taxi constitutes a rank— and Sam gets there, leans in, and gives directions I don't hear. I pile in with him in the back of the car, and it takes off with a jerk of acceleration. The cab driver isn't chatty. That's a good thing.

Sam passes me the file that he'd taken from the manila folder on board. I hadn't asked then what was in it, because I didn't want to push him. I still don't, but I have to ask.

"Home or office first?" I ask. It's almost five o'clock; depending on work hours, Suffolk could be at either place, or en route.

"We're trying the office first. I like surprising people there. They're not as likely to try to kill you in front of the boss." Sam's dry sense of humor is forced. I feel like I'm in free fall. I try not to look out the windows as we drive, because everything we pass has a memory attached to it of my old life. The park where I used to take the kids. The store where I bought my favorite dress.

The restaurant where Melvin took me to dinner for our last anniversary.

My mouth feels dry, and my throat clicks when I try to swallow. I wish now I'd guzzled more water on the plane. Sam and I haven't talked about it, but it isn't too likely that this Suffolk will put up much of a fight; he doesn't seem the type. I just want to do whatever Rivard wants and stop anyone else from ever seeing that video; I don't know if I can trust Rivard to keep his promise to buy it and keep it from spreading, but it's the only option I have. It doesn't matter that it's faked. What matters is that it feels real, even to me, as if I've repressed the memory. People like to say that *cameras don't lie*, but they can.

And when they do, everyone believes.

It's a short ride to the address that Sam gave the taxi driver, and we glide to a halt in an industrial area that looks thriving. There are multiple-story office buildings, but Imaging Solutions seems to be a small operation located in a multistore strip mall. I pay the taxi driver from my diminishing stash of money and follow Sam to the store.

Inside, the place smells sharply of chemicals and ozone. The carpet is a basic industrial, with no padding beneath; there's a faux wood counter, a register, some colorful posters about various services for signage and printing. I can hear the grumble and chatter of machines from behind a wall; there's an open doorway to the left that leads to the work area. The wall is fitted with a row of glass blocks, and through the watery distortion, I see people moving back there.

The door has sounded a bell, and now a young man emerges from the back, wiping his hands. He's wearing a short-sleeve white shirt and black tie, and even his haircut looks conventional and straight out of the 1950s. "Hello, folks," he says. "How can I help you today?"

Sam says, "We're looking for Carl David Suffolk."

The young man smiles. "Well, sure, but he's at work right now, so we don't allow any visitors in the work area—"

"I'm not a visitor," I tell him. "I'm his sister. There's been a family emergency."

"Oh. Oh, sure. Okay. Let me go get him—"

"I'll go with you," Sam says. As the manager turns away, he whispers to me, "Go around back in case he runs."

"I hope everything's all right," the manager says. "Mr.—?"

"Suffolk," Sam lies easily. "I'm his brother. And you are . . . ?"

"David Roberts. I'm the assistant manager."

"Great. Thanks, Mr. Roberts."

Roberts flips up the counter where it's hinged, and Sam walks around the corner with him. The second they're out of sight, I exit at a run and race around to the end of the strip mall, down the alley, and around the drab back. It's lined with dumpsters and loading docks, and as I run, I count off stores. Luckily, most are labeled at the back doors. When I find Imaging Solutions, I slow down. No trucks at the loading dock at the moment.

The rolling garage door is closed, and so is the solid metal door next to it, but as I reach the foot of the steps, the door bursts open with a bang, and a hefty white man in his midforties bursts out. Like Roberts, he's wearing a short-sleeve white shirt and black tie; unlike his boss, he hasn't been as careful with it, and there are smears of black toner around his waist. He looks pale and frantic, and his eyes widen when he sees me standing there blocking the steps. He spins, but it's too late. Sam's come out of the door behind him. He closes it and says, "Carl, let's be smart about this—"

I don't even have time to yell a warning, though I see it coming; Carl lunges at him. Sam dodges with the ease of a matador, and Carl barrels past. He stumbles. Sways.

And then he falls off the dock with a howl of panic.

He hits on his back, and the impact dazes him; he's still lying there when we reach him. He seems okay, and when Sam offers him a hand up, he takes it. "Anything broken?" Sam asks. "How's your head?"

"Okay," Carl says. "I'm okay. I'm—" The shock snaps, and he realizes his situation. He stumbles back, but he's limping, and Sam and I look at each other as Suffolk starts a lumbering, lurching run for slow-motion freedom.

I say, "Hey, Carl? Look, just give it up. Don't make me shoot a kneecap off you."

Suffolk turns. He seems ashen, and for the first time, he looks at each of us in turn, with real focus. When he gets to me, his face changes. It turns malignant, as if some demon has drifted to the surface and altered his skin. His forehead reddens. He lowers his chin, and his eyes have a cold delight in them that makes me want to step back. I don't.

"You," he says softly. "You're his *bitch*."

And then he lunges for me, and because I didn't step back, I'm easily in his range. I think he intends to knock me down, and I'm ready for that.

I'm not ready for a full-on killing assault.

His hands close around my throat, and without any hesitation at all, he starts a crushing pressure. This isn't a game, and it isn't tentative. He intends to kill me. My rational mind breaks into a white storm of panic. I can feel myself being lifted right off the ground by his strength, and the pain, the suffocating panic of my lungs laboring for air, robs me of any kind of real thought at all.

I hear a whisper in my ear. It's as clear as if he's standing next to me. *This is how you die, Gina.* Melvin's voice. It seems to have been an eternity already. I try to fight, to twist, I try to keep my neck muscles stiff against his crushing grip, but I know that's only going to prolong my agony.

Melvin's voice comes again. *It takes a long time, strangling someone. Three or four minutes at least. Maybe longer.*

It seems like an eternity, but it's only been seconds, I realize; I see Sam punching Suffolk, solid blows to his kidneys. Suffolk doesn't even notice. His rage has become armor.

Shoot him, I want to scream at Sam. *For God's sake . . .*

I scrape my toes along a hard surface. My flailing fingers catch onto something soft. I thought I was trying for his eyes, but this isn't his eyes, it's a lip, and I dig my fingernails in and pull and twist as hard as I can. I hear a bellow as loud as thunder wash over me . . . but his hands don't relax.

It's getting darker. I can hear tissues crunching, compressing. I'm listening to my body break.

And then, suddenly, I'm falling. My flailing feet hit the ground, but my knees are weak, and I tip backward as they give way. I'm pulling in a sweet, burning breath even as I fall.

Sam catches me.

I collapse against his chest, and his arms go around me to hold me upright until my knees steady, and all I can do for a moment is pull in air, push it out, even though it hurts. Once my body has its demands for breath satisfied, I start to take it all in again.

Carl Suffolk is down on the ground, bleeding from a head wound. There's a pipe next to him. Sam clocked him hard enough to finally break through that shell of rage.

"Gwen?" Sam asks me. "Can you breathe?" He sounds scared. I manage to nod, though I'm sure the bruises around my throat are going to be black in a couple of days. I swallow. Nothing feels broken. If Suffolk had managed to collapse my larynx, snap my hyoid bone, I'd be beyond anyone's help. I think he almost managed it.

The rolling back door of the business is up, and there is a crowd of white-shirted employees—men and women both—staring out at us from the loading dock. Roberts shoves his way through with a phone in his hand. "Yes, right now!" he's saying. "I need police right now. One of my employees is being assaulted—"

"Uh, sir, that's not what happened," one of his employees says. "*He* attacked *her*!"

"I always said he wasn't right in the head," one of the others says, and more nod. "Creepy asshole."

"All right, all right, settle down!" Roberts says. His face is flushed, and he's clearly out of his depth. "Let's let the police settle this—"

"Back inside, folks!" calls a deep, cheerful voice, and I look back down the alley to see Mike Lustig, of all people, striding toward us. He's wearing an FBI protective vest and windbreaker, and he's got his badge prominently displayed; it catches the low western light and flashes like real gold. Behind him, he's brought two other agents, who look stone-faced and dangerous. They're all in sunglasses against the glare of the setting sun. "Roll that door down. Go on now. Thank you for your cooperation. Nobody leaves. I've got agents on the front. Just sit tight."

He sounds so incredibly self-assured that Roberts ushers his people back inside and rolls down the door without so much as a protest. I can see him curiously peeping out the window, phone still in his hand. Probably on with the local police again.

"Jesus, son, you clocked him good," Mike says, crouching down next to Suffolk. The man's groaning and stirring. "Going to have to get him checked out before we do anything else."

"Trust me," Sam says. "Cuff him first."

"This guy?"

"He choked Gwen half to death," Sam says. "That's why I used the pipe."

Mike looks up at me, and his face goes still for a moment. Then he nods. "Okay," he says. "Cuffs it is. Closest emergency room, and then the nearest field office. Nobody say anything until we're on the record. Gentlemen, you go get everything that he touches in there. Computers, printers, desk, *every goddamn thing*. I want it all. If the manager fusses, call me."

I send a frantic look at Sam and manage a rough whisper. "But Rivard wanted us to—"

"I know," he says. "I gave Suffolk Rivard's message. He opened it and ran for it. Nothing else we can do."

"Have you got the envelope? What did the message say?"

Sam produces it from his pocket. It's been torn open.

There's nothing inside.

◆ ◆ ◆

Claiming federal agent privilege skips the ER waiting list and gets us immediate attention from a doctor who pronounces me okay, except for the pain, swollen vocal cords, abrasions, and a neck that will look like I'd survived a hanging for the next couple of weeks. He thinks I'm lucky to be alive. I do, too.

X-rays and a head CT scan reveal that Suffolk has a mild concussion, thanks to either his original fall to the ground or Sam whacking him soundly on the head, but either way he's released, as am I, and half an hour later we're in a plain interrogation room at the FBI's Wichita field office. The old days of reinforced one-way glass are gone. These days it's cheaper to mount multiple cameras in the room that capture every angle of the conversation.

I don't get a seat at the table. Me, Sam, and our escorted-visitor badges get to park ourselves in the monitoring room with an FBI staffer who lets us watch as Lustig sits down with Carl Suffolk. There's a good half an hour of chitchat, lulling Suffolk into a sense of security, before Lustig looks up at the camera and says, "Would you please run that video we talked about for Mr. Suffolk now?"

The tech in the monitoring room, who's only glanced up long enough to see our prominent visitor badges, presses some buttons, and a flat-screen TV in the interrogation room begins to show something I can't make out, but I can see it running on a separate screen here in the studio. I've never seen what's being shown, but it's obvious on the face of it that it's . . . horrific. And familiar.

It's video taken in Melvin's garage, before the wall was broken. Before his secrets were out. I recognize everything, down to the oval braided rug on the floor.

There's a woman standing on the rug with her hands bound and a metal noose around her neck, and for a frozen second, I thank God that this time it isn't Sam's sister. I think it would break him if it was.

Lustig pauses the video on a close-up of the young woman's face. She's a pretty blonde, with big, pleading, terrified eyes. I recognize her. It's my husband's fourth victim, Anita Jo Marcher.

"Every once in a while, our teams stumble over some really dark shit," Lustig is saying to Suffolk. "We all know about the child porn—and yes, Mr. Suffolk, we've got your phones, tablets, and computers, work and home. Everything with your digital fingerprints on it is about to get autopsied. That ship has sailed all around the world. Clear?"

Suffolk doesn't say anything, but he nods. He's back to looking pallid, lost, and completely helpless. I'd feel pity for him if I hadn't seen the demon under his skin. If I didn't still feel the scraping burn of his fingers around my neck.

"So tell me where this *particular* video came from," Lustig says. "Doesn't seem your usual perverted taste."

"I don't know," Suffolk mumbles. But I recognize the way his chin goes down, the way his eyes take on a hard, dark shine.

"Sure you don't. By the way, your work computers were clean, but funny thing, we found this video on a thumb drive in your desk at work. You watch it on the computer sometimes when you're on the night shift all by yourself? You just like to keep it on hand for dull moments there, Carl?"

Suffolk's chin is working up and down now, like behind those closed lips he's practicing a biting motion, again and again. He doesn't blink. And he doesn't answer.

"Maybe you haven't thought this through, but either you're going to jail today for federal charges of possession and distribution of child pornography, or you start playing let's-make-a-deal like your damn life depends on it. That time would be right now, my man. This minute. Who provided this video?"

Suffolk suddenly looks away. Up toward the camera. "Is she watching?"

"Who?"

"Her."

Lustig doesn't say anything. Suffolk stares at the camera, and it feels like I'm right in the room, feet away from him.

"You fucking bitch," he says. "He should have killed you, too. I hope he does now. I hope he films every bit of it because if he does, I'll pay to watch that shit. You hear me? I'll pay to watch!" His voice rises to a scream at the end. I have no idea why he hates me so much, but I feel it like acid burning my skin.

Mike Lustig doesn't move. Doesn't even so much as raise an eyebrow. His body language continues to be loose, open, relaxed. I don't know how he does it. Once the screaming stops, the silence stretches for a long moment before Lustig says, "You let me know when you're done with your tantrum. I can wait. 'Cause guess what? No matter who else is involved, nobody's sitting here but you. Nobody's going to be doing hard federal time but you, unless you start answering some questions. So tell me. Where'd you get this video?"

Suffolk has gotten quiet. Staring down at the table. The demon has gone back to its lair, somewhere deep inside. He fidgets, looks uncomfortable, and finally, he mumbles one word. "Absalom."

"Uh-huh," Lustig says. "And?"

"Absalom sold me the video. I sold stuff to them, they sold stuff to me. You know. A market exchange."

"How?"

Suffolk lifts one shoulder and lets it fall, like a sulky kid. "I paid in Bitcoin. That got me a link."

"So you're not part of Absalom. You're just a customer."

"And a supplier." He gives Lustig a sudden, unsettling grin. "I get discounts."

"What do you supply?"

"You know." He shrugs again. "Retouched photos. Edited videos. Commission stuff."

"We'll have a long talk about that in a bit, but let's keep moving. So who do you know in Absalom, then?" Another shrug. No answer. "How about the name Merritt Van Der Wal? You know him?"

"Nope."

"Napier Jenkins?" I've never heard either of these names, but I can only assume that he's making them up . . . or he already uncovered more Absalom members without us. That's probable.

"No."

"How about Lancel Graham?"

The hesitation gives Suffolk away. He hadn't expected that name, and of course he knows it. We all know it. I flinch all over at the name, but I keep my focus on Suffolk. "Don't know him, either."

He should. That name, of all of them, absolutely ought to ring a very loud bell for him.

"Carl, I'm disappointed in you. I know you know Lancel Graham, because you didn't buy that damn video with Bitcoin from Absalom. You got it straight from Lancel Graham, copied right off his hard drive. You know we can track that digital footprint, right? You're not stupid. So now you're going down for a federal slam dunk of criminal conspiracy, and possession and distribution of child porn, plus you'll be enjoying the great state of Kansas's tour of its legal system for conspiracy to murder."

"I never murdered anybody!"

"Roll the other one," Mike says, then looks up at the camera. The tech in the room with me presses buttons, and a new video begins. Same set, but subtly different simply because of the proportions of the room it's crowded into. This one, I realize, was filmed in the cabin basement up above Stillhouse Lake. Lancel Graham's place. It's his re-creation of Melvin's torture chamber . . . and there's a girl shown in this one, too.

The girl with the butterfly tattoo, the first one Graham killed and dumped in the lake to implicate me in her murder. I catch my breath, because I remember her from around town in Norton. She sat across the restaurant from me and Lanny as we ate cake, and she'd been a normal, smiling, sweet young lady.

I'm seeing her last, awful minutes on earth in this video.

The tech shuts it down once it's made an impression, and I realize I'm shaking. I turn away so I don't have to look at the freeze-frame of her face.

Mike Lustig is saying, in the same calm voice, "That video is Lancel Graham murdering his first victim, and the time stamp tells me you had it on the same thumb drive before the second young woman was killed. So yeah. Conspiracy to murder, Carl. I don't think you're going to see a computer screen again before we're all jacked into the net by our brains. Unless you want to *talk to me*."

Suffolk is shaking, I can see it. He's a sadist and a coward, and he knows damn well that all of those charges could be leveled at him, and possibly more.

He's also dangerous. The way he went after me, the unhesitating way he choked me, tells me it isn't the first time he's tried to kill someone. It might actually be the first time he's *failed*.

"I don't know anything about Absalom," Suffolk finally says, and Lustig sighs and starts to kick his chair back. "Except a couple of names, that's all! Just some names. Screen names, not even real ones. You know. Graham made some side deals with me, that's all. He and I had . . . common interests. We swapped videos. I didn't know he was the one killing those girls! I thought he got 'em from somebody else."

"Sure you didn't. Let's start with screen names," Lustig says, shoving a pad of paper and a felt-tip marker across to him. "And throw in anything else you can come up with that might save your ass from twenty-five to life in a federal penitentiary, too. Because I can predict with a fine degree of certainty how pleasant that vacation stay's going to be for you. Bet you can, too."

It takes half an hour for Lustig to get a full picture of the things Suffolk collected, beyond the photos and videos he supplied to Absalom's marketplace. He enjoyed a very special kind of horror: graphic videos of torture and murder. Snuff films. The official FBI position has always been that they don't exist, but it comes as no surprise to me that they do, and that there's a marketplace for them on the dark web.

It's a nasty surprise, though, that Absalom deals in those, as well as child pornography. Their sideline in blackmail and Internet tormenting is just that: a hobby, though it helps them attract and identify potential customers. Psychopaths recognizing psychopaths and then catering to their particular pleasures. Layers and levels to all this evil, and at its core, a heartless, soulless greed.

Melvin Royal, Suffolk said, was a gold-level supplier. When he was still active, he'd filmed his crimes, and Absalom found a market for them after the fact. I'm sickened, but not surprised. Only his still pictures were found and presented at trial, but a video camera was in the garage. Just no tapes or digital files.

What *really* frightens me is that if Melvin's real video cache surfaces now, the fake one that links me to his crimes will only have more credibility. There'd certainly be an official investigation—Mike might even head it—and I'd be exonerated, eventually.

But as I already knew, being found innocent of a crime doesn't mean much to most people . . . and it means even less if they have something tangible to convince them differently.

"Yeah, Melvin Royal sold his shit directly to Absalom," Suffolk tells Mike. "They ran a pay-per-view event for every new video, and then sold downloads. Thousands of 'em. If it works like my deal with them, the money they paid him is in a Bitcoin account he can access from anywhere. But I don't know for sure. I told you. I'm just on the fringes. A customer."

A customer who collects the murder and torture of innocent victims. I want to throw up, remembering those hands around my neck.

Mike finishes writing his notes. "Anything else?"

On the screen, Suffolk leans back in his chair and says, "One more thing." Then he looks up at the camera and smiles. Just *smiles*. It's eerie, and chilling, made more so because then he actually winks. "Make sure you watch the whole recording of that first video you showed me, the Royal one. There's a treat for you right at the end."

Lustig gets up from the chair and slides it neatly in at the table.

"Oh, I'll be sure to do that," he says. "But if you think you're going to get a last good-time jolly watching it with me right now, dream on. You get used to being alone in a locked room for a while. Call it a preview of the rest of your life."

He's in the monitoring room in another minute, nods to us, and goes straight to the tech. "Raj? You got me a seat?"

"You can watch in the back; I'm queuing it up now," the tech says. He looks up and past us and gives Lustig a concerned look. "You sure you want to see it?"

"Wouldn't be doing my due diligence if I didn't. Have you seen the whole thing?"

The tech looks away. "I haven't finished yet."

"Tough work, I know," Lustig says, almost gently. "I'll finish it up. I'll log the time codes as I go."

Raj looks unspeakably relieved—this, I realize, must be part of his job. Watching horror after horror reduced to pixels, to light and shadow and sound. "I'll queue it up to where I stopped logging. Headphones are next to the monitor, sir. Thanks."

Sam catches Lustig's arm as he passes. "Hey. Are you seriously going to play his game—"

"I have to," Lustig says. "Believe me, I wish to hell I didn't. Wait here."

We wait. I glance over at Lustig every once in a while. It takes a long time, and there's no movement in the room except for the creak of our chairs and the sound of Lustig's pen scratching on paper, and after nearly half an hour, the sudden, sharp sound of Lustig's chair rolling back from the small, gray desk. I look up. So does Sam. Lustig's gotten to his feet, headphones still on. His face is, for just that moment, completely overcome with surprise. He'd have steeled himself against the horror, the anguish, the brutality, so what surprised him enough to bring him right to his feet?

Lustig hits a key on the computer, rips off the headphones, and charges over. *To me.* He takes my arm and tows me back, fingers digging in painfully, and when I try to resist, I get dragged. All my instincts put me on alert, and I have to fight the urge to hit him hard, fast, and with brutal force. I don't let people handle me like this.

But this is an FBI agent, and I know resisting will only make it worse.

"Hey!" Sam shouts, but Lustig ignores him. Sam follows as I'm pulled toward the computer. "Mike, what the hell are you doing? You—"

His voice fades as we both see what's on the screen.

A hot, needle-pricking sensation of unreality washes through me. I feel dizzy again, and I'm suddenly glad for Lustig's hard grip holding me in place, because on the screen, frozen in time, is the bleeding, screaming victim. In front of her, Melvin reaches for an evil-looking knife.

Someone is handing the blade to him.

That someone is *me.* I can see my profile. I'm standing just in front of the camera, next to a wall full of knives and hammers. Melvin's tools.

And I'm *smiling*.

"I'd arrest you right fucking now," Lustig tells me, "except that I don't have jurisdiction, and Kansas already acquitted your sorry ass.

Now you sit down and tell me everything you know about Melvin Royal. *Right now.*"

I'm numb. I'm just . . . empty. I sit down, still staring at the screen. At my face—Gina Royal's face. It hurts to talk, but I force the words out anyway. "It's a fake," I tell him. "I wasn't there. *I was never there.* Absalom faked—"

"Shut up with that bullshit," Lustig says, then rolls my chair around so he's leaning his weight on the arms, shoving his face close to mine. "*You were there.* All this, this victim act? I've had my doubts all along, and believe me, I'm very done being played. You tell me what you know!"

"That's not me!" I scream it in his face, out of sheer panic and desperation—it's a raw, rough, broken sound, and it hurts. God, it hurts. "I don't know! I am *not* part of this!"

He shoves my chair, and it rolls back and smashes against the wall with such force I'm almost pitched out of it. I get up, ready to fight, but Lustig doesn't come closer. He stares, and then he turns and walks away. Raj is turned toward us, mouth half-open in astonishment.

Sam hasn't moved toward me, either. He looks calm and blank, right up until he picks up the monitor and throws it against the wall. It smashes into sparks and broken plastic, and Raj lets out a yell of protest, coming up out of his chair.

"Sam!" I cry that out, and wish I hadn't, because the look he gives me flays me to the spine. It destroys me. I wonder if he's about to finish the job that Suffolk started.

Lustig pauses at the office door to say to Raj, "You don't let her leave this room until I come back. Understand?" He charges through. Raj nods and gets himself together. He blocks the way out.

I feel trapped. Hunted. My throat is on fire, and when I swallow, I taste blood.

Sam heads for the door, too. I want to call after him, but I'm afraid to do it now. Raj is in his path, until Sam says, in a voice that I don't even recognize, "He said *she* had to stay. I don't."

Raj reluctantly edges out of the way, and then Sam is gone. I'm alone with the tech agent and the smashed monitor. The room smells like ozone. Raj won't look at me. I can see he's nervous; his throat is working, and he's tracking me out of the corner of his eye in case I make a move. But I don't. I just stand there, numbly. I don't know what else I can do.

Mike Lustig opens the door. He looks grim and furious, and Raj gratefully sinks back into his tech chair. "You can go, Gina," he says. He bites the words off in chunks. I'm no longer Gwen Proctor to him. "But don't you get comfortable. You won't be out walking free for long. Now get the fuck out of my building before I do something I'm going to regret."

There's another agent standing next to him, stone-faced, and I can tell that he's my escort out of the building. Everything feels unreal now. I wonder what they'll do if I just lose control and start screaming. Probably drag me out anyway. I don't make a conscious decision to leave; I just do it. I'm suddenly out of the darkness of the monitoring room, and into a hallway. The agent has a grip on my arm—firm, not abusive.

He escorts me out, unclips my badge, and walks me to the lobby, where the FBI receptionist takes the identification from him. Both of them look at me expectantly.

I don't know where I'm supposed to go now. What I'm supposed to do.

I finally realize that I'm expected to leave, so I walk out the front doors, which automatically lock behind me. It's dark, the sun long down, and the wind's cold. I stand there in bewilderment, thinking I've fallen out of time. Out of space. This is *Wichita*. I've driven these streets. Walked in that shopping center visible in the distance. Gotten gas at the station on the corner.

I shouldn't be here.

The enormity of everything that's just happened rolls over me, and I stagger to one of the broad concrete blocks that guards the approach to the ground-floor lobby of the building. It's not low enough to sit on, but I lean against it, trembling, gasping for breath. The past is cascading down on me now, in smells and colors and tastes and horror, and *could it be right,* could it possibly be right that I was ever part of what Melvin did, that I'd been in that garage prior to the day it all cracked apart? That I helped him, and I've forgotten *all of it*?

Am I insane?

I don't know how much time passes. Minutes, but it feels like hours, and there's the scrape of footsteps, and someone's coming toward me. For an instant, I think it's Melvin. I think, *this is how it ends.*

But then he passes beneath a streetlight, and I make out Sam's face. He isn't reaching out, but he's here. His gaze is fixed on the offices behind me.

"Get up," he tells me. "I talked to Rivard. The plane's waiting. It'll drop us in Knoxville. I'll drive you back to Javier's."

"And then?" I ask. It comes out in a rough whisper.

He doesn't answer. And he doesn't wait for me. I'm left to scramble along in his wake, lost, but grateful to have a path out of this nightmare.

I will never come back to this place.

I realize that the way I whisper the words, it's become a prayer.

15

LANNY

When we hear the crunch of gravel outside, I grip my brother's hand tighter. I haven't let go for the past hour, and neither has he; we're back to our little-kid days, after Mom and Dad went away—both arrested, the same day. I still remember that more vividly than anything else: me and my brother sitting in the backseat of a police car. It felt like being in a cage, and it smelled like sweat and feet, and we held hands the whole way. We didn't talk. I don't think either of us knew what to say. I remember not being so much terrified as dazed. I kept expecting it to be over, that Mom would come get us, and we'd get ice cream and go home. Brady—now Connor—had been the one who'd cried, and I remember being impatient with him being such a baby. I kept telling myself it was nothing. We would be home soon.

But there was no home by then.

It had been Brady, not me, who'd asked endless, anxious questions once we were at the police station. *Where's my mom? When can we see her? Can we go home? Where's my dad?* It had been clear to me, in all my older-child wisdom, that the police officers weren't going to answer any of those things, and I kept telling myself it didn't matter because it was all a big, stupid mistake.

The police gave us drinks and snacks and put us in a room with some toys and games that were all too broken or too young for us. I had a book I'd been reading that day, I remember, but I never finished it. Brady—*no, stop thinking of him as Brady, his name is Connor, it's Connor now*—took the book out of the trash when I threw it away; I don't even remember the name of it. I think that was the first book he read, really. He started reading the day our lives went down in flames.

That's the one book I know I can never bear to finish. Maybe that's why I can't remember what it's called, or anything about it.

Grandma came for us, after flying all night to get there, and took us back to her house. She'd been the one who'd had to explain to us about Dad being a murderer, and Mom being arrested for helping him. *Your mom didn't do anything wrong,* she'd told us over and over, and it had seemed true then. They'd let her out of jail. She'd been found innocent, and when she came back, I was so glad, so glad I finally cried.

Everything's broken inside me now, and I can't cry. I can't feel anything except pure, drowning anger.

She lied to us. All this time. She's a damn liar.

I look up when Javier, standing at the window with a cup of coffee in his hand, says, "She's here." He turns to look at Kezia, who's in the kitchen. She's dressed for her job, which means a jacket and nice pants and a gun and badge, and it makes me remember that she's a detective, like her boss, Prester. Good. Maybe she can arrest Mom and take her away again, for good this time. "Sam's with her."

"Keep it low," Kezia tells him. "Let's hear Gwen's side of it."

I look at Connor. I'm holding his hand, but it's lying still and limp in mine. I wonder if he's even heard, but then he takes my hand from mine, slides a bookmark into place in the book he's reading, and puts the story aside. When he stands, I do, too.

Boot barks, low and threatening chesty sounds, and it makes me feel safe. My hands are cold. I put them in my pockets. Everything seems very clear to me right now, and at the same time, everything's destroyed. I know I can't trust her. I can't trust *anybody*, ever again, because *I believed her*, and my mother lied to us.

I just want this to be over with, and at the same time, I can feel part of me wanting to cry, punch something, run away, collapse, and curl up into a ball. It's like all the pieces of me are shattered, and I don't know how to put anything back together again.

Connor seems calm. Way, way too calm.

Javier steps out, and Boot goes quiet. There's some low conversation, and then the door opens. It's Mom.

My first thought is, *She looks tired.* My second thought is, *Why is she wearing a scarf like that? She doesn't like scarves.* I'd bought her one, once. She'd been nice about it, but had only worn it once. This one is a dull, gunmetal gray, and she's wrapped it close around her throat.

Maybe she's sick. I don't care. I hope she dies. I hope she falls over right now and dies, and I can step over her and leave.

She rushes to hug us, and her relief collapses into confused hurt when Connor and I, without communicating, both step back from her. She slows down, stops, and says, "Sweetie? What is it?" She's talking to Connor first, and her voice sounds wrong. Scratchy, deep, weak. Maybe she really is sick. I want to punch her in the throat, and the thought seems so real to me that I see red, and I shake all over. *Don't you dare touch him.*

Connor doesn't say anything. He hasn't said much since we found him. Mom looks at me. There are tears in her eyes, *fake* tears from a *fake* Mom, and I hate her so much it makes me want to puke.

"Lanny? What is it?"

And just like that, I scream. It comes out of me in an uncontrolled, high-pitched burst. *"Screw you!"*

Javier steps between us, which is good because I'm throwing myself at her, and he's holding me back. He's trying to say something, but I can't hear him. Weirdly, I do hear Kezia say, clear as anything, *So much for keeping it low.* She hasn't moved from where she's standing, but she's ready to. She's watching Connor.

I need to take care of my brother, so I stop screaming, and I turn away, and I get myself together. I put my arms around Connor, but he doesn't seem to even notice.

He's staring at Mom like he's never seen her before.

Mom's trying to talk. Her voice sounds whispery and raw. "Oh, honey, God, what's wrong, what did I do wrong—"

"I don't know, *Gina*, what do you think you did wrong? Lie to us *forever*?" My voice is back to normal, but loud, and I want to shove her, push her right out of our lives. I want to defend my brother because I know this hurts him in ways I can never make right again. It's my job to protect him, and I didn't. I couldn't.

Because *she* did this to him. To us.

Mom's crying. Tears are streaming down her face, and she keeps reaching out, and we keep backing away. Javier's still blocking her. He says, "Sit down, Gwen."

"Her name's not Gwen," I tell him. "It's *Gina*. Gina Royal. That's who she always was."

"I don't know what's going on," Mom says. But there's something in her eyes—a kind of blind, trapped panic—that makes me think she already knows. I'm used to seeing my mother as almighty, strong, nearly superhuman; I've seen her throw herself into a fight even if she knew she couldn't win it. *For us,* some part of me whispers, but I shut it up fast.

I know she's not a superhero. She's human, like me. Like Connor. Like everybody else. It feels like I'm learning something important, and something sad, too. She's just another person, in the end.

And she's evil. She's *just like Dad*. No, she's worse than Dad, because he didn't screw with our heads and make us believe down was up and wrong was right. Dad never made us think he was innocent.

She did. That's so much worse, and I'm never, ever going to stop hating her for it.

"Sit down," Javier says to her again. He sounds like he's had enough. Mom glances at Sam, who isn't even facing toward her anymore, and she sinks down in the armchair. Javier walks over with his tablet device, taps, and hands it to her. "Explain this."

Mom's face goes so pale that I think she'll collapse, but she doesn't. She stares, but I don't think she's watching, not really, and when the video's over, she hands it back to Javier and bends forward to put her face in her hands. I think for a second she's crying, but when she comes upright again, her eyes are dry and almost dull. "That's not me," she says. Her voice sounds like torn metal, rough and sharp. "It's fake. Absalom created it."

"Sorry, no," Javier says. "This is too good for some casual hater to do. I see *you*. Helping *him*."

"It's *fake*! If it's real, why wasn't it shown at my trial? Think, Javi, please! I know it looks bad, believe me. It makes me sick, and it makes me angry. But *that is not me*. This never happened!"

"Just shut up," I tell her. "It's right there. It's staring you in the face. *You did it*."

"Lanny, honey—"

"Don't," I say sharply. I want her to leave now. I can't stand to look at her. She makes me want to vomit. "Shut up. I'm sick of your bullshit."

She's crying again now. Good. I'm glad it hurts. She has no idea how much it hurts *me*.

"How did you get this?" she whispers.

Connor lifts his head for the first time and says, "I found it." He doesn't sound angry. Just empty. I'm scared of that, because my brother isn't as angry as I want him to be, at least not that I can tell. It's like he *expected* the world to fail us.

"Where did you—"

"Doesn't *matter*, does it?" I break in. "Because he did. It proves you're a liar."

"It proves people want you to believe I am," she says. "Please, Lanny—"

"Don't *talk to me*!"

Silence. We're all looking at her, except Sam; he's busy pouring himself a cup of coffee, trying to pretend everything's normal, but I can see the stiffness in his back. His expression is so blank it looks like a Halloween mask. Is it him, too? Is he a liar? He lied to us in the beginning. Maybe we shouldn't trust him, either. Or Javier. Or Kezia.

Maybe there's nobody in this world left for us to trust but each other.

Mom turns to Javier and Kezia. "Where did he get this? How?"

"I found it," Connor says again. He's not looking at anyone.

Kezia's watching him like she wants to come and scoop him up and hug him. I think she would, if this wasn't so tense. "I checked his phone," she says. "He hacked the parental locks. Smart kid. Unfortunately, this is where it led him. And us." She transfers her stare to Mom. "And you're not helping yourself by focusing on where he found it. Question is, what are you not telling us?"

"The FBI knows about the video," Mom says. "They're analyzing it. They'll prove it's fake, because it is."

Sam says, in a voice so cold that I feel it even through all my anger, "There's more than one video. There's a second one that shows Gwen helping him in the garage."

"That's not me!" Mom nearly shouts it at him.

He just shrugs. "Okay. *Gina*, then."

"No, Sam, it was never me, I didn't do—"

Sam turns on her and slams the coffee cup down on the counter. "Goddamn it, you walked away from murder and accessory charges, so just *stop lying*! Why the hell would Absalom fake those videos? The one on Suffolk's USB has been there for a whole year!"

Mom draws in a pained breath and says, "And Absalom has been attacking me and my kids for *four* years. Photoshopped pictures. Harassment. Death threats. Vigilante justice. They've made my life a living hell, you know that! Why do you think this is any different? Why can't you believe me, Sam?"

"Because I can see what's in front of me," he says. "Unlike your jury." Sam turns to me, then. To Connor. His tone goes gentle. "Kids, I'm sorry. I really am. This isn't your fault, not at all. I wish I could help you. But this—" He shakes his head. "This is just . . . enough."

"Sam!" Mom comes to her feet as he walks for the front door. "Sam, please don't!"

"Leave him alone," I tell her. "You've hurt him enough."

I don't know if she even hears me, but she stops trying to talk to him. She watches as Sam leaves. The door shuts behind him.

She looks helpless now, and lost, and afraid. "You can't believe this. I understand why Sam would. But not you, Lanny, you know better. You know who I am."

She reaches out to me, and I don't come toward her. I pull back.

"I never want to see you again. You're not my mother. I don't have a mother." I mean it. I mean every word, and I can hear the rage shaking my voice. I want to slap her so hard that just thinking about it makes my hand feel hot. I want to punish her. I want her to feel like I do. Beaten and wrecked.

And I think she does now, because the shock and horror I see in her face is almost enough. Almost.

"I never helped your father!"

It comes out as a strangled sort of cry, and I don't believe her. I don't even think she believes herself.

Connor says, "You did. We saw. Stop saying you didn't. We're never going to believe you again." That's it. That's all. It's the most he's said since he saw the video.

It hits Mom hard, and she gasps like she's been punched in the stomach. She looks at Javier. At Kezia. Nobody has anything more to say to her. I see something break inside her, and she sits down again. My mother looks like she wants to die.

It hurts me to see that, but it's the weak part of me, the one that still, stupidly, *always* wants to believe things will be all right, and they never will. They never were right from the start. Maybe, finally, this is the last time I'll believe stupid, childish bullshit.

"What do you want me to do?" Mom finally asks. She sounds defeated now. She's given up. I wait to feel good about it, because I should, but I just feel empty. The anger that's been driving me is starting to drain away. All that's left is silence and ruin, and I've never felt so alone in my entire life.

"I need you to go, Gwen," Javier says. "Don't come back until this is over and you've got real proof of what you're claiming. You shouldn't be around your kids right now. It's not healthy." That surprises me, somehow. I didn't think he'd be on our side. Or that Kezia would, really. But they're standing with us, against Mom.

It helps.

Mom can't believe it, either. "Javi—"

"If you can prove what you say, that Absalom is behind this, then we can talk," Kezia says. "I'll be the first to say I was wrong. But right now, I'd be a fool not to believe what's right in front of my face, and what I see is you helping Melvin Royal carry some poor girl in to cut up. If that's true, any part of true, you don't deserve to ever see these kids again."

Mom puts a hand to her mouth, like she might scream, or vomit. The look on her face—shock, panic, I don't know. But she's in pain. *I don't care,* I tell myself fiercely. *Good. I hope it hurts.*

"If I'm really what it shows on that video, why am I out hunting for him now?" Mom asks. Her voice is shaking so badly it sounds like it might fall apart. "How does that even make sense?"

"Makes sense if you're trying to get back to him and join up," Kezia replies, and that stops my mom cold. It also makes me feel sick to my stomach, because maybe it's true. Maybe Mom and Dad have always been working together. Maybe whatever sick thing they had is still there.

"I'm not," Mom says. It sounds weak. It sounds like a lie, and I start to hate her all over again.

"Yeah, you say. Maybe all this innocent-victim act was a lie from the start, and Absalom had you right all along. Which is another reason to keep these kids away from all that mess."

One image suddenly comes through to me, and it stops the flood of anger inside me. Mom, coming down the steps in Lancel Graham's basement. The horror on her face when she realized what she was looking at.

The joy when she saw me and Connor, unharmed.

It doesn't make sense with everything else, and it's the truest moment I know, the moment where I saw, really *saw*, how much she loved us both. Mom came for us in that dark place when I thought we were going to die alone. She was bleeding and wounded, and she'd fought her way back to save us.

That isn't something a liar and a killer does. Is it?

Maybe she does love us, I think. And then, *But maybe she just loves Dad more.* That's an awful thought, one that makes my stomach drop, and I put my arm around Connor. I can't take any chances. I have to protect him. And that means I have to make Mom go away.

I'm tired all of a sudden. I just want to curl up in a ball on my bed and cry.

Mom's scarf slips enough that it reveals a whole universe of bruises—dark red spots, threads of broken blood vessels connecting them. Somebody's hurt her, and for a second I'm scared, and I'm worried for her, and I have to stop myself from feeling that because *she's a liar* and she probably deserved it.

My head hurts, and I hate this—I hate all of it. So I say, "Just get out, Mom. We don't want you." I meant to say, *We don't want you here,* but it came out the way I really felt it. *We don't want you.* It's the worst thing I could say to her, and I know that. I really do.

Mom draws in a sharp breath and puts a hand on her stomach, like I've stabbed her there. Her lips form my name, but she doesn't say it out loud. Maybe she can't.

Kezia says, "Lanny's right. Go. Don't come back until this is over."

"I swear to you, I'm going to protect these kids like they're my own," Javier adds. "I'm going to protect them from every kind of threat, and right now, that includes you. Get me?"

Mom's eyes fill up with tears, but she doesn't cry. She says, "That's all I want."

And then she looks at us, and I can tell she wants to come to us, hug us, cry. I can feel her need to do that shivering in the air around her, like thunder.

I can feel my whole body craving it, too, because bodies are stupid; they just want to be loved. But I'm better than that. I'm stronger. Mom taught me to be stronger, and I am. No matter how much it hurts, I just stare at her and will her to go away.

And Mom leaves.

She *leaves.*

I wait for her to look back, but she doesn't. The door shuts behind her. Even though I wanted her to go, demanded it, the fact that she did it still feels like she betrayed us all over again. My stomach hurts. My chest feels tight. Nothing's good anymore, nothing in the whole world.

I keep my arm around Connor, holding him close. He usually squirms away when I do that, but not now. My hug is telling him, *I'm here, I'm with you, I'm not letting go of you.*

It's saying, *I'm not like her.*

We're all quiet for a while. I guess Sam was waiting outside, because we hear the engine start, and the gravel crunch, and when it's gone,

Kezia lets out a deep, gusting sigh and says, "Damn. I'm sorry. That was rough. You kids okay?"

I nod. Connor doesn't do anything. He's staring down at the floor, wearing that mask he gets when he's just too overwhelmed to feel anything at all. I don't know what this is going to do to him, but I know it can't be good. Kezia turns to Javier, and though she says it quietly, I hear her anyway. "I can't leave now. I'll call Prester."

"You can't keep tap-dancing around him on this," he says. "Kez, he already checked in here, trying to figure out what was making you and me take so much time off work. He's either worried about you, or suspicious. Neither one's good. You haven't been a detective long enough to get a free pass. Go to work."

She gazes at him for a long moment, then shakes her head. "No, I have a better idea."

"Kez. *Querida.*"

"I'm serious."

Javier shakes his head, but he doesn't say no when she pulls out her phone and dials. I watch her numbly as she walks back and forth. My anger's gone now. It's like it left with Mom, and all I have left is a chilly, empty space where my guts should be. I sink down on the couch and pull the heavy knitted afghan from the back to wrap around my shoulders, because I'm shivering now.

Kezia says, "Prester? I need to tell you something. And I'm thinking maybe you should come here to Javier's house to hear all of it."

◆ ◆ ◆

Detective Prester is an old man, so old I'm surprised he's not retired, but he's still smart. You can see it the second he looks at you.

He takes everything in with one long glance, including the two of us on the couch. We haven't been told to go and hide this time, and I'm not sure we would have, anyway. "Well, damn," he says, then closes the door behind him. "Guess that answers my questions about the kids. Where is Gwen?"

"Not here," Kezia says. "Have a seat."

Prester does, at the kitchen table. Javier's made coffee, and he pours three cups and sits in the third spot. Prester accepts and sips, but he keeps looking over at the two of us. I wonder what he sees. *Little orphan children,* I think, and I hate that. But it's true. We're alone now. Mom isn't coming back, and even if she did, I wouldn't go with her. I can take care of myself, but what about Connor? He's not old enough. He needs help. I'm smart enough to know they won't let me be his Mom stand-in.

We need help.

For the first time, the size of what happened hits me, and I feel the wobbly burn of tears in my throat and my eyes. I look over at Connor. He's staring at his book again, but he hasn't turned the page in minutes. He's not reading. He's hiding. He's good at that.

I envy that right now, because I don't know what to *do.*

"Gwen and Sam—" Kezia begins, but Prester holds up a hand. It trembles a little.

"No, Claremont. I been doing this awhile now. I think I can solve this little mystery. Gwen and Sam went running off on their own investigation. They figured the kids would be safer here, with you. How am I doing so far?"

"You're on it."

"And from the look on all these faces, something's gone pretty wrong," he says. "Pretty damn wrong. They missing?"

"No," Javier says. "But things are getting complicated. I didn't want you thinking Kezia isn't a good cop, or we've got some family trouble, or something. This isn't that."

"Looks exactly like family trouble to me," Prester says. "Just not your own."

As an answer, Javier powers up his tablet and hands it over. Prester watches the video, and I can't tell if it affects him at all. He just nods and hands it back. "You believe it?"

The question hangs in the air for a long few seconds, and then Kezia says, "I don't want to. It does seem really damn convenient that this video was out there and somehow nobody got it to the cops before her trial. Why'd they hold it back?"

"People do," Prester say. "Answer's always the same. Money or power. Somebody was hoping for a payday, if it's genuine. If it isn't, it's about power. And that all depends on who benefits."

I think about that. What did that mean? Who could possibly *benefit* from something that horrible? What good did it do?

I don't work it out until Javier says, "Having this hanging out there puts Gwen on the defensive. It makes people look for her, and she has to stop looking for her ex to watch her own back."

Dad. It benefits Dad. My head hurts. It doesn't make sense, but it does, too. I just can't believe anyone would do something like that *deliberately*.

"Benefits Absalom, too," Kezia says. "Right?"

"It does, since she must be on their trail, too," Prester agrees. "Not saying it can't be real, but like you said, Kez. Seems too easy. And you have to ask yourself: Who the hell was creeping around in the bushes filming this in the first place? Seeing them carrying an unconscious girl in, and not calling the police? If that landed on my desk, I'd have to first ask where it came from, and why."

I'm starting to feel a little sick now. He's making it sound like some story out of a movie. But it isn't. Not at all. He's making it sound like she's innocent.

She can't be. Because I made her go away.

"I already walked Connor through how he found it," Kezia says. "I can show you. Apparently, he's been on a message board that talks about his dad's crimes. There was a link. It's been taken down now, but that's where he got the video."

"You really buy her story about it being faked?" Javier says. "It looks so *real*."

"You gone to the movies lately? People with PCs and a decent skill set can make impossible things look damn real nowadays. It takes forensic analysis to work out what's real and what isn't. I think this hit everybody in an emotional place, not a logical one."

"So you don't believe it," Kezia says.

"I'm saying that I'll keep an open mind until the tech geeks tell me different, one way or the other." Prester drinks some more coffee and cuts his gaze toward me and Connor. "You sure this is the best place for these kids?"

"No," Javier says. "But I'm sure it's better than being dragged out there on some road trip looking for trouble. If Gwen finds it, last thing any of us wants is them in the cross fire."

Prester nods in agreement. "Appreciate you bringing me in on this. I'll keep it quiet." He turns to Kezia. "Far as I'm concerned, you can be out in the field most of the time. If the field means you're here looking out for them, that's all good, too. We get something to investigate, I'll call you. Otherwise, you stay close. I don't want anybody else coming after them. Might look bad on my record."

He takes his cup to the sink and rinses it, and then he shakes hands with Javier and Kezia before he goes. He never talks directly to us.

When the door closes behind the detective, Kezia and Javier look at each other for a few long seconds, and then Kezia comes to sit down in the armchair, across from the two of us. "You guys okay?" she asks.

I want to laugh. Seriously. We are not okay. How could we be okay? I'm shaking all over.

"I'm fine," I say. She doesn't know me well enough to know that when I tuck my chin in and let my hair droop over my face, I'm lying.

"What do you want us to say? She let us down. She let us all down. She ought to be in jail with Dad."

Kezia doesn't like doing this. She, like Javier, is good at protecting people, but not so much at comforting. But she tries. "I thought maybe you can tell me how you're feeling about everything."

I roll my eyes. "Mad. Pissed off. Disappointed. What else do you want me to say? It's done already! She's *gone*!"

Even I can hear how my voice gets raw at the end of that, and I shut up, fold my arms over my chest, and slump back in the couch. My entire body screams, *Don't talk to me*, and Kezia accepts that. "Okay. Connor?"

"She shouldn't have lied to us about what she did with Dad," he says.

"I know that, but are you sad? Or are you mad?"

She's trying too hard, and I think she probably is as pissed at Mom as we are. We're not a favor she and Javier are doing gladly anymore. We're a responsibility. I'll bet they're both thinking the same thing: *How did we get into this? And how do we get out of it?*

I'll bet we're all thinking it, but me and Connor, we're not going to say it. We're our mother's children. We don't want to talk about our feelings. When Mom dragged us to our counseling sessions after she got out of jail, I think I broke a record for the number of hours without talking in talk therapy.

If I want to blab about it, *if*, I don't want to do it here. And not with Connor listening. I have to be strong for him.

Connor's shrugged in response to Kezia's question, and she gives us a sad little smile like she knows. She doesn't. "Okay, but you know you can come to either one of us, right? Anytime. About anything. This is a hard day, and we want to be here for you."

"Yeah. Great. Are we done now?" I say. "Can I go to my room?"

"Sure," Kezia says. She sounds gentle. "You go rest if you want. We'll be here."

Before I do, I bend over and put an arm around my brother's shoulders. I whisper, just for him, "You can come to me, you know that, right?"

He nods slightly. He will, when he's ready.

I walk into my room and slam the door. I lie down on the bed and stare up at the ceiling; I twist and turn and put my headphones on, but nothing works. I can't rest. I can't sleep. So I pace. I think about Mom. I remember all the things she's done for me, with me, all the fun and light and laughter she gave me, and I wonder if I've made a terrible mistake. That makes me angry at myself, first for hurting her, and then for not sticking to being angry.

I feel so alone right now, and empty, and I want someone to care. Not in the abstract. I want someone to look right into my face and tell me they care what happens to me, and I want it so bad it hurts. But not Kezia. Not Javier.

No. Who I really want to talk to is Dahlia, and I'm not allowed to go to town, or call her. I know why, and it's smart, but I don't feel smart right now. I feel desperate. There's an empty place inside me that's choking me, like there's not enough air in the room.

So I pick up my phone, put her number in from memory, and text her where to meet me. I sign it *Tana*, which is short for lantana, her favorite flower, and she nicknamed me Lannytana a while back.

She hits me back in seconds. ½ hr ok?

K, I type back, and then I end the call.

She didn't hesitate. It makes me feel warm and nervous.

Connor's shown me how to do this. I climb out the window and shut it behind me. Boot barks as I hop the side fence, but only once, as if he doesn't quite know how to communicate that I'm breaking the rules, or he doesn't really want to rat me out. He finally paces the edge of the fence, then climbs back on the porch and lies down. Guarding Connor, I think. Good. I need him to do that for me.

I haven't run in a long time, and I need to feel that again. The control. The burn. The stillness inside that comes when you focus everything on that one effort. It doesn't leave room for all the noise.

So I run. I take off through the woods, watching my footing but keeping to rough game trails until I hit a road, and then running at stride. I see the blue glitter of Stillhouse Lake through the trees in less than half an hour, and I slow down to a walk because my legs are starting to shake. I'm coming up from the far end, by the gun range where Javier ought to be working, except he's taken an extended vacation to make sure we're safe.

I wonder how long it'll take him to realize that I'm not safe right now. And how long to find me.

I stay in the woods, moving carefully and hiding whenever I see any hint of cars or people. There aren't a lot out today. It's cold and a little cloudy. Indoor weather, for most folks. The wind's too sharp for boating.

I'm passing Sam's cabin now. It's standing empty, I guess; he locked it up and left it just as it was, so in an emergency I have somewhere to hide. But I don't want to be guilty of breaking in, either.

From his cabin, I can see our old house.

It's set back from the road and the docks—close enough to be considered lakefront, but far enough up the slope that we don't have to worry about flooding or casual visitors. *Our house.* Except it isn't, really, I guess. All our good times, all our memories of cleaning the place and painting and making it our own, of evenings at dinner and watching movies and being a family . . . all that's wrong now. I don't know how to feel about any of it.

It's like a museum of someone else's life.

I slip out of the trees and break into a run, trying to look like I'm just out for exercise and, nope, totally not the kid of the most notorious serial killer in the past ten years—nope, not at all. I don't see anybody.

I speed up as I get to the driveway and race up it, and I get a real good look at the place.

The house was tagged by vandals before we left it, after word about Dad got out and people knew who we really were. The paint's still there, splashed in insults over the garage and wall. New tags have been added. One's a crude drawing of a hanging woman and two smaller figures on the same scaffold. Gee, subtle, guys.

I stop on the threshold, breathing hard, and try to get my heart rate down. *This is dumb, Lanny. Super dumb. You know it is.* Yeah, and I was starting to think it was a bad idea, too. But I've come this far. I don't really know why, but it feels like this is the only place in the world I can still feel normal.

The front window is smashed. I see wind blowing in. The blinds are broken and fluttering like wounded birds.

I'd stuck keys in my pocket, and now I unlock the door, which still has old crime scene seals on it. I use the keys to rake that seal apart, then push in. No lights, and when I try the switch, no power, either. Oh, and also, no alarm. The pad is dark when I look at it.

I shut the door, lock it, and the smell hits me. *Gross, God, what is that? Is it a dead body?* For a second, stranded in the living room with only the dim light coming in from the crooked, flapping blinds, I imagine one hanging in the hallway from a rope, and if I hadn't just locked the door, I'd have been out of it in the next second.

Don't be an idiot; there's no dead body in here, I tell myself. I look around. The living room isn't really disturbed, except for the brick that came through the front window. Well, and some creative spray painting on the walls. The TV is gone, along with the game console, and most of the games. They came in to do some damage, but they got distracted with stuff to steal.

The stench gets worse when I go in the kitchen, and I see the mess in there. More scrawls of red spray paint, dripping like fresh blood, but whoever did it wasn't good enough with a paint can to make it readable. I think it might say *bitch*, but only if I squint.

The kitchen is the reason for the smell. Someone's opened up the fridge and thrown food all over the floor; it's a molding mess, crawling with flies even in the cold. I want to throw up, but I grab the broom and dustpan and trash bags, and I scoop up as much as I can. The garbage still in the can stinks, too; we never had time to empty it before we left.

Somehow, I never thought I'd be inviting Dahlia into a crime scene. I do my best to get it cleaned up before she arrives.

I bag it all up and take it out back to throw it in the big metal locking bin that's supposed to keep bears away, not that I've ever seen a bear up here. It keeps raccoons frustrated, at least.

I'm shutting the lock on it when a shadow falls, and I realize that there's someone right behind me. I turn and get ready to scream and jam keys between my knuckles just like mom taught . . .

But it's her.

"Hey," she says, flipping her hair back out of her eyes. Dahlia, just like I remember, except her hair's gotten a little longer. God, she's pretty. Prettier than I'll ever be. I want to cry because it's so good to see her, and at the same time, I want to hug her, but I'm not sure I should. "So, you kind of vanished on me, bitch. What's up with your crazy ass?"

She hitches up onto the picnic table that's on the back deck, the one Mom and I built but never really got to enjoy, and I go up and sit beside her, close enough our thighs touch along the side. My heart's racing. I'm not supposed to be seen by anybody at all, certainly not someone who knows me. I've broken all the safe rules.

But this feels so right. So very right. The emptiness inside of me is gone, and right now, in this moment, I have peace.

"I had to go," I say. "I'm sorry. I wanted to call you, but things got crazy. And then people were kind of out to get us. You heard, right?"

"Yeah," she says quietly. "Is it true you killed Lancel Graham?"

Graham was dead all right. But it was a shock to hear my friend thought I'd done it. "What? No! God! Who even said that?"

"Everybody," she says and shrugs. "Well, they buried him, so it kind of sounded true, right? And you're badass. They said he was some fucked-up killer. And so was your dad . . . ?" It's kind of a half-ass question, and I don't want to answer it. At all. It's such a quiet question, and it feels larger than the whole world. I'd never told Dahlia about Dad. Not that I hadn't wanted to, but there were rules. Mom's rules.

Screw Mom. Mom's made a career out of lying—to us, maybe even to herself. But I don't want to lie to Dahlia, ever again. Sitting here with her in the sun, feeling something real even if I don't quite know what it is . . . that means something.

I reach out and brush her fingers with mine. She doesn't look at me, exactly, but she turns her hand, and our fingers twine together. My pulse jumps, because this feels strong. It feels *right*. We used to hold hands like this, sometimes. I thought it was because we were just BFFs.

But now I think it's something else.

I can trust Dahlia. I have to trust her, because if I don't, I'm just like Mom. A liar.

"My dad is a monster," I tell her. "It's all true. He raped and tortured and killed girls just a little older than we are."

She turns to look at me, wide-eyed. "God. That's shit. Weren't you scared?"

I shrug a little. "I didn't know. To us, he was just . . . you know, Dad. He'd lose his temper sometimes, but he never hit us or anything. He just liked his rules."

She bites her lip, a habit she has when she's nervous. I can see the half-hidden flash of her teeth. "I heard he did stuff in your house."

"Not in the house. In the garage," I say. "He kept it locked."

"Still."

"Yeah," I say quietly. "I know. It's pretty screwed up."

It feels like I'm dropping boulders off my back, telling her this. It makes me dizzy how light I feel. How *safe*.

Dahlia is still holding my hand, and I can feel every ridge of her fingerprints, every beat of her pulse. I'm hot in the sun, and lazy, and for the first time in a long time, all the chaos stops.

"Hey," I say. "You still failing Spanish?"

"So much fail," she says, and then she laughs—not because it's funny, but out of relief that we're changing the subject. "*No se habla*, for reals." But the laughter dies quick, and she gives me a look from under her thick, velvety lashes. Dahlia's eyelashes are lush and soft, not spiky like mine when I apply mascara. I don't have any makeup at all on today, and now I feel naked. Dahlia's got blue eyes, very clear, the color of the lake in the heat of summer. Just a hint of green at the center. She's wearing a thick sweater and a hoodie over that, with fingerless black gloves, and her blonde hair is streaked with deep strokes of green that start out emerald and fade before they reach the tips. She looks like a punk mermaid.

"So," she says. "I texted you about a trillion times. Stalker-texted. You never answered."

"Couldn't," I tell her. "We had to throw all our phones away and get new ones."

"Because . . . because the cops were after you?"

"Not the cops," I tell her. "We didn't do anything wrong. No, it's because of my dad. He escaped."

"Yeah, I know, but I thought they caught him?" Dahlia's eyes have gone wide, and she's staring at me like I'm wonderful and tragic and terrifying all at the same time.

"No, they caught all the other ones who got out. He's still out there. Somewhere." I sigh. "That's why I wasn't supposed to text you, or call you, or anything. Because we're trying to make sure he doesn't find us."

"So . . . should you be *here*?"

"Hell, no, and they'll be super mad if they find out."

"Oh . . . where are you staying?"

I want to tell her. I really do, and I would if it was just me . . . but telling her means putting Connor's life in her hands, not just mine, and I can't. I have to look out for him, especially since Mom's . . . whatever she is now. "Around," I tell her. "I can't tell you, though. It's not because I don't trust you, it's just—"

"No, no, I get it. I won't say anything. I never saw you here." She turns and looks at me directly, and it's dazzling. "I don't want anything to happen to you, Tana."

It makes me catch my breath, and shiver, and I hope she doesn't feel it. I change the subject again. "Who trashed the house?" I wave a hand back toward the hall, the kitchen, the damage.

"Oh. *That.*" Dahlia twirls a finger in her hair and tugs it down. It's cute. "Yeah, well, you know that ass cancer Ernie, from town? Him and some of his baseball buddies from high school. They got run off by the cops two or three times. I'm sorry. I was going to come and clean it up, but I was scared I'd get arrested, too. My parents would never understand. They don't understand most things." She glances at me again, and there's something in it that I instinctively know, and then I don't, but I feel warm suddenly, burning up inside the smothering clothes I'm wearing.

"That's okay. At least the cops got them before they did more damage. Hey, come inside," I tell her. "I shouldn't be out here where just anybody can see us."

"I—" Dahlia thinks about it for a few seconds. I slide off the table and walk to the back door. *She's leaving,* I think, and I'm not sure how I feel about that. Bad, I think. I don't know. When I look back, though, she's following me. "Sure."

I open the door and go inside, then lock the door after. "Sorry," I tell her. "It's a rule. Door's always locked. I mean, you can get out and everything. I'm not holding you hostage."

"Freak show, you realize there's a great big hole in the window, right? What good does locking up do?" Dahlia coughs and makes a face. "Ugh. What's that smell?"

"Ass cancer Ernie and his friends dumped food all over the floor. I cleaned it up. I guess the smell's going to take a while to go away."

"Ernie's got your games and stuff, by the way. He's been bragging about it all over town, like the strutting dick he is. God, I hate him. I've been thinking about slashing his tires."

"Really?"

"All he talks about is how evil you are. I want to take a baseball bat to his windshield. I mean, slashing his tires is pretty mild, comparatively. Almost a good deed."

While we're talking, we're moving down the hallway, away from the stench. Not like either one of us is planning it. I don't feel so scared now; Dahlia always changes the world around me into something better, something almost normal.

My door's still half-open, and I swing it back.

Ernie and his goons didn't get this far, apparently, because it's like stepping into a dream. Everything's where I left it, and just as messy. I freeze for a couple of seconds, and Dahlia crowds in behind me; I feel the heat of her skin against my back, and the warmth of her breath on my neck as she says, "Oh God, is it trashed? Did they—"

I move forward, because I don't know if she could feel me shiver, and I pick up stuff from the floor and stack it in the corner just to have something to do. Clothes, mostly. There's my favorite black tee, and it smells like old sweat, but I put it aside anyway to take back with me.

I can hardly smell the rotten-food stench in here at all, and when I shut the door and open the window a little, it's fine. I sit down cross-legged on the bed. Dahlia flops down next to me and hugs my pillow. I miss my pillow. Javier's aren't soft enough. Maybe I'll take that with me, too.

"Hey, that's mine," I tell her, and she tosses the pillow at me with an expressive eye roll. I catch it before it hits my face. It still smells like detergent, which reminds me of Mom, and how she did the laundry twice a week, and I helped fold stuff. Sheets and towels, every week. Routines. Safety.

Why did she have to be such a *liar*?

I avoid the pain. Change the subject. "So, what are you doing today?"

"Heading up to the Rock."

Oh. Right. The Rock is a big, jutting boulder that rests about halfway up the hill; it's heavily graffitied, and a gathering place for local kids who want to smoke and drink and generally do stuff their parents wouldn't like. I don't go very often, but I know where it is. Everybody knows.

"Oh. So that's where you're hanging out now?" She hunches her shoulders forward, which sort of counts as a shrug that can't be bothered. "You're going to get busted if you keep that up." I hesitate, then continue. "Were you meeting somebody?"

She grins suddenly, and I wish I hadn't asked. I think. "Nobody special. I was just seeing who was up there, and if they had anything good to share. Sometimes Mary Utrecht has her mom's Valium."

"Oh, so now you're into pills? I leave, and you go all dark side?" I throw the pillow, and she catches it in midair.

"Relax, it's casual. It's not like I go to pill parties or anything." She sends me a quick glance. "Hey, how did you get here, anyway? I didn't see your mom's ride on the road."

"Yeah, well, I walked," I tell her, then immediately wish I hadn't said that; if she tells anyone, they'll know I'm living somewhere in walking distance of this house. I wish we were somewhere else. I love my room, but everything in it reminds me of Mom, of how she's always been here, ready to give me a hug when I needed one, or fix a problem, or protect me with her life. Having Dahlia here helps, but it doesn't stop the truth from coming through.

I'm not angry at Mom anymore, I realize. I'm sad. I'm disappointed. I'm confused.

"You okay?" Dahlia asks me quietly.

"I don't know." I swallow, and it hurts, and my eyes burn. "I—my mom and I had a fight. I said some things. I was pretty cruel."

She leans over to look down at me. "I yell at my mom all the time."

"No, it's—I think I really hurt her. And maybe she deserved it, I don't know anymore. But . . ." I can't help it. I start to cry, and I roll on my side and hate that I'm crying and that Dahlia can see me doing it, but it feels good when she touches my shoulder and ruffles my hair and rubs her hand in slow circles on my back.

"You're a good person, Lanny Proctor," she whispers in my ear. "You'll get it right. Okay?"

"Okay." I gulp back tears. I'm weeping for a lot of things: Mom lying to us; me cutting her to pieces with words; this ruined house that used to be such a sanctuary. I'm even crying because I've lost Dahlia, but I haven't lost her at all. Stupid. I feel stupid.

Dahlia knows how to snap me out of it.

The pillow hits my nose, and I claw it off and yell, "Hey!"

"No more sad face. Time to get happy, girlfriend!"

I'm half-angry with her, and half-giddy. I taste tears and laughter at the same time. I grab the pillow and smack her with it, and we wrestle for it, and then I'm on top of her, and we're looking at each other, and she's laughing like a dropped silver bell and I think . . . I think . . .

I don't think.

I just kiss her.

It's like everything explodes into quiet around me, and all I can feel is *her*, her lips (so much softer than the boys I've kissed, smaller, sweeter), her body arching up against mine, our breasts pressing together under the layers and layers of cloth, and *God*, this feels like the best moment of my life. Like until this moment I've been doing it all wrong, and finally I've figured out something so important it makes everything fall into place inside me. It's wonderful, and it's terrifying, too. I'm shaking with the shock of what I've done, and I pull back, wondering if Dahlia's going to scream at me and call me names now.

She doesn't scream. She doesn't cry or yell. She's smiling like she's just waking up from the most wonderful dream, and she's looking at me that way—the way that Javier looks at Kezia, the way Sam has sometimes looked at my mom, and my breath catches because I was right, it's beautiful. It *feels* beautiful.

"Well, *hello*, I've been wondering when you'd finally get around to that," Dahlia says, which makes me laugh in panic and wonder. Her lazy, lovely smile fades. "I've been crying myself to sleep since you left. Did you know that?"

"No. Why?" I mean it honestly, because this is all coming at me fast, and I can't quite get hold of it.

"Because I love you, fool." She grabs the pillow and whacks me with again, which makes my hair fly in my face, and I start to laugh, and she kisses me again.

It's still stupid. I *know* it's stupid. And dangerous. But it doesn't feel wrong.

I don't feel wrong anymore.

16

GWEN

Everything's wrong. I feel like I've been cut open and emptied of everything that matters, and I can't even say that it hurts, because what I feel is . . . nothing. No anger, no fear, no rage, no love, nothing but echoing silence from my head and my heart.

Not a person, but a shell of one. Maybe I've always been a shell, because if those videos are real, then I've never been who I thought I was.

Sam's driving. He says, after a long, rough silence, "Where do you want me to drop you?" It's clear he doesn't even want to say that much, from the abrupt tone of it. I swallow hard and shut my eyes.

"So that's it," I say. "We're finished now."

"We've been finished since Atlanta," he says. "Did you honestly think anything else?"

God, it hurts, but at the same time I can't deny that he's right. Clearly, he ought to get the fuck away from me; he can't tell who I am anymore, or even what I am. For all Sam knows I could be some secret accomplice of Melvin's, or working against him, or some weird, psychotic combination of the two. "I understand," I say. I mean that.

I'm off balance. The loss of my kids has taken my world away. I don't care where he leaves me—by the side of this country road, or in the middle of a city. He could shoot me and dump me in the ocean, and I don't think I'd care. I feel dead inside. I want my kids, and my kids don't want me, and how do you live after that?

Sam says nothing to me for a long time. We let the miles hiss away beneath the tires as we take the turnoff away from Norton and back toward the freeway. The numbness doesn't go away, but something else begins to grow. It's a wild sense of recklessness. Purpose. If I can't protect my kids one way, I will protect them another.

Absalom has made me into the worst kind of enemy: one with nothing to lose, and nothing left to fear. The only hold Melvin had on me was my kids, and if their safety is out of my hands, then there's no longer any reason for me to be careful.

Or invisible.

I ask Sam, "How far to the next town?"

"Half an hour to one big enough to matter," he says. "Why?"

"Drop me off," I say. "He'll find me."

"What are you talking about?"

"Melvin will find me. I'll make sure he does." I can imagine how it would go: a moment of inattention, and suddenly he's there. He's on me, beating me down or shocking me senseless. I'll wake up the way his victims do: helpless, suspended, terrified, in agony. And the pain won't stop until I die from it. "I just need to make sure you find him and kill him. I don't care what he does to me. I can get him out in the open for you."

"You don't mean that."

"I do. He'll keep me alive as long as he can, so you should have time. Even if it's too late to save me, he'll keep my body with him, after; he won't run until he's satisfied. I'd be the last, Sam, even if you can't get to me before it's done. You can stop him. I can make him take his time, make it last until you find him. *He cannot get to my kids.* That's all that matters to me now."

He suddenly pulls the truck over to the side of the road in a rattle of gravel, and the chassis rocks as a fast-moving eighteen-wheeler blasts past, then another. He puts the gearshift in park and turns in his seat to face me. I can't tell what he's thinking, until he says, "Goddammit, Gwen. If you're telling the truth about that video—" He closes his eyes for a second, and then I recognize the expression, finally. It's a frozen, distant look of someone who's staring into the face of something awful. I wonder if I have it, too. "You need to be there for your kids if you didn't do those things. You know that."

I'm doing nothing *but* thinking about the kids. Thinking about Lanny staring into my face and rejecting me once and for all. My children deserve my last, best effort to preserve them, even if it takes me away from them forever. I can't prove that I'm innocent. But I can save them, whether they believe in me or not.

"This is the right way," I tell him. "It's the only way."

"I can't let you do it."

"You can't stop me."

He shakes his head and says, "Your best bet is to go back to Rivard. Rivard gets to Absalom. Absalom leads to Melvin. You don't have to do it this way."

"That takes too long."

"You can't put yourself out there like some . . . sacrificial goat."

"Why not?" I turn toward him, and I see him flinch from what he sees there. "If I'm already dead to the people I love, I might as well die for them."

It's bleak, and it makes perfect sense to me. I think that for the first time Sam Cade really pities me now, as if I'm broken. But I'm not. I'm forged hard out of pieces, like a bar of solid steel. There's nothing soft left.

I'm too broken to be broken anymore.

"If you want to leave me here, then do it," I tell him. "I'll go it alone. But I'm going after Melvin Royal. It's all he's left me in the world to care about."

He swallows. I don't know the last time I've seen Sam unsure, but here it is, right now. I have a thousand-miles-away view of the desire I felt for him before, the hopeless wish that we could cross the minefield between us and let the past go, just for a while.

But the past never leaves us. It's in every breath, every cell, every second. I know that now.

"God, Gwen," Sam whispers. "Don't do this. Please don't."

I unbuckle my seat belt, open the door, and step out into the cold, misty air. Rain's on the way, the kind of wintry stuff that turns to ice in the blink of an eye. Black ice, the kind you can't see coming. The kind that spins your life out of control and into disaster.

I start to walk in the direction that traffic is headed, along the side. It's a dangerous spot to be on foot; there isn't much shoulder between the gravel and the road surface, and on the right, the land drops in a steep curve. Nothing beyond but the sharp points of trees.

Everything hurts. There is nothing safe, nothing good, nothing kind anymore. If I fall, it won't hurt me. If Melvin cuts me, I won't bleed. I'm not here. *I'm not here.*

When Sam puts his arms around me from behind, I fight. I struggle. From the passing cars and trucks, it must look like he's attacking me, but no one stops. No one cares.

Everything *hurts*.

I scream. It goes up and into the misty air and is swallowed up like it never existed, and everything crashes in and down, and I am crushed under the weight of a grief so large that it's the earth itself.

I have a wild desire to run into the constant traffic, and *I should. I should just end it in a blare of horns and lights and squealing brakes and blood*, but that doesn't save my kids.

"Easy," Sam is saying, his lips close to my ear. He's holding me too tight for me to break free. "Easy, Gwen. Breathe."

I'm breathing, but it's too fast. I feel light-headed. Sick. The world is gray and nothing matters, but his body is warm and solid and holding me here, to life. To pain.

I hate him for it.

And then the hate melts, and what's underneath is something raw and hurt and desperately grateful. My panting slows. I stop fighting him.

The tears start slowly, just a trickle, and then a flood, and then he loosens his grip enough to let me turn and lean on him. He's always let me lean on him, and I have never deserved that grace. I don't deserve it now. His presence is the only thing that's real in this mist, fog, pain, ice.

"I've lost my kids," I gasp out between sobs. "Oh God, *my kids*." The pain is in my heart, in the empty space of my womb where they grew, and it's so primal that I don't know how to live through it.

"No, you haven't," he tells me, and I feel the scrape of his beard stubble as he presses his cheek against mine. "You haven't lost anybody. But do you really want their mom killed by their dad? Do you think that saves them? I *know* what it feels like to be the survivor, and it turned me inside out. Don't do that to them." I feel him swallow. "Don't do it to me."

We stand there in the cold, buffeted by traffic and smothered by mist, for a very long time, and then I say, "I'll try." I mean, *I'll try to live*.

I almost believe it.

Just because Sam doesn't want me to fling myself into traffic, or give myself up to Melvin, doesn't mean our friendship is healed. I don't know if there is anything between us anymore. The bridges we'd built, out of time and care and kindness . . . those are ruins, and the rapids run deep.

We drive for about an hour, and the silence hangs heavy, until Sam says, "We need gas. Food wouldn't hurt, either."

I can't imagine eating, but I nod. I don't want to argue. I'm afraid the slightest disagreement will send us both tumbling down the river, out of control.

He pulls off at a truck stop, one of the big chain affairs that accommodates dozens of cars and features extravagant convenience-store selections, plus a sit-down restaurant and showers for tired long-haulers. We take a booth in the diner and eat chicken-fried steak and mashed potatoes, and the food revives me a little.

"Are you going back to Stillhouse Lake?" I finally ask him. "Or . . . home?" I don't know where his home is, I realize. We've never really talked about where he's from.

"I haven't decided," he says. "I'm thinking about it." I get a glance that's so fast I barely register it as a look. "If you didn't do what those tapes show you did—"

"I didn't." Somehow, I manage to say it quietly. I want to shout it. To smash my fists into the table until they bleed.

"If you didn't," he repeats, without any emphasis at all, "then I can't let you put yourself in danger without someone to watch your back."

I'm biting the inside of my cheek, I realize, to keep myself from doing something stupid. I taste copper and realize I've drawn blood. I have a mad, stupid urge to tell him that I *did* do those things, and to just fuck off and *let me go*, because I know right now that it would be the kinder thing to do. This is tearing him apart. I can tell from the careful way he moves, as if he has to think out everything he does, no matter how normal. We seduced each other into the idea that we could overcome all this, and now . . . now we can't.

"Someone you can recommend?" I ask him.

Sam puts his fork down and leans back against the worn vinyl of the seat. For the first time, he looks me square in the eyes, and I can't read him at all. All control, nothing on the surface. "Lots of people," he says. "But nobody I'd trust you not to screw over."

"Sam—"

"Don't." It's a soft, sharp cut, and I see the flicker in his eyes to go with it. Violence, suppressed. "If you're lying to me, swear to God, I will walk away and leave you to die, because you will deserve what you get. Do you understand me?"

I should tell him to just drive away, right now. I know I should. Sam is a good man who's had a hard road to this point. But I can either be honest and cruel, or I can be kind and a liar.

He wouldn't thank me for being kind. And the truth is, I need him.

"I won't lie to you," I say. I mean it. "I never helped him. I never will. I want him dead. And you can help me get there."

He doesn't blink. Doesn't move. I can see that he's waiting to see any sign in me of deception, or weakness.

Then he nods, spears a bite of steak, and says, "Then that's the deal. We find him. We kill him. And we're done."

My scarf, I realize, has slipped down and exposed the darkened bruises around my neck, and as the waitress stops to refill our water glasses, I see her giving me a worried look. I readjust the fabric, say nothing, keep eating. When she brings the check, she turns it over in front of me. Handwritten on the back is, *Is that man hurting you?*

The irony is so thick I want to laugh. I shake my head and pay the bill in cash, and she moves on, still frowning.

I don't tell Sam she thought he was abusive. It's the darkest possible joke, because I'm the one hurting *him*.

By that time, Sam's staring out the window. It's fogged over, but when I wipe a spot clear, I realize that the sleet is coming down thick. It's already started to coat the cold surface of the sidewalk; the freeways won't be much better.

"We won't get far in this," I tell him.

He nods. "There's a motel next door."

We drive the SUV over to the parking lot. This chain isn't as anonymous as the French Inn, and I have to use a prepaid card as a guarantee, even though we're paying cash.

"One room?" the clerk asks, and it isn't really a question until Sam says, "Two." That earns us both a curious look, and she books us in that way. It's twice the expense, but I understand. Space is better now.

In the silence of the anonymous room, I sit on the bed and stare at nothing, and I wonder when this emptiness will start to fill. All my panic and pain is gone now, but all that's left is . . . nothing. Nothing but a desire to *find Melvin*.

My room shares a connecting door with Sam's. I take off my shoes and wrap up in the covers, and I'm still staring at that silent closed door when sleep drags me away.

I come awake in the dark, heart pounding, and I don't know why until I feel the phone buzzing next to me. My eyes are tired, and it takes me a second to focus on the number. It's familiar.

It's the same one Melvin used to call me before.

I press the button. I don't say anything.

"Rough day?" Melvin's voice.

"Yes," I say. "You meant it to be." I slip out of the covers and turn on the light beside the bed; for a heart-stopping second I'm sure I'll see him there, sitting in the corner, but there's no one here. I move quickly to the connecting door and open my side, muting the phone as I tap lightly on the wood.

"You brought this on yourself, Gina. You keep pushing and pushing, and pretty soon you're going to end up somewhere you don't want to be. Or . . . I don't know. Maybe it's exactly where you want to be. Maybe you've got a taste for it now, too."

Sam isn't answering, and for a hollow second I think he's left me behind, changed his mind and driven off into the night . . . but then I hear the lock turn, and he opens the door. Like me, he's fully dressed. He doesn't look like he's slept, from the bruised circles under his eyes, and light silvers the rough stubble on his chin and cheeks.

"You want to end this?" I ask Melvin. I see Sam get it, and he shifts his weight, as if he's bracing for a fight. It helps, having him standing here. It pushes the gut-deep horror of Melvin's voice to arm's length, even if it's a temporary kind of relief. "Fine, let's end it. You come get me. I won't fight you. We can finish this right now. All you have to do is agree to leave our kids alone."

He's tempted. I can feel he is; it quivers in the air between us, a horrible attraction so perverse it makes me feel sick and faint. I recognize the deeper pitch of his voice when he speaks next. This is foreplay to him. "We will finish this between us," he says. "But not until I'm ready. You get to wait for it, honey. You get to wait, and watch, and worry when I'm going to come for you." There's double meanings in all of that, sexualizing and fetishizing my fear. "I want you to wait. I want you to imagine it, over and over. When you can't stand it anymore . . . that's when it'll be time."

"I'll tell you where I am right now. All you have to do is show up."

Melvin says, in a dismissive tone, "I'm not hunting you. Not yet."

"Do it or I'll find *you*."

"You know why I married you, Gina? Because you're the perfect wife. You're blind, deaf, and dumb to anything that doesn't concern you, and you have the spine of a worm. You're never going to come after me."

"That's Gina you're talking about," I say, low in my aching throat. "I'm Gwen. Gwen will find you, and she will put a bullet in your diseased brain. That's a promise."

"Brave when you're on the phone and Mr. Cade is nearby. But maybe I'll just pay him a visit, and leave you to clean up the mess."

"You don't kill men," I say. "And you don't have the guts to try anyone who might be a fair fight. Including me."

He's silent. I think I've made him angry, but when he finally replies, it's quiet and controlled. "First time for everything. And the firsts are exciting."

He hangs up before I can think of some other way to taunt him and keep him pointed at me, *only* at me. I feel like it's a failure, and that shakes me hard. I can't let him find the kids.

Sam silently takes the phone from my hand. Gets his keys.

"Where are you going?"

"I'm dumping this," he says. "A long way from here. I'll get you another one on the way back. Lock up. Shoot anybody but me who comes in."

"No! If I can keep him talking—"

Sam grabs my arm as I reach for the phone. He's gentle about it, which is at odds with the emotion I can feel rising off him like smoke. "If you keep him talking, you'll get yourself fucking killed," he says. "And me, too. We're hunting *him*. Not the other way around."

Then he's gone, and I have no choice but to lock the doors and go back to sit, and wait, for what comes next.

17

SAM

I can't help but wonder how Melvin Royal keeps finding her, keeps getting her phone number. It doesn't make sense. These are disposable phones, and the number has to be shared out. He can't search through records to find her; not even Absalom is that good, that fast. So how the hell is he finding her? *Maybe she wants him to find her. Maybe she texted him the goddamn number and you're the biggest fool in the world for even starting to believe her.*

I can believe a lot of things about Gwen. I can even believe that, once upon a time, a terrified wife might have done things that she wants to block out from her memory.

But I know she's totally sincere about wanting this man dead. So I have to write off the possibility that she's working with him.

The first time he called, that had to be Absalom providing him with the intel. But somewhere, somehow, someone else has cherry-picked her number, and it's ended up in Melvin Royal's hands again. How?

I can't solve the puzzle. I drive carefully, well aware of the slippery road conditions, the cars spun off in ditches, the hazy glitter of ice still drifting down in the glow of streetlights. I'd like to drive a hundred miles to ditch this phone, but it's too dangerous. I settle for twenty-five miles, which takes nearly two hours of tense effort. I wipe the contacts and history and texts, destroy the SIM card, pull the battery, and pitch the shell as far out into an empty field as I can throw it. It's useless junk now, and if by some weird sorcery he can still track it, let him dig for it under the ice.

I'm on my way back when my own cell phone rings, and I pause a second, then pull off into a gas station parking lot and answer. "Yeah." No name, no friendliness.

"Shut up and listen." It's a distorted electronic voice, and when I look at the number, it's blocked. "We can help you get revenge on the one responsible for your sister's death, once and for all."

I wait a second before I say, "I'm guessing this is Absalom I'm talking to."

"Yes."

"I'm not interested in anything you've got for sale. Not your porn, or your torture, or whatever other sick garbage you have—"

"We're not selling anything. Not to you. We want to offer you something for free."

I think about hanging up, but having Absalom *talking* seems like a victory of some kind. They're scared enough to reach out. The least I can do is keep them on the line. The longer they're engaging with me, the less they're spending protecting Gwen's ex. "Not sure I want anything from you, free or not."

"What if we offer you Melvin Royal?"

"You think I can't get him without you?"

"We know you can't." This Absalom motherfucker is coldly smug, and I want to reach through the phone and pull his guts out through his mouth. "He's always going to be faster and smarter than you. Without us, you won't get close."

I watch traffic move past on the highway. Nobody's going full speed, especially big trucks; they're all aware of the ice, the danger. "And why are you turning on him now? You were helping him before."

"He was making us money before. Now he's costing us."

That makes a weird, cold sense. "So what do you want from me?"

"Fair trade," the voice says. Flat, modulated, inhuman. "You give us the wife, we give you the husband."

"Why do you want her? Don't give me any bullshit about good deeds and punishing the wicked. We both know that's not who you are."

The voice of Absalom—and I'm eerily convinced that I'd *know* this voice without that digital filter—says, "You don't need to know why we want her. All you need to know is that she'll get what's coming to her. You've seen the videos. You know she earned it."

I'm silent. When I blink, I can see that terrible, *normal* smile on Gina Royal's face in the video as she's handing her husband a knife to cut his victim. I can imagine that same smile when it's my sister hanging there, helpless. Those videos might be fake, and God, I pray they are, but they *feel* true, and that's hard to fight. They appeal to all my buried hate and rage, the same anger that pushed me into online harassment, into stalking, into planning Gwen's death. I never acted on any of it.

But I can't deny that those feelings are still there, still bubbling under the surface.

What I say is, "How can I be sure you're going to give me anything at all?"

"Half a mile up, there's an exit to Willow Road. Take it. Turn right. There's a coffee shop on the corner two blocks up. Tell the barista you left your tablet there. There's one waiting under your name."

Shit. The phone feels hot in my hand, and I'm shaken more than I should be. Of course they can track me. They've got this number. I'll have to ditch my phone, too. I should have already done it, but I was so worried about Gwen that I didn't consider *both* our phones would have been compromised.

"Okay," I tell the voice. "I'll look. Where do I call you back?"

"You don't." The voice remains flat, expressionless, but I can imagine the man on the other end is smiling now. Grinning, maybe. "Just watch what's on it. The password is 1-2-3-4."

The cold's creeping into the cab of the SUV now, or maybe that's the shock finally taking hold; either way, my down jacket doesn't feel warm enough anymore.

I hang up, drop the phone on the seat next to me, and pull out into traffic, heading for Willow Road.

◆ ◆ ◆

At the coffee shop—a local place, nothing nationally branded, and nearly empty in the poor weather—I order a coffee and ask for the tablet. It's behind the counter with a sticky note on it. When I ask who found it, I get an indifferent shrug.

It powers on when I hit the button, and I enter the password the voice gave me. I've taken the precaution of taking a seat in the corner of the shop, at an angle where no passersby or bored baristas can take a look at what I'm seeing. Not that anyone seems remotely interested.

There's a file that comes up immediately. It's video; I pause it to dig out earphones and plug in. The figure on the screen is shrouded in a black robe with a hood, and there's a red devil mask concealing the face. Blank white wall behind it. The lighting's poor, and the sound isn't much better, but it's clear enough.

"If you're seeing this, you know what we're offering. You know who this is. We will give you location upon agreement."

It's a brief intro, designed not to give anything up if anybody else watched the video by accident . . . but I know the context.

The scene changes in a jump cut. I recognize Melvin Royal immediately. He's facing the camera, but it's clear he doesn't know he's being filmed. He's got on a ball cap and sunglasses, and he's grown a scruffy beard. He blends well: jeans, a flannel shirt, a down jacket that's a dead ringer for the one on my back. He doesn't look like a man on the run. He looks, if not like a local, then someone who might be a casual visitor.

He's standing near a corner, looking through a rack of postcards under what probably is an awning. The sun's out, so it isn't anywhere around here, but it's cold enough that everyone passing is wearing something heavier than a sweater.

He isn't postcard shopping. He's watching people. I see as a young woman passes that she catches his attention. He pulls a card from the rack and pretends to study it, but behind the sunglasses, he's following her. Assessing her.

He puts the card back in the slot and steps out in pursuit. Casual. Natural. A hunter in his environment.

It's fucking awful to watch, and I can't help but think, *That girl's dead now.* It brings back dark nightmares of my sister walking oblivious into the darkness of a parking lot, then vanishing forever. Snatched away by a predator as fast and ruthless as a praying mantis.

I can't tell where he is, not from this narrow-focus video. I try blowing up the postcard rack to see details, but nothing's clear enough. Could be anywhere winter chill has taken hold, but likely still somewhere south and west of here; I can't see any snow or ice on the ground.

Of course, I don't know *when* it was filmed. I try the metadata for the file, but it's clean. Not Absalom's first ride.

A chat window opens on the tablet. The contact name is Abs, for Absalom.

I watch as a message appears: we give you location if you give us Gina.

Give her to you how exactly? I'm just killing time, trying to think. Struggling against a tidal wave of memory and sickness and the feeling that if I *don't* do something, more women are going to die, sure as sunrise.

Motel address and room number, the next message says. **Stay out of the way. Let us have her.**

What are you going to do with her?

What you wanted. The answer comes fast, and in the next second, another window opens, piling documents one on another, faster and faster. Screenshots, and with a sick jolt I recognize what they are.

My words. Posts on message boards. E-mails I sent to Gina Royal. Letters I wrote to her mailbox, every time she moved and tried to hide. The hate is right there, in pixels and pages.

> . . . helped slaughter my sister like an animal . . .
> . . . never be done with you. You have no hiding
> place . . .
> . . . guilty as sin and I will never forget, never
> forgive . . .
> . . . hope you suffer the same torture she did . . .

It's me. It's my sick fury captured and on display. Nightmare made real. I wrote those things. I meant them.

She's guilty as sin, Absalom says, quoting my own rage. **She deserves to pay for the girls who died.**

Fuck you, I type back with shaking fingers. **You're helping Melvin Royal.**

Now we're helping you. Everything has a price. She's yours.
We'll give you Melvin. You give us Gina.

I take a long moment of silence. I stare at all the evidence of my madness, and I know it's still in me; I still half believe those videos of Gina Royal. I wish to hell I didn't. I want to rip that part of myself up

223

by the roots, but I can't; it's the part that holds the memories of my lost little sister, too. It might be toxic, but it's important.

I think. My coffee sits undrunk, cooling, as the sleet hisses against the windows and the night grows darker. I remember Gina Royal saying she never helped her husband. Swearing it under oath. I remember the video, fake or not, that says she lied.

I remember Gwen screaming into the cold wind while I held her back from plunging into traffic.

And then I type two words.

I'm in.

18

CONNOR

Dad said that Javier and Kezia would never figure out what I did, and he was right about that. He sent me all the instructions: how to download the video onto his phone, how to transfer it to the one Mom gave me, how to take off the parental lock that kept me from using the Internet so I could pretend I found it on a message board. He even posted a fake message there so Javier could find a broken link when he went looking. I already knew Mom's code to take the lock off. It wasn't hard to figure out.

Dad told me to do all that and hide his phone before I watched the video on the one Mom gave me.

He knew it would hurt. He said me it would, and that he was sorry.

Dad's been right about everything.

He proved it.

I'm texting him regularly, whenever I can. I'm sitting in my bedroom now with the door locked in case Lanny decides to check on me, reading his latest message. I wrote to you, kiddo. I sent you letters, birthday cards, presents. Did you get any of them?

There's only one answer to that. No.

Because she was determined to poison you against me, son. I'm sorry. I should have tried harder.

Were there really presents? Cards? Letters? I don't know, but I remember Lanny saying that she'd seen one he sent to Mom. Not to us. But it talked about us. Mom never intended to show us any of it.

Maybe she kept everything from us. Everything Dad said, wrote, sent.

It makes sense to me. Everything he says disturbs me, and everything makes sense.

But I still don't know whether or not to trust him. Mom lied to us. Maybe he's lying now. I don't know how to trust anybody, not anymore. So I don't text back. I just keep rereading his apology.

After another minute, another text pops up. Well, think about it, Brady. You can ask me anything you want, remember that. This is Dad, signing off.

I text back Bye and shut down the phone. Then I take out the battery. I'm still careful about that. I don't want anybody hurt. Especially Lanny.

I should stop texting him, I know that. I know it's wrong. Lanny would be furious. Mom—I don't want to think about what Mom would do. Mom doesn't matter anymore, and I can't pretend I ever even knew her. At least Dad hasn't lied to me. Dad says she helped him. He has evidence. All Mom has is *Please believe me*, and I don't anymore.

The phone from Dad is like a secret promise, an escape hatch, and I keep it on me constantly now; I only put it on charge when I'm asleep, and I shove it under the pillow.

I'm living a double life now. Brady has a cell phone. Connor has one. But I'm almost two different people.

Dad only ever texts back. He doesn't text me first, and we've never spoken, not yet. He told me it was my choice, and if I never wanted to call, that was fine, too. He wasn't going to push me, and he hasn't. Not like everybody else does.

He lets me make up my own mind.

I'm holding the phone, thinking about turning it on and calling Dad, when I see Lanny slipping over the fence. She's not leaving; she's coming back. I didn't even know she'd been gone. She's quick and good at it, but Boot still barks and chases after her, as if he's arguing with her. She picks up a stick and tosses it for him to chase, which I guess is a pretty good excuse in case Javier looks out the window.

Dad doesn't sound crazy in these messages. He sounds like a father. He asks how I'm doing, what I'm feeling. What I'm reading. He lets me tell him the stories of the books I really like. He tells me stories, too—nothing weird, which I guess people would expect. He tells me about growing up and looking for arrowheads, catching frogs, fishing. Normal stuff that I don't do. I'm not the one who runs and jumps. That's Lanny's job. I live mostly in quiet, and I watch things happen. Maybe that's bad, I don't know. It's just how I like it.

Dad hasn't once asked me about Mom, or where we are. I wouldn't tell him that; I know I can't really trust him that far. But sometimes I wish he *would* ask, which is weird, and I wonder why I want that. I guess I have this fantasy that he's going to come in and take me away, and somehow, we'll be . . . better. He'll be a good dad, and we'll go on adventures. I even imagine what kind of car he'll be driving, what he'll be wearing, what kind of music will be on the radio. Dad liked weird oldies from the 1980s. So probably that stuff. I sometimes listen to it, too, not because I like it, but because I wonder why he does. I could teach him to like new music. I could make him a playlist.

That makes me remember that I used to make them for Mom, and she'd sit and listen with me and say, *Oh, I like that one, who is that?*

And she wasn't just playing along, she'd remember later. That memory hurts now, and it makes me feel sick and wrong for doing this. But it's not my fault.

Mom left *us*.

I go out onto the porch and sit down in the chair.

Lanny comes to a stop when she sees me, and I see her hesitate before she throws the stick again for Boot and nods to me. "Hey. What are you doing out here, goofus? It's cold."

"Reading," I tell her. It's not a lie. "What are you doing?"

She's got red in her cheeks, and I don't think it's from the cold. "Nothing."

"Meeting your girlfriend?"

"No!" she immediately shoots back, and in a way that I think might even be true. But the red in her cheeks gets darker. "Shut up, you don't even know what you're talking about. Besides, we know we're not supposed to go anywhere people can see us. Right?"

"Right. And we always do what we're supposed to do. Right?"

"Well, *I* do," she says, with an older sister's superiority. "You know, you're going to ruin your eyes squinting out here. It's dark."

"I was just going in," I tell her. "And that's not how you ruin your eyes. If you'd read more, you'd know that."

"*Stop* reading a book, is what I'm saying. Come on. Let's go in."

"Wait," I tell her. "Are you okay? Really? About Mom?"

"Sure," she says, and I see the stubborn shift of her chin, the angry level of her eyebrows. "I'm glad she's gone. We agreed. We talked about this, Connor."

"Do you want her to come back?" I ask her. "I don't mean now. I mean . . . like, someday."

"No. Never. She lied to us."

"Everybody lies," I say.

"Who told you that?"

"I heard Kezia saying it. Everybody lies."

"She means when they're talking to the cops. Not to their kids. Not to each other."

But you just lied to me about where you went. And I lied to you about the video. Everybody does lie. So now you're lying about that. It's making my head hurt, thinking about it. I miss Mom. I miss having a normal place to go where I knew it was safe.

I miss having a home. A for-real home.

I miss Mom.

No, I don't. I don't miss Mom. She's a liar and she left and I'm not going to cry about it, because crying doesn't fix things, it just makes a mess. Dad said that to me once, and like some of what he told me, it's even true.

I'm glad Lanny was doing something that made her feel better. My minutes I spend on that phone don't make me *happy*, exactly; they make me feel something, but it isn't that. I'm just less alone. Less confused.

Maybe I'm not built to be happy. Like Dad isn't. I want to ask Lanny about Dad, but I know she'll just yell at me and tell me Dad's a monster.

"Come on," Lanny tells me, and I follow her to the steps and up into the house. Boot follows us inside and runs to jump into his fleece bed next to the fireplace. I pat him on the head, and he gives me a lick before sitting up to look out the window.

Javier isn't inside. Well, he isn't anywhere I can see him, which isn't the same thing, I guess, but it feels weird. I go into my room and look out the window, and I see him out by the barn, pacing. He's talking on the phone. It seems kind of intense.

I feel like a ghost. Like nobody sees me anymore. Mom did, once. But Lanny just mostly sees me as someone who takes up space, I think. She still sometimes calls me ALB, Annoying Little Brother. Sometimes she means it.

I matter to Dad, though.

And though it isn't smart, I keep taking the phone out of my pocket, wondering what it would be like to hear his voice.

◆　◆　◆

It's after dinner, and I'm in my room reading, when I overhear Lanny talking to Javier. It's not like she's particularly loud, and normally I wouldn't pay attention anyway, but she's talking about Dad. I guess Javier and Kezia are still trying to do therapy for us. I hate to tell them how long my sister resisted saying anything to anybody the last time she was seeing a counselor. She doesn't share.

Well, that's not really true. She doesn't share about *herself*. But she's sharing about me.

". . . not really a big deal for me," she's saying when I start listening and put my book facedown on my chest. "Dad, I mean. He never really scared me, exactly. He never cared much about me. It was always Connor more than anything else. He babied him, when he paid attention to anybody at all."

Liar, I think. The idea of Dad scares her a lot. And the rest, about me? That's kind of a lie, isn't it? I'm not sure. My memories of Dad all have a weird flexibility to them, like I might have made them up.

Maybe Lanny's are like that, too.

I can't make out what Javier says. He's farther away, and his voice is too low. But I can hear my sister's reply.

"He's always quiet, but since we left our house, it's been way worse. He's being weird. Maybe it's just that he's still dealing with being scared so bad, or maybe being in a strange place. I don't know. Connor never says what he feels. He can be kind of sneaky." She laughs a little, but it sounds flat.

Sneaky. She means like Dad.

I hate her in that instant. Pure, white hatred that makes me feel like I'm suffocating. *You're the sneak. You snuck out over the fence today. Don't you dare say that.*

I don't like being angry. It makes me cold again, and shaky, and I wish she'd *stop talking*.

But she goes on and says, "It's not Connor's fault. He always thought Dad was okay. Probably because Mom was always too worried to tell him the truth, all the truth. He's old enough now to know it. Dad's a monster. I'm never letting Connor go near him."

She says that like she's in charge.

She's not in charge.

As long as I have this phone, *I'm* in charge.

19

GWEN

I feel naked without my phone, small comfort though it is. The motel room feels cold and empty and generic, and Sam's gone too long. Way too long. I try watching TV, but everything irritates me. People treat life and death as entertainment, serial killers as a delicious Halloween joke, and it disgusts me. I watch part of a horror movie and feel dirty, and finally I end up staring blankly at the news, watching the slow disintegration of the world I used to know.

Sam finally calls me on the hotel phone. It's near midnight. I'm aching with exhaustion but too tense to sleep; I feel breathless as I grab the heavy receiver and lift it to my ear. It's old-style, tethered to the phone by the coiled cord, and I almost immediately pull the whole assembly off the table and onto the floor with a clang. "Hello? Shit! Sorry. Hello?"

There's static for a second, and I think that I've broken the damned thing, but then I hear Sam's voice. "Hey. I thought I'd better call."

He sounds odd. Maybe that's the poor connection, but I go still, as if I'm waiting for the hammer to fall. "What's wrong?"

"Weather's way worse now," he says. "I had to pull off the freeway, it's an ice rink. It might take me hours to get back. I just wanted you to know . . ."

"Know . . . ?" It feels like there's more there. More than he's saying.

"Not to expect me back until the morning," he says then. "I'm going to get a room here, try once the sun burns some of this mess off. Okay?"

"Does it matter?" I ask. "You don't have a choice, then I don't, either."

"Yeah," he says. "Sorry, Gwen. I'm really sorry."

I wonder, then, if he's really never coming back. I can't blame him if he's not, if he's changed his mind with a little distance and time. I'm a black hole of trouble and pain and need, and just being around me has to be agony for him right now. He deserves better than to be dragged into the hell I live in.

It doesn't really matter, I tell myself. I intended to go on with or without him.

"Okay," I say. I don't sound right, either. "It's fine. I'm fine. Thanks, Sam. For everything."

That's final. I hear the ending in the words, and it makes me catch my breath because though I hadn't believed anything else could ever touch me, this *hurts*. This time it leaves a scar.

"Gwen . . ." There's something in his voice, and I can feel him wanting to tell me—and then the silence stretches, rattled with static. "See you soon."

It feels false. I force a smile, because I know if you smile when you're talking on the phone, it sounds cheerier. Something about the shift in voice pitch. Nothing magical about it. "Okay," I tell him. "Be careful out there."

He doesn't wish me the same. A quick goodbye, and I'm listening to a dial tone. I slowly lower the phone into the cradle. The phone cord immediately coils up into an unmanageable knot, and I unplug it from the receiver and smooth it out until it slips free, then reconnect it.

A little order in a world spinning out of control.

I have a wild, dark need to call my kids. They wouldn't know this number. They might answer the call, and I'd get to hear one of their voices. I want that with such force it feels like I might burn up from the blaze of it.

I stretch back on the bed, turn on the TV, and wait. In the morning I'll make a plan.

In the morning, I'll find a way through this.

◆　◆　◆

I try to stay awake but as the night drags on, my eyes drift shut. When I open them, I see Melvin Royal leaning over the bed.

He can't be here. *He can't.* I think for a beat that I'm imagining it, and that's long enough to cost me.

I go for my gun. It isn't where I left it. I spot it tossed on the other bed. Too far to reach.

I fight. My first punch, off balance and robbed of power by the springy mattress beneath me, still connects.

It knocks Melvin's face askew, and I pause for a dim second in horror. Unreality slips over me in a cold rush, and I feel my skin tighten, as if shrinking from the impossibility of it.

It isn't Melvin. It's someone wearing a fright mask of Melvin's face.

His punch doesn't have the disability of being thrown from a bed. It lands hard. The mattress does absorb some of the shock, but not enough. I'm dazed from the blow, and my ability to resist is down by half as he drags me off the bed and onto the carpeted floor, where he rolls me on my stomach. I use the chance to shove myself up, and I lift my right leg in a fast, vicious mule kick.

He's straddling me, but he's too far forward for the kick to do damage, and then he puts a knee in my back and forces me down again. I scrabble for anything I can reach, and I find the phone cord. I pull, and just like before, the whole thing crashes off the table. It hits my shoulder, but I hardly feel the pain. I grab for any part of it I can reach, find the weight of the ancient old device, and twist to swing it at his head.

He dodges backward, traps my left arm at the end of the swing, and wrenches until I drop the phone again.

He hasn't said a word, whoever he is. Not Melvin. He's wearing one of those ghastly Halloween masks that were sold for a couple of years after Melvin's show trial; my ex was a popular douchebag costume, especially among the frat boys. But seeing one in the flesh is a horrible shock.

Like a nightmare come to life.

I'm totally focused on fighting, but it hits me then: I'm in a *motel*. One that's likely at full capacity, thanks to the winter storm.

I open my mouth to scream bloody murder.

He jabs the contact points of a stun gun into the back of my neck, and the volts roll through me. The world doesn't go dark, it goes bright; every nerve in my body fires, and I see a volley of silent fireworks go off behind my eyes. The pain is familiar. I've been Tasered before. *Hold on, hold on . . .*

The second jolt, fired longer, puts me past any resistance.

I feel him manipulating me like a rag doll while I tremble. My hands are pinned behind me with some kind of cuffs. I'm picked up and thrown over his shoulder. He stops to take my gun, and my pack from where it leans, and he's out the door in seconds. He shuts the room and readjusts the mask so it hangs straight to conceal his face. I see a blur of rusted iron railing moving past. Sleet has left a thick, watery coating of ice on it. Sam and I took first-floor rooms this time, and just on the other side of the railing, the parking lot is full of parked, silent, ice-slicked vehicles. I see one or two lights on in rooms. I try to get myself together. *Scream,* I tell myself, but I can't. I can barely see. My body feels like a locked cage.

I feel my captor slip a little on the ice as he loads me in the rear cargo area of a van, and I hope he'll go down, but he catches himself on the open door. He climbs inside, drags me forward, and does something I can't see, but I feel a tug at my limp, bound hands. I hear a click. I'm lying on fraying carpet, but under that is cold metal.

I'm stupidly grateful when he grabs a thick fleece blanket and throws it over me. At least I'm not going to freeze to death.

Though that might be far kinder than what's in store for me now.

I don't have a phone. Sam isn't here.

No one will ever know where I've gone. Unless they review surveillance video, if there even is such a thing, they won't even know I didn't leave of my own accord.

My captor finishes, and I hear the hollow boom of doors slamming behind me. The van smells of rust, oil, old fried food. My body's starting to come back to me, and it hurts everywhere, but that storm is a summer rain compared to the fear that's choking me. *I'm alone. I'm alone, and Sam won't know where I've gone.*

A new thought crowds in, and it brings a bloody, ripping despair with it. Sam's odd behavior on the phone. His hesitations. What did he want to tell me? That they were coming for me?

Did Sam do this?

I try not to think about what's going to happen to me, but I can't avoid it. I know. I've seen the results of Melvin's frenzies. Tears leak from my aching eyes, and I realize I'm not crying for myself. I'm crying for my kids, who will never know how much I love them now. I'm disappearing into the dark. I will end up bones on the bottom of a lake, and they'll never find me.

Please, I pray to a God I can't be sure is listening. *Please, don't let them think I abandoned them. Do what you want to me, but don't give them that pain. Let them know I fought for them. Please.*

I hear him get in the driver's seat, and then, with a lurch, we're moving into the ice-locked night, and I don't know where we're going. The terror and shock are starting to recede just a little, enough to let me breathe. Let me think about what to do.

This is what you wanted, I tell myself. *You wanted Melvin to come for you. Now you just have to live long enough to be useful to your kids.*

Stay alive.

I can't depend on Sam now. I can't depend on anyone but myself. All my life has been coming to this.

I'm not ready.

But I begin.

20

SAM

"Steady," Mike says to me. "Stay focused."

I'm watching from the cold interior of his black Jeep. We're in a far corner of the lot, parked under a security spotlight that doesn't illuminate us, but blinds anyone looking that direction. Somehow, I wasn't surprised to find that Mike had come back to Knoxville; he'd known where we were heading when we left Wichita, and I thought he was tracking Gwen, waiting for the FBI evidence to come in that would let him get a federal warrant to arrest her.

But instead he's sitting with me in the freezing, icy night, watching as Gwen is abducted.

He's right to warn me, because it takes everything I have not to draw my gun and go shoot this man wearing a Melvin Royal rubber mask in the head, and then kick the guts out of him. My sick anger is pulsing in my head, ready to blow the top of it off.

It isn't just because he's beaten Gwen down enough to have her hanging limply on his shoulder, but because he wore *that disguise* to do it. It's fucking vile, and it makes me imagine what went through her mind when she saw it.

I've done this to her. I hate myself as much as I hate that asshole who's hurt her.

"It could still be him under that mask," I tell Mike. Words are tough right now, but I force them out anyway, so I don't lose it completely. "Melvin would think it's funny."

"Could be. Probably isn't. Just hang in. She's all right. They want her alive." He cuts his gaze swiftly to me. I know he can see the rage. "You can call this anytime you want, Sam. Anytime."

I wish I already had. I've been second-guessing this decision from the moment I said yes. I'd never intended for Absalom to actually *take* Gwen, but for this to work they had to think that I was carrying through on the bargain. In the abstract, all it took was nerve.

In practice, I was watching a woman I still cared about get dragged away, limp and bloody, to what was certainly going to be her death, and this didn't feel like a clever gambit. It felt like I was complicit in her murder. *If he gets away . . .*

"He's not going anywhere," Mike says. His voice is calm and steady, and it helps tamp down my adrenaline shakes. "This ice will keep him slow and easy. We've got him whenever we want to take him. You know that. Don't blow it now. Did they send it yet?"

I check the tablet that I got at the coffee shop again. The battery's still at 80 percent. It's got a cell signal, but there are no new messages. Not yet. As soon as we have Melvin's location, we'll move. Christ, this is hard, watching this asshole take her. It wakes echoes of my sister, and they're trying to drown me.

I know Gwen's willing to risk herself. She'd be the first to tell me that. She'd look me in the eyes and tell me, *Let me do this.* She'd say that getting Melvin is the first, the *only*, priority we should have.

But it isn't, and knowing that breaks the shell of doubt I've grown around my feelings for her. Shatters it completely. Doesn't matter what she's done. It matters who she is, and how I feel about her.

Come on, you bastards. Send the message. The air's frigid, but I'm glad; I feel like my skin is on fire, and the pressure of fear for her is burning inside my chest like phosphorus. Every second they delay is another second she slides deeper into danger.

"We should move," I tell Mike. "If we lose her—"

"Not gonna lose her," Mike says. "I don't like using her as bait, but either she's the bravest goddamn woman I ever met or she's a psychopath, and either way it's the best move we can make. Let Absalom think they got her, they give up Melvin Royal, we get her back."

I wish this was an official FBI operation, with covering vehicles and drone support, but on this, we'd agreed to go without that sanction. Mike's already way out on a limb, the way he'd involved us in Wichita, not to mention the cabin in Georgia. If he gets results they'll forgive and forget, but meanwhile, drawing federal resources—or even local ones—is out of the picture.

Another thing that rasps against my nerves: Mike's confidence. He's good at throwing up false faces.

"Nothing yet," I tell him. The tablet isn't giving anything up. We watch the man in the Melvin Royal fright mask make his way carefully to a white panel van, and he nearly goes down as he shifts his weight to toss Gwen inside. I feel it like a punch in the guts, the way she falls like a sack of sand, no attempt to catch herself. *Is she alive?* God, what if he killed her in the room? The thought almost makes me lunge forward, but I get control with an effort. *Absalom wanted her for something special. They won't kill her out of hand.*

That sounds desperate, even in my head. I could have misjudged this completely.

I could have gotten Gwen killed.

The man's slip on the ice means that Gwen's only halfway in the van, and I see her twitch, and her feet move slowly, as if searching for a floor.

"She's okay," Mike's saying. "She's moving, man. She's fine."

No, she's not fine. I know Gwen. She'd be up and fighting this maggot with everything she had, cuffed or not, if she could. As we watch, the man in the Melvin Royal mask climbs into the back of the van and disappears, and there's that gut punch again, only this time it rips deeper. What the fuck is he doing?

Gwen's weakly moving feet are dragged into the dark, and for a long, suffocating moment, we can't see what's going on. I hear Mike say, "Hold on, wait," even before I know I've got my hand on the door release. His hand grabs a fistful of jacket and yanks me toward him. *"Wait."*

"Wait for *what*? You know what kind of people we're dealing with!"

If she couldn't move much, she probably couldn't scream, either, and that thought makes me strike his hand off me and pull my gun, and Mike slowly holds up a hand to signal his surrender.

But when I turn my attention back to the van, I see the bastard climbing out again. I can just barely see the soft bottom of Gwen's socks, ghostly pale in the reflected light.

I see her move. Thank God, I see her move.

"Any word from—"

"You check it," I tell him, shoving the tablet at him. I don't want to take my eyes off this man. He's concentrating on keeping his balance as he slams the doors closed, and as I watch, he uses a key to lock them. No windows in the cargo area. She's invisible now.

But she's alive. She's still alive. And now we have to make sure she stays that way.

"Nothing yet," Mike says. There's a thread of tension in him now, I can feel it. For a guy who keeps it completely locked down, that means he feels this is as wrong as I do. "Give it a minute."

"It's been a goddamn minute," I tell him. "They're screwing me. They're not going to give him up."

"We knew that was a possibility. We'll take him once he's out of the parking lot. They may have somebody else watching. We've got to try to get that intel."

"Not if we risk losing her."

"We're not going to lose her."

The red light of the van's taillights comes on a second before his headlights do, and then he's moving backward, careful on the ice though he's got winter tires to combat the skids.

I take the tablet from Mike. *Come on, come on, you assholes . . .*

"Mike," I say. The van makes its way through the parking lot to the exit. Taillights flash again, red as a demon's eyes, and it makes a right turn. *"Mike!"*

"Trust me," he says. "We're not going to lose him. But there isn't a lot of traffic out there to cover us. We need a lag."

"We need to keep her in sight! *Go!*"

He fires up the engine and puts the big vehicle in gear, and we glide out, too slowly. I want to jam the accelerator. The parking lot is bathed in chilly white light that reflects off the ice. He turns right and corrects a slight slide with ease.

Mike nods at the shape of the white van ahead. It's taking a left turn under the freeway. In that lane he'll be making a U-turn and taking the access road the other direction.

Mike takes his phone off the dashboard and hands it to me. "Watch the screen," he says. "Make sure we don't lose the signal."

I'd been the one to put the tracking device under the van, once the man in the mask had disappeared inside Gwen's motel room; I'd barely made it back to the Jeep when her attacker came out again, carrying her. But having her go untracked wasn't an option, no way in hell. And, thank God, the marker on the screen shows a steady green. The van's emerging from the other side of the freeway underpass, turning left again. Heading north on the map.

I give directions to Mike in a low voice, all my concentration on that light. The light represents safety. As long as we can see it, she's okay, and I can hold on to that.

We take the first left turn. The sudden grit and bite of clean asphalt under the freeway is a shock after the smooth glide of ice, but it only lasts a few seconds, and then we're turning left again, and Mike has to control another skid.

The green signal flickers.

I look up from the screen. I can't see the van, but there's a slight rise ahead. It must be on the downhill curve. We have to slow down, because there's a spun-out sedan blocking the right lane of the access road, with a frustrated-looking woman in the front seat trying to get traction with tires that are too bald to grip. In other circumstances I'd feel sorry for her, but right now all I feel is fury that she's in the way. I see her stark, terrified face as we glide past her. Mike's an expertly trained driver, but I'm praying we don't end up blocked by something bigger.

The signal blinks again. It's still ahead, though. "What the range of this thing?" I ask Mike.

"Couple of miles," he says. "Why?"

"It's flickering," I tell him.

Mike doesn't say anything. No reassurance. When I look over at him, his face reminds me of those times back in the service, when he pretended everything was all right so convincingly that even I believed it.

We crest the slick hill, and I look for the van ahead.

It's not there. But there's another hill. It seems to be staying just ahead of us, just out of sight. Still on the map.

"Goddamn it, speed up," I tell him. My heart is pounding, my palms sweating. Lot of adrenaline, and no good way to burn it off. All

I can think about is her in that van, mixed with flashes of the pictures from Melvin Royal's crime scenes.

"We're okay," he says. "Calm down. You're not going to help her by freaking out."

I want to see that van. I want to know where she is. I *need* to see it.

The glide downhill feels like a controlled skid; I can feel the back tires trying to pull free. The sleet's stopped. Thick clouds capture the city's orange-tinted lights and reflect them back to form an unreal, science-fiction sky.

Everything feels wrong, and dangerous, and . . . *Where the hell is that van?*

The signal flickers again, and as we make our way up the next hill, a steeper one, it looks on the map as if the van's stopped about half a mile ahead, because we're gaining on it. I don't tell Mike. He won't go any faster in these conditions anyway.

I see the truck coming off the freeway just before it loses its shit. The driver's going too fast, and when he skids, he panics and wrenches the wheel; the pickup—too light, too unbalanced for these conditions—spins violently, hits a guardrail, tips, and spins midair over the barrier. It lands with a violent crash on its roof and slides right at us. Mike shouts a curse and tries to get us past. He nearly does.

The truck clips the rear bumper of the Jeep, and we lose traction, and I grab for handholds as our vehicle spins out of control, picking up speed as it slides. Mike manages to ease it sideways, then straight again, and we both look back at the pickup behind us. The roof's half-crushed, and there's no movement inside. The driver's hurt in there. Maybe dead.

"Don't stop," I tell him. I hate saying it, but there's no choice. "Can't help him, Mike."

"Fuck," Mike says. "Where's the van?"

I look at the phone. "Stopped," I say. "Half a mile ahead." We've lost a minute already, but at least the van's not moving. They must have pulled off the road.

"Fuck!" He grabs the phone from me and makes a call, reporting the accident and adding his badge number and contact information in clipped, crisp words that are fired like bullets. It takes a full minute we don't have, and I'm fighting a desperate need to pull that phone out of his hand. He disconnects and tosses me the phone as he eases forward again. Our Jeep took no damage, it seems. Or not enough to stop us.

I flip the display back on again to the map.

There's no blip.

It's just intermittent, I tell myself. *Wait.* I do. I stare at the screen for a second. Five seconds. Ten. I feel the sick, hot weight condensing in the pit of my stomach. Sweat on my forehead. *No. God, no.*

There's no signal.

She's gone. *She's gone.*

"Mike," I say. I think he can hear the desperation in it.

"I'm going as fast as I can," he says. He is. The hill is steep, and slick as glass, and if he gooses it at all, we'll break traction and slide back.

"The signal's failed," I say. I feel sick. Empty. "Get us there. Now."

"They're right up ahead," he tells me. "Hang on. We're going to see them as soon as we come up to the top. Just hang on."

I keep watching the screen, praying for a blip, a flicker, *anything*. *This can't happen. It can't.* They can't just make a whole van disappear.

They can if they found the tracker and crushed it.

We crest the hill. We can see for miles ahead. There are four vehicles in view, inching their way along. A red sedan. A police SUV, lights flaring as it makes a slow-motion progress. A black Jeep older than the one we're in, cruising at an unsafe speed. An eighteen-wheeler, sticking to access roads and slow, steady miles.

I can't see a van. Any van. In these conditions, they couldn't get that far ahead of us. They can't disappear.

I feel sick now, and I'm sweating. The flashing lights of the police car paint everything in lurid splashes.

"Could be just ahead of the truck," Mike says. His control isn't as perfect now, and I can hear the worry. "Son of a *bitch*, where is he?"

"Just go," I tell him. "Push it." I sound desperate. I am.

We take off, moving faster now. We match the black Jeep's progress, which takes us past both the sedan and the cops; the latter give us cold looks, but I don't give a shit if we get stopped now. I put Gwen at risk. I stood by and watched her get abducted. I will fight anybody, badge or no badge, who gets in my way right now because *we have to find her*.

There's no van in front of the tractor trailer.

There's no van anywhere.

There's no signal.

There's no Gwen.

We've lost her, and I can feel panic closing in, cold as sleet.

"Go back," I tell him. I hear the edge in my voice. "They must have pulled off. Maybe they took a side road. Changed vehicles."

"Sam—"

"Just do it!" I feel like cut meat inside. I remember the rubber Melvin mask and taste bile. I manage to swallow it back. "We have to find her!"

We do. We turn back on the slick road, find a way back. We check every side road, every lay-by, every building.

The van is gone. I feel his hand roughly pat my shoulder, but I don't want comfort. I want this *not to happen* because if I'd done this, if I've killed her . . .

The tablet I've almost forgotten lights up. A message has come in. I grab for it, and Mike puts the Jeep in park in the empty lot of a closed restaurant as I thumb the device on.

The text is from Absalom. It says, You cheated. You think we wouldn't know? But we keep our word.

A link comes in the next message. I click it.

A map opens. It zooms in, and with shaking fingers, I pinch in to get an overview. What am I looking at?

It's a map of Kansas. There's a pin in the map, in a rural area outside of Wichita.

I look up at Mike. His face is blank. I wonder if he feels the same deep, scorching guilt, or if this is just a goddamn maneuver to him. A gambit that didn't pay off.

I switch back to the message window. Where is she? I can't scream it at them in a text, and the letters look stark and desperate. Fuck you, you assholes, what's in Wichita? It makes an awful kind of sense that Melvin would go back to his old hunting ground. And that he'd take Gwen there.

There's no response for a long moment, and I want to break this thing, destroy it into pieces too small to find, because there's no one else to punish. No one but myself.

The reply suddenly pops back. Forget the bitch. She's not your problem anymore.

I let out a shout and punch the dashboard so hard that I feel something pop in my hand with a firecracker burn, but I don't give a shit. *No, goddamn it, no, not like this, not like this . . .*

I type back, Wrong, assholes, she is my problem, and I'm going to find her. You hurt her, I'll make it my mission to put bullets in every one of you.

That's my rage talking. I don't have a clue how to find any of them. It's an empty threat, but I can't help making it.

There's another long pause, and then a message comes back. You want to play? We told you where to find Melvin Royal. Get him fast enough, maybe she lives.

The breath goes out of me. You're lying.

No. We want you to be there. To see.

My hands are aching. I'm panting for breath, and I want to break the tablet in half, feel that glass shatter and splinter like breaking bones.

But that's what Absalom does. Taunt. Misdirect. Threaten.

"They want us to go to Wichita," I say aloud. Mike's looking at me with real concern when I turn to look at him. "Why?"

"Keeps us from looking somewhere else," he says. "I've been smelling a rat since Atlanta. They've been playing you *and* me. Sending us where they want us, getting rid of their deadwood, like Suffolk; son of a bitch was already on the FBI's radar anyway. We got too close, and all of a sudden they're working on dividing us up. Sam, we need to *think* right now."

I don't want to think. It's the last damn thing I want. But deep inside, I think Mike's right. They've got Gwen. We can't stop that by chasing bait. We have to get ahead of them.

I take in a deep breath, hold it, let it out. "Okay," I say. "What first?"

"We rewatch that video you got at the cabin," he says. "Because I think that's where they got us heading the wrong direction."

I stare at him. "You think they *meant* for us to find that?"

"No. I think they *didn't*, and everything since then has been countermeasures. We get that lead and suddenly there's a video implicating Gwen. Then a second one, when we grab Suffolk—and I'm pretty sure Absalom wanted to get rid of that rank bastard anyway, because he was careless. Somebody's leading us on a pretty little path, and we need to get off that trail, now."

I force down the need to argue, to kick Mike out and grab the wheel and *drive until I find her*. Because he's right.

Slow down. Cut loose. Reset.

Because that's the only way we're going to find Gwen now.

We need to get ahead of them.

21

CONNOR

I hear Lanny go into the bathroom. She likes to take a shower at night, and I wait until I hear the water running before I shut and lock my door, pull out the Brady phone, and turn it on. It takes a full minute to come up and search for a signal, and I get a barely audible chime when it's ready. The sound of running water will cover my voice, as long as I keep it quiet.

I go in my closet and shut the door. The clothes and blankets in here will muffle things more. I don't want anybody hearing me. The dark feels comforting, and when I put in the battery and turn on the phone, the TV-blue glow of its screen throws everything into sharp shadows around me. I sit down, cross-legged, and lean against folded blankets in the corner. The closet's made of cedar, and the warm, sharp smell of it makes me want to sneeze.

I can't do this, I think, but the bad thing is, I know I can. I know I have to. I have questions, and I want to hear his voice when he answers them. Lying in texts is easy. Maybe it's not so easy on the phone.

I dial the only number in the phone book. My heart is pounding so hard my chest hurts.

It rings, and rings, and then it goes to a voice mail that just has a mechanical voice that says, *Please leave a message*, and I hang up. I feel hot and sweaty and disappointed, and at the same time, I feel relieved. I tried, and he didn't even answer. I don't know if I'll ever be able to do it again. That was hard enough.

Being in the closet feels like being sealed off from the world. It's weird and kind of peaceful. I'm wondering how long I can stay in here before someone comes looking when the phone buzzes in my hand, and I almost drop it. I answer the call and say, "Hello?" My voice sounds high and uncertain and quiet. It's less sure than I am that this is the right thing to do.

Dad says, "Hey, son, I'm sorry. I couldn't get to the phone in time. Thank you for calling me. I know that's a big step for you to take." He sounds like he's been running. I imagine he had the phone across the room, maybe in a coat pocket, and it was ringing and ringing and then stopped when he reached for it. If he's out of breath, he cared enough to hurry to get it. That means something. I think.

"Hi," I say. I'm not quite ready to call him *Dad*, not like out loud. "Maybe I shouldn't have called . . ."

"No, no, this is good," he tells me. I hear something like a door slamming. I hear wind over the phone speaker, like he's stepped out into the open. "Are you alone?"

"Yeah."

"Good." He pauses for a second, and I hear his breath. "How are you?"

"Okay." I know I should say something more than that, try to really *talk* to him, but suddenly now that he's on the other end of the line it feels wrong. The fantasy was better than the reality. So I rush on. "It's cold out, maybe going to snow or something. I was out for a while today."

"Did you go for a walk?"

"No. I just went out."

"You should get out more, Brady. You should go explore. Go for a hike, if you're somewhere that's possible. I always used to like hiking."

I'm not like him, not a loner who goes off on adventures. I like stories where I'm part of a team, where I'm important not because I can run fast or fight well, but because I'm smart and clever and can solve a problem when someone else can't. I wonder if he would understand that. "Yeah," I say, because I don't want to disagree with him. "I guess. I could take the dog."

"Do you have a dog now?"

"Boot," I say. "He's a rottweiler."

"He know any tricks?"

"He can fetch and lie down and roll over," I say. "I'm teaching him to shake hands."

"Is he a good hunting dog?"

"I don't know."

"You like to go hunting?"

There's something about the way he says that . . . I don't know. It feels ugly. So I hurry past it, the way you're supposed to hurry past a graveyard at night. "No, I just—I got lost, and Lanny and—" I stop myself, because I almost used Javier's name. "Lanny got Boot to help find me." I wasn't lost, not really. After watching that video, I'd been so angry and hurt that I just wanted to *leave*. But I hadn't gotten far before I realized I didn't have anywhere to go. Dumb. I should have kept going. "So I guess he can hunt. He's a good dog, and he's smart, too."

"I like dogs," Dad says. "Not cats. I always think of dogs as boys, and cats as girls. Don't you?"

I don't know what to say to that. It sounds weird, like he wants to go somewhere with that, and I don't want to follow. It doesn't feel right. I shift position, and hangers clink above me. The smell of cedar is tickling my nose. "I called because I need to ask you something," I say.

I've only just now realized that I'm going to do this, *really* do it. I feel sick, but I make myself do it anyway. "You know how they said Mom, uh, helped you kill those ladies?"

"Uh-huh."

"Did she?"

"Kiddo, I'm sorry. I just—son, I believe you're old enough to know the truth. You've been lied to most of your life about me, didn't I tell you that? But what's worse is that it's your mother who's been doing the lying. She's no innocent, believe me. I felt like you should start to know what really happened when you were little."

The way he says it makes me feel stupid for being upset about what I saw. Like I should be better than that. Stronger. "Okay," I say. "Well, I watched the video, you know that."

"And you made sure they didn't know you have this phone, right?"

"Just like you said," I told him.

"And your sister saw the video, too?"

"Yeah." I wish I hadn't done that. I hate seeing her cry, and I hate seeing her *not* cry when she should want to. But I needed her to know what I did: that Mom couldn't be who she said she was.

"Nobody knows you're talking to me?"

"No." I take in a breath and let it out. "Is it true? That you killed that girl later, the one you were carrying?"

"You mean the one your mom *helped* me carry?" His correction is a little sharp, and then he softens immediately. "Sorry, Brady. It's just that I've been spit on and lied about for so many years. And your mother got away with everything."

"Did you do it, though?"

"Did I what?"

I swallow. My mouth is dry. I don't want to ask this. But I do want to, and I make myself. "Did you kill them? All those ladies?"

He doesn't answer, for long enough that I'm listening to the wind through the phone speaker and his quiet, even breathing on the other end. Finally, he says, "There are things you just won't understand. It isn't what you think."

"It's a simple question." I sound suddenly pretty adult now, I think. "Did you kill them, or not?"

"I did kill one girl, but that was an accident. We were going to hold her for ransom, that's all. We needed money for you and your sister, and her family was rich. It was an *accident*."

"But all the other ones . . ."

"There were no other ones. The other stuff they say about me, the other girls—that's all made up. Faked—I'll send you links to articles about it, how the scientists in the police lab switched my DNA for the real killer's. That's why I had to get out of jail. I need to prove my innocence. Nobody would listen to me while I was behind bars."

The real killer. My heart speeds up, because this sounds right. It makes sense. *My* dad can't be a killer, not really. TV shows, they always have people who were accused but didn't really do the crime, and the real killer gets found in the end. So why can't that be true now? Why can't Dad be innocent? Didn't that make more sense, that he and Mom did something stupid to help *us*, and then the police decided he was guilty for everything else? And Mom lied to us so she could stay with us and take care of us?

I'm glad I think of that, because I didn't like to believe Mom lied just to hurt Dad. No, she was trying to help us, that's all.

If it *was* an accident, it makes more sense than trying to imagine that my dad, the big, warm shadow who took me to my first baseball game and watched TV with me and sometimes read me stories at night . . . that my dad is a monster.

I can distantly hear the shower cut off. Lanny's almost done in the bathroom. She'll blow-dry her hair, and then she'll come knock on my door to say good night. She always does.

"I have to go," I tell him quickly. "Sorry."

"Wait! Brady . . . Son, I just wanted to say thank you for talking to me. I know it isn't easy. But it means a lot to me." I can hear that it does. He sounds like he's about to cry. "I never thought I'd get to hear your voice again."

"Okay." I feel weird now, and sick to my stomach. Is it better, knowing that my dad loved me, still does love me, when everybody expects me to hate him? "I've got to go."

"One more thing," he says. "Please."

"What?" My thumb hovers over the button to end the call, but I don't press it. I wait.

"Just call me Dad," he says. "Just once. I've been waiting such a long time to hear it."

I shouldn't. It's a line, and I shouldn't step over it. I texted the word, sure. But I haven't *said* it. It feels like admitting something to myself that's too big to understand.

But I don't have time to think about it. So I quickly say, "Goodbye, Dad," and I shut it off. My heart's hammering, and my hands are shaking, and I can't believe I *just talked to my dad.*

Someone knocks on my door. It isn't Lanny; I can hear the hair dryer just starting up. I turn the phone off and open the closet door to say, "Yeah?" I'm watching the little circle spin around. It takes forever to shut this thing off.

"Connor? Can I come in?"

It's not Javier. It's Kezia. When I don't answer, she tries the doorknob, and I'm glad I locked it, because this phone *isn't turning off* . . . and then it suddenly does, it's dark and silent, and I put it in my pants pocket and go to open up. "Hi," I tell Kezia. "Sorry." I go back to the bed and sit down, cross-legged.

She doesn't come in, just watches me. "I've been worried about you."

Everybody's worried about me. Except Dad, who thinks I'm okay.

When I don't answer, Kezia goes on. "You know, it's okay to be mad with your mom. But you have to know she still loves you. A lot. Okay?"

"Sure," I say, then shrug. "You don't have to worry about me. I'm fine. Just waiting for the bathroom. Lanny takes forever in there." I hope I sound okay. Normal, at least. On the inside I'm shaking, and I feel like I'm flying apart. *I talked to him. I heard his voice. I called him Dad.* I don't know how I feel. Elated, because I got away with it. Terrified. Happy. Worried. All those at the same time.

I can get rid of the phone now, part of me says. *I've talked to him. So that's done. I should go smash it now and bury the pieces.*

But I can't. Because this piece of technology in my pocket, it's like a magic button I can press and feel . . . kind of normal. How can I get rid of it now? But it's a risk. If they find out, everybody will be mad at me.

I remember his voice shaking as he asked me to call him Dad, like it was the only thing he wanted in the world, and I think, *I don't care if they're mad.*

I need my father. And now, I really think he needs me.

◆ ◆ ◆

I sleep well for the first time in weeks. I don't even dream. It's like hearing Dad's voice silenced something inside me that was screaming all the time.

And I know that's probably wrong.

When we get up the next morning, everything seems normal, except me. We have waffles and bacon. I convince them to let me try some coffee with lots of milk and sugar, and I can't decide, once I have it, whether or not I like it, but I drink it all anyway. Lanny's milk-only now with her coffee. Javier and Kez just drink it black.

"Why don't you have anything in it?" I ask them, just to have something to talk about. Javier laughs and exchanges a glance with Kezia.

"Probably the same for both of us," he says. "When I was in the marines, we were lucky to get coffee. Almost never got it with anything else. You only have so much room in a pack, and when you're carrying everything you need on your back . . . you skip the luxuries."

"I got used to black coffee at the station." Kezia nods. "You grab it quick to go. Creamer's always out, and mostly the sugar is, too. After a while, you just adjust your taste."

That sounds grown up. Maybe someday I'll be drinking it black, too.

After waffles, there's washing up, and then I take my bath. When I come out, Javier is gone to the range for the day. Kezia's staying with us. Good thing Norton is a low-crime area, I guess. She gets two calls in the next hour, but neither of them is important enough for her to change plans.

Lanny's busy making some kind of braided bracelet. She's been try-ing all day to pretend like everything's fine, it's all cool, and this is the latest thing. She doesn't even look up. "Stop staring at me."

"I'm not staring."

"Yes, you are. God, go do something else already."

"I hate just sitting around here."

"Just be patient."

I laugh, not very happily. "Really? When did you become Saint Patience? Because if you have to wait thirty seconds for the microwave, it's a national crisis."

"About the same time you became Sassy McQuipperson," she says.

"Who's the bracelet for?"

Her fingers miss the next braid, and she hisses under her breath and unravels the knot. "For me," she says, which has to be a lie. Lanny's never worn a braided bracelet in her life. Especially not one in black and pink. Black, maybe. But pink?

"No, it's not."

She doesn't say anything for a few seconds, then says, "A friend."

I'm only asking about it because it's making her uncomfortable. She's shifting around, shooting me burning *Drop it* looks. "Look, it's cool if it's Dahlia you're making it for, you know."

She looks up and gives me a long, weird look. Then she says, "It is."

"Isn't she the one you hit in the nose?"

"She's been my friend for . . . for a long time."

I shrug. "You still punched her in the nose when you met her. And it wasn't a *long* time. Wasn't even a year ago." I pretend to read, but I'm watching my sister. She keeps retying that one twist, over and over, and then she growls and shreds the whole bracelet into separate pieces of yarn and gets up to look out the window. "So. You really like her?"

"Maybe," she says, which means yes. She crosses her arms. "Yes. None of your business."

"As long as you don't tell her where we are." I see her straighten, and I put a bookmark in and close the cover. "Don't tell me you told her! You're not supposed to tell *anybody*, you know that!" I lower my voice so that Kezia can't tell what we're talking about.

Lanny just shrugs. Her jaw's gone stiff, like she's expecting me to hit it. "That was Mom's rule, and Mom's gone. Besides—she won't tell anybody."

"She's going to tell *everybody*!" I'm angry now. *I* haven't called any of my friends. Or gone to look for them. I've been doing exactly what Mom said I was supposed to do. Well . . . except for the phone. Except that. "Is that where you went when you were over the fence?"

"No, I went—" She catches her breath and bites her lip, and I see tears in her eyes, but she wipes them away. "I went to go look at our house. That's all. I met her there." She glares at me with such sudden venom that I feel like she's hit me. "Why don't you go read your stupid book!"

I'm so mad by then that I slam it down on the table, and I say, "It's *your stupid book*, didn't you even notice?" Because it is. It's the book that she was reading on the day that our lives went wrong. She was reading it, and she didn't look up even when Mom stopped the car for the police, and all I could think about was *what was so great about that book*, because she was reading it the day Mom got arrested, the day our house and our dad got taken away from us. She was reading this book on the last day when there were no monsters, and parents could still protect us. I rescued it when she threw it away. I wanted to hold on to something, something from *home*. Something from *before*.

I've kept it.

I'm shaking now. And I'm breathing really fast, so fast my stomach hurts. I've been reading and rereading this book for so long that pages are falling out of it, and two of them have broken loose and are sticking out like broken teeth now.

Lanny reaches over and draws her fingers over the cover, like touching the face of someone dead. Then she takes the book and she walks over to the fireplace, and I realize she's *going to burn it*, and I charge over and rescue it and hold it close to my chest.

We don't say anything. We just look at each other. And then she slumps down on the floor and starts to cry. I'm her brother. I should try to make her feel better. But I don't.

I go into my bedroom and slam the door and lock it. I can still hear Lanny crying. I pace back and forth, and then I grab my coat from the closet, and my gloves and hat.

Kezia's been watching the fight from the kitchen table, not interfering, and when I walk out in my winter gear, she says, "It's freezing out there, Connor."

I don't feel like Connor right now. I just want something warm.

I want my dad.

"I won't be long," I tell her. Boot has come up out of his lazy sprawl by the crackling fireplace, and he's bouncing around my legs. "Boot needs to go out."

She doesn't like it, but she nods finally. "All right. Inside the fence only." She stares at me for a few long seconds, and I don't dare look away. "Connor? Can I trust you?"

"Yes," I tell her. I mean it. She can trust Connor. Just not Brady.

"Okay." I can tell by the way she looks toward Lanny now that she believes me.

As I open the door, she's already putting her arm around my sister, who's crying like her heart has broken.

I go outside, and she's right, it's freezing—the kind of dense, damp cold that feels like snow is falling even though it isn't. The clouds overhead are deep gray, so heavy they seem ready to crash down on top of us. Mist hangs in the top of the trees. It'd probably be foggy on the lake today, too, and starting to freeze over.

Boot is bouncing up and down, and I pick up an old, badly chewed tennis ball and throw it for him. As he's gnawing happily on the toy, I put the book in my pocket, and I take out the phone. This time, I don't worry about it. I don't think about *what if* or *why not*. I just dial my dad's number.

He answers on the first ring. "Son?"

I feel pressure behind my eyes, and in my throat, but I'm not going to cry, I'm not . . . and then I am crying, like Lanny was, and I say, "I just w-want it all b-back." It bursts out of me, this thing I've been holding back for years. I want to go home to Wichita. To have my old name back. To live in our old house and have a mom and a dad and for things to be *right*.

My dad sounds worried when he asks, "Did something happen, Brady? Are you okay?"

"N-no." It was a good answer to both those questions. "Where are you, Dad?"

It's the second time I've called him that, and it comes naturally now. I needed to hear his voice, to hear him really care about me.

"You know I can't tell you that. I wish I could. But you can tell me where *you* are. I can come see you if you want me to—but only if you want me to, okay? I'd never do that without your permission."

I try to remember the last time my mom asked me for my permission. She didn't when she moved us, or when she told us we'd have to get called by different names. She didn't when she brought us here and went off without us. Mom orders. She orders, and she lies, and she was never what she pretended to be.

Dad's *asking*.

But I'm not that dumb. However I feel right now, Dad's a criminal on the run, and I can't just tell him where I am—not because of me, but because of Lanny. Dad would never hurt me, I know that, but there's something that whispers deep inside me that I shouldn't take chances with Lanny's safety.

"Son?" I've been silent too long. Dad's voice is shaking again. He coughs. "Son, I swear, I don't mean you any harm. You don't have to go anywhere with me. I just—I just want to see you, that's all. I miss you so much. You're important. I want you to know that. Believe that."

I'm not important enough to Mom to make her stay here. But Dad thinks I'm important enough to risk being caught to see me.

It matters.

"I can't go with you, Dad," I tell him. It hurts, but it's fair. I don't want to lie to him. "I do want to see you, though. Can we just . . . talk? Just one time?"

He's quiet for a second, and then he says, "Yes. Yes, I can do that. But, Brady? We have to be *very* careful about this. If you tell anybody about it, even your sister, you could get me killed."

"I won't," I say. I sniffle and wipe my nose on my sleeve. "I won't tell anybody."

"Not even your sister?"

"No."

"I love you. You know that, right?"

I change the subject. "So . . . when?"

"I have to ask you where you are to tell you that. Is that okay?"

"Don't you know?" I'm surprised. I think he's probably been tracing my phone. Mom always said he could do that.

"I don't," he says, and I believe him. "I wouldn't try to find you without your permission."

She lied about that, too. I'm too angry to care about whether it's right or not when I say, "I'm in Norton. In Tennessee."

He's quiet for a few seconds; then I hear a quiet little laugh. It sounds bitter. "She never even moved you away, did she? Smart. She knows everybody will be looking other places. Not so close to where you were last living."

I don't want to talk about that. About Mom. It makes me feel terrible. "So when?"

"I'm not that far away right now," he tells me. "Listen, son . . . we'll meet somewhere you feel safe. Where is that?"

I don't feel safe anywhere, ever, but I don't tell him that. I try to think of somewhere, and the only thing that comes to mind is what Lanny said. *She met Dahlia at our old house.*

That's safe. Kind of. And it doesn't give anything away.

So I tell him, "Come to our old house at Stillhouse Lake. You know where that is?"

"I can find it."

"When?"

"I told you, I'm not far. So . . . how about in a couple of hours?"

I'll have to walk to get there, which means it'll take me at least an hour. Less, if I run, but I'm not like Lanny. I don't enjoy it.

"You're that close?" Suddenly I feel weird. Like I *really* shouldn't have said anything. Shouldn't have asked for this. I want to throw away the phone and go inside and tell Kezia what I've done. I never knew you could want something this bad and still be afraid of it, too.

He must have heard it in my voice, because Dad says, "I don't want to push you, kiddo. If you want to wait, I can wait. I won't come looking for you, I swear. Just like I don't call you. You call *me* when you want to meet. Is that better?"

I suck in a breath so deep it hurts to hold it. I let the cold air get warm, and it comes out white when I breathe again. "Okay," I say. He sounds completely normal. *I'm* the weirdo here. Dad's doing everything he can to make me feel like I can trust him, and I'm being the asshole. "I'll be there in two hours. But Dad? I'm bringing the dog."

He laughs. "I'm glad. I want you to feel safe. You bring Boot. You have your sister on speed dial. You do exactly what you have to do to trust this is okay. I don't hold any of that against you." He falls silent for a second, and his tone shifts. Gets quieter. A little darker. "But, Brady . . . if you tell your Mom, or another adult, or even Lanny, you're putting me in serious danger. These cops, I'm telling you that they'll shoot me on sight. I'm trusting you with my life. You have the power here. I'm in your hands, son."

I feel like I'm drowning. I *want* to do the right thing, but I don't know what that means anymore. He's my father. He hasn't asked for anything. I asked *him*. He's willing to put himself in danger for me.

And he loves me. I can hear it in what he says, how he says it.

"Okay," I say. I still don't sound like I'm sure, so I try again, louder. "Okay. I'll meet you there."

"I love you, Brady," he says.

I gulp down another wave of nerves and say, "I love you, too."

I shut the phone down and put it away. Boot crawls over, still destroying the tennis ball, and puts his warm weight over my legs as I sink down to the ground. I hug him, and he squirms and turns his big, brown eyes on me with his jaws crushing the tennis ball, then drops it and licks my face clear of tears.

"Am I stupid, Boot?" I ask him. He just keeps licking. "I shouldn't go. I should go tell somebody."

If I'm going to do this, I have to be smart about it. So I go back into the house and tell Kezia that my stomach hurts, and I want to lie down and go to sleep. She asks me if I want anything to help with the stomachache, but I say no, as politely as I can, and then I go into my room. I make my bed messy and pile clothes in to make it look like I'm there, and then I write a note that says, *I'm sorry, but I'm going to meet Dad at our old house, please don't be mad. I've been talking to him, and I think I need to see him. I'm being careful. I took Boot.* I put the note on top of my clothes. That way, someone will find it if anything happens and I don't come back. I put the number of the phone Dad gave me on the bottom of the page, too. Just in case. Then I lock the door, turn on the TV, open the window, and climb out. I close it behind me. I whistle Boot around to the side of the house, and I clip on one of the leashes that Javier keeps for when he takes him out for walks outside the yard. Boot seems excited, but he balks when I lead him to the gate and open it.

"Come on, boy," I whisper. "Come *on*!" We can't stay here. If Lanny or Kezia looks out . . .

But Boot decides it's okay and romps through the gate like it's a great adventure. I close the gate, and we run into the shadow of the woods.

It's a long walk to Stillhouse Lake.

I run.

◆ ◆ ◆

The house is trashed. I guess Lanny said that, but I wasn't really listening. I didn't bring any keys, so I don't go inside; I lurk in the shadows on the side of the house, trying to look like some local kid who's just out for a walk with his dog. I don't see anybody. The cold and the feeling that the snow will start any second keep people away from the lake.

Kezia's already called twice. I haven't answered.

I've missed the lake, and I sit against the side of the house awhile and stare at it. It's got a slow, drifting mist on top, but the water's starting to take on a thick, opaque look. It's already slushy, and by tonight it'll have a crust of ice on top. It won't freeze very deep. It's pretty here, and quiet except for the birdcalls and the distant sound of somebody using a chain saw on some logs. Storing up firewood for the storm.

I fiddle with Brady's phone, and I think about calling Dad and saying, *Don't come.* This idea sounded okay before, when I was angry and scared and upset. Now it feels weird. I don't know when things are right, but this feels like I've made a mistake.

I'm about to call him when the phone rings again. I quickly dig it out of my coat pocket and look at the number.

Oh shit. I seriously consider not answering it, but I press the button and put it to my ear.

Lanny is already yelling before I can even say hello. "What the *hell* do you think you're doing, bonehead? Where are you?"

"Lanny—"

"I got your stupid note. I went in to wake you up for dinner and, *Oh my God*, Connor—where are you? Kezia's freaking out!" My sister's still yelling, but I can tell she's scared. Really scared.

Brady, I think. *My name is Brady.* But I don't say it. "I'm okay," I tell her. "I just want to see him. He'll be here in a few minutes. I just want to talk to him, and then I'll come back. Besides, I have Boot. I'm okay."

"Dad is a murderer, and you don't know him! You barely remember him! Connor, I want you to promise that you'll come back, *right now*—"

She's cut off. Well, she's still talking, but there's static, and the phone moves away from her voice, and I realize someone's taken it. I hear voices in the distance: Lanny, and Kezia. *What's going on? Where is he?*

Lanny didn't tell Kezia she found the note before she called me.

There's another few seconds of silence, maybe while she reads the note, and then Kezia's calm voice says, "Connor, are you at the old house right now?"

"Yeah," I say.

"Is your father there yet?"

"No."

"Okay. Here's what I want you to do. I want you to walk over to the closest neighbor's house and knock, and get inside if you can. I'm sending a patrol car out, and I'm coming as fast as I can, too."

The way she says it, it's not even an order, it's a fact. I'm *going* to follow her orders. She seems cool and confident and in control, and it reminds me of how my mom says things sometimes.

"But I want to talk to him," I tell her. "That's all. Please don't send the police." I know she's going to, she's a police detective, and now I've screwed everything up by leaving that note because she'll have to report it. I've put my dad in danger. "Please don't shoot him!"

"Connor, nobody wants to hurt him," she tells me, which is a lie. She's moving. I hear the door slamming, and Kezia's breath is coming faster now, but her voice is still level. "Your father's been convicted of real serious crimes, and he's a dangerous man. He needs to be in jail so he can't hurt anybody. Are you walking? Because I can't hear you walking. You need to be heading for the neighbors, right now."

I take about three or four steps away from the house. The nearest house is over the hill, near the cutoff drive. I move slowly. "I'm going," I tell her.

I hear a car start on her end. "Connor, I'm going to stay on the phone with you," she says. "Hey, did you walk all the way from the cabin? That's a long way. Aren't you tired?" She's talking to keep both of us calm, I think. I go another four or five steps, and then I stop, because I hear her whispering to my sister. She probably thinks I can't understand, but I have very good hearing. Like a bat, Lanny says.

She's telling Lanny to call the Norton police on her own phone.

It hits me then that I'm *bait* now, that they're going to get my dad, and it's all going to be my fault. Because I did this, and when he comes and gets trapped, he's going to blame me.

I don't go toward the neighbor's property. I hang up on Kezia. I stop in front of our house, and I think for a few seconds. Somebody broke the front window, and the curtains are blowing in the cold breeze off the lake. Rustling like dry leaves. I dial my dad's number. He doesn't answer. I get voice mail, and I tell him not to come, but to text me when he gets the message.

Minutes go by. Long minutes. I keep checking. No text from Dad. No calls. Kezia keeps calling, but I just keep sending it to voice mail.

Fifteen minutes. Kezia won't take much longer to get here, even if the Norton police take their time.

I dial my dad's number again. *Come on, come on . . .*

It goes again to generic voice mail, and I blurt out, "Dad, please don't come, I'm sorry, don't do it, please don't, the police will be looking for you—"

The phone rings, and the phone asks if I want to hang up and accept the call. Kezia. I ignore it, take the phone, and run forward, to the edge of the slushy lake. I try Dad's number again. Again. Again. When I get voice mail the last time, I say, "I'm getting rid of the phone, Dad. I don't want them to find you with it! Please don't come here!"

I throw the phone as far as I can out into the lake.

It lands, then breaks through the hardening crust on top of the water. It disappears without a sound, and without a ripple. It's too cold for ripples.

I hear a car engine. I think, *The police are here*, and I turn around, ready to take my punishment. Boot has gone still at the end of the leash, and he's facing the road.

It isn't a police car. Not even an unmarked one, like Kezia drives. It's a white van, a big, long one with no windows on the sides. It's got muddy stains all up on it, like it drove through a lot of slush.

There's a man in a black coat with the hood up behind the wheel. He parks on the road and gets out, and I can't see his face, but I know who it is. Who it has to be.

Time slows down. I know time doesn't really do that, but that's how it seems, like I'm in one of those movies where everything goes slow motion and the hero steps out of the path of a bullet. Only there's no bullet.

I can't think what to do. Part of me says *run*, and that part is strong enough to make me take a couple of steps back, but where can I go? The lake's behind me. I should run left, around the van, and head for the neighbor's house, like Kezia said. But the other, bigger piece of me says, *Stay. It's your dad.*

The man stops about five feet from me and puts down his hood. It's not Dad.

The man's old, with thick white hair on the sides, bald on top. His eyes are a mean, muddy brown, and when he smiles at me, it's just teeth. "Hey, there, Brady," he says. He has a Tennessee accent, like he's from somewhere close. "Your dad sent me to get you. You just come on with me now, and I'll take you to meet him."

I hear a distant wail. A police siren. This is all wrong, and I don't know why Dad isn't here. Was he scared? Didn't he trust me? Maybe he was right, because I screwed it all up by leaving that note. This is my fault.

The sirens seem a long way off.

Boot growls. It's a low, rumbling sound I've never heard before, not like *this*. The growl he gave us back at Javier's when we first came was just playing, but this isn't. When I look at him, he's staring at the man, and Boot's lips are pulled back from his long, strong teeth.

"Son, you need to tell that dog to stop." The man tries a smile. "I done told you, your dad sent me. But I'm not going to fight that dog. I'll kill it if it comes near me."

He has a gun. I see it now, shoved in the waistband of his jeans. He puts his hand on it.

Boot lets out a loud, scary series of barks and lunges to the end of the leash. He's big, and strong, and I can't hold on.

"Boot, no!" I yell, but the dog isn't listening to me. He's jumping forward, hitting the ground, jumping again. Like flying.

The man jerks his gun out, but it isn't a gun at all, because when Boot lands on his chest, he puts it up against the dog's chest and I hear something like sizzling, and Boot yelps, high-pitched and awful, and rolls off. He falls, all his legs twitching and his head jerking. His eyes are wild and round.

I scream and run toward him, but the man is right there, in the way, and he grabs my arm and swings me around. His fingernails are long and dirty, and *he isn't my father*, and something's all wrong, Boot's hurt, and *I can't get in that van*, Mom always told us to never get in anybody's car, to shout and yell and fight every step.

I try to pull free, but he wraps me in both arms and lifts me off the ground. I'm struggling, but he has my arms pinned under his. I kick at him. Boot's still twitching, yelping like he's in pain.

"Shut up, you crazy little shit," the man shouts. I can smell toothpaste on his breath, and coffee. "You shut the fuck up or I will knock you out, you hear me? Cops are coming! We got no time for this. Don't you want to see your daddy?"

I keep kicking. He can't cover my mouth if he's going to keep my arms pinned, and I start yelling again, but the man is rushing me toward the van, and even if someone hears, they won't get to me in time, and I have to do something.

Mom wouldn't let this happen to her. I don't think about Dad at all. I remember my mom, who always, always stood between us and danger. She wouldn't give up. I'm not giving up, either.

I kick again, harder, and this time, my boot heel connects hard with the man's groin. I hear my knee click, and I get a flash of pain, but I don't care, and when he yells and lets go, I start running. I can hear the sirens. I can see dust coming up in the air just on the other side of the hill. They're almost here.

He hits me from behind with something before I'm more than half a dozen steps away. I stagger a couple of steps, and then I fall down.

Everything goes gray and soft, and then red with pain, and I can't think. I can feel him dragging me by the feet.

I hear the siren get louder and louder, and I think it's just in my head until I see Kezia's black car come flying over the hill and barrel toward us, with built-in blue-and-red lights flashing in the front grille.

I can't let him get me in the van. I know that. I twist and try to jerk the man off balance as he pulls me.

I see Kezia throw open her door and lunge out almost before the car stops. She has her gun drawn in the next second, and she's aiming, and shouting, "Police officer, let the boy go!"

The other door is opening, too, and Lanny hits the ground running. She shouldn't come at us, but she does. She's running straight for us.

She's getting in Kezia's way.

Lanny is screaming my name—*Brady*, not Connor, because she's so angry and so scared—and she tackles the man trying to pull me so hard it knocks his grip loose, and I bang my head hard into the road from the recoil. Everything goes soft. I scramble up, but the world keeps moving, and I can't get to Lanny because she's fighting with the man in the coat. I see Boot; he's trying to stand up on shaking legs now, and he's barking, but it sounds frantic, strangled, and he can't help much, either.

Kezia fires into the air and yells, "Lanny, goddammit, *get down!*"

Lanny tries, but then the man grabs her by the hair and yanks her backward to hide behind her. He climbs backward up into the open doors of the van and pulls her in with him. I hear the sizzling sound again. He's shocked her.

I try to get to her, I do, but he's dragged her all the way up front, and now he's dropping into the driver's seat, and *I can't reach my sister . . .*

The van screeches away. He hasn't even closed the back doors, and they flop around until they slam closed as he accelerates around the turn by Sam Cade's cabin. He's going around the lake.

He's going to get away.

Kezia is suddenly there, and I feel her warm hand on my face, turning me to see how much I'm hurt. I think I'm bleeding. I don't know. All I can think is, *I did this.* I must say it out loud, because Kezia presses her hand to my forehead, and says, "No, baby, you didn't. You're okay. We're going to find her. You just relax, it's all right." Her voice is shaking, and she takes her cell phone and dials. "Goddammit, where's my backup? White van, heading around the lake! Confirmed child abduction, I repeat, *confirmed child abduction*, victim is Lanny Proctor, white female, fourteen years old, wearing jeans and a red down jacket, black hair, *do you copy that*?"

My head hurts so much I throw up. I can feel Lanny's old book digging into my ribs.

I can feel when Boot limps over and starts licking my face.

Then I don't feel anything else.

22

Gwen

Pain comes in a slow, thick wave.

It's just a red wall at first, an announcement by my entire body that things are not okay, and then it recedes a little, and I begin to identify specifics: my right ankle, throbbing in hot pulses. My left wrist. My right knee. My jaw, and I don't remember being hit there, but you don't in a real fight; it all becomes a blur. My shoulders ache horribly.

There's something in my mouth, tied tightly enough that it's forced between my teeth. Cloth. A gag. That's why my jaw hurts.

I remember . . . what do I remember? The motel room. The man in the Melvin mask. Taser. Van. It all feels distant and smeared, but I know it's real, because it terrifies me. Nightmares aren't frightening once you wake up.

Memories are.

I remember being in the van. Tied up with . . . something. I remember the rattle of chains. We drove, and then we stopped. The van went up a sharp incline, and then it was all very, very dark, and we started to move again.

I remember a flashlight in my eyes, so bright it hurt, and a sting on my arm. He's injected me with something, I realize. Maybe more than once to keep me sedated. That accounts for the horrible, bitter taste in my mouth, like poisoned chalk. I'm so thirsty my lips are cracked, and my throat aches horribly. I can't summon up enough spit to swallow.

I'm in the dark, and I'm so cold that I'm shivering convulsively, even though there's a blanket wrapped around me. I'm not in a van now.

I'm in a box. I'm curled up, legs pressed against my chest, and my hands are still cuffed behind me. That's why my shoulders hurt. My head throbs so badly that I wish someone would cut it off and spare me the agony, and I think that's the aftereffects of the meds. It's pitch black, and I can't see the box I'm in, but when I scrape my fingers over the surface, I feel rough wood. Splinters. The air smells stale, but I feel a breeze coming in on one side. There are airholes, and when I twist and look in that direction, I can see a dim glimmer of light.

Funny how a little whisper of hope can steady you.

Okay, I tell myself. *You're cold, you're hurt, but you're still alive. First thing: get out of this box.* I wonder if I've been dumped somewhere to die, a long and ghastly torture. But that isn't Melvin's style. If he can't see it and can't get his hands dirty, it won't be good enough just to kill me. And I know this is his handiwork. If anyone intends to see me dead, it's my ex.

I try bracing myself and pushing against the lid of the box, but I have no leverage the way I've been confined. I try working my feet up against the sides, but the box is just too small.

I try screaming. The best I can do is a broken, muffled cry that won't be heard even a foot away, and I can hear engines and machinery.

Now that my head is clearing, I realize that I'm not near cars, though that's my first guess.

I'm near airplanes. *I'm at an airport.*

I start shouting again, trying to make myself heard; I try rocking the box, but it's heavy, and I don't have much space in which to try to shift my weight.

My elbow bangs hard into the side of the box. It explodes a little stick of dynamite up my nerves and into my aching shoulder, but I do it again, harder. Maybe someone will hear me knocking.

Someone does. The top is pried off, and a flashlight glares in at me. I can't see past it. I can only try to scream for help and struggle to get up . . .

And then I hear a male voice say, "Shut her up, and keep her out until we get there."

"That's a high dose." Second voice. I don't recognize either of them. "There's a risk she could arrest, or stop breathing. If we kill her—"

"Shit. Yeah. Okay. Give her as much as you can. We can dose her once we land."

No no no . . . My heart starts thudding faster, adrenaline kicks in, and I dig my shoulders back into the splintery wood and slither up, trying desperately to make it out of the box . . .

A Taser slams lightning through me, and I drop.

I barely feel the sting of the needle.

By the time the box closes again, I'm slipping away on a dark tide, and the last memories I hold on to, the only ones that matter, are faces.

My daughter. My son.

If they're the last things I ever see, maybe that's enough.

23

LANNY

I'm in the dark, and for a second when I wake up, I think I'm back in that cramped little cell in the basement of Officer Graham's mountain cabin. I reach out for my brother.

Connor isn't here.

My head is pounding, a sick, purple-red pulse that makes my stomach twist. I don't remember what happened. I remember seeing Brady fighting with a man, and running to save him, and then . . .

Then what? I can't grab the thought. It slips away. I remember the man shocking me, finally. And then hitting me because I kept trying to get up.

Brady! Is he okay? No, I remember, I can't call him that. His name is Connor. Did I call him Brady when I was yelling for him? I think I remember that.

Someone else was there . . .

Kezia. I *do* remember that, all in a rush. The car jerking to a stop, me flinging open the door and running for my brother. Kezia—Kezia had her gun out.

I ran in front of Kezia's gun. Mom's going to kill me; she's always taught me not to do something stupid like that. I realize with a sick surge that I want my mommy right now. I want her to hold me and tell me it's okay, I'll be okay.

Because I realize now that I'm inside of a big metal space that's jolting and swaying back and forth. I can hear engine and road noise, and my head keeps banging painfully into metal. I try edging a hand forward to cushion it, but that hurts, too, when my skull crushes down into my knuckles. I'm afraid to let him—whoever *he* is—know that I'm awake, so I open my eyes just a little, just enough to see a vague, blurry outline of where I am.

I'm in the back of a van. There's some carpet on the floor, and an old fleece blanket. There are also chains welded into the side. Every bump he hits—and there are a lot of them—the chains fly up and clank down with a rattle.

I'm not chained down. I test that by moving my arms and legs. Maybe he didn't have time. Maybe he's scared of getting caught.

I'm here. Connor isn't. That means he got away. He's safe. I'm scared—scared to death—but I'm fiercely proud that I fought for him. If anything happens to me, I didn't let Connor down. Nobody can take that away from me.

I hear the man who's driving, muttering. He's talking to someone on a cell phone. "I'm telling you, it didn't go the way you said! . . . Yeah, the dog was a goddamn problem! And then the kid didn't want to go, not like you thought. And then the girl, and the cop—I didn't sign up, you know. I'm just in the business of transport. That's all. I'm not going down with this . . . No! You can fuck right off with your damn bonus!"

We're heading uphill, on a rough road. A mountain trail, I think. Something like that. We can't be too far from Norton, but there are hundreds of miles of wilderness out here, and if he managed to slide out of Stillhouse Lake before they had roadblocks up . . .

He's talking on a cell phone. That means something. My sluggish, hurting brain finally reminds me why that's important: because I have one, too. I slowly slip my left hand down, down, all the way to the pocket of my coat.

My own phone is gone.

I try the right pocket, in case I've forgotten where I put it. No phone. He must have ditched it. That's Abductor 101, I remind myself. I've studied all this stuff. I wanted to know it, in case Dad ever came for us. First, they ditch cell phones so we can't be tracked. Next . . .

I try not to think about *next*.

Who's he talking to? That's a question that trickles in, and I realize that it's important. What I find out now could matter a lot. This man isn't my boogeyman father, he's . . . just some random creeper. Strong, fast, but a creeper. Mom would outsmart him. Dad would chop his head off and not slow down. I am the child of two scary, scary people, and I have to remember that now. I have power.

I just have to figure out how to use it.

You're a kid, something scoffs at the back of my head. *You don't have any power. You're going to die.* That voice. It's the same one that tells me I'll fail the next test, or that I'm not pretty enough, or that I'll never be happy and I should just give up. I've listened to it sometimes. I sat in the bathtub with a bottle of pills one time, counting them out, thinking, *It would be better if* . . . but I knew it wouldn't be. My life is worth something. I shut the voice up that day in the bathroom, and I'm shutting it up now.

I'm going to *live*.

"Listen, I'm not in this for your goddamn revenge, you *owe me*, and you'd better get these cops off my ass right now, because if they get me, I am going to tell them every goddamn thing, and you'd best believe that's enough to—" He stops talking for a second. I feel the van slow down, as if he's taken his foot off the gas a little. "Uh—no, no, Jesus, I don't want her, what the hell would I do with her? I'm not one of those freaks, okay?"

I'm trying to file away everything he says. I wish he'd say a name. Any name.

And then he kind of does. "No way. I'm damn sure not taking the chance on driving her all the way to Atlanta, so she goes in the pit. I don't care what the old bastard wants."

He's just hung up the phone. I hear him drop it on the seat next to him. There's a thick metal screen separating me from the front of the van, so there's no chance I can lean over and grab it. I'm going to have to get out and run for it.

The van's still going uphill. I start sliding myself back, hoping that it looks like it's just the vibration and momentum moving me. I keep my head down, turned sideways, in case he looks in the rearview mirror. He's muttering under his breath, but I only catch one word in ten . . . *stupid . . . prison . . . Atlanta.* He wasn't talking about my full name— Atlanta Proctor. He meant the city.

My boots touch something solid. I'm up against the back doors.

I let the bouncing of the van move me so that I can get a good look at the doors. There's a simple grab-and-pull door latch on the inside. But is it unlocked, or did he use some kind of remote lock on it? The second he sees me go for it, he'll know I'm not unconscious, and I don't know what he'll do then. He didn't shoot or stab me back in front of Kezia, but Kezia's not here anymore.

I can't just wait for the situation to get worse. If the door's locked, it's still going to be locked when the van stops.

I lunge upright, grab the latch, and yank.

It's not locked—I can hear the door move—but it's stuck.

"Hey!" He yells it, and I know I'm out of time. I twist over on my back, pull my legs up to my chest, and kick out with all the power I've got. Once. Twice.

Both doors fly open.

The van's stopping, but I throw myself forward and land on rough, muddy ruts. I don't hesitate.

I run.

The old man gets out and tries to catch me, but I leave him behind. I run like my mom does, as if death is trying to catch me, and I don't look back until the road curves and I can risk a quick glance.

He's back behind the wheel, and he's turning the van around.

I'm on a broad, sloping hill. I can't see anything but trees and the dirty ribbon of road, but that doesn't matter now. If I stay here, the van's going to catch up. I have to get off the road. I'm shaking, and my skin feels like it's all ants and sunburn, maybe from the Taser, and I'm having trouble thinking, but I *have to try*, because nobody knows where I am, I'm all alone, and all I want to do is scream and run and find my mom . . .

Mom. I spent so much energy being angry at her, but she's the first one I think of. The only one. And as if she's there with me, standing next to me, I feel suddenly calmer. I hear her voice say, *You have to run, baby. Get away from the road. Go now.*

I pull in a gasp and stumble over the dry, cold ruts into winter grass. I run, and I stumble where the snarled, dead stalks catch at my feet. I can hear the van coming back down the road, but I don't slow down, I *can't*. I run like my life depends on it, because it does, and all of a sudden, I'm in the cold, dark shadows of the trees.

I go far enough that I'm covered, then crouch down. I'm still shaking, and I'm not sure if I can run in this forest very well; there's not much light coming down through the stiff pines. I can't afford to fall, smash my head, break my leg. I have to go carefully. I wish I had a flashlight, or even the pale light of a phone screen, but I've got nothing at all. I start to freak out; the tremors become real shakes, and I feel cold under my thick down coat. *My red coat. Why did I wear the stupid red coat?* I can't take it off. I'll freeze.

Mom, help me.

Her voice doesn't come this time, but that warm feeling of being safe does. Mom doesn't panic. She plans. She finds weapons and gets ready, and when the time comes to fight, she *fights*. I have to be *her* now.

I keep going, farther into the darkness, moving slowly. I come across a pretty good broken branch with about the heft and thickness of a baseball bat. Even better, the splintered end has sharp points on it. I keep a good grip on it and move on. I can't tell the directions. It's too cloudy. I start looking for moss—isn't it always on the north side of trees?—and once I find some, I start angling in the direction that I think will take me toward Norton. All I need to do is get to a highway and flag somebody down.

The van keeps going. I hear it move down the road. It rattles and creaks, and the brakes squeal at the turn.

I stop when I realize I'm doing exactly what he expects me to do. I'm heading for Norton, for safety. Down the hill.

But from what I glimpsed of the road, that curve will take him cutting across that path. He'll be able to find me. The trees are thick here, but I can already tell they're getting thinner on the way down. My red coat will stand out like a torch.

I need to go *up*. He was taking me somewhere, wasn't he? Maybe even where he lives. And if it's a cabin or something, there could be a phone, a computer, even a ham radio.

I don't want to do that. I feel sick, turning away from what looks like possible safety and into the cold, dark unknown. But I know it's what he won't expect.

I go a long way in the trees, but I keep watch on the road. The van hasn't come back. Maybe he's patrolling for me down the hill. I'm starting to feel better now; the shakes are wearing off, and though I'm still scared, at least I have a club, and I'm not staggering anymore.

If something happens, I'll run. I'm fast. I can make it.

I glimpse something up ahead. Some metal, like a fence. My heart skips, then thuds harder, because a fence means something behind it. I was right. There *is* something up here.

I check down the road again. I can see, in the distance, a random glint of glass that I think is the van. He's a long way down. I have to take the chance. If I go to the road, I can move faster.

I break cover. I run so hard I think my tendons might snap, but my body knows this, it's trained for it, and it settles into the easy, efficient motions of distance running as I eat up ground. There's a pretty sharp slope up, and my lungs burn before I'm halfway up it, but I round a broad, rising curve and see that the road is opening up into what looks like a turnaround.

End of the line.

There's a thick fence of welded-together scrap metal, rusted almost paper thin in places. Ancient **KEEP OUT** and **NO TRESPASSING** signs, one of which is staying on by one fragile bolt that looks ready to give way. But I don't see anything on the other side of the fence. I climb over it and listen for the sound of dogs. Dogs would give me away, and if they attacked, I'm not sure I could outrun them. I keep low and to the trees, which are still thick beyond the fence, and run parallel to the barely visible ruts in the road that leads right up to the barrier. I'm not sure this is what I should do, but I am sure of one thing: getting lost in the woods, in the dark, in this weather, means dying. When the snow starts to fall, I'll be frozen for sure.

I see the cabin only because of a glint of broken glass in the distance. It's a sagging, half-destroyed thing, windows busted out and door gaping open. Nobody lives here. Nobody's lived here for years. I slow down and look at it closely, because I am absolutely sure that if there's ever been a place that was haunted, it's *this* place. It has an awful feeling about it, a kind of terrible gravity. *People died here. You can feel them screaming.*

Come on, I tell myself. *If there's no phone in there, you can still go down-mountain. But you have to look.*

I cross the weedy ground that used to be a yard. There's a covered round spot that I suppose was once their well water, or maybe a septic system. Roses are growing wild around the side of the house in tangles of thorns the size of animal claws. Nothing blooming now.

The door's open, and I step inside. My heart is hammering, and I'm *sure* there's someone inside, waiting; I want to run so badly my legs shake with it. But I edge into the darkness, and I nearly do scream when I see the glint of what seems like eyes in the corner.

It's not eyes. It's a video camera. It's new tech, nothing from the Betamax generation that this cabin hails from. There are lights, too, all hooked up to a small diesel generator. *What the hell is this?* The feeling of dread is so strong in here I can taste it, and everything, *everything*, is telling me to run, get out of here, and never come back.

I stop dead when I see the princess-pink canopy bed on the other side of the room. It's new, or new-ish. Neatly made, with a pink ruffled bedspread and fluffy white pillows. It's wrong, and sick, and incredibly creepy, and I don't go any closer at all. Couldn't if I tried. I back up toward the camera and the lights, and I find a closed laptop sitting on a warped apple crate. I open it, and it boots up without asking for a password. It has an Internet connection. It's using a cell-signal USB.

I pull up the messaging program, and silently thank Mom for making me memorize phone numbers. I quickly type in Kezia's, Javier's, Connor's, every number I can think of, and tell them to track the cell address on this connection. I can't tell them where I am, but if the computer's sending, this should work. IP addresses can be faked. Cell signals have to be routed through towers. Harder to fake.

I check the other programs and find FaceTime. I quickly boot it up and call Kezia's number. She accepts in seconds, and her face resolves on the screen out of a blur of moving pixels. "Lanny? Jesus, where are you?"

All of a sudden, I'm in tears. Seeing her has made it all real, and I can't hold it back anymore. I want someone to come get me. *Now.* I try to talk. I can't, for a few seconds. When I finally manage to, I say, "I'm okay, but come get me! *Please!*"

"I will, I promise. Can you tell me where you are?"

"Up pretty high," I tell her, swiping at the tears still streaming hot down my cheeks. My voice keeps breaking, and I can hear the terror in it. "I didn't see the road. But this is some old cabin. I don't know what it's for, but . . ." I pick up the laptop and pan it around to show them the room, lights, camera, bed.

When I turn it to face me again, Kezia looks shaken. For just about the first time since I've known her, I see real fear on her face. She tries to speak and can't. She swallows and tries again. "Okay. Okay, here's what I need you to do. You keep this connection open. We're going to trace this signal."

"It's a cell signal," I tell her. "I think there's only one road up. We're somewhere west of Norton. The road kind of curves in a big S coming up."

"Good," she says, and she tries to smile. "That's good. We're going to find you. Is there any way you can lock the door of this place?"

I swallow hard. My nose is dripping, and I wipe at it with a corner of my shirt. My eyes are swollen, and they ache now. I just want to curl up in the corner, but I get up and take the laptop across with me to the door. "There's no lock on it," I tell her.

"Can you brace it with something?

I put the laptop down, and I look around. I try pulling the bed, but it's big and heavy, and I can only move it a few inches. I come back and see that she's talking to Detective Prester now. And someone else.

Connor.

My brother's head is bandaged, and I can see some dried blood on his chin. But the first thing he asks when I come into view is "Lanny? Are you okay?"

"Yes." I realize I'm whispering. "I'm okay. I just—" I swallow. "I'm afraid he's coming back." Something terrible occurs to me, and I stand up and look around. Really look. There aren't any closets. No hidden places for my dad to be hiding in. "Did Dad tell you he'd meet you *here*?"

"No," Connor says. He looks so miserable. "He was supposed to meet me at the house. I never meant this to happen, I swear, I just—" He starts to cry like his heart is breaking. "He said he loved me."

I can't imagine what that feels like, or how big it seems to him. I just want to wrap my arms around him and hug him until he stops feeling so bad. Until he's my annoying little brother again.

He's the one who's been quietly, constantly suffering, and I didn't even know about it.

Connor gulps and says, "Please come back. Please. You have to."

He backs away from the camera. Kezia leans in, and I see her looking at him in concern for a second before she transfers attention back to me. "Honey, I need you to find yourself a place to hide. If you can't find one in there, get out of that cabin. We're triangulating the signal, and we're sending police as fast as we can. I'm going to stay here and stay on the line with you. Take the laptop with you if you can and keep it on."

I have to keep the lid open, and that's awkward, but stepping out of the cabin feels like intense relief. It only lasts a few seconds, though, and then I start wondering where the van is. Is it coming back? I can't see anything through the trees. I can't hear anything.

What if he comes back on foot? I had to leave my club behind.

"There's no place to hide," I tell Kezia miserably. "It's just the cabin and trees." I pan the camera around.

"Stop," Kezia says. "What's that?"

I take a look at what I moved past. "I think maybe it's a well? Do you want me to open it?"

"See if it's some kind of basement," she says. "But don't go down there. Just look."

I reach out and wrap my hand around the metal cover, then slide it back. I can't see anything much. There's a ladder on the side, rickety iron, but I can't tell if there's a room down there.

I turn up the brightness on the laptop as much as I can, minimize the Skype screen, and go to a white page. Then I angle the laptop awkward over the edge and shine the light down.

It's not as deep as I thought. If it was once a well, it's been filled in part of the way. About fifteen feet down, the ladder ends in a concrete floor.

There's a white pile of sticks down there. Lots of sticks. I don't know what it is until I see the pale curve of something that looks . . .

. . . like a skull.

I'm looking at bones.

I almost drop the laptop. I hear a high, thin hissing in my ears, and I stumble backward and sit down, fast. The laptop falls on the ground next to me, but the lid doesn't close. Everything looks grainy and weird, and I feel like I'm floating.

I'm fainting, I think, and that's so stupid. Why would I do that? My heart isn't pounding, it's almost fluttering, and I feel sick. Cold sweat has broken out on the back of my neck, on my face, my neck, under my breasts and arms. It smells rancid.

I don't know what's happening to me.

"Lanny!"

I blink. Kezia's been calling my name for a long while now. I turn toward the laptop. I tilt it so the camera can see my face, and I bring up the Skype screen. Kezia's practically filling the camera, she's leaning so close.

"There are dead people," I tell her. "In the well. They're dead."

I see her swallow. I want to cry again, but everything feels wrong side out now. I don't know if I have tears. I can't feel anything but cold.

"Are you coming?" I ask her. "Please come. Please."

"We are," she promises. Kezia's got tears for me. I can see them rolling down her cheeks. "You just breathe, sweetheart. We've—" She pauses to listen to something someone's shouting in the background. Takes in a deep, unsteady breath. "Okay, we've got your signal triangulated. We're coming, Lanny. We're coming right now. I'm going to send Connor with Detective Prester, and I'm going to stay right here with you. Right here. I'm not going to leave you alone, okay?"

"I'm okay," I say. It's automatic. I'm not okay. I'm glad she didn't shut down the call. I don't know what I'd do if someone wasn't looking at me. Scream, probably. Or just . . . vanish. This feels like a place where people just . . . disappear.

Kezia keeps telling me I'm safe, but I don't feel safe at all.

I sit and stare at that open pit until I hear the sirens coming. All this time I thought I knew what evil was. Mom knew. I pretended. But now I know it's that room in the cabin. That pile of bones. Evil's a quiet place, and darkness.

Kezia says, "Can you see the police cars? They're coming up that road. They're coming now. Don't worry about the man in the van. They got him down toward the main road. He's in custody. He can't hurt you."

I nod. I look away from the pit. I look at her, and I say, "He was going to bring Connor here. Wasn't he?"

She doesn't answer.

I'm glad she doesn't.

24

SAM

Mike Lustig and I sit in the coffee shop where I'd retrieved the tablet, and a few customers trickle in as the leaden sun rises. Some of the cloud cover begins to thin. Ice will melt off by noon, the news is promising, but commuting will still be a mess. Flights are starting in an hour out of the airport, which is now packed with stranded travelers.

Gwen is gone. There's no tracking her now. We lost any chance at it the second that van went over the hill and disappeared into thin air. There's nowhere for me to put my grief and fear and anger except to bottle it up inside. That pressure cooker will only hold for so long, but it *has* to hold for now.

We have to find a way to get to Melvin Royal that they can't foresee.

Mike and I ignore the slow resumption of normal life and sit in the corner watching the video as we try to find something, *anything*, that we've missed. The tablet has a provision for two sets of earphones, and he has his own. When we get to the end of the video the first time, Mike nods and makes a circling motion with his hand. *Play it again.* I do, all the way through. We watch it over and over again, and I've lost count of the screams, the pleas, the questions and answers. I see nothing I didn't see before.

And then I do.

It's a flash of memory rather than what's on the screen, sparked by the sight of a dirty eighteen-wheeler moving past the coffee-shop windows. And from that random glimpse, my viewpoint shifts, and *I get it*. I know why all this is happening. Why I've been feeling this shadow, this weight, almost from the beginning.

I wish I could feel relief. I don't. I feel real horror twisting my guts into a knot. *This can't be happening. Can't be right.*

Mike sees it in me as I take my headphones off, and he pauses the video midscream. "What? What is it?"

"We got it wrong. No. No, *I* got it wrong from the start." My voice sounds rough and distorted. *It's my fault.* That fact yawns in front of me in a black, bottomless canyon of blame. "Christ, I did this, Mike. It's—"

"Hey, man, focus. What did I miss?"

"You didn't miss anything," I say. "Come on. We've got to move, *now*."

I'm already on my feet. He grabs the tablet and shoves the headphones in his pocket. "Where are we going?"

"The airport."

"*Airport?* Tell me you're not taking their bait and going to Kansas, man. You're smarter than that . . ."

The walkway's been coated with rock salt, and it crunches under my boots as we head for the Jeep. The air tastes heavy, sharp in my lungs with ice crystals, but the sun's a thick, hazy glow behind the clouds. The front will burn off soon. I'm thinking about that because I'm trying to figure logistics. Logistics is better than the guilt, because if I fall into that chasm, I'm never climbing out of it alive.

"Let me ask you a question," I tell him. "What was the name plastered on that eighteen-wheeler on the access road last night?"

Mike pauses to stare at me over the hood of the Jeep. "The hell are you talking about?"

"Last night we were following the white van. It was about a half a mile up when the pickup wrecked, remember? When we came over the hill, we saw a red sedan, another black Jeep going too fast, a police SUV with lights burning. And an eighteen-wheeler."

He's frowning now, and I can tell he thinks I've completely dropped my marbles. Maybe I have. Maybe coming at this crazy is the only way to understand it. "What about the eighteen-wheeler?"

"Rivard Luxe," I tell him. "The truck on that road had Rivard Luxe written on the side of it. Mike, it's big enough to fit a van inside."

I see it when I blink: fancy gilded script on the dirty side of that eighteen-wheeler, as if it's suspended on a jumbotron hanging right in front of me. The most vivid memory I've ever had. I noticed, but I didn't *pay attention*. I was too focused on Gwen, on that van, to see what was right in front of me.

Mike still isn't getting it. I open up the driver's-side door and get in, and when he's inside, too, he says, "Even if you're right, what the hell does the truck have to do with the video we were just watching?"

"The first time we talked about the video, I asked if you knew the name Rivard," I say. "And you told me that Ballantine Rivard is famous. From that moment on, we were making the wrong assumptions. We just did it again, while we were watching it."

"Jesus." Mike drags out the word, and it's so reverent it's almost a prayer. "That poor bastard PI wasn't hired by Ballantine Rivard. He just said *Rivard*."

"Exactly," I say, firing up the Jeep. "He wasn't hired by the old man at all. He was hired by Rivard's son. The dead one."

"And that's not a coincidence," Mike says. He gets it now. All the way. "*Fuck.*"

So now we know. The problem now is . . . what can we do about it?

There's a reason I want Mike on my side. FBI agents carry weight.

Mike has a backroom conversation with an airline manager who magically produces two tickets for us, despite the backlog of travelers, and we're rushed through security on the strength of his badge and into business-class seats to Atlanta on the first available flight.

I'm reminded of the plush seats on the Rivard Luxe plane we took to and from Wichita, and I feel angry and sick that I fell for it. I keep chewing on it. I can see it all now, every step. Ballantine Rivard has gone out of his way to mislead us, misdirect us, threaten Gwen, sow doubt and fear to split us up.

I'd lay heavy bets that Rivard's son was never hounded to his death by Absalom. Not the way his father described to us, anyway.

"Rivard's never going to talk to us," Mike says. "I don't have a hope in hell of getting a warrant based on a supposition and a wild-ass guess."

"I know you don't." I sound bitter and angry, and I am, because I've been a damn fool. I've left the idea that Gwen's guilty in the rearview. I don't know why I ever fell for it in the first place, except that I was already conditioned to believe it. She's only ever been straight with me. *I'm* the one who lied. *I'm* the one who came into her life intending to tear it apart.

And now I've done that, and I need to find her and help her put it back together. It's the only way I can even start to make up for what I've just done to her.

"How do you feel about helping me out without that badge?" I ask Mike, and he sighs.

"I'm not too likely to be carrying one, anyway, once this is all done; the Bureau doesn't much like agents going rogue, and brother, I am as rogue right now as it gets. But I'll stand with you." He's silent for a second, maybe just contemplating the breathtaking mistake we've both made to get us here, and then he asks, "You think Rivard's behind his son's death?"

"Has to be," I say. "That tower is his fortress, and if I had to guess, the stores are nothing but an elaborate money-laundering operation. Absalom's dark web is his real business, and he wasn't about to let anybody kill his golden goose. If his son got too close, maybe grew a conscience, that explains his 'suicide.'" I air-quote. I'm basing a lot on an eighteen-wheeler and a guess, but it all rings true. It all, finally, makes sense to me.

I *knew* something was off about that slick old man. I'd felt it from the beginning—the effortless way he'd conned us into the tower, then gotten us to do his bidding in Wichita. He wanted a plausible way for the second false video about Gwen to be discovered, and maybe Suffolk had been getting a little difficult. Two birds, one stone.

This goes deeper and darker than I ever imagined. Melvin Royal, vile as he is, is just another tool for Absalom—fulfilling his own sick fantasies, and there was Rivard, ready to pay him to do it. I feel dizzy and sick with the scope of it, and the cruelty.

"I don't care what we have to do," I tell Mike in a low, dead-quiet voice. "I want Rivard to tell us where Gwen is. Whatever it takes."

"Whatever it takes," Mike says. "But you need to gear down a little, son. Save that edge for when you need it."

I sit in impatient, jittering silence as the plane is deiced, as we wait for our turn for a runway, and finally, we launch upward toward Atlanta.

◆ ◆ ◆

We land at three o'clock. The weather is crisp and clear and barely qualifies as fall, much less the winter we just left. We rent another SUV, this one on Mike's personal credit card, and he takes all the damage insurance. "Screw it," he says. "I'm not worrying about the paint job."

We get to Rivard Luxe and park in the visitor's area in the garage. We sit for a moment, and Mike says, "You got even the vaguest idea what we're going to do now?"

"Sure," I say. "I'm just trying to think of a better one, because this tactic is liable to get us adjoining cells. Mike . . . I'm talking federal offense."

"You're selling this plan hard. Well, I said I'm in, so let's get on with it. Don't spell it out for me. I don't want to know." I know he feels every tick of the clock, just like I do. Gwen's out there, and in the back of my mind, I can't help imagining what might be happening to her already. I have to keep that locked up. If I don't, I'm going to rush, make bad decisions, and all this will be for nothing.

"Okay," I say. "I need you to go across the street to that convenience store we saw on the corner. Buy a ball cap, a clipboard, a manila folder, bottled water, sunglasses, and a pen. If they have any hoodies, get two—one for me, one for you. By the way, do you have evidence gloves on you?"

"Sure," he says, then reaches into his coat pocket. He pulls out a set and hands them to me. "I'm guessing what you're asking me to get is a disguise. Anything else?"

"Baby powder."

"What kind of party are we starting, here?"

"Just shut up and get it."

"Where are you going while I'm off doing the shopping?"

"Copy shop down the block," I tell him. "Meet you back here in fifteen minutes."

Fifteen minutes later I'm standing by the SUV with a thick cardboard documents envelope in my hand. Mike comes walking down the ramp with a plastic sack stuffed with items. He's got everything, even the hoodies.

As we get back in the rental and shut the doors, I take the papers I've printed out of the envelope. "Here. Put that on the clipboard."

"Sure," Mike says. He slips the paper under the spring clip. "Sign-off sheet. I assume we're doing a delivery. That only gets us to the front desk."

"We need to make them evacuate the tower," I tell him. "In a building like this, the fire alarms are zoned, so only certain floors get evacuated first. Keeps the whole place from being shut down at once, and makes evacuations easier. But to trigger the fire alarm for his floor, we'd have to be *in* his penthouse, or the security center."

"That's not going to happen."

"No. Which is why we need the whole building out at once. We need Rivard to come to us." I hold out my hand. I see him register that I've got on the latex gloves he gave me earlier. "Baby powder."

"Oh shit," he says, even as he hands over the small container. "You're not serious, Sam. *Shit.* You get any prints on that envelope?"

"No," I tell him. I pour a generous amount of powder into the manila envelope and use the bottled water to wet the flap and seal it. Then I slide everything in to the thicker cardboard envelope, turn it over, and press on the printed label I created at the copy shop. It has a bogus but official-looking address from a local legal firm, and it says Personal and Confidential: Ballantine Rivard, and on a separate line, Urgent: Open Immediately. "Trust me, I don't want adjoining cells."

"Okay. So what do I do?" Mike asks.

"You wait here. Only one of us needs to be on that camera." I zip up the hoodie, put on the ball cap and sunglasses. I secure the cardboard envelope under the sign-off sheet so all I have to handle is the clipboard, then strip off the latex gloves. I have to be careful now with what I touch. Clipboard's okay. I can't put my fingers on the paper, or the package.

Mike knows I'm doing it to keep him out of it, in case this goes bad. "Keep your head down and sunglasses on. Good thing you're an average-looking white boy."

When I hit the lobby, I'm walking fast. It's nearly quitting time, so a lot of people are already streaming toward the doors. I head like an arrow straight for the reception desk. I don't recognize anybody on duty, and as I shove the clipboard across the desk at the man behind the computer, he barely spares me a glance anyway. "Sorry," I tell him. "Signature. Package for"—I pretend to squint at the label—"Ballantine Rivard. Personal and confidential. Urgent delivery."

He doesn't miss a beat. Why would he? He scrawls a signature, fills in the date, prints his name, and takes the envelope without any prompting from me. He shoves the clipboard back. Now the man in the Rivard Luxe jacket looks harassed. "Great," he says. "You know it's almost five, right?"

"Must be nice," I tell him. "I got four more stops before quitting time, man."

That's it. I exit fast out the front doors and walk around to the parking garage. I get back in the SUV and toss the clipboard in the back. Mike's got his own blue hoodie on now. "Went about as well as it could. So what's standard protocol for these things?"

"In a high-rise building? When somebody identifies possible anthrax in the mail, they pull the alarms and call hazmat, cops, FBI, everybody. It's a big scramble. Building security evacuates everybody, all floors, to a safe distance. Circulating air gets shut down. It's a zoo and a circus, and the bigger the building, the bigger the chaos."

Sounds perfect. "And I just committed an act of terrorism," I say.

"Better make that *we*," he says. "This had better fucking work."

"Rivard must have a private elevator," I tell him. "They'll bring him down that way. We need to find it."

"Oh, I already know where it is," he says. "When Rivard got involved in all this, I dug into him, top to bottom. Didn't find much, but I remember the elevator. It's one floor above us in the parking garage. A secured exit, but we don't need to go in. They're going to come out."

I nod. "Then we disarm his guys, and we make him talk. You got a problem with that?"

"Nope," Mike says. "Let's find your lady."

◆ ◆ ◆

It takes another twenty torturous minutes for the alarms to start sounding, and I can't stop thinking about where Gwen could be. If she's in Wichita, if Absalom gave us the right info from the beginning . . . but why would they? No, that's a misdirection. It has to be.

But I can't turn my brain off. Gwen's alone, and she thinks I abandoned and betrayed her. Every second we're waiting counts in drops of blood, and screams, and I have to work to keep my nerves in check. Not moving feels like another betrayal.

We wait in a corner by the unmarked private exit, and finally we see a sleek, oversize Mercedes SUV pull up the ramp and park. It's been fitted for a wheelchair, and the driver gets out to open the back and pull down a ramp.

I exchange a look with Mike, and Mike shrugs. The chauffeur is a black man of approximately Mike's height and build. This area of the parking garage is relatively clear of other vehicles—probably a badge-only level—and nobody's come in or out of the place since we took positions. It's a risk.

But it's worth it.

With the unconscious chauffeur tied up and left behind a retaining wall, Mike stands right out in the open in the tireless stance of someone used to waiting. His cap shades his face, and in my experience, people see what they expect to see. Shapes, not features. When the exit door opens, a flood of security men piles out—more than we could take without gunplay, and even then, I don't think it would be likely we'd come out on top. But we no longer need to.

Ballantine Rivard's wheelchair glides out at top speed. He's wearing a dark-blue suit with a pale-yellow tie. No comfortable sweat suit today. He's angry; I can see that from where I slump in the passenger seat up front. All the windows are darkly tinted, which is useful just now. I have my gun out, in case I need to use it, because now my nerves are all firing, and I know we are one smart security guard away from this blowing up.

But they're not looking at us. They're looking outward, for threats. Rivard ignores his guards and stops, spins his chair backward, and drives it in reverse up the ramp. Rivard is practiced at this. His back is to the driver's compartment, and I hear him snap some restraint system in place. Mike pushes in the built-in ramp and gets into the driver's seat. I don't think Rivard has so much as glanced at him.

"Where to?" Mike asks Rivard.

"We're heading to the disaster office. Go," Rivard snaps.

Mike nods as if he knows exactly where that is, and the whole thing is unbelievably smooth. Rivard still hasn't realized that Mike isn't his usual driver, and he doesn't know he has a silent passenger up front. I was worried one of his guards would ride along, but they're moving toward another vehicle entirely.

We come out of the garage. There's a barrier in place, but the men on duty—who aren't police, not yet—move it to let us pass. The place is still being evacuated. Rivard Luxe holds close to two thousand people in its offices, and this is going to disrupt Atlanta traffic for hours. *If they catch us, we're definitely going to jail now.* Terrorism and kidnapping.

It'll be a while before anybody misses Rivard, but now the clock isn't just ticking for Gwen . . . it's ticking for us.

I don't know when Rivard works out that something's wrong— maybe when Mike doesn't follow the expected route—but because I'm watching him in the rearview, I see him take his phone out of his pocket. I put my gun to the back of his head. "Drop it," I tell him. "Now."

The phone bounces to the floor and slides all the way to rattle against the back door. Rivard is silent for a moment. When he finally speaks, he doesn't sound the least bit afraid. "Mr. Cade. I suppose I should have anticipated that you'd come back. I just expected you to try something more conventional."

"Glad to disappoint you," I tell him. "Where is she?"

"Melvin Royal's wife?"

"Gwen."

"You mean Gina. She'll always be his wife first. Surely you realize that by now."

I feel my muscles tightening, and I have to make a real effort to relax. "You really *want* a bullet?" I ask him. "Because, hey, keep going."

"Do you want to explain to me why you've taken me hostage?"

"You're going to tell me where Absalom's taken Gwen."

"I have no idea." That rich, thick Louisiana accent feels like mockery right now. I never wanted to pistol-whip an old man before, but the urge is pretty strong. "Why in the world would I know?"

"Sam?" Mike's voice is quiet, but tense. "Ease it down, man. Where are we going?"

"Where he left Rodney Sauer," I say. "Seems appropriate."

Rivard doesn't keep talking. Maybe he's trying to figure out what buttons to press this time, and not finding any. I keep my gun pressed close and tell him to keep his hands up. He's an old man. His arms tremble, and the shakes get worse the longer we drive. Good. I want him tired and afraid.

We park in a darkened alley between two warehouses. Everything on the block is derelict and empty. The only tenants are rats and pigeons.

While Mike takes a turn holding him at gunpoint, I open up the back, grab his phone, and strip the battery. I wouldn't put it past a man this rich to have a fail-safe tracker in it, so I find a handy brick and batter the phone into bits, then drown the bits in a muddy puddle. The violence feels good.

I climb in, then kneel down so I'm on Rivard's level. When he studies me, Rivard's face changes. It tightens, and for moment I see a skull under the skin, and hell in those eyes. "You'll go to jail for a long time for this," he says. "And I'll still be free. You know that."

"I know that if you don't tell me what I want to know, you're going to die here," I say. I mean every word. I'm already in this deep.

"You'd kill a helpless old man in a wheelchair. That's sick."

"You should know," I tell him. "Billions of dirty dollars in your bank account from worse than that. You think we don't know?" I put the gun under his chin. "Because we do."

Rivard's eyes dart to Mike. He's unnerved now. Mike's stripped off the Rivard security jacket and thrown it in the van, and now he's zipping up the hoodie. "You, I recognize you. You're a federal agent," he says. "You can't let him do this!"

"Which part?" Mike says. "The terrorism threat, the kidnapping, or the murder? First two are my problem. Last one's all yours. Murder's not a federal crime."

Rivard's lips are pale and compressed, and his eyes dart from one of us to the other. Starting to realize, I think, how deep the shit hole is.

"You're Absalom," Mike says. "The rest are just minions. You're a bloated white spider getting fat off the dead. How long's that been going on? Five years? Ten? I'm guessing before Melvin Royal strung up his first victim. Finding out how to use the dark web to find your customers and make your money must have been like tapping a river of pure gold."

Rivard's silent. If looks could kill, all of Atlanta would be a mushroom cloud. But I don't care about finding out more about Absalom. "Gwen," I say. "Talk. Now. Because I promise I'll start shooting pieces off you. I'll be nice. I'll start with the ones you supposedly can't feel anymore." I move the gun to tap the barrel against his kneecap. His raised arms are shaking wildly now. Ready to drop. "Keep those hands up. I'm counting to five, and then you lose a leg."

It's almost a normal tone of voice, but there's nothing right about the corrosive hate that's churning inside of me. I thought that Melvin Royal was a monster, and he is, but this man . . . this man is the one who uses monsters to make money. And if I have to pull this trigger, I'm not going to care.

"She's gone, Mr. Cade," he says, then licks his pallid lips. His tongue looks like a worm crawling on a wound. "You already know where. Absalom told you, just as I ordered them to do."

I don't blink. I start counting. Because I don't believe him. She isn't in Wichita.

When I get to five, my finger tightens, and Rivard blurts out, "Stop! All right! If you want to know, I'll tell you! But *please*, let me put my arms down!"

"Tell you what," Mike says, taking out his handcuffs. "I'll make it easier for you."

The bitter rage that flashes over Rivard's face confirms for me that he had a plan, and once Mike has his hands secured to the strap that keeps his chair in place, I search Rivard.

There's a sleek, small gun in his breast pocket. Fully loaded. I toss it to Mike. "Engraved," he says. "Only assholes put their initials on a gun. Go on. Shoot him."

Rivard is sweating now. Everything he's counted on is failing, and he has to know I'm serious. If he doesn't, he's going to find out when his kneecap hits the floor. "All right," he says, in an oily tone that manages to be desperate at the same time. "Let's just calm down. We're all men of reason here. And I can be reasonable. You know the resources I have at my disposal. What exactly is it that you'd like me to do? Turn over some of our more creative suppliers? I'm happy to do that. I'm sure the FBI will find me *very* useful."

"I'll bet," Mike says. "And you know what? We're going to get it all without your help. Shoot him, Sam."

"I can't even feel my legs. Shooting me is just theater!"

"I think the sight of the inside of your knee might make an impression," I tell him. "One, two—"

Rivard blurts out, "There's a pay-per-view event at midnight!"

"And why the hell do we care?"

"It's how we do things," Rivard says. "For . . . premium content. A live event, a thousand virtual passes, fifty thousand dollars per pass."

I already feel sickness boiling up. I can see the shape of this thing coming, and it's a horror. "You have two seconds to tell me how this helps me find Gwen."

"It's her!" he blurts, and he flinches when he sees what crosses my expression. The loathing I feel is making me sick, it's so intense. I want *so badly* to kill this man, so badly I can taste it. Murder has a sharp, metallic taste, like biting tinfoil. "Her and Melvin Royal. We wanted it recorded. It starts at midnight. We sell the recordings later, but the live event is—special."

"Fuck you," I say, and I come so close to pulling the trigger; the tidal wave of fury that's breaking inside me nearly drowns my sanity. "Where is it?"

Somehow, impossibly, he *smiles*. It's a sickly thing. Sweat glitters on his forehead. "You can buy a seat, Mr. Cade. It's not quite sold out yet. I think we have five tickets left."

Shoot him. Shoot this piece of rotten meat right now. I don't know whose voice that is, but I think it's my sister's, and I might have done it if Mike hadn't stepped in by the end of that awful little taunt and slammed his fist squarely into Rivard's mouth. The surprise shocks me out of the urge to kill, and I think he just saved Rivard's life. And mine. My skin feels like it's going to burst, the container of a bomb that's going off inside me with too much force to contain. I've never felt hate like this before, not even for Melvin Royal. Everything's tinted with it, tastes of it.

Mike's punch leaves Rivard rocked back in his chair, and his mouth is bloody. He looks shocked, and vulnerable, and all of a sudden, I see a pathetic old man.

I take my finger off the trigger.

"Let me tell you one true thing, Mr. Rivard," Mike says, and I know that tone in his voice. That's the Mike who kills. That's the Mike who walked me out of a war zone when my plane went down in enemy territory. The Mike who put down every bastard in our way. "Sam Cade's the nice guy in this van. So you think real goddamn hard about the next thing you say, because I don't care anymore about my badge, or my career, or how much time I have to spend in prison."

I believe him. I don't know if he's lying, but I know that Rivard *certainly* doesn't, and there's a savage joy in that, in seeing the real, liquid fear in his eyes.

"Louisiana, outside Baton Rouge. There's a derelict house there, right on Killman Creek. Triton Plantation. That's where it will be held." He tries a smile. "You need me, though. You need me to order it to stop. You can't get there in time."

"We don't have to," Mike says. "That's the great thing about modern police work. All I have to do is make a phone call and get everybody out there arrested."

Rivard's not *quite* broken. He bares bloody teeth now. "In Louisiana? I don't think so. We own many, many police officers down there, and we're not careless. You have no assurance that the police on the other end will do *anything*. Even if you get lucky, find an honest cop, that area is very well defended. You'll never get her out alive. Or Melvin. You need me to—"

Mike yanks the expensive silk handkerchief out of Rivard's pocket and shoves it in his mouth, then roughly strips off the man's tie and cinches it in place as a gag. "Sick of your voice," he says, then turns to me. "I'm calling a guy. He can keep Rivard on ice until we have enough proof to put him away."

My throat's dry, fried with anger and adrenaline, and I have to try twice before my voice works properly. "You believe him about the police?"

"I think it's possible. Worst thing we could do is call the local cops and tip his men off down there."

"You think he's telling the truth? That he can call it off?"

"I think if we let him near a phone, the first call he's going to make will burn that place to the ground and kill everybody in it," Mike says. "Because a cockroach like this? He knows how to survive, first and last."

Mike steps out of the van and makes a call, and I hear Rivard making muffled noises, but I ignore him now. He's meaningless. I'm trying to calculate how far it is to Baton Rouge from Atlanta, and what the chances are we can get there in a few hours. Not good. The flights up and down the East Coast are a mess from the storm, and even if Mike can somehow work his FBI magic again, the storm's moving southwest, which means it's between us and where we need to be. It'll cause rolling chaos.

We have to get Gwen out of there. The idea that she's in that house, with *him*, makes my skin crawl and my stomach turn. I don't care how it happens, but I want her safe. I want to hold her again and tell her how sorry I am that I let this happen to her.

And every passing minute means the chances are smaller I ever will.

Mike's first call is brief, and when it's done, he says, "My guy's on the way. He'll make the van and Rivard disappear until I say different."

"He understands who Rivard is, right?"

"He knows. He's solid, and he owes me."

I wonder what kind of person is solid against the wealth Rivard has, but I have to trust he's right. "What about the cops?"

"I'm calling the New Orleans FBI office instead," he says. "Rivard could well own half the cops in that parish down there, but I know the NOLA folks. He doesn't own them."

Except, when that call ends, I can tell it doesn't go well, and my blood pressure spikes up again, pounding my temples. "What?" I ask him.

"Major stuff going down in New Orleans. Terrorist alert," he tells me. "My guys say there's no way they can break loose to help us. They say call the locals."

"What about the state police?"

"Most of them are going to be stretched thin, and dispatched to New Orleans to assist. Besides: same problem as the locals. We don't know who Rivard's bought off, and I don't have any personal friends down there I can count on."

I check my watch. It's just gone six o'clock. Gwen's murder starts at midnight, streamed live.

We have seven hours to get to her. Time zone change gives us the extra hour.

Hold on, I think. *Jesus, Gwen, hold on for me. You promised.*

Hold on.

25

GWEN

When I wake up this time, I wake up in bed.

The nausea hits me immediately in a violent rush, and I curl in on myself to try to hold it back. My head pounds so hard I think my skull will crack, and I can feel myself trembling—not cold now, but shaking from the aftereffects of the drug. Once that begins to recede a little, and the burning bile calms in my stomach, I feel other things. The same pains from before, but with more added. My back feels raw. I think the rough wood of the crate left a small forest of splinters.

When I open my eyes, I try to make my foggy mind tell me where I am. The room's dim, but I can make out white sheets over me. They feel damp and smell like someone else's skin. A stench gradually creeps over me: mold, an *old* smell: bodies in the ground. The reek of age and decay.

The fear creeps back sluggishly, too tired to continue . . . but it brings clarity with it. Purpose.

I shift to relieve a torturous cramp in my hip, and I feel the bed shift in a way that isn't due to my motion at all. I freeze. *There's someone next to me in the bed.* I can feel the animal warmth of his body, and every instinct in me screams at me *not to move*, as if like a child, I can make myself invisible. Staying still won't help me.

I have to help myself.

I try to edge away, hoping to slide out of bed quietly, but I stop when I realize I can't move my left wrist.

The one that aches so badly.

My wrist is tightly handcuffed to the old wrought iron bedstead. I must have broken something, maybe a small bone in my hand, because trying to pull at the restraint, however gently, earns me a pulse of agony so bright it takes my breath. I want to scream, and I can't.

I'm not in my clothes. Someone's changed me into an old, stiff nightgown. The nylon feels brittle, as if it might crumble into dust if I move too aggressively.

The light outside the window is getting dimmer. The sun's going down. I turn my head, and I can just make out the features of the man who's lying next to me.

I suppose I shouldn't be surprised that it's Melvin Royal, but I am. Seeing him here, asleep without a care in the world, is such a shock that it feels like a punch to my heart. A fatal blow. I feel a scream gathering in my throat.

Kill him is the next thought that rushes into the void of my mind, and I bend my right elbow and lunge. I'm trying to bury it in his throat, lean my weight on the point of it until I shatter his hyoid bone, and for a second it feels like I'm going to accomplish that. I feel my elbow bear down on his throat and I start to push . . . and then he's rolling away. *Laughing.*

I claw at Melvin, drag my fingernails through any piece of him I can reach, and take strips of flesh off him as he escapes. I'm yanking savagely at my pinned wrist now, and every pull sparks an agonizing burn, like fireworks in the palm of my hand. I don't care. The fury in me is stronger than the fear, the pain—stronger than *anything*.

Melvin, rolling to the far edge of the large bed, stares at me as I flail at the edge of my reach. He props himself up on one elbow and watches me with awful fascination. I'm livid with rage, burning with it like a candle, and it doesn't leave room for more sensible emotions, like fear or confusion or horror.

I just want to kill him.

"Is that how you thank me for letting you have one last comfortable rest?" he says to me. "I should have put you in the cellar. Let you worry about the rats and roaches for a while." He twists and looks at the deep fingernail gouges I've left in the flesh of his side. He's lean now. Fit. He's been spending his prison time lifting weights, I think, but he's the pale color of something that lives in caves. He was only allowed an hour of yard time a day, I remember. It didn't do him much good. He's grown a beard. But other than those changes, he's exactly as I remember him.

He's capable of anything, and I damn well know it. I've seen it, in decaying flesh and broken bones and drying blood, a sculpture of horror and agony he made. But cowering isn't something I do anymore. "Put me in the cellar. Rats and roaches would be better company," I say. It comes out more like a growl. I wonder if my eyes are bloodshot. It feels that way. Feels like every vein in my body is bursting with fury. "You *bastard*."

He shrugs, and that slow, cool smile makes me want to claw it off his face. "You were such a nice woman when I married you. Look what being single's done to you. I don't like the muscles, Gina. When I start cutting, I'll get rid of those first. I like my ladies delicate."

My white-hot anger flickers a little, but I deliberately feed it images of his victims. I'd rather be enraged than terrified, and those are my only choices now. This is what I signed up for, back on that road in Tennessee when I thought about darting into traffic and ending it all. I told Sam that I'd rather give my life this way, keeping Melvin occupied, tied down, so that he could be found.

Rage is better than fear. Always.

"I'm not one of your ladies," I tell him. I wonder how many bones I'll have to break in my hand to pull it free. Three? Four? He's put the cuff on very tightly. But he's too calm. Too prepared. This is a trap, and I think he *wants* me to hurt myself.

"You're my wife, Gina."

"Not anymore."

"I never accepted that," Melvin says, as if that settles everything. He checks a watch he has on the nightstand on his side of the bed. "It's nearly seven. You should have something to eat. It's going to be a very long night."

I realize now that he's wearing faded old pajama bottoms. They're a little large on him. Antiques, like the gown he's put on me. "Where are we?" I ask. "How did you get me here?" It's not Tennessee. It doesn't feel like that, smell like that. There's a different weight to the air here, and it's warmer.

"This place belongs to a friend of mine," he says. "A grand old place, back in the day. The front of it used to look like the White House, but you can't tell it anymore, between the rot and the kudzu that's taken over. As to how I got you here . . . let's just say I had some help."

"A plantation," I guess, because this all feels Southern Gothic, and the kudzu gives it away. "You think you're the lord of some decaying manor now?"

"Think of it as a place where special events are filmed. Commission pieces get done here. My friend's got a few other location sets around. You've even found a couple of them. The warehouse was one. That cabin you blew up was another."

Special events. I remember the darkest trade that Absalom does, in rape and torture and murder on film, with a sick, gritty taste in my mouth. "You were part of it," I say. "Absalom."

"I was a customer who graduated to being a supplier," he replies. "I had talent. Made a good career out of it for nearly ten years. I was careful. I suppose I got careless, at the end. I should have put that last

306

one in the lake while I had the chance. If I'd cleaned up the garage the night before, like I intended, we'd still be married." He pats the mattress. "Still sharing the marital bed, too. I know you've missed it. I have."

He sounds so normal. Wistful. It's disorienting. Who would I be now if he'd kept hold of me for these past nearly five years? What would he have done to our children? I don't want to imagine it, but I do: poor, passive Gina Royal, afraid to meet anyone's eyes for long, scuttling through life with rounded shoulders and the mentality of a victim. Showing her children nothing but submission.

My kids might be damaged now, but I have fought for them. I've made sure they're strong, independent young people. He can't take that from them. Or me.

"You going to rape me, Melvin?" I ask him. "Because if you try, I'm going to rip as many pieces off you as I can reach."

"I'd never do that to you. Not to the mother of my children." I've gotten to him a little. He stretches and tries to make it look natural, but I can see he's frustrated. I'm not playing the role of cowed victim. I'm not *submitting*. "Not that I can see her much in you now. Look what you've done to yourself. And for what? To survive? Not worth it, Gina, especially since you're going to die this way." His eyes take on a wet, opaque shine, like ice. He's already started taking me apart in his head.

"Fuck you," I tell him. I start working on the cuff. The pain is extraordinary, a supernova of red-and-yellow flares that burn like phosphorus as I twist my hand. Something gives with a wet, crisp snap, and the sensation is so overwhelming that I don't feel anything for a blessed second. It's like my body is trying to give me time to escape.

I break another bone, and my fingers burn like I've lit them on fire. I let out a cry, but it's an angry one. A victorious one. Pain is life. Pain is victory.

I'm going to get free, and I'm going to kill him.

"Gina," he says. "Look at me." The tone's almost gentle. "I'm sorry it has to be like this, in front of the cameras. I didn't want that for you.

I wanted it to be just you and me. But Absalom wanted to get paid back for what they've done for me. And what they're going to do."

"You're apologizing?" I can't help it. I let out a bitter, barking laugh. "God, what next. What's Absalom going to do for you, do you think? Get you out of the country? Set you up somewhere with new victims? They're using you, you idiot. When they get what they want, they'll kill you, too."

"Don't call me an idiot," he says, and the gentleness melts out of his voice and leaves it flat and cold. "Don't *ever* do that. I played you, Gina. All the way down." His chin lowers, and his eyes almost seem to shutter. There's no humanity in them now. Just the monster. "Brady's been calling me. Did you know that?"

It hits me under the shield I'm holding up, and all my wonderful, freeing anger gutters out in an instant. I stop trying to get free. I don't want to give him an inch, but I can't stop myself from asking, "What are you talking about?"

"Our son. Brady." Melvin sits down on the edge of the bed. "I arranged for him to be given a phone when our friend Lancel had him—remember that? That phone was Brady's lifeline, if he needed it. Turns out he did. First you abandoned him. Then he discovered you lied to him. Just enough doubt to exploit, to get him talking. It almost worked." There's a terrible, bitter disgust in the twist of his mouth now. "But you made him a weak, sad little rag doll, our son. You did that to him. He's worthless to me the way he is. I'm going to have to toughen him up now."

This is not the calm, polite Melvin that other people knew. It's not even the Melvin *I* knew, back in Wichita; he never would have said these things, not about his own son. This is the toxic sludge at the bottom of a black lake spilling out of his mouth. Hearing him talk about my son this way makes me sick, and it also makes me terrified.

"You're lying. You couldn't have been talking to him," I say, because that's the only thing I can cling to. "He would have told me."

"He didn't use the phone right away—you kept him on a tight enough leash. But once he started, he just couldn't stop." Another cold smile. "Like father, like son, I suppose."

I remember suddenly who found that awful video. *Connor.* It wasn't an accident. It wasn't Absalom. Melvin did that to our son. He did it deliberately. "You *son of a bitch.*"

"It's not my fault you left him with strangers," Melvin says. "You made him vulnerable. Easy to break, and I broke him. I was planning to have him here with us. I think that would have been fitting, for him to see you break, and then I could take him with me and teach him how to be strong. But it didn't work. Instead of Brady, we got Lily."

It's coming too fast, and it's too much. I don't have time to feel the shocks. I'm drowning in them. "You mean Lanny?" I've said her name, and I wish I hadn't, because he can see the cracks now. The fear. He feeds on it. "You don't have her."

"You're right. I don't. She got in the way when Absalom's transport man went to get our son. By now she's up in the hills, at another of our . . . special places." He shrugs. "I told them to make some use out of her, one way or another. She's not as marketable as she would have been younger, but—"

"*Shut up!*" I scream, and the raw edge to it surprises me. I feel heavy and cold, like my body is already giving up. I want my rage back. The fear is too hard. Too heavy. *Lanny, oh my sweet precious girl, where are you, what's he done . . .*

I remind myself, somehow, that Melvin Royal is a liar. A deceiver. A manipulator. And he knows where my undefended weaknesses lie. My children are how he hurts me. I have to believe they're safe. *I have to.*

"You're a very bad mother," he says into the weighted silence. "I'm going to get my son and make him mine again. I've already got your daughter. You think about that until I'm ready for you."

He knows when to strike and retreat. He stands up and goes to the door, and for the first time I realize that this bedroom has other furniture in it—an old, leaning dresser, some framed prints half-eaten by mold. A cracked mirror that shows the world in two badly reflected pieces.

In it, I'm torn in half, as if he's already started destroying me.

I know I should get myself free. I know I should fight. *I have to fight.*

But all I can do, as Melvin leaves me, is lie there, shuddering. I claw the sheet over me, because the cold seems so intense, despite the thick, tepid air. I need my anger back.

I wonder if anyone knows where I am. If Sam might be looking, or if he even cares to try.

Maybe this is how I end.

Maybe, before he destroys me completely, I'll buy my children's safety with my blood.

That's all I can wish for now.

26

SAM

It costs Rivard three broken fingers, but he finally agrees to call the airfield and has them ready his private plane for us. That gets around the impossible tangle of canceled flights out of the commercial lines, but it throws us another curve: it takes time to get the plane fueled and ready, and when we board, we find that the pilot's not there yet. He's going to be another hour coming in.

I tell the flight attendant to take the day off with pay. We aren't going to need drinks and dinner. She seems surprised, but nobody ever argues against an unexpected bonus, and her quick departure leaves us on the aircraft, alone.

Mike's watching me as I check the time. It's already eight o'clock central time. Flight time to Baton Rouge is about an hour and a half, but the weather between us means diverting around it, and that adds at least another half an hour. If we're not wheels up until nine, that's eleven on the ground, and no time to get to where Gwen's being held. *We should have tried having Rivard call it off.* But I knew he'd screw us on that. It would be his only sure revenge.

Every second we waste now is blood in the water. "I'm taking the plane," I tell him. He nods; he's been expecting that. He knows I can fly it, and it's fueled and ready. "Lock it up and let's get in the air."

I slide into the pilot's chair and start preflight checks. The cockpit's different—sleeker and more automated than most—but I've driven enough birds that everything's clear at a glance. Tens of thousands of hours behind me. This plane's a piece of cake. I plot the course and lock it in, and the onboard computer automatically loads the weather stats and adjusts. I was right. Two hours' flight time.

I know how to clear the plane for takeoff, and I'm not surprised that the tower doesn't notice the pilot change; small airfields like these, they thrive on people knowing their own business. I get on the com and tell Mike to take a seat, then taxi the plane out. Focusing on the work keeps the jitters at bay, and the images of what's happening to Gwen a distance, at least for now.

Takeoff feels like victory, like speed, like we're finally beating Absalom at their own game. But I know that's an illusion. Being in the air is freedom to me, and the vibration of the plane is a familiar, soothing rhythm. It keeps the fear in check.

I lock in the autopilot and step away to talk to Mike. "Anything else we can do?"

"I called the FBI's Baton Rouge resident office," he says. "Both agents stationed there are coordinating with New Orleans. I'm trying Shreveport. We might have to go to the state police. Last resort, because I don't know if they'll take it seriously, but we're running out of options."

I leave him to make the calls. There's nothing else I can do now but wait, and I'm not good at it.

Keep fighting, Gwen.

Keep fighting.

27

GWEN

The despair lasts until a ratty-looking, thin woman, arms pocked by a junkie's scars, brings me water. The second I see it, I realize how desperately thirsty I am, and I take the bottle and guzzle it thirstily.

It's a mistake, and I know that as soon as the drugs hit my system. In just a few minutes, I feel the chemical wave of them rushing through my veins, and though I try to pull my broken hand the rest of the way through the cuffs, I can't seem to stay focused. The pain keeps holding me back, and no matter how much I try to concentrate, it's like sand through a screen.

By the time the drugs take a real hold, I'm panting, sweating, moaning, and everything is smeared and blurred around me. Spiders in the sheets. Eyes on the ceiling. The terror is like something alive inside me, fighting to get out. I imagine it clawing through my skin, bursting through in thick, black streaks that choke and blind me.

When I finally pass out, it's a mercy.

I don't know how many hours go by. When I'm finally aware again, I'm not handcuffed anymore. My left hand is swollen, and I can barely move it. The drugs keep me soft-focused and weak, and I see the thin woman again. She shouts at me, a red cascade of sound, and then roughly scrubs me down with a wet towel. She takes off my nightgown and throws clothes at me. I can't manage it myself, so she dresses me like a doll, slaps me when I start to lie down in the bed, and makes me lie on the floor. I don't care.

I'm barely aware that she chains me to the bed's thick iron leg. I'm gone again before I can work out what to do next.

The next time I wake, I'm much clearer. My left hand is massively swollen and bloodied now, and locked back in the handcuff. No chance now of pulling it loose. I've made a real mess of it, and I'm still not free.

I need to find a way out of this and get back to my children. Their faces are so clear that I feel I can reach out and touch them, and I'm seized by a feeling of loss so intense it tears me apart, and I start to cry. *I lost them. I lost my kids.*

I bang my left hand against the floor, and the pain that shatters through me is breathtaking. It destroys the grief, drives a bright shard of alertness into my brain.

I do it again.

I bite my lip to keep from screaming, and my whole body shakes from holding it inside. I think I'm going to fly apart, but I don't. My head's clearer when the storm's passed. Pain helps. Pain drives out the last of the drugged fog.

I hear creaking footsteps, and I see the thin, bare legs of the woman who gave me the drugs. She stands over me. I nod like a junkie, and she watches for a moment, then leaves. I make sure she's gone before I look around.

I'm in the same room. It's the same bed. Did I really wake up here with Melvin, or was that some hideous drug dream? God help me, I wish I could believe that, but I know this is real. He's real.

This is all grimly real, and I need to *get it together* because time is running out.

He told me something about the kids. Something awful. I reach for it, but it slips away like oil in water, and I'm almost grateful for that, because I can only remember the *feeling* of that despair, not the shape.

I focus on what's in front of me. My puffy, wounded hand. The handcuff digging into swollen flesh. Purple-tinted fingertips.

The other half of the handcuffs is fastened around the iron leg of the bed.

I stare at that for a long few seconds, and then I slowly realize why I'm staring.

I can slip it off.

The bed's heavy, but that leg? Thinner than the cuff. If I lift the bed, I can slip it under. The junkie girl isn't careful. She thinks I'm beaten.

I inch over, careful not to make much noise, and I slowly lift myself up to take the weight of the heavy bed on my back, pushing it up. It's awkward, and agonizing, and I have to concentrate hard to keep my trembling muscles from just giving up and letting the bed slam down again . . . but I slowly pull the empty side of the handcuff free, and then I bend back down, inch by inch, until the iron foot touches the wood again. Silently.

Somewhere deeper in this house, I hear bells. No, they're chimes. A clock. I've missed some of the chimes, so I can't tell what the time is, except that it's later than ten. Could be eleven. Could be midnight.

Floorboards creak across the room. I get ready. *Come up fast,* I tell myself. I want to cry, I feel so lost, so tired, but part of me is still that forged steel that Melvin has made of me. *Come up fast. If it's the girl, swing the metal handcuff into her face. Get her down. Take her weapon, if she has one. Keep moving. Don't stop.*

I don't know where I can go. I don't think there's anywhere to run. But I'm not stopping.

I tense up as the footsteps come nearer.

It's not the junkie girl I see first. It's Melvin, and the sight of his broken smile shakes me once more. "Look who's awake," he says. "Annie. Get her up. We need to start on time."

Start on time, like this is some Broadway production, and he's the stage manager.

I come up with all the power I have and slash the handcuff at his face, but I fall short. I'm off balance, and he easily dodges it. He grabs me by the forearms and shoves me at Annie, who takes my left hand and squeezes so hard my knees give way. I don't scream. Not quite.

"Do what I tell you," she says. "Walk."

She shoves me into a stumble, and she keeps her iron grip on my injury, reminding me she can inflict pain anytime she wants. Outside the room, I realize that we're on the second level, and there's a wooden railing on the right overlooking the room below. Everything smells of neglect and rot, and the floor creaks and groans with every step. There's a large, gaping hole ahead, and above it, the ceiling's fallen in. Water drips from the sagging, blackened edges to patter on broken boards. I can see a cloudy night sky up there, and when I tilt my head back, the drugs threaten to lift me up into the faint, glittering stars.

Annie leads me around the hole and close to the banister. The railing isn't in any better shape than the floor. If she was on the side closest to it, I'd push her over. It would probably break loose and send her crashing down to the atrium below.

But *I'm* on the railing side. *Go over,* I tell myself. *It's better than what he has planned.*

But I know the fall won't kill me, and I'm afraid I'll break a leg and lose any chance to run, or fight.

I stumble over the torn carpeting and fall forward so suddenly that Annie lets go. I catch myself on my hands. The left one gives a searing stab of agony, and I cry out and lurch over to my right . . . and my fingers catch on a loose piece of floorboard. It's splintered at the end, and I feel the sharp edge. I don't hesitate. I dig my fingers in and pull on the break, and a piece splits off. I grab it as Melvin jerks me upright by my hair. I don't use it yet—not yet. I press it flat against my right wrist, out of sight.

Wait until you can be sure. You won't get another chance. I know what's coming for me will be slow, and brutal, and horrific, and the worst part, the *worst part*, is that I don't think it will do any good to hold out. I don't think anybody can help me now. I have to help myself. As long as he's focused on me, he isn't going after the kids.

The kids.

I remember what Melvin said now. *Brady called me. We have Lily.* I feel a wave of pure horror, like cold honey over my skin. *No. No. No.*

We're approaching a closed door, and I slow down. Annie's hand grabs my left wrist and twists hard, but it doesn't affect me as much now, because there's a greater pain. A greater horror. I can't let this happen. I can't let him *have my children.*

Melvin steps ahead and swings the door open. A gentleman's gesture from a monster.

It's his torture chamber. I don't even need a glance to see that; it comes at me as one thing, as inevitable as winter. I don't look at the details.

I'm looking at the girl. The girl who stands on that oval, blood-stained rug, with the wire noose around her neck. The girl with dyed black hair, coarse and clumped with sweat, which hangs over her features.

For that one, horrible, irrational second, I think that it's Lanny.

I scream. It bursts out of me in a shocking rush, all of the agony and grief and horror so real and present that I feel everything in me has been cut to the bone and flayed open, spilling out like blood. I swallow the cry a second later, but I know what it reveals to him.

The girl isn't Lanny. She's not my daughter. But she's someone's daughter.

She's standing on the balls of her feet, straining to keep her balance, because if she relaxes at all, the noose bites into her neck. It's deliberate and cruel and finely calculated, just like the tools hung on pegboard, arrayed in order on the walls. On the wooden workbench, toolboxes stand open to display wrenches, screwdrivers, pliers . . . all color-coded, aligned in precise rows in the drawers.

Precise in his barbarity.

There are two other people in the room. One man adjusts lighting, ignoring the girl and her horrible struggle. Another one adjusts the focus on a video camera on a tripod. Both look completely *normal*, and it's horrifying to see that this is just *work* to them. Just another day.

"Shit," the video guy says. "I wasn't rolling. I wish I'd gotten that scream. That was something."

"Are we close?" Melvin asks.

"Ten minutes out. You can start with the daughter stand-in, but keep it short. They're paying for the main event, not the opening act." He's just so . . . *normal*. He's wearing a Hawaiian shirt with hula girls on it, and cargo shorts, and slip-on sandals. But nothing about this is normal. Not one of these people has a soul. There's something missing in all of them.

I turn my head. Melvin's stopped next to me. He's staring at that poor girl with horrible, fixed intention, but he tears himself away to transfer that look to me. It's the worst thing I've ever seen. The pupils of his eyes have dilated, and in the light from that room they look almost . . . red. Monster's eyes. "She looks a lot like her, doesn't she? Our Lily."

I can't breathe. I can't move. There's something so dangerous in front of me that it paralyzes even my voice. I knew he was evil. I never knew he was *this*. There's . . . nothing in there. Nothing I can identify as the least bit human.

"Yes." It comes out in a shaking whisper not out of fear but rage. "But this girl isn't Lily. There's no point in hurting her. It won't have the same impact."

"Won't it?" He considers me, like a bird considering a bug. "I'll let you choose."

The video operator has quietly turned the camera on. I'm blinded as lights suddenly flare hot against my face. But I don't blink. I can't. If I show any weakness at all, he'll have me.

"Choose what?" The small shard of wood's pressed hard against my skin, and I can feel the gouge it makes. I shift, put my weight on my left foot. I make sure he can't see my right arm.

"I'll let this girl go if you ask to take her place. But you have to *want it*, Gina. You have to *ask*. Beg me for her. If you do, I'll turn her loose and let her leave. It'll take her hours to get to a road. Lots of time before she can find anybody to listen to her. She's a junkie whore. Maybe nobody will ever believe her." His lips twitch, and a slow smile overtakes them. "But she'll be alive. I know how much you want to save people."

Breath turns to poison in my lungs. He has me. He knows what I'm going to do. But before I do it, I say, "You're never going to have Connor."

"Oh, Connor's all yours," he says. "But I'm going to have *Brady*. Count on that. What's your answer? Because either way, you're going to die tonight. This one doesn't have to. Clock's ticking, Gina. Choose."

I don't want to look at those dreadful eyes anymore. I let my lids drift shut, and I say. "Please, Mel. Please let her go. I beg you."

It burns in my mouth to do that. Worse, I've just called him Mel. It's the first time since the day our lives shattered apart. I wonder if he even notices.

"Good girl," he says. I feel sudden heat against my skin. He's put his hand on my cheek. "All right. She gets her life. I always knew you'd give in, if I found the right motivation."

He bends close to me. His breath flutters against my skin. His fingers are gentle as they trace the line of my chin, my lips. I keep my eyes closed. *God, I can't look. I can't.* I'm trembling. The drugs make me dizzy, and unsteady. I wish Annie would twist my broken hand again, just to clear my mind.

"Let the girl down," he says. He's not talking to me, but his lips are so close to my cheek they brush my skin. "Get her out of here. Put her on the road and tell her to run."

The spell breaks, but it isn't me who breaks it. It's the sound of the winch control activating with a whine, and the choked gasp of the girl. She's crying. "Oh God, thank you, thank you—"

"Out," Melvin says. "Or I kill you."

I hear the rush of running feet. She's leaving.

Now, I think. *Now.* I can't miss. He's right here.

I open my eyes and adjust my grip on the wooden dagger.

Someone laughs.

It shocks me. It shocks Melvin, too, and we both look toward the doorway. Annie's leaning there, high as a kite from the look of her, and she's giggling as she watches the other girl run for her life. "Son of a bitch," she says. "I thought you were some fuckin' badass, man. Here you are letting people go, making deals. Don't you already own this sorry bitch?"

"You're talking about my wife, Annie," he says. His tone is mild, and calm, but the eyes . . . he's deep in whatever fantasy he's cultivated. "Don't disrespect my wife."

"Her?" Annie's lip curls. "She's nothing."

"No. She's mine."

When he moves, it's like the strike of a snake, too fast to be seen. He smashes her head into the door frame, again and again and again, a flurry of moves so shockingly violent that I can't even think to act, to attack him, to try to save her life. He's a tiger, pure bloody rage, and I'm terrified. Everybody's frozen, even the film crew, who must have seen horrors I can't imagine.

I don't want to see this, but I can't close my eyes. It's as inevitable as a nightmare.

Annie collapses, gasping, eyes blind with blood. She crawls toward me.

I back up. I can't help the instinct. Panic is howling inside me, a black tornado of despair because my thin piece of wood is nothing, *nothing* against this madness, it's a paper-thin lie I've told myself, and nothing can stop Melvin Royal.

Melvin steps over Annie, grabs a screwdriver from the rack, and with one viciously powerful blow, he drives it through her skull.

Then he loses control.

My vision grays out. I can't see this. I can't know it. My mind is trying to run, trying to hide like a child in a maze, and I hear myself screaming because Annie can't, she doesn't make a sound, and all I want to do is *run*.

But I can't make it past him. The second I move, I'm a victim.

When Melvin stops, it's because he's tired, not because he's finished. I can see that in the way his chest heaves, and his hand shakes, and the butchered woman lying on the floor is barely recognizable as human from the neck up.

The lighting and camera operators haven't made a sound or a move. They've frozen in place, too, as if they know they're in the presence of an animal who could eat them just as easily. When Melvin sits back on his haunches, he looks at the camera operator. He's dripping with Annie's blood. He still has the screwdriver.

"Keep rolling," he says to the cameraman, and, oh *Jesus*, he sounds so normal, so like the man I married. The man who took vows to love and cherish and protect. "I'm just starting."

I feel myself going away. It's not a faint; I know I can't make myself vulnerable that way. I feel my mind leave my body, drift up like a balloon only loosely tethered to this heavy, shaking sack of flesh. From this distance, looking down, I don't feel the horror or the sickness. I don't watch. Somewhere, I have to believe that my children are still alive. Safe. That somewhere, Sam is okay.

Somewhere, people still live in the light.

But here in the dark, I'm all that stands between Melvin and the people I love.

And I have to keep standing.

When I open my eyes, I'm still in that putrid, dying place, and Melvin Royal is turning toward me. His bloody face looks calm, and his smile looks hungry.

"Gina," he says, "I'm sorry, but this is how it has to—"

I lunge forward, and I jam the sharp piece of wood into his eye.

It goes deep, rupturing the fragile surface, and I feel the warm fluid from within sluice over my fingers. It's all I have. All I can do. It's isn't enough, I know. Everything inside me goes silent.

It's almost peaceful.

The wood breaks in my hand off as he screams and twists away. He's alive. Blinded in one eye, in agony, but alive.

Melvin pulls the wood out of his destroyed eye and screams in rage.

The silence inside me snaps, and the fear roars back in, black and silver and cold as sleet, and I know I have seconds, *seconds*, to save myself.

I'm already lunging forward. It feels like I'm moving in slow motion, every motion crystalline clear and *too slow*, and something inside me is screaming to *hurry, hurry, God, run, go*.

I'm past him before he realizes I've moved, but he's only a step or two behind me, screaming my old name, my dead name, and I know if he gets his hands on me, there won't be any carefully curated torture streamed out to enrich Absalom; it'll be pure, bloody slaughter, just as it was with Annie. He'll rip me to pieces.

I see the camera operator moving out of the room behind us; he's brought the video recorder with him, and he's filming me as I head for the stairs. I hear Melvin roaring. It sounds like hell is ripping open behind me.

The screwdriver that Melvin used to kill Annie has rolled out into the hall, kicked there at some point, and I bend and pick it up without breaking stride. Someone's charging up the stairs, a new man, and he has a gun in his hand.

I need that gun.

I can't feel the pain of my wrist anymore, or anything else. I feel incandescent. I burst with power, and I close the distance faster than I thought possible. I bury the screwdriver in the guard's neck, and the gun falls to the floor as he staggers back and starts to tumble down the steps. I dive for the weapon, twist over on my back, and as I roll, I see Melvin taking a last step toward me. He has his right hand clamped over his bloody, mutilated eye, but he sees the gun just in time to throw himself to the side as I aim and fire. Adrenaline or not, the shock of recoil sends a brutal stab through my arm, and I yell in pain and fury. My first shot misses him by less than an inch. I try again.

Melvin ducks into the room where he intended to kill me. He has weapons there. Maybe even a gun. I can't stop now, even if my wrist shatters off my arm, I have to *hold the gun and shoot*, and pain doesn't matter.

I fire more bullets into the wall, walking the shots methodically across. I don't know where he is. My heart is racing so fast that it feels like a dying bird in my chest, but my brain feels slow. Calm. Almost peaceful. The gun in my hand is a semiautomatic, so it has a minimum of seven bullets. I've fired four.

The video operator is still standing there filming me. Maybe he truly doesn't understand that he isn't just *crew*, that he's a guilty accomplice to horrors. Maybe he thinks his camera is a magic shield.

I shoot him, and he goes down. *Five.*

I scramble forward. My legs feel weak and loose, but somehow I stay up. I dodge drunkenly around the hole in the middle of the floor, step over the dead camera operator, and pray there's still at least one more bullet in the gun so I can put it in Melvin's head.

I make it to the door of the torture room. There's a man curled up motionless on the oval rug: the lighting tech. I got him with the shots I put through the wall.

Melvin isn't here. *Melvin's gone.*

There's a door to the left. I missed it before; the camera tripod was blocking it. But the tripod's on its side, and a broken laptop is sparking and flickering next to it.

I sense someone behind me. A shadow, moving fast.

I whirl and pull the trigger.

I realize just one second too late that it isn't Melvin.

It's Sam.

The gun clicks.

Empty.

Sam's breathing hard as he skids to a stop. He's staring at me with wild eyes, and he's standing in the spreading pool of Annie's blood. He's got a gun, too, and he's holding it on me as if I'm a dangerous creature he can't trust. Then he yells, "Put it down, Gwen! Put it down!"

I drop the gun, and it hits my leg painfully enough to jolt me out of my momentary trance. Everything floods me at once, a storm of emotion that I can't even understand. It rips away the focus, sends me reeling, shaking. The pain is back. So is the fear.

"He's still here!" I scream at Sam. "Melvin! He's still here!"

Sam's staring down at the ruined body of Annie with an expression of pure, visceral horror. It takes him a second to tear his gaze away and fix it on me. "No. He's out in the hall. He's dead."

"What?"

"He took a bullet in the eye. It's okay. Gwen. He's down." He catches me when I fall against him. I feel such an immense sense of exhaustion I think I might die. My heart is hammering like an engine; my body is still intent on running, fighting, even when there's nothing left to fight. I feel tears shredding me, wild and desperately intense.

"You got him," I whisper to Sam. "Thank you. God, thank you."

He holds me so tight it feels like we're fusing together, and I want that, I want that. "No," he says. "I didn't shoot him. You did. Didn't you?"

It takes me a long, icy second to understand what he's just said, and why it's important.

I didn't shoot Melvin in the eye. I stabbed him. With the gore and blood, it would have looked like a death wound. A shot to the eye. All Melvin had to do was lie down and let Sam go past him.

I grab Sam's gun and use his shoulder as a rest to aim, because there's the monster coming just behind him, there's the tiger, and death is in his eyes.

Melvin is lunging for Sam's back with a knife.

I stop him with three bullets through the forehead.

He folds at the knees, and then he's down on his face. He's still breathing. I can see his back rising and falling, and I want to put another bullet in it, but Sam's turning now, taking the gun from me.

It's good he does, because I likely would have shot Agent Lustig, who enters the doorway with his own gun drawn. Sam lowers the weapon, and Lustig takes one look at the two of us, then at the dying man stretched out on the floor. The dead man near the lights. The ruined body of Annie.

"Christ," Lustig says, and lowers his weapon. "My good Christ, what the hell is this?"

We stand there in silence. Lustig kneels next to Melvin, and we watch my ex-husband's back rise and fall for three more gasping breaths, and then there's a long, rattling exhalation that trails into silence.

The devil's dead. *He's dead.* I want to feel . . . what? Good? But there's none of that. I'm just grateful. Maybe later I'll feel satisfaction, vengeance, the fulfillment of a long-burning rage.

But right now I'm so grateful I am weeping. I can't stop.

"Please," I gasp. I reach for Sam, and he puts his arms around me again. "Please, please tell me they're okay, please, please . . ."

"They're okay," he whispers to me. There's a stillness to him, a peace, that I need right now. "Connor's all right. Lanny's all right. You're safe. We're okay. Just breathe."

My knees give way when we're halfway down the rotten stairs, and Sam carries me the rest of the way. I'm so tired. I can't keep my eyes open anymore. When I manage to look, he's putting me in the passenger seat of a sedan, and I'm looking at the rotten, spoiled colonial splendor of Triton Plantation House. It does look like the White House, destroyed by rot and time. A creek runs by the side of the road, sluggish and choked with mud. Bayou country.

Sam and Lustig are outside the car, talking in quiet voices. They're both shell-shocked. I can hear it. But I'm not. Not anymore.

"Rivard was right. State police never showed. If we hadn't made it—" Lustig breaks off. "It's a bloodbath in there. God only knows the bodies we're going to find around here. How many of these places do they have?"

"Dozens," Sam says. "But we've got Rivard, and once this thing breaks, it'll shatter everywhere. We'll find them. All of them."

I wish they'd burn it down. All of it, ashes and bones. But I know there's more to this than what I want, and I know that. I'm just so tired that I feel tears sliding cold down my cheeks. I wipe them away with a clumsy, bloody right hand.

That's Melvin's blood.

Melvin's dead.

Mike Lustig leans in and says, "You should thank our boy Sam," he says. "Saved your life."

"No," I tell him. I feel everything slipping away again. "I saved him."

I sleep.

And I don't dream at all.

28

Gwen

One month later

To most people, I look like I've recovered. I try hard, for my kids. If I still feel fragile as glass inside, I think only Sam can see it now. Sam, who sees everything. That might have bothered me once, but now I'm glad. I talk to Sam. I even see a psychologist who specializes in trauma recovery. I'm getting better. So are the kids. I made sure they got their own therapy, whether they admitted to needing it or not.

I don't check the Sicko Patrol anymore, but when I ask, Sam quietly tells me that it's continuing to roll on with more fire and energy than before. Despite my wishes, I'm the subject of a lot of articles and blogs again. Some think I'm a hero. Many think I got away with murder.

One thing I have to accept: now there's no hiding from it anymore.

The symbol of that is this house on Stillhouse Lake that we're reclaiming as our own. It's not just the four of us; our friends have been here helping. Javier and Kezia. Kezia's dad, Easy Claremont. Detective Prester and several Norton officers I now know by name. Some of the kids' school friends and their parents came, too; they all pitched in to repaint the outside of our house and get rid of ugly reminders of the past.

I expect new hatred to come at us, but for now, at least, this house is our fortress again.

Today, it'll be finished.

"Mom!" Connor holds up something I can't see from across the room. "Is this trash?"

"Does it look like trash?" I call back, and I manage a smile. He smiles back. It's hesitant, and stutters a little in the middle, but it's a start. We have work to do, Connor and I. Miles to go. He blames himself for too much, and now he's grieving his father. I know Melvin doesn't deserve that, but this isn't about him. It's about Connor, and letting him go through all the stages of grief for a man who never truly loved him. "Thanks, baby. Why don't you take a break?"

"Why don't you take a break?" Sam says, then takes the trash bag from my good right hand. My left is wrapped and splinted, and it hurts too damn much, but the doctor says it'll heal. Eventually. "Because you need to sit. Stop pushing."

He's right. It's done. Sam and Lanny have teamed up to repaint the damaged kitchen walls, while Kezia and Javier installed the new front window. Connor and I have picked up the last remnants of garbage. The front curtains stay down for now. I want to look out at the snow and the lightly frozen lake. It seems clean out there, in a way I don't think it ever has before.

Lanny is sitting with her girlfriend—maybe they're not quite calling it that yet, but I can see the looks—and they're wearing matching braided bracelets. When she thinks we're not looking, I know Lanny's holding Dahlia's hand. She needs this. She needs to be loved. I'll do everything I can; I'll love her more fiercely than any lioness, but I can't give her gentleness, and sweetness, and Dahlia seems to have that for her, at least for now. I stop to hug my daughter, because I can't *not*, and she lets me cling for a long, long moment before she pushes back and rolls her dark-rimmed eyes. I kiss her dark hair and try not to think about the girl in the noose. The one who got away, I think. I keep asking. They haven't found her, but she wasn't dead at the plantation, either.

Maybe she's found safety. Maybe something good came out of it for her.

Sam's waiting with a beer for me, and I gratefully take it and sink down next to him on the new couch. The old one was filthy, and anyway, it's time. It's time for new things. Fresh starts.

"Mike called," Sam says, then takes a deep pull of the beer. Connor settles in on the other side of him, and when Sam puts an arm around his shoulders, he doesn't flinch. He takes out a book and starts reading, but that's expected. It's a new book, I realize. One I haven't seen before. That seems significant, but I don't know why. "He's going to be tied up in DC for a while, but he says hi. Rivard's executive assistant rolled hard the second he knew the old man was locked up. He gave Mike the keys to the kingdom."

"Everything?" I ask, giving him a look. The trauma of Baton Rouge sometimes seems like a nightmare, a month out, but suddenly it's vivid again. Memories of empty, hungry eyes. The gun kicking in my hand. I can still feel the shock traveling through my arm, up my body. Feel the blood on my face. I take a breath. "You're sure? *Everything?*"

"Almost a thousand arrests just this week," he says. "All over the world. Including the ones who bought tickets to the show that night."

That's code, and I understand it. *The show.* The one where I was to be tortured to death. I shiver a little and huddle closer to his warmth. "That sounds good."

"They're going to get all of them. Rivard was a businessman; he kept excellent records. Even the trolls are getting hauled in and booked." Sam laughs a little bitterly. "Not that it's put a dent in your hate mail, but give it time."

"So Mike's okay?"

"Mike," Sam says, "is the new golden boy of the Bureau, and I think he likes it. Oh, one more thing. The forensic work on the videos finally came in: faked, of course. Not that you had anything to prove to us about that. Any of us." He looks over at Kezia, at Javier, at the kids, and I feel gratitude well up inside. Over this past month, each of them has come to me and told me when and where they'd come to the realization that they were wrong. Predictably, maybe, my daughter was the last.

Sam apologized first. Not that he had anything to be sorry for. Oh, the kids *believed* me first, I think, but it took an adult admitting it before they were comfortable saying so. I think they get that reluctance to show vulnerability from me. I hope that I can show them something else, now.

I tip my head up and look at him. He kisses my forehead, a quick brush of lips that leaves me warmer. This is sweet. And I'm so grateful for that. "Thank you."

"You're welcome," he says, offering me his bottle. We clink glass. "The FBI's putting out a public statement tomorrow that completely clears you. The end."

I sigh a little. It was a minor issue, given everything else that's happened, but I'm glad it's settled now. "You and I both know that isn't true," I tell him. "There will always be some people out there who don't believe it. Any of it."

"In a fight between some *Infowars*-swilling neckbeard and you, I know who to put my money on," he says. He takes another drink, and I can tell that he's trying to make it casual when he says, "About my cabin. Seems like the owner wants me to sign another lease starting next month. Rent's going up, too."

"I see."

"So I might be homeless pretty soon." There's a slight, teasing question in his voice. I smile, but I don't look up.

"That would be sad."

"So sad."

"And I suppose you might need a place."

"Now that you mention it. Got any leads?"

Lanny and Dahlia are whispering together. Giggling now. "Oh, just get it out there," Dahlia says. "We all *know*."

"Yeah," Connor says, turning a page. "It's pretty obvious."

"Okay, okay, fine. Mr. Cade, you're welcome to move in here." I feel a tremor, though I mean it. This is a huge step for me. An expression of trust I wasn't sure I could ever give anyone again.

"You sure?"

This time I do glance up. His eyes are steady and kind, and I catch my breath, because there's a look there I've never quite seen before. Intense, as if he's seeing me for the first time, all over again.

"I'm sure," I say. There used to be a minefield between us, but all those bombs are gone now, blown up, and what's left in its place is good ground. A good place to build. It'll take work, but I've never been afraid of that.

"Dinner's ready!" That's Kezia, from the kitchen. "I didn't cook it, so it's safe, I swear." The running joke of the past few weeks has been Kezia Claremont's inexplicable talent for ruining absolutely everything she tries to cook. It's a gift.

"She made an effort, though. She burned some toast," Javier says as Kez carries a big pan of roasted chicken and vegetables to the table. "Let's eat before Boot gets it all."

Boot rolls over at the mention of his name and licks his chops. I pat him, and he grunts and closes his eyes. He's recovered better than any of us.

"Yeah, get everything on the table," I say, then slip out from Sam's warmth to put on my coat, hat, and gloves. "I'm just going down to check the mail. Be right back."

"Be careful!" That comes from everybody at once. Sam is watching to see if I need company. I shake my head.

I'm smiling as I make my way—carefully—down the hill. The house is secure. Clean and new, all the bad stuff gone. I know it's symbolic. I know healing will take time and love and care.

But we're family. We're survivors.

I open the mailbox. There's a lot stuffed inside, and I stand there next to the recycling bin at the end of the drive and dump off junk catalogs and mail until I'm down to a light handful of bills and a letter. I look down at the last envelope, and I stop moving. For a moment I stop breathing. If I could pause my heart, I would.

It's Melvin's handwriting. I look at the postmark.

Someone mailed it after he died. Maybe somebody in Absalom, one last, bitter stab out of the dark.

I look at the way he's written my name in careful, precise block letters, and I remember seeing the frenzy that came over him when he killed Annie. I can't forget that. Ever.

I think about it for a moment, and then I put the other mail in my coat pocket and walk farther down the hill, across the road, and onto the shore of Stillhouse Lake.

The water's glassy and still, frozen into ripples. I look around on the shore and find a sizable rock about the size of a grapefruit. I hold Melvin's letter in my healing left hand and toss the stone out with my right. It breaks easily through the thin ice and reveals dark, freezing water.

I get another stone, a smaller one, and I search in my pockets. The mail came with a rubber band. I use it to wrap Melvin's letter around the rock.

I throw the weighted, unopened letter into the water. For a second I see the pale flicker of the paper, and I imagine the ink starting to bleed. In a few hours what he wrote completely gone, and the paper reduced to drifting fragments of pulp.

"Mom?" It's Connor, calling from the house. I turn and wave. "Mom?"

"I'm coming," I call back.

The last of my ex is at the bottom of the lake. No one will ever know what Melvin wanted to say.

And maybe, if he's burning in hell, that will hurt him worst of all.

SOUNDTRACK

I choose music for each book I write, because it helps me find the right tone and tempo of the story. Since it helped inspire me, I thought you'd enjoy seeing the music that goes along with Gwen's journey in *Killman Creek*.

I hope you enjoy the musical experience as much as I did, and please remember: piracy hurts musicians, and music aggregation services don't provide a living. Buying the song or album direct is still the best way to show your love, and help them create new work.

- "Eminence Front," The Who
- "Sledgehammer," Peter Gabriel
- "Poker Face," Lady Gaga
- "Staring at the Sun," TV on the Radio
- "Games Without Frontiers," Peter Gabriel
- "Hate the Taste," Black Rebel Motorcycle Club
- "Box Full o' Honey," Duran Duran
- "Red Rain," Peter Gabriel
- "Time of the Season," The Ben Taylor Band
- "Mama," Genesis
- "Welcome to the Circus," Skittish
- "Beneath Mt. Sinai," The Stone Foxes

- "Whatcha See Is Whatcha Get," The Dramatics
- "Human," Rag'n'Bone Man
- "Believer," Imagine Dragons
- "Jockey Full of Bourbon," Joe Bonamassa

Rachel Caine's website contains more information about her books, her appearance schedule, and more: www.RachelCaine.com.

Follow her on social media:

Twitter: @rachelcaine

Facebook: rachelcainefanpage

ACKNOWLEDGMENTS

To my friend Steve Huff, most especially, and my coconspirator Ann Aguirre. Special thanks to the mighty Liz Pearsons and the great T&M team, who just plain rock.

ABOUT THE AUTHOR

Photo © 2014 Robert Hart

Rachel Caine is the *New York Times*, *USA Today*, and Amazon Charts bestselling author of more than fifty novels, including the Stillhouse Lake series, the *New York Times* bestselling Morganville Vampires series, and The Great Library young adult series. She has written suspense, mystery, paranormal suspense, urban fantasy, science fiction, and paranormal young adult fiction. Rachel lives and works in Fort Worth, Texas, with her husband, artist/actor/comic historian R. Cat Conrad, in a gently creepy house full of books.